SNOW DAYS WITH YOU

LEONIE MACK

First published in Great Britain in 2023 by Boldwood Books Ltd.

Cover Design: Alice Moore Design

Cover Photography: iStock and Shutterstock

A CIP catalogue record for this book is available from the British Library.

Paperback ISBN 978-1-80415-854-8

Large Print ISBN 978-1-80415-853-1

Hardback ISBN 978-1-80415-852-4

Ebook ISBN 978-1-80415-856-2

Kindle ISBN 978-1-80415-855-5

Audio CD ISBN 978-1-80415-847-0

MP3 CD ISBN 978-1-80415-848-7

Digital audio download ISBN 978-1-80415-849-4

Boldwood Books Ltd
23 Bowerdean Street
London SW6 3TN
www.boldwoodbooks.com

For Tatiana, for being there with me on the journey of this book from start to finish

1

'You're an odd duck, Luna Marie,' she muttered to herself and allowed her forehead to fall to the steering wheel. That was what her mother used to say in her fond, exasperated tone. Luna had rarely disagreed with her, but that afternoon the description was particularly apt.

She'd reached the end of the road. Unfortunately, that didn't mean she'd arrived anywhere. Her car had conked out at the end of a narrow road that stopped abruptly at a rushing river with snow-covered banks. There was an abandoned warehouse to one side.

And when she peered up out of the windscreen... her eyes couldn't grow round enough to comprehend the *other* obstacle right in front of her. Thick forest powdered with snow rose steeply on the other side of the river and between two sloping hills, she glimpsed a jagged rock face, soaring into the cloudy, late afternoon sky. It wasn't just a mountain. This was what geographers meant when they wrote about a 'massif' – a giant agglomeration of peaks, wild and impassable.

Luna shuddered. She wasn't supposed to be here. Obviously,

she wasn't supposed to be *here*, at the end of this lonely road with nowhere to go but up. She'd taken a wrong turn somewhere while her phone had struggled to pronounce the French street names. But she also wasn't supposed to be 600 miles from England on Christmas Day, in *Chamonix* of all places. Now, she was stuck here.

Over the past two days, she'd headed steadily east in her old Astra, spending hours on motorways and a night in a 500-year-old hotel in Troyes, disturbed by vivid dreams. She'd got confused at roundabouts and been too nervous to overtake anyone, driving on the wrong side of the road – or the wrong side of the car.

At some point in the last hour or so, as her distraction had increased with her proximity to the place she fervently hoped held some answers, she'd forgotten that the fuel light was broken – something else she hadn't managed to deal with recently. When the car had made an alarming cough as she'd turned into this dead-end road, she realised she hadn't filled the tank since Troyes that morning.

Her phone rang, startling Luna out of her misery. Her cousin's name flashed up for the tenth time that day and she muted the call with a grimace. She'd have to call Lydia later and give her an explanation, but it was difficult, since she'd surprised even herself by making it all the way here, when she had been expected in Sheffield for Christmas lunch.

Taking another peek at the mountain and swiftly looking away again, she thought to herself in grim amusement that this definitely wasn't Sheffield.

When the phone stopped ringing, she cancelled the missed call notification and flicked back to the maps app to find a service station. Locating one just over two miles away, she decided it could have been worse, although lugging a jerry can for forty-five minutes wouldn't be fun. At least she could get herself out of this mess without calling a tow truck she couldn't afford.

Well, technically, she could afford it. She had an unfathomable lump sum sitting in her bank account, so much that she didn't want to look. She still didn't know what to think about the fact that she'd been the beneficiary of a stranger's life insurance policy. She'd benefited from someone's sudden death. The thought of spending any of the money – especially without knowing anything about her unfortunate benefactor – was abhorrent.

It was absolutely quiet and Luna listened to herself breathe for a moment. The tightness in her belly that hadn't gone away since she'd received the letter from a French insurance company was already easing. She'd *had* to come here. She'd *had* to know why a man called Robert Durand had died and she'd become €750,000 richer. If she found out who he'd been to her, visited his grave, perhaps she'd be able to use that money to set herself up for the future.

She'd been so distracted by the mystery in the three months since she'd found out, she'd neglected her few friends, done nothing about the imminent end of her teaching contract and completely lost track of real life – including keeping her car serviced. Lyd had accused her of searching out dead people instead of living.

Lyd would think it was just like her to take off with nothing but a suitcase of clothes and her mother's ashes in the back seat. Luna glanced apologetically at the beautiful handmade urn that housed June Rowntree's cremated remains. How many times had Luna been told to leave them in a cabinet at the cemetery? It had never felt right – something was unfinished, even though that thing was probably just Luna's grieving.

She shivered as the car grew colder, the longer the engine was off. Opening the glove box where she'd stowed her gloves, she caught sight of the photo that was the other reason Luna had fled here instead of following the moving boxes up to her cousin's house, where she'd planned to live until she sorted her life out. Holding the photo up, she smiled at the image of her mother, sunshine glinting off her blonde hair and the reflective ski goggles up on her forehead. If the face hadn't been so dearly familiar, Luna would never have believed her mother had held a pair of skis in her life. June Rowntree had rarely left Kent. Driving on the M25 had been her idea of an extreme sport. And yet, there she was, looking casually comfortable at the top of a mountain, in a photo with the words *Chamonix, 1992* written on the back.

'I'm here, Mum,' she murmured. 'Why didn't you tell me you'd been here? And who the heck was Robert Durand?' Speaking to the photo was just as strange as speaking to the urn, which she occasionally still did, but it was more difficult *not* to say something when she saw her mum's face. Tucking the photo back into the glove box, she pulled on her stripy gloves and opened the car door, ready to start out on her quest for petrol.

What she wasn't ready for was the shock of the temperature. The ice in the air flew at her face and her nose felt as though it was full of liquid nitrogen. Her coat might as well have been riddled with holes, for all the good it did in protecting her from the cold. When she stepped onto the road in her ancient leather brogues, she could feel the frost through the soles.

Hauling herself upright like a clockwork toy that needed winding, she slammed the door shut and focussed on breathing and not panicking. Two miles. That was all she had to manage. *Crap*, her calf-length skirt and thin cotton tights with a hole in the knee were *not* appropriate for sub-zero temperatures.

Darkness was falling rapidly and she could only imagine the cold snap that would follow. Tiny flakes of snow swirled as she turned away from the river – and the mountain – to head for the main road. She'd just taken her first few, slippery steps, when a throbbing whump-whump started up in her head.

One gloved hand flew to her temple. Not now! She couldn't handle a cancelled Christmas, a wild-goose chase, unemployment, lack of petrol, freezing temperatures *and* a migraine. But the pain didn't shudder through her skull, as it usually did. In fact, there didn't seem to be any pain at all, just a persistent throb – which she realised, a minute later, was not in her head at all.

A navy-blue helicopter swooped over her with a blast of wind, blowing her already unruly hair into her face and showering icy particles over her. The aircraft banked sharply and hovered over what she'd assumed was the old loading area of the warehouse. Floodlights blinked on and Luna noticed the squat buildings weren't abandoned at all. She held her arms over her head as the helicopter descended, sucking the air out of her lungs.

As soon as the runners touched down, the door slid open and a man in a helmet and a blue uniform emerged, followed by another, heads down as they hurried out from under the blades.

The second man turned back and hesitated and it took Luna several heartbeats to realise he was looking at her. He changed directions and jogged to the fence near where she was standing, tugging off his helmet and goggles as he did so.

'Madame!'

She picked her way across the icy road so she could hear him better over the throb of the helicopter.

'Madame,' he repeated, 'vous ne pouvez pas rester ici.' *You cannot stay here, madame.* Even if the uniform hadn't suggested he was in the military, with a patch on the breast that read 'PGHM Chamonix', his posture gave him away as a gendarme. She wondered if he said 'madame' to every woman out of professional habit, or if she'd crossed over into 'madame' territory now she'd reached thirty.

'I'm sorry – désolée,' she corrected herself, cranking her French brain into action. 'Je suis en panne d'essence,' she explained, feeling heat rise to her cheeks. She must have sounded like an idiot to have run out of petrol and it would challenge more than just her French to explain that she'd left on a whim and driven across the country in a state of distraction, with her mother's urn in the back seat.

The soldier regarded her blankly. His thick, straight hair stood up in unkempt spikes. He had a broad chin and ears that protruded just a little and Luna thought he looked like such a friendly, neighbourhood gendarme that she might get over her embarrassment sometime this century.

'You... 'ave no petrol?' he confirmed, switching to English.

'I forgot to fill it,' she mumbled. 'I'm going to go to the *station-service*,' she said, feeling even more of an idiot for not being able to decide which language to speak in.

'You cannot stay here,' he repeated. 'This is an emergency street.' He gestured behind him to the sprawling buildings, where she now read, 'Section Aérienne Gendarmerie de Chamonix' on a sign. 'Why did you come here?'

Wasn't that the question of the hour?

A gust of wind bit her skin through her coat and she glanced warily up at the mountain and the sky that was rapidly turning from purple to grey. As she watched, a wispy cluster of cloud dissipated to reveal a crescent moon, hovering next to a rocky summit as jagged as a tooth. The moon looked enormous, slowly taking shape in the dimming sky.

'Have you ever thought about what happens after you die?' Luna's words slipped out so quietly the wind nearly whipped them away before the gendarme could hear them. It might have been for the best if it had.

2

As soon as she'd uttered the sentence, she realised how it must have come across. 'I didn't mean—sorry that sounded all wrong. I didn't mean after *you* die, or me! I mean a general "you". I've just driven a long way today and...'

A baffled smile crept onto the gendarme's face, lopsided and full of even, white teeth. His features were too asymmetrical, his brow too strong, too craggy to be swoon-worthy, but he did look entirely trustworthy.

'You need help.'

She swallowed a dark laugh at his statement. Did gendarmes have highly trained intuition as well as great posture? Perhaps she did need help. Perhaps what she was doing wasn't normal.

'I can help you,' he said and that's when she realised he'd been asking a question. Add French grammar to that earnest smile and it made sense. 'Petrol, yes? Not diesel?'

'Yes, but I can get more petrol. I'm sorry my car is in the way—'

'I can get you enough petrol to drive. Wait here?'

Before she could stop him, he turned and jogged back to base or the station or whatever it was called for the gendarmerie. A whole team of two-tone blue soldiers had appeared to wheel the helicopter into the hangar for the night.

As she waited, Luna stared up at the moon, the celestial body that was her namesake. She didn't remember her father who'd died when she was three, having abandoned the family before that. She only knew that he'd been French, had lived in Corsica and that he'd given her the name Luna Marie.

Seeing the glowing crescent moon suspended over rugged needles of rock, hanging so low it seemed to cast a spell over the valley, she could understand why someone would name their child after the moon.

Shaking herself out of her thoughts, she squinted at the activity on the helipad, but couldn't make out 'her' gendarme. Then she noticed a figure holding a jerry can and a length of hose striding swiftly over the tarmac towards the car park to one side.

She blinked in astonishment as he fed the hose into the petrol tank of an unmarked SUV and sucked on the hose to start the flow. She was worried for a moment, wondering why he could so confidently siphon fuel out of a car, but, when he returned a few minutes later with that lopsided smile and cuddly brow, she suspected he was merely competent, not criminal.

'Open the... bouchon,' he said, gesturing at the fuel cap. Then he poured the pungent petrol into the tank with steady hands.

Luna stood by and tried not to watch too closely, nor to appear too appreciative of the impressive capability of those weathered hands. The back of his jacket read, 'Secours en Montagne', mountain rescue, and his belt was hung with a short length of rope, several carabiners that clacked when he walked, a pair of leather workman's gloves and a tool like a hammer, but with a jagged head. When she looked more closely, she realised it wasn't a belt at all, but a climbing harness, encircling his waist and thighs.

He glanced at her and she snapped her gaze back to his face.

'Can I help with something else?' he asked as he screwed the cap back onto the empty jerry can. She couldn't answer for a moment, his smile was so distracting. She didn't think it was possible for anyone to be sweeter than this gendarme who smiled with his whole face and siphoned off petrol for stranded strangers. Add a kitten and she'd buy a whole calendar of pictures of this guy completing practical tasks ridiculously competently. She wasn't brave enough to imagine him shirtless, but even fully clothed she'd be guaranteed twelve months of swoon.

'Was that your own car?' she asked. 'Did you give me some of your petrol?'

His answer was a self-deprecating nod, lines wrinkling at his eyes. He made her think of big hugs and kisses on the cheek and she should leave before she remembered how lovely those things were and how long it had been since she'd experienced them.

'Taking fuel from the base would be too much paperwork,' he supplied drily.

'Well, merci encore. I'll... be on my way.'

'Pas de souci, madame.' No worries, spoken in earnest, clipped French.

* * *

The woman took one last look at the moon, her expression luminous, before giving him a self-conscious smile and climbing back into her car. *Mission accomplished*, Yannick assured himself as she started the engine. He'd cleared the obstruction on the road. He didn't need to understand why her car had conked out in front of the drop zone, or why she'd been talking about life after death – or perhaps he had misunderstood her. He'd been thinking about Jim again, about the way his friend had stared at the moon just before he'd died.

Yannick stepped back to allow her to drive away, until he noticed her tyres. Tapping on the bonnet with a frown, he gestured for her to cut the engine.

Her dark eyes looked huge in the fading light when she opened the door questioningly. Her short brown hair was a mess around her face and she struck him as a mystery he needed to solve. No, not 'needed'. He certainly didn't need a mystery, in addition to everything else he was juggling.

'You have the wrong tyres,' he told her sharply.

'They're not that bad, are they?' she asked, examining the front one critically.

'The roads in Haute-Savoie require winter tyres from November or you face a fine – do you have snow chains in the car?'

'Oh, no, I don't have chains,' she said in dismay, her gaze flitting to his uniform. 'Do you have to give me a ticket?' She sighed and dropped her hands limply, as though expecting him to produce a pair of handcuffs and arrest her.

He slammed his mouth shut, not sure what to say. He'd never seen anyone so accepting of a traffic fine. 'My shift is over,' he muttered. 'But you need to address the problem,' he added with what he'd intended to be a stern look, but she was looking up at him with such a bright smile that he lost his train of thought.

'I will, I promise,' she assured him. 'I'm not going far. You won't have to rescue me again.'

He wanted to insist that he hadn't rescued her, but, upon reflection, he supposed he had, although it had been nothing like the mission he'd just completed, retrieving an off-piste skier who'd fallen fifty metres down a rock face. He gave her a brief nod in concession.

'Faites attention,' he said, switching to French out of habit for the phrase he uttered nearly every day: *take care.*

'D'accord, monsieur,' she said, tucking herself back into the car and closing the door.

He knocked his fist on the roof in farewell, while she wiggled her fingers in a wave. He squinted at her as she drove off, cocking his head. With a deep breath, he headed for the hangar.

'Friend of yours, Yanni?' Emilien called out, tossing him a rope to pack away as soon as he entered the equipment room. 'Or a hot date?'

'Neither,' he grumbled. 'A lost tourist.'

'Ah, probably a groupie, then – or a helicopter spotter. Did you get her number?' It was true, very few tourists were genuinely lost when they turned up at the drop zone. Usually it was families with kids, wanting to gawk at the helicopters.

'I'm not going to ask a tourist for her number.'

'That's where you're going wrong, mon vieux,' Emilien said, calling him 'old man' and giving him a playful shove. 'You don't have to marry every woman you date.'

'Do you want to go? I can finish, here,' he offered, ignoring the jibe. 'Louise is probably waiting for you.'

Emilien gave an exaggerated grimace and stroked his chin. Ten years younger than Yannick, at twenty-eight, his partner had the looks and attitude of an adrenaline junkie – when he was off-duty – and the revolving door of women to match. Yannick hoped he'd got the name of his latest girlfriend right.

'I'm late for dinner with her parents, but that's fine by me!'

Yannick slapped him on the shoulder and roughed him up on the back of his head. 'I thought you liked Louise. Go!'

'Are you going home to Valérie and Maëlys?' Emilien asked, his tone cautious. 'Home' was an interesting choice of word.

Yannick shook his head. 'I saw them yesterday. They've gone to his parents in Haute-Marne.' He didn't need to explain who 'he' was. In a tightly knit unit like this, everyone knew his ex-wife had a new partner. He didn't mind them knowing; it was important to share potential distractions, but he still struggled with the fact that most of the servicemen at his age were either happily married or had remained single by choice. He'd expected to be the former, with a wedding band tattooed on his ring finger for the times when climbing and handling ropes prevented him from wearing one.

'Alors,' Emilien said, 'get yourself on one of those dating apps and find someone new. Use a photo of you wearing the uniform and all the ladies will be after you.' The prestigious mountain rescue unit had a mythical reputation in the Chamonix valley, but Valérie certainly hadn't thought much of his calling.

He responded with a grunt and an eyeroll to discourage further conversation on that topic. 'Go,' he repeated to Emilien, shooing away the others, too, when they came to help. 'It's Christmas. Go home.'

Much later, as he ambled back to his jeep in the car park, absently jingling his keys, he caught sight of something colourful on the road where the woman's car had come to a stop. Changing course to look, he found a single, knitted glove with multicoloured stripes. It was soaking wet and had possibly been run over, but he picked it up carefully with a sigh.

He'd wash it and put it into the lost property bin in the equipment room, even though she probably wouldn't come back for it.

3

Luna awoke suddenly the following morning to the sound of her phone ringing. After a moment of disorientation, she fumbled for the device on the bedside table, squinting at the screen to see her cousin's name flash up. Oops. Lydia probably thought she was lying in a hospital bed somewhere, rather than this stylish bedroom at an alpine B&B.

'I'm sorry I didn't call you back,' Luna said as soon as she put the phone to her ear. She hauled herself upright, feeling ancient after the adventure of the day before. When she rubbed her eyes and tried to pry them open further, her gaze fell on her mother's urn, which she'd placed on the bedside table.

June had chosen the urn herself from her bed in the hospice and that made it even more precious to Luna. The polished stone was beautiful, but Luna knew it was still strange how often she needed the reminder that June Rowntree's remains were in there and her mother was no longer walking the earth. Perhaps taking her mother's ashes across Europe with her was a peculiar thing to do, but it didn't seem strange when she had so many questions that might never be answered.

'You're sorry for *not calling*!' Lyd howled. 'Are you okay? We were so worried we couldn't eat Christmas dinner!'

'Gosh, I'm sorry. I didn't think. I'm... I'm in France,' she admitted with a wince.

The silence that followed was even more worrying than Lyd's howling. 'No, Luna,' she said firmly. 'Please tell me you're not looking for your mysterious benefactor. You've done nothing but look for him for the past three months – with no luck. He's *dead*. What's he going to tell you from his grave? And if he wanted you to visit his grave, he would have left instructions – or maybe an inheritance instead of an insurance payout.'

That was the part that disturbed Luna the most. Why had he paid the insurance premiums? Lyd was right she'd done little else but search since she'd found out about the money, writing letters and making endless phone calls, checking municipal records and paying for access to official databases, but her research had ended much the same way as the road yesterday: in a dead end. There were hundreds of people named 'Robert Durand' in France and data protection legislation had foiled her at every turn. All she had was an address in Chamonix and mail that had been returned when she'd tried to send a letter there.

The insurance company hadn't been interested in her questions, only assuring her that the policy was valid, that there was no doubt she was the correct recipient, not least because the policyholder had updated her address over the years.

'I *have* to look for him. I know you don't understand, but it's got something to do with Mum, too. She was here. There's a connection.'

Lyd's sigh was deep and loud. 'Lu, I know you struggled with your mum's death. We all understand that and it's okay to hold on for a while, especially when it was always just the two of you, but...' Luna braced herself. 'You have to find a way to move on.'

Luna gritted her teeth to hold in her response. Her ex-boyfriend, Aiden, had told her something similar, when he'd explained why he wanted to have 'a break' and never contacted her again. She'd rather have her mum's ashes than a flaky boyfriend.

'I'm sorry I ruined Christmas,' Luna said earnestly.

'It's okay. We managed some of the turkey, in the end.'

'Oh... good,' Luna muttered. 'Give the boys a hug from me.'

'You should get back here and give them a hug yourself. They're looking forward to you moving in for a while. Did you take a look at the real estate listing I sent you a couple of days ago?'

Luna had looked – and swooned and cried at how gorgeous the little stone cottage at the edge of the Peak District was and how much her mum would have loved it. For the first time, she'd allowed herself to imagine buying that perfect little house and a cat and living mortgage and rent-free for the rest of her life. The prospect had been very appealing – until a wave of guilt about Robert Durand and his life insurance had washed in afterwards.

'I thought that cottage was just what you'd want, but I've got lots more houses to show you. With your budget, you could buy something really special,' Lydia continued, oblivious to the dilemma boring a hole inside Luna's heart.

She needed to change the subject before she got more upset. Luna couldn't buy a house with money that shouldn't belong to her and she couldn't think of the insurance money as hers until she understood what had motivated her benefactor – or at least until she'd found a way to pay her respects.

'Did you talk to Aunt Julie over Christmas?' Luna asked.

'I spoke to Mum briefly,' Lydia began. Luna's cousin was dealing with the absence of her own mother for entirely different reasons. Instead of helping Lydia care for her brood after retirement, Aunt Julie travelled for months at a time and was terrible at messaging. 'She said Auntie June didn't keep in touch very often back then, especially not with Grandma and Grandad. They wanted her to stay close by and get a permanent job, but she'd insisted on taking short-term contracts all over Europe, and then she got pregnant with you and they didn't talk at all for a year.'

Could it have been a contract that had brought her mum to Chamonix? It struck Luna how little her mum had talked about that time in her life.

'So no one remembers her talking about someone called Robert Durand?'

'Mum didn't even meet your father, Lu. She didn't visit June when you were born. They wouldn't have chatted about her friends. And Mum kept getting Corsica and Chamonix mixed up, so I don't think she knows too much about those few years Auntie June was away.'

'Thanks for asking, anyway.'

'*You* aren't going to come back with a French boyfriend and a baby on the way, are you?' Lydia asked with a laugh. 'I mean, I wouldn't mind some playmates for my kids, but it didn't work out so well for your mum, did it?'

Luna shared her laugh, thinking of the Gore-Tex and ski-boot crowd at the hotel – or the gendarme who'd leaped out of a helicopter and used his mouth to siphon petrol out of a car – taking a romantic interest in *her*. 'I don't think you have to worry. If Aiden the office manager thought I was boring, I'm pretty sure the thrill-seekers in this town won't take a second look.'

'You're not still bemoaning the loss of Aiden, are you? But you're not staying there long, anyway, right? A couple of days to look for clues and you'll be back here where you belong.'

Back where you belong... Luna tried not to let those words hurt. Luna hadn't *belonged* since her mother had died and before then, their little family of two had been an island.

Her brain whirred, trying to come up with a convincing response. 'It might take more than a few days to find the answers I need.'

'You don't need answers. You need to move on with your life. You'd better come back by the beginning of term. I've told all the schools in the area that you'll be available for substitute teaching and they were over the moon! And that French teacher I told you about, Mrs Goode, has said she'll retire early now you're coming. She wants to finish at Easter. Plus, you never know how long that cottage will stay on the market.'

'Great. Thanks, Lyd,' Luna said, trying to sound as though she meant it. It had been difficult finding work over the past two years, unable to move out of Kent because of her mum's illness, and it was always a struggle to find enough teaching hours in a subject that many schools didn't even offer. The upside of her precarious employment status had been that her part-time contract had come to an end in time for her to traipse across France on a wild-goose chase at Christmas. 'I've got to go,' she murmured.

'You have an appointment with your dead guy?'

'Lyd!' she scolded her cousin.

'It is kind of weird, you know.'

'Weird or not, I have to look for him. I'll keep in touch.'

Luna disconnected the call with a deep sigh. Perhaps she should prioritise the future, since she wasn't sure where to even start looking for Robert Durand, but she couldn't give up without trying. Yes, she was looking for a dead man, but she might also find some traces of her mother at the same time.

The two weren't necessarily connected, but Luna didn't believe both trails could lead her to Chamonix by coincidence.

She'd checked into a little gîte, a B&B in les Bois, a residential area on the outskirts of Chamonix, after her petrol drama. She'd been terrified to drive too far with her inappropriate tyres and, as she nearly skidded on the ice in the driveway of the hotel, she understood how grave her mistake had been. She would take the bus, today, and be thankful for the warning, the emergency petrol – and the kind smiles – from the evening before.

The B&B thankfully didn't believe in making do with a Parisian breakfast of a coffee and croissant and Luna tucked into a boiled egg, fresh rustic-style bread with a little too much from the cheese buffet, slices of fresh apple and a crispy, buttery pain au chocolat. Suitably fortified, she was hopeful she'd find her answers and be able to live happily ever after in the countryside cottage of her dreams.

Wrapping up as best she could, draping an extra cardigan around her neck when the loose knit of her scarf seemed certain to let in the wind, she stepped out into the cold. Even though she'd been expecting it, she still shuddered violently and pulled a muscle in her neck as she cringed. The air had *teeth* at these temperatures.

Hurrying to the car to collect her gloves, she was dismayed to find only one. She checked in the footwell, the centre console, rummaged in the glove box, but there was no sign of the other one. With a groan, she stuffed her hand in her pocket and set off anyway.

The only clue she had to Robert Durand's identity, an address not far from the gîte, proved to be useless, but at least she discovered why her letters had been returned unopened. It was a small apartment complex and the name 'Durand' had obviously been removed from the letterbox. Although she knocked on all the doors, only three people answered and none of them had heard of Robert Durand, making Luna think he must have been a very private person – or perhaps they were unfriendly neighbours.

It was another dead end and the visit hadn't been worth the onset of frostbite in her little finger. Even after holding it near the fan heater on the bus for ten minutes as she travelled into Chamonix, her hand felt stiff and swollen.

But the cold wasn't her biggest immediate problem. It turned out it was rather difficult to go around asking complete strangers, 'Do you know a dead guy called Robert Durand?'

Even though she could comfortably ask, 'Connaissez-vous un mort qui s'appelle Robert Durand,' the French term 'un mort' sounded even more gruesome to her. She managed to ask the man in the tourist office without mentioning that Robert Durand was dead, but he responded in the negative and obviously hadn't appreciated that €750,000 hung in the balance.

'Est-il moniteur de ski ou guide de montagne?' the man asked blandly.

Luna blinked. Could Robert Durand have been a ski instructor or a mountain guide? For all she knew, he'd worked at the local supermarket.

'You can ask at the Compagnie des Guides,' the man suggested.

Perhaps Robert Durand had been one of these mountaineering types, with ice picks and snow shoes, and that made her wonder what her mother had found here all those years ago. The cold still-ness, the cosy town full of wooden chalets and historic stone hotels, the jagged mountain peaks, were rather overwhelming.

Luna stepped back out into the cold to make her way to the Maison de la Montagne, where the historic Compagnie des Guides was located, in a sweet, rendered building with brown shutters and a green copper roof, next to a pale stone church, its bell tower dappled with snow. A sign informed her that it was also the office of the Chamoniarde, the volunteer mountain rescue society. Hope-fully one of the two historic institutions would have a lead.

But after waiting her turn in the busy office, the answer was another disappointing one.

'I'm sorry, I don't have anyone by that name listed as a guide and the clients in the system do not have addresses in Chamonix,' the middle-aged woman behind the counter informed her.

Luna nodded slowly. She shouldn't have expected anything different. A photo of her mother with skis meant nothing in a place like this and she'd been naïve to think she could find him so easily.

Robert Durand, with his commonplace name, could have been anyone. Every day here would cost her more of his money and her investigation might be a long one. Going back to England before term started would be a more sensible option than staying here, looking for links to her mother that might not exist.

'Thank you anyway,' Luna mumbled to the woman. 'Erm, he would be... deceased. Does that make a difference to your search?'

The woman blinked at her. 'You're looking for a dead mountain guide?'

'I'm trying to find out... he might have had a connection with my mother. He died in March.'

The woman frowned. 'Are you sure he was a mountain guide? In the past year we've only lost Jim.' The way the woman said 'Jim', full of affection tinged with sadness, made Luna pause.

'I'm sorry for your loss,' she murmured, her throat thick. Her mum had been gone over a year, now, and Luna had grown somewhat accustomed to pushing through when the emptiness came rushing back, but part of her welcomed it each time it did – welcomed it and wanted that ache, because it was at least something that connected her to her mum.

'It is a part of life when you live in the shadow of Mont Blanc,' the woman said with a faint smile. 'Unfortunately, people die up there every year – although not often one of our guides.'

Luna froze – from the inside, this time. People died on Mont

Blanc *every year*? She wouldn't look up at the peaks the same way again. Why would people go up there if it was possible that they would never come down alive? She gulped.

'Robert Durand might not have been a guide,' she muttered, 'but I thought it was a good place to start.'

'Let me check in the system of the Chamoniarde,' the woman said kindly. 'Perhaps he is listed as a volunteer.'

But the second search proved equally fruitless and Luna trudged to the door of the office in a daze without taking note of any of her surroundings – not the intrepid adventurers with their jagged-looking hammers tucked into their backpacks, nor the rosy-cheeked families looking at brochures. She'd been stupid to come.

Outside, it was a sparkling, sunny day, the piles of snow crunching under her feet. The town was a strange place, with pedestrianised lanes, slate roofs and a relaxed, summertime atmosphere, even at freezing temperatures. Every street, every hotel, even the cheesy souvenir shops, were dwarfed by the presence of the mountain behind: the sparkling white of fresh snow and the shadows of a glacier tumbling towards the valley. The place didn't feel real – except that Luna now knew there were people up there risking their lives. She deeply understood that death was very real.

And hunger. Hunger was real. The scent of caramel and butter wafted out of a nearby pâtisserie, reminding Luna of how long it had been since breakfast, as well as the importance of enjoying life while it lasted. She hesitated for a moment, before deciding that Robert Durand, if he'd been here showing her Chamonix himself, would probably have stopped here for cake.

She drifted towards the pâtisserie nose-first and took a seat under a heater at the outdoor tables – after she got over her shock at the presence of outdoor tables. Tucking the blue fleece blanket tightly around her, she ordered one of the many varieties of herbal tea and a twisted pastry sprinkled with sugar crystals. Macarons formed a colourful pyramid in the window and the clientele of the café fascinated her: rugged men and women with sunburn and blunt fingers, slurping coffee, and well-heeled older women in pairs, sharing gossip over a café au lait.

Biting into her treat, she garnered a few sidelong glances as she – rather unsuccessfully – tried to stifle her squeaks and murmurs of enjoyment. The pastry held the same buttery, crispy magic as a genuine French croissant, but with the addition of a soft pudding centre.

For twenty minutes, she soaked up the sunshine – and licked up the crumbs – and thought Chamonix might not be so strange after all, until she realised she could no longer feel her toes. Now that her tea was finished, her fingers were starting to hurt, too.

She stood in a hurry, preparing to return to the B&B to regroup. She was discouraged and concerned about the money and clearly out of her depth, if her haphazard arrival the night before was any indication. She'd never been comfortable in the cold. If this was adventure, perhaps she'd been better off without it, she thought morosely as she watched one of the sunburnt men gather up his battered rucksack, complete with ropes and hammers and skis.

Luna felt entirely alone and rather stupid. Others came here for the camaraderie of skiing, of exploring and taking risks and having adventures together. All Luna had was the name of a dead man, a photo of her mother and a single, woollen glove.

If she was going to stay here longer, she would need something more – at the very least her other glove.

As she trudged back in the direction of the bus stop, a woman emerging from a small boutique caught Luna's eye. She had long, wavy hair, shot with grey, and a spindly frame. With her heavy-duty hiking boots and rough woollen pullover, she didn't look like the swishy tourists with their high-tech gear. She peered at something in the window and then disappeared back inside.

The boutique was in a small wooden chalet, with a hand-painted sign above the door that read, in art-nouveau lettering, 'La Fontana: cristaux, minéraux, bijoux et bonbons'. Luna did not need any crystals, minerals or jewellery – and certainly not any sweets, after her recent sugar hit – but browsing for a few minutes would help her warm up and she was curious about whatever the woman had been studying so critically.

There was a sign in the window.

Recherche prof d'anglais pour adultes en petit groupe, free-lance, contrat à court terme.

Someone was looking for an English teacher for short-term freelance work. It felt like a sign.

Of course, it was actually a sign. But it was also *a sign*. Perhaps Luna's quest wasn't a lost cause after all. Lydia would call her dotty with fond condescension, but perhaps she needed to be a bit dotty to find her way in this town.

Luna headed for the door of the shop with a prickle of anticipation. A bell tinkled over her head as she stepped inside and then froze. There was an entire ecosystem inside the little boutique.

Set in the middle of the space was the silver trunk of a dead tree. Some parts were smooth and others covered in moss and lichen. Alongside the gnarled wood were woollen throws and wicker baskets full of pebbles and aromatic pinecones and one full of wizened red rose hips.

Instead of little boxes of stones with prices on, the shiny crystals and various minerals flowed in a river along two sides of the shop, with price categories indicated on wooden boards. The back of the shop boasted an array of larger crystals, some clear, others smoky and some in shades of pink.

Tucked in the nooks and crannies were stands of earrings, bracelets and little packets of boiled sweets that looked like rocks as well. Even shopping could be an adventure in Chamonix.

'Puis-je vous aider?' A voice sounded suddenly, offering help. Luna turned to find the woman she'd seen outside standing surprisingly near, studying Luna intently. 'Attendez,' the woman said, holding up a finger as she instructed Luna to wait.

With thoughtful humming and hahing, the shop owner rummaged in the stream of rocks, making a soothing clack. When the woman had found what she was looking for, she took Luna's hand.

'Sens, ne regarde pas,' she instructed. *Feel, don't look.*

Luna closed her hand around the stone the woman placed in it. The shape was irregular, with smooth edges and polished curves. Her hand was so cold, the stone felt warm.

'What do you think?' the woman asked, still in French.

'C'est... agréable,' Luna tried out. *It's nice.*

The woman clucked in disapproval at her answer and snatched the stone back, making Luna snap her eyes open again. She hadn't realised she'd shut them.

'This one,' the woman said emphatically.

The next stone was rough, rugged with bumpy facets, and the edges were quite sharp. Luna suspected she wouldn't have picked that one up herself.

'Intéressant,' the woman said as she took the stone back. Luna caught a glimpse of reddish brown with white patches. 'Don't look,' the woman admonished, and Luna snapped her gaze back up. 'Your eyes often give false signals. I'm interested in your heart.' The stranger had a striking face – lean, weathered and lined but stunningly beautiful when she fixed Luna with a smile. 'Hmm, perhaps that one,' the woman mused.

Returning to the crystal river, she picked up another rock and hid it in her palm. Luna held out her hand and obediently closed her eyes. The third stone was smooth, but not as polished as the first. Her thumb traced a seam in the rock. Luna wasn't sure what she was supposed to say about it, so she opened her eyes and glanced questioningly at the shop owner.

To Luna's surprise, the woman smiled warmly. 'That one. Pierre de lune, for healing the past and new beginnings – and intuition for making good decisions.'

Luna froze, the rock suddenly heavy in her hand. She glanced down to see an unassuming white stone, flecked with grey. Pierre de lune – moonstone, it must be called in English. She refused to believe the stone signified anything more than the woman's insight, but she couldn't stop the fresh surge of determination in her veins. She would find *something* here, even if it was only a grave where she could pay her respects.

She cleared her clogged throat and asked, 'How much is the stone?'

The woman considered Luna for a long moment. 'You are English?' she asked in French.

Luna nodded. 'I'm a qualified teacher. I saw the sign in the window and—'

The woman's smile widened. 'You manifested very quickly. Keep the stone for free. Can you work legally in France? Can you take a class next week?'

'Well, yes, I... I have a French passport. I c-can teach next week.' Luna struggled to assemble the sentence in the conditional, the difficult form of grammar that expressed uncertainty, so she accidentally sounded more confident than she would have in English.

'Meraviglioso! I am Silvia, by the way,' she said, grasping Luna's shoulders and pressing two enthusiastic kisses to each of her cheeks. 'I come from the other side of the mountain, in Piedmont, but I have been here in Chamonix for many years now. I have this shop and I coordinate language classes for private clients. What is your name?'

Luna couldn't help returning the woman's smile with a wry one of her own. 'Luna. My name is Luna.'

4

Luna had expected Silvia to be amused to discover that she was named after the moon, but she hadn't expected to be received like a long-lost daughter. After wrapping her arms around Luna in a hug that lasted long enough to feel awkward, Silvia had made her an espresso, opened a box of chocolates that looked like works of art, and asked Luna to recount her life story.

Luna's answer was rather boring until she got to the past two years. Silvia listened with such intensity that everything tumbled out: the death of her mother, Robert Durand, the insurance payout, even the photo of her mum skiing.

'Do you think this could have been a romance? A man she met before your father?' Silvia prompted.

At first, all Luna could do was splutter an inarticulate response. 'I don't know. She never said anything about Chamonix, but this photo is dated the year before I was born.'

'Do you think he could *be* your father?' Silvia asked gently.

'No!' Luna insisted immediately. 'My father lived in Corsica and he died years ago. His name *was* Robert, but Robert Favre, not Robert Durand and if I've learned anything over these past few months of research, it's that there are *thousands* of Roberts in France.'

Silvia grasped her hand as she listened and gave it a squeeze when Luna described her arrival in Chamonix the night before. 'We will find this man. I'm certain of it. I don't know who he could be, but *someone* will know, and that someone will find you – if you don't find them first.'

'I haven't had any success so far,' Luna mumbled miserably.

'Perhaps the moonstone will help,' Silvia said with a smile. 'Show me the photo – the one of your mother.' Luna fetched it out of her handbag. Silvia studied it closely from several angles, before exclaiming, 'Aha!' in a very promising tone. 'This is at La Flégère, one of the ski resorts on the Aiguilles Rouges. I see a little part of the restaurant here in the corner and the view of the Aiguille du Midi also fits.'

Luna swallowed, staring at the photo. 'It's so strange,' she began. 'I can't believe she used to ski.'

'Why not?' Silvia asked.

'Well, she wasn't very active. We used to go rambling occasionally, but she always got so worried about getting lost or falling, so we stayed on well-established routes. After I went to university, she... she didn't look after herself very well, I suppose,' Luna admitted. 'I think I took up running to compensate for how inactive she was – although I realise that makes no actual sense. She had heart problems, but she was okay until...'

Silvia squeezed her hand and said softly, 'It never gets any easier to speak of the end.'

Luna nodded glumly. 'It wasn't her heart that made her sick, though. It was ovarian cancer. A few months and she was gone and now all I have is the name of a stranger and—' She cut herself off before she admitted she had her Mum's ashes on the bedside table at her B&B. She suspected Silvia would be the last person to judge, but funerary urns didn't seem like an appropriate topic of conversation this early in a friendship.

Perhaps, if Luna discovered something important about June's past, it might help her decide on a permanent resting place and her impression that something was unfinished, her intuition, would be vindicated.

'L'intuition,' Silvia said softly. Luna's gaze snapped up to hers in surprise. Did Silvia read minds, too? 'The moonstone helps refine your intuition. Follow your mother's footsteps and you might find Robert Durand, find out why you received this money.'

'Follow in Mum's footsteps? Go to the ski resort?' Luna said, her voice fading at the end. 'I can't ski. Even the cable car would scare me.'

'You can do it, Luna,' Silvia said with certainty.

'You wouldn't say that if you knew me better,' she muttered in English in reply. She couldn't even safely drive around here – or maintain her own body temperature. But Silvia's smile seemed to hide a secret Luna couldn't hope to understand – the same secret she sensed when she looked up at the mountains.

'Are you staying in a hotel?' Silvia asked suddenly. 'Or have you rented a holiday apartment? It's nothing fancy, but I can rent you a room on a monthly rate, if you need. I live just outside Chamonix, but the bus connection is good. You'll be doing me a favour by taking on some classes while you're here.'

'That's... w-wow, that's very kind of you,' Luna stammered. Lydia would tell her she was crazy all over again, when she heard she'd taken a job and was staying with a woman from a crystal shop, but it was a way forward – something Luna hadn't had for a long time. 'Are you sure?'

'I am certain you are here for a reason and who am I to ignore that message?'

Luna had to agree she'd received a clear message to stay. She had a way of earning some income and cheaper, longer-term accommodation. She had a location for the next step of her quest: La Flégère. Most importantly, she'd made a friend, which was a miracle in itself, given she'd lost touch with everyone except Lydia during her mother's illness.

She was oddly reluctant to leave the beautiful little shop when Silvia turned the sign to 'fermé' for an extended lunch break, but she was curious to see the room Silvia had offered to rent to her. Silvia bundled Luna into a little blue jeep and left the bustle of restaurants and hotels in Chamonix for a town nestled higher in the valley and the most charming chalet she had ever seen.

Tucked behind a row of bare silver birches, the chalet was encircled by tall pines clutching snow in their branches. The house itself showed its age, with chipped mortar and darkened wood, weathered shutters that had once been pale blue. But the carved pattern under the eaves, the faded red shield with a white cross and the hand-carved falcon looking down from its perch by a first-floor window appealed to Luna far more than the chalet chic of her gîte. A pillow of snow clung precariously to the slanting roof and, as the jeep pulled into the driveway, three startled deer took off for the nearby bushes.

Along the valley, the ever-present mountain peaks glowed glaring white.

'Do you know which is Mont Blanc – or Monte Bianco as I called it as a child?'

Luna shook her head, gazing at the seemingly gentle roll of the peaks. Her unease returned, as she thought of the guide who'd died and those ropes and carabiners on the mountain rescue gendarme. She thought of life insurance policies and that made her stomach roil.

'That peak that is a nice triangle, you see? That is the Aiguille du Goûter. To the left, there are two domes and the higher one is Mont Blanc.'

Although Luna tried to tell herself the mountain summit was no different from any other – isolated and cold – that twinkling, white dome whispered invitingly, making her imagine what it would be like to stand there in the wind and the ice and *achieve* something.

She blinked back the unexpected thought. Scatter-brained Luna would trip over her own skirt in the valley. She was glad Robert Durand hadn't been a mountain guide.

'Have you been up there?' Luna asked hesitantly.

'You want to go up there?'

'Noooo,' she said with a firm shake of her head. 'I'm just making conversation.'

Silvia patted her arm and motioned for Luna to follow her inside. 'Yes, I have been up there – once, in summer. But I am a hobby climber. I don't need to test myself against the summits, like a mountaineer. Usually, I just look – and dream. "L'alpiniste est un homme qui conduit son corps là où un jour ses yeux ont regardé",' she quoted with a chuckle, 'as said by one of our famous guides from the past, Gaston Rébuffat.'

A mountaineer is a man who takes his body where his eyes once looked, Luna translated silently as she glanced back at the peaks.

'Alpiniste' was a word she had rarely heard in all her years of French study and teaching, but the vocabulary came to life, standing where she was, traversing the summits with her eyes.

'Well, *I* will only ever look,' she said with a wry smile.

'Perhaps it is best so,' Silvia said, suddenly thoughtful as she followed Luna's gaze.

Luna trailed Silvia up the steps to the carved hardwood door which opened into a warm alpine paradise. A fire flickered in a brick stove in one corner and the thick air swaddled her in relief after the solid cold of the outdoors.

Inside, the chalet was just as charmingly dilapidated as outside, the immense wooden beams, blackened with age, contrasting with blue patterned carpet that had seen better days and a Formica kitchen.

Silvia's eclectic taste was evident in every corner. There were throws in bright green and pink, with stripes and swirls. Metal artwork and ceramic bowls decorated the shelves and side tables, along with thick-woven wall-hangings, strings of beads and pieces of wood and rock. It was chaotic and joyful and felt gloriously lived in.

'Mon chou!' Silvia called loudly. 'I have a guest.'

After a muffled response from behind a door that was ajar, a man appeared, wearing a short-sleeved thermal shirt and trousers, rubbing a towel over thinning grey hair. Although he appeared close to sixty, he was wiry and looked fit and full of energy.

'This is Guy, my amant,' Silvia said, casually calling him her lover and lifting her face for a kiss. Luna's eyebrows flew to the wooden ceiling. It wasn't a passionate kiss, but it lingered, along with Luna's embarrassment as she averted her eyes too late. Ending the kiss with a sigh, Guy turned to Luna and held out his hand, his smile warm and his eyes twinkling.

'This is *Luna*,' Silvia introduced her with emphasis. 'She is an English teacher and the solution to all my problems.'

'Actually, I'm a French teacher, but I am English,' Luna mumbled, a touch confused by the introduction.

'I'm sorry, but I'm on my way out,' Guy said. 'Duty calls, I'm afraid.' He disappeared back into what must have been the bedroom and returned buttoning up a pale blue shirt with several patches and a few rows of honours over the left pocket. He shrugged into a coat of two-tone blue that Luna recognised with a start. After giving Silvia another lingering kiss, Guy waved and pulled the door shut behind him.

'He's a gendarme,' Luna blurted out.

'I can't resist a man in uniform,' Silvia said with a wry chuckle. 'Yes, he's the capitaine of the mountain rescue unit and one of my best clients,' she continued with a wink. Luna was fairly certain the wink meant the suggestive comment was a joke.

'Are you sure I won't be in the way, if I stay here?' Luna asked doubtfully, trying not to wonder if any *other* gendarmes ever came around to talk to their capitaine.

'Definitely not. Guy doesn't live with me; I'm not good at sharing my life full-time. I really needed a new teacher, so your arrival is a great relief to me.'

'Why do you need someone at such short notice?' Luna asked warily.

'The teacher I wanted to send to the new class, John, is in hospital.'

'Oh, I see. That is unfortunate.'

'It certainly is. He broke his femur skiing. It will be a long time before he walks again.'

Luna nodded mutely, dismayed that she had benefited from other people's misfortune far too often lately. 'Would you like me to fill in some forms, or see some ID or something?'

'Come and see the room first.' Silvia took her arm and ushered her in the direction of the stairs that led to the floor below. The house seemed to be designed in the opposite way to what she was used to, with bedrooms *downstairs*. On the ground floor was a little wooden sauna and a series of doors, one of which opened to reveal a room with a bunk bed and a solid wood wardrobe. It was spartan and a bit chilly, but that was oddly satisfying after she'd felt so guilty for spending the insurance money on an expensive hotel.

'I had dreams, when I bought this house, of making it a basic hostel for hikers and climbers, but I don't have the money to finish it. The room is small, but if you don't know if you will stay here permanently or not...'

'Oh, I'm not planning to *move* here,' Luna contradicted her immediately, wondering how she'd given Silvia that impression. 'I'll stay a few weeks, until Easter at the latest, if you need me. Then I have to get back to England for...' *my cousin, and a dream of a cottage.* 'The summer term,' she said instead.

'It's harder to leave this valley than you think, once you've found your feet,' Silvia said softly.

'I'm not... an outdoors type,' Luna insisted. 'It's beautiful here, but I can't even ski. Usually I jog for exercise, but in Chamonix it's so cold I can't breathe. If I lived here I'd just eat pastries all day and drink hot chocolate.'

'We can get you skiing – no problem.'

'You don't need to help me, really. I appreciate you renting me the room—'

'Luna, I have a feeling about you,' Silvia announced. 'I always listen to my intuition. Whatever you find here, it will change your life – if you let it.'

5

It was the strangest sensation, dappled sunlight on her face through the tall trees swaying gently above her, the soft snow cushioning her on all sides – and the searing cold on the back of her neck. She should haul herself up and check for broken bones, but she took a moment to indulge her wounded pride instead.

A morning at an adult ski class and an afternoon of practice and she'd ended up here: cocooned in a snowdrift after slipping off the end of the beginner's slope. The only success of the day was that she'd learned to fall safely. She was even less able to imagine herself calmly swooping down a steep slope than she'd been that morning, when she'd set out with stubborn determination, wearing this old set of burgundy-and-yellow ski clothing she'd borrowed from Silvia, feeling like a cross between Bridget Jones and the Michelin Man. She certainly felt more Bridget Jones now with her skis askew and sticking up, the snow melting into her neck warmer.

How did you do this, Mum?

Hauling herself upright, she glanced up to see the tape barriers at the end of the slope just above her head. She hadn't fallen far.

Her skis were still attached, but she had to pop them off to move her leg into a more comfortable position.

At least the skis didn't appear damaged. Silvia had helped her source some second-hand equipment, insisting that Luna would spend so much time on the slopes that renting skis would be too expensive, as doubtful as that sounded. The only thing Luna had truly splurged on was a pair of super technical mittens, since she valued her fingers and had been suffering since she'd lost her knitted glove.

Her new friend was the first person who hadn't encouraged her to throw around her newfound wealth. It was refreshing to spend time with someone even more peculiar than she was – although Silvia didn't seem exactly peculiar. She just seemed to have a different kind of wisdom from other people.

But Luna questioned the wisdom of learning to ski. She was thirty years old, the only snow she'd ever seen was the occasional dumping that caused traffic chaos on the M20 and created dirty piles in suspicious colours on the footpath and she hadn't even known what a 45 per cent gradient looked like until she'd glimpsed the crazy skiers hurtling down the more difficult pistes. Talk about pitting yourself against the mountain.

Luna took a deep breath and tried to convince herself she was okay, there was no need to panic. She'd tumbled a few feet off the baby slope, not a thousand feet down an unforgiving piste noire. After taking stock and finding that only her wrist hurt a little, she dug her boots in and clambered back up. That was when the real accident occurred.

In a blur of red-and-blue ski clothing, something went flying past her, and came to a stop further down the slope with a crash and a groan. If there was one thing former A&E nurse June Rowntree had drilled into her daughter, it was how to act in an emergency. Luna ripped off her mittens and pulled her phone out of her pocket, dialling 112 without hesitation.

She tried to gather her French, but the operator prompted her in English, so she gave up. 'A skier has fallen into the trees at the bottom of the Trappe chairlift at La Flégère,' she said clearly, ignoring a scream and panicked voices from above.

'Has the resort rescue been notified?'

'I-I don't know.'

'I will alert them. Can you reach the victim safely?'

She took a step, hearing another panicked groan from below her. Picking her way from tree to tree, Luna's heart pounded from the effort and her concern for the fallen skier, as she made slow progress down the slope. After another few metres, however, her boot slipped and she fell onto her knees, jarring her wrist again.

The gravitational forces dragging her down – and down and down – were alarming as she teetered on all fours. Swallowing a whimper of panic, she collapsed onto her side, breathing hard. The slope was steeper here, the bottom of the ravine looming before her.

A weak cry of, 'Help!' in a woman's voice snapped Luna back to the present. She snatched up her phone, where it lay half-buried in the snow, relieved to see the call was still connected.

'Allô? Allô?' she heard when she put the phone back to her ear.

'Sorry, I tried to reach the victim, but I can't. She's too far down and it's very steep.'

'She is not on the ski slope?'

'No, she fell from...' Luna glanced up, seeing a sheer rise with rocky outcroppings. As she watched, another skier zig-zagged down the mountainside and her alarm stuck in her throat. 'Uh, I'm guessing off-piste. It could have been a big fall. I don't know. Maybe fifty metres.'

'It's very important to stay where you are and do not take any risks. I have alerted the emergency services, but I transfer you now to the peh-jeh-ash-ehm.' Luna's panicked brain tried to translate the last word, but it didn't sound like any French she knew.

The line rang briefly and then a man picked up who seemed to have the details of the accident already and prompted her with more questions. Less than a minute later, the throb of a helicopter sounded over the valley.

As a recognisable, navy-blue rescue helicopter rose above her, whipping up snow, she realised what – or rather who – was coming. 'Peh-jeh-ash-ehm' was the French pronunciation of 'PGHM', an acronym she'd seen before, on the breast of the gendarme with the soft smile and Silvia's 'amant' Captain Guy.

She covered her head with her arms as the wind from the rotor blades whipped over her. The helicopter touched down and left again immediately, but activity above heralded the arrival of the rescuers. Two men, attached to ropes, approached Luna swiftly, moving with ease as though walking along the slope that had nearly sacrificed Luna's body to the angry mountain gods was nothing more than a hillside ramble in Sussex.

One rescuer spotted her and headed in her direction. She came face to face with his crampons first, vicious-looking spikes attached to big boots, stamping heavily into the snow. He was wearing a helmet and goggles and a hi-vis vest over his jacket. Each step he took rattled and clinked as the ropes and carabiners attached to his harness shifted.

'Vous êtes le témoin?' he asked. It was a simple sentence, but she didn't immediately understand the words, because they'd been spoken by a voice she recognised. Her gaze snapped up. Despite the helmet and reflective goggles, she knew that chin, remembered a smile on those lips.

Her gendarme.

'Madame?' he prompted her. 'Vous êtes blessée?' He didn't

appear to recognise her, but that was understandable – even if she hadn't been wearing goggles and a helmet.

'Non,' she said, giving herself an inward shake. 'Je ne suis pas blessée,' she said, confirming that she wasn't injured.

While the other rescuer made his way towards the victim, her gendarme peppered her with questions, trying to form a picture of what had happened from her disjointed description. She tried to explain in French, but it came out in a confused mix of both languages.

'La chute – cinquante mètres? Cent?' He asked about the height of the fall and then the angle. 'Up there, you say?' he continued, in accented English. 'The victim lost... conscience... consciousness?'

'No,' she replied. 'I heard her all the time.'

'Très bien. You are safe here?'

She nodded, even though her fingers curled frantically into the snow every time she glanced towards the bottom of the ravine. Time ticked by unnoticed, while the action seemed to slow down. The gendarme spoke into a radio, relaying the information to his partner. A doctor in a red jacket, attached to the safety rope, made his way down the slope to the other gendarme, clasping a folded stretcher.

Luna was so distracted watching the flurry of activity around the fallen skier that at first, she didn't react when the gendarme slipped an emergency harness around her torso, fastening it at the front. With a few efficient movements of his expert hands, he hooked her up to his own harness and urged her to her feet. She slipped and wobbled in her ski boots that weren't designed for climbing, pulling her rope line taut, but the gendarme didn't so much as stumble under her weight.

Tugging her in front of him and reconnecting her harness to the system of safety cords and pulleys the rescuers had hastily strung together, he grasped the ropes and hoisted them both up towards the slope. His arms surrounding her, Luna realised with dismay that *she* was being rescued – again.

'All-ez! Nous montons!' he said in a clipped voice, with a little grunt of effort, announcing their ascent. She wasn't sure if he was talking to her or into his radio. She slipped and slid her way through the snow, colliding with him when her boots lost grip. She might have been embarrassed to be rescued again, except for his murmured reassurances as they ascended. 'Oups! Doucement, madame. C'est ça. On y est presque,' he crooned. *Gently, that's it. Almost there.*

Luna snorted a laugh. What an end to her skiing adventure: being rescued by the most adorable gendarme in the world, who said, 'Oups,' in a soothing tone, called her 'madame' and felt as solid as a rock behind her, his feet planted in the snow with ferocious-looking crampons.

He deposited her onto the ski slope, unclipping her with quick movements of those capable hands, and headed off over the side again. A moment later, he reappeared with her skis and poles, setting them down beside her. Luna gawked, marvelling at the full-service rescue.

Her gendarme gave her a brief smile that took her right back to Christmas night, before disappearing backwards over the side, rappelling down to his colleagues.

The buzz of the helicopter sounded again, hovering over the trees and dropping a hook on a cable with astonishing precision. A moment later, the stretcher emerged above the treetops with the doctor attached, sailing over the ridge as it was winched up to the helicopter. Then the aircraft banked neatly and disappeared into the valley.

The small crowd that had gathered dispersed with excited murmurs. The rescue was over, after barely ten minutes. But Luna still felt the loopy effects of pounding adrenaline. Her wobbly knees gave out and she sat heavily, wincing at the sting in her wrist.

Hearing clinking and the crunch of snow, she glanced up to see the two gendarmes emerging under the tape and unclipping themselves from the safety rope. They talked and laughed as they packed up their equipment – just another day at the office. At least that must mean the skier would be okay. One was holding a billowing piece of coloured cloth, but Luna's tired brain was too tired to process what it was.

She shivered violently, whether from the shock or simply because the sun had disappeared behind the peaks, she wasn't sure. Exhaustion crept over her thoughts. She must have given a sigh or made some other sound, because the gendarme looked up sharply. He tramped over to her and crouched down.

'Ça va, championne?' He'd called her 'champion' – which she thought was a bit much – and asked if she was okay. He lifted his goggles and peered at her.

Now that the pressure of the rescue had dissipated, she couldn't stop herself staring up into his face and blurting out, 'Hello, again.'

6

He paused, his smile frozen. With a furrow of his brow, he lifted her goggles up onto her helmet and studied her face with a huff of surprise.

'Rebonjour,' he said. Thankfully, his smile was back, the one with all the teeth that was a bit lopsided and entirely sweet.

'I'm sorry. I said you wouldn't have to rescue me again,' she said, continuing in French.

'I didn't rescue you. I assisted you.'

She gave a doubtful smile. 'How is the victim?' she asked.

'Stable, probably a broken tibia. She was bleeding, but the doctor was able to treat her on site and give her something for the pain. They will take good care of her at the hospital – thanks to you.'

She glanced away, unable to keep her gaze on his face as he regarded her warmly, tilting his head. Stupid adrenaline. She would start to think he was handsome and dashing in his uniform in a minute. It was easier to keep her eyes on the crampons, the unfamiliar equipment that marked him as a different species of human. He'd just helped pull an injured woman off the mountainside, while Luna had fallen off the beginner slope.

'But next time,' he continued, 'don't go down. Leave the rescuing to us.' He brushed his fingertips under her chin, softening the criticism, and Luna had the strange thought that she was glad this person existed, that he was out there saving people, reassuring them with his gorgeous smile and peering at them from beneath those thick, dark eyelashes.

Making to stand, she gasped when her bare hand touched the freezing snow and the twinge in her wrist sent another ripple of pain up her arm. The gendarme's warm smile became a concerned frown that was unfortunately just as endearing.

'You are hurt? Can you move your fingers?'

Her hands were stiff from the cold, but she wiggled her fingers and tried to stand again. He stopped her with a squeeze to her shoulder.

'Where are your gloves?'

Luna glanced around, frowning when she didn't see them. Then she remembered tugging them off to make the phone call and peered down the slope in dismay.

'Down there? Attendez.' He instructed her to wait while he slipped back under the tape and returned a moment later, brushing snow off her mittens. She reached for them, but he crouched down again and took her good hand in his. Chafing it for a moment between both of his, which were miraculously warm with rough fingertips, he then tugged her glove carefully into place. 'Show me your wrist.'

'I think it's just a... sprain,' she said, the last word in English, when the French wouldn't come. 'C'est pas grave,' she said, insisting the injury wasn't serious.

He examined it anyway with cautious fingertips. The thump of the helicopter sounded again and Luna realised it had come back for the two rescuers and their gear. 'Her' gendarme – although she chided herself for thinking of him that way – shouted to his comrade to bring him something and a moment later, he strapped a piece of orange plastic around her wrist that moulded to her skin to form a splint when he pumped the air out of it.

'There is one more patient to transport to the DZ for first aid,' he spoke into his radio and helped her to her feet.

Luna shook her head fiercely. 'I don't need transport. It's not serious. I'll go to a clinic when I get back to the valley.' But the gendarme propelled her gently in the direction of the helicopter, holding her head down as they approached the spinning blades.

'Let's be cautious, hmm?' was all he said in reply.

Another gendarme stood on the runner of the helicopter and greeted her gruffly, giving her a firm push into the cargo area. She stumbled into a fold-down seat at the back as the gendarmes stowed her skis and the large piece of cloth she'd seen earlier and hopped aboard. The machine took off again before they'd even closed the door.

'What is that?' she asked the gendarme as he took his seat opposite her.

'This? A parachute,' he explained. 'The woman we rescued was speed riding,' he added when she only stared blankly in response.

'Speed riding?' she repeated, feeling obtuse. The word was in English, but it meant nothing to her.

'It's a combination of skiing and paragliding.'

Luna's stomach whooshed towards her ankles. 'Is that a *thing*?' she asked in English, her voice high.

'A... thing? Que voulez-vous dire?' he said.

'Never mind,' she muttered, gritting her teeth and slipping into her harness as the helicopter roared off over the treetops.

Clutching the seat with her good hand, she swallowed as her stomach leaped, gawping as the helicopter rose and left the ski resort behind. She glimpsed the summit at the top of the resort, isolated and swept with snow. The aircraft banked and the rocky needles of the Mont Blanc massif looked almost close enough to touch. Below the treeline, powdered white, the cluster of roofs nestled safely in the valley, just beginning to glow with evening lights.

Luna's heart expanded in her throat. The landscape was so beautiful she couldn't catch her breath, but the pounding of the rotor, the constant whine and the speed at which the helicopter manoeuvred through the air made her nauseous, not to mention her thoughts of crazy people jumping off those mountains with parachutes.

'Okay?' she heard faintly over the roar of the engine. She blinked at her gendarme. His partner sat next to him, a younger man with a beard and a polite smile that was much less reassuring. Far from helping, she'd caused them more trouble. Perhaps she shouldn't have accepted the 'lift', but it was also no use arguing with gendarmes, she supposed.

She nodded to assure them that she was okay and peered out of the window as the helicopter tilted again – and there was the moon, rapidly taking shape in the dimming sky. It was just shy of a half-moon now, even more prominent than it had been the first time he'd rescued her.

If this was the trouble she'd caused him during a crescent moon and a half-moon, she didn't want to imagine what could happen on a full moon, she thought to herself with an amused smile. Perhaps Silvia should give him some protective crystals, although he'd probably think she was foolish for thinking about crystals and signs and fruitless quests for dead people.

Her cheeks felt hot – which couldn't be right, since her entire body was cold. Perhaps she'd lost the ability to sense temperature after a day out in the elements.

'The moon is so close up here,' she said, satisfied that she'd managed to say something halfway normal.

His answering smile was a touch rueful. 'The moon looks close in the mountains, but it isn't any bigger than usual,' he said. 'It's an optical illusion.'

'A what?' she asked. Although the meaning of 'illusion d'optique' in French was clear, she struggled to believe that such an extraordinary sight would have a mundane explanation.

'It's your eyes,' he said, gesturing to her face. 'Your eyes make you *think* the moon is big.' If he hadn't had such a trustworthy expression, she might have suspected he was pulling her leg. 'Là,' he said, holding one hand up against the window and making a circle with his thumb and forefinger. 'Look. The moon is small again.'

When she closed one eye and peered through his fingers, she was amazed to see he was right. The looming celestial object she'd marvelled at a moment ago was replaced by the familiar little circle of light she glimpsed high in the sky most nights. When he moved his hand away, it looked enormous again. She rubbed her eyes with her gloved hand and looked again.

'I don't believe it,' she muttered in English. 'I thought you had a special moon in the mountains.'

'Not a different moon – a different point of view,' he continued in French. 'A clear night with a moon is always lucky for alpinists,' he said, leaning across to peer out of her window. 'Although not many are up there in December – only the hardiest.'

A different point of view... Perhaps that was the magic that mountaineers tried to grasp.

The helicopter swooped below the tree line surprisingly quickly, the twinkling lights and slanting, snow-covered roofs rising up to meet them as they touched down at the helipad where Luna's car had conked out a week earlier. She felt decidedly wobbly as the gendarme ushered her out again, gripping her elbow as though he could tell how jelly-like her knees had become. He escorted her to the base and sat her down on a bench outside the door, crouching in front of her and peering critically into her face. He turned her head from side to side and it took Luna a moment too long to realise he was examining her for symptoms of shock and not just studying her with interest, as she was helplessly staring into his broad face.

'I'm okay,' she insisted again, a shudder undermining her words.

'A car is coming from the hospital to collect you – just to make sure. You need to be careful with the wrist,' he said.

At that moment, a van arrived, marked as patient transport for the Hôpitaux du Pays du Mont Blanc and Luna resigned herself to ending her day in the hospital, hoping she'd never have to admit to Lydia how disastrously her first attempt at skiing had gone. Helping her up, the gendarme led her to the vehicle, where a nurse was waiting.

'Here is today's heroine,' he said to the nurse. 'Possible wrist sprain – and she's a little cold and sunburnt,' he added.

Her gloved hand flew to her cheek. That would explain why her skin felt so hot.

The gendarme squeezed her shoulder. 'Merci bien. Thank you for your help. You saved that woman some pain by helping us find her quickly. Take care of yourself, d'accord?'

'Thank you,' she said with a nod, meeting his gaze once more before he turned back to the base. When he'd taken a few steps away, a sudden thought gripped her.

'Um, wait!' she called out before he could go. 'This is a strange question, but I'm looking for someone called Robert Durand. Do you know anyone by that name?'

She held her breath while his brow slanted in thought. But

when he raised his gaze to hers, he shook his head. 'I'm sorry. The name sounds familiar, but it's a very common one.'

Her shoulders slumped and she released all of the breath she'd been holding in a misty gust. So much for Silvia's ideas about the right person finding her. 'Thanks anyway,' she mumbled.

'Come with me, please,' the nurse prompted Luna.

She couldn't help sneaking another glance over her shoulder as she followed the nurse towards the van. Her rescuer headed for the door of the base, carabiners clacking. Of course he didn't look back.

'What is your name?' the nurse asked in French, distracting Luna from her disheartening thoughts.

'Luna Rowntree,' she answered with a sigh.

She didn't see the gendarme's steps falter when he overheard her name.

7

'Hé là, les gars!' the helicopter winchman, André, called out in greeting as he stepped into the operations office where Yannick and the rest of the day's crew were finishing up. Yannick was working on the never-ending reports and his colleagues were distracting him as usual. 'I found this in the hélico.' He held up a single, black mitten. 'The Englishwoman?'

Yannick blinked at it in disbelief, thinking of the stripy woollen glove in his car, freshly washed. Not only had she crossed his path twice in the strangest of circumstances, but she also seemed to lose an accessory every time. Would it be shoes, next? A scarf?

'Give it to Yanni,' Matthieu said, slapping him on the shoulder. 'She's your Cinderella!'

'Here you are, Prince Charming,' André said with a chuckle. 'I thought you liked her.'

'I didn't *like* her,' Yannick insisted as he accepted the mitten without thought. 'It's called "keeping the victim distracted". She was more shocked than she looked. And I don't know why you all think I want a girlfriend,' he finished with a grumble. The word 'girlfriend' made his insides clench.

'Calm down,' André said soothingly. 'I'm only teasing. Are you okay?'

Yannick sighed and turned away from the computer, even though he wasn't finished. The damn paperwork was never finished.

If André was asking, he deserved a straight answer. 'Her name was Luna,' he said thoughtfully.

'Unusual name,' André commented. 'And that struck you... why?'

Yannick grimaced and gave André a sidelong glance. The winchman would work out the answer soon enough. André had been there that day. He'd winched the other victim to safety once Yannick had freed him.

'You're still thinking about Jim?' André asked softly. 'I heard the boss put you into professional development training. Is that... where this is going?'

Shit. He knew the group, the whole team, had his back, but it was difficult to take their sympathy – first for his divorce, and then for the loss of Jim and his struggle to get past it. The incident was nine months ago, now. He'd been through counselling and passed the psychological assessment with flying colours. He didn't get flashbacks or experience the fear of history repeating itself, but the team couldn't take any chances.

If he was moved to a desk job... He wasn't sure how he'd feel in the unit if he wasn't out there with the guys. The job was the one part of his life that made sense. Bringing people back down the mountain – in any state – was the only thing he'd ever been able to do about the fact that his brother was still up there, lost forever – and now he'd lost Jim too. This woman had appeared and reminded him of that day again – reminded him that he wasn't any good at letting go. He needed to do something to make up for the way he'd failed Jim.

He dropped his voice so the others wouldn't hear him. 'You know Jim's last words were—'

'I know,' André cut him off, which was probably for the best. Yannick didn't need to relive the moment his old friend had taken his last breath, staring at the sliver of sky visible through the gap in the ice, delirious, and mumbling something about seeing the moon – la lune.

It hadn't been the first time Yannick had seen someone die – it hadn't even been the first time he'd cut a dead body out of the ice for transport back to the valley. It was the decisions he'd made that day, that still bothered him.

He'd told the story over and over again during the investigation; his actions had been scrutinised at several levels of command. He'd even received a medal for his conduct. Decisions were taken by the whole team, on the mountain, and every man there had stood behind him. But it didn't change the fact that he'd been the only one down in that crevasse.

'This woman, Luna, said she's looking for a man called Robert Durand and for a moment it felt like too much of a coincidence.' André didn't seem to follow. 'You didn't know Jim's surname was Durand? "De Montagne" was just his nickname. I keep wondering if she's looking for a relative of his.'

'It's a common surname,' André pointed out, which was exactly what Yannick had been telling himself since the woman had asked him. She couldn't be connected to his old friend, the legendary mountain guide, but it was concerning how quickly his mind had latched on to the possibility.

'You need to go for a drink?' André asked him.

He shook his head. 'I'm going to go for a run – after I finish up the paperwork and put this in lost property.' He shook the mitten, dropping it next to the keyboard.

'Where are you headed on Friday?' André asked.

'Guy wants to check out Tour Ronde, if we don't get more snow.' It was part of the job to go out – and up – to check conditions on the more difficult routes in the massif – a part of the job Yannick loved.

'Look after the old man,' the winchman joked.

'Don't let the commandant hear you say that,' Yannick warned with a smile. 'You can only hope to be in such good shape when you're nearly sixty.'

'Who's nearly sixty?' came a voice from the next room. Guy's sense of timing was almost as legendary as his ice-climbing skills. 'You might feel old, Yanni, but that's because of Valérie. It's not your fault.'

Yannick swallowed a groan as he received a slap on the back hard enough to make him double over in the chair. He wasn't sure if the 'patron', the boss, was joking or not. André met his gaze with a silent guffaw. Turning slowly, Yannick arranged a dry smile on his face. 'Hey, patron,' he greeted Guy with a handshake. The commandant was a weathered old mountain dweller with the stamina of an ox and the heart to match. They might joke around, but Guy easily inspired the kind of loyalty the unit was famous for.

'Which of you is in the English class on Thursday?' Guy asked, pointing a finger from one face to another.

'Me,' grumbled Matthieu. 'Yannick, too.'

'Good,' said Guy. 'I'll see you at Cordial at 0900,' he said. 'No grumbling. The teacher is a guest of the PGHM – and a very kind young woman who's new in Cham.'

Yannick ignored all the meaningful glances in his direction. Being one of the only first responders who was single really sucked sometimes.

He could see Matthieu stifling a snort. The team hadn't taken it well when a visiting colonel had commented that some members of the unit seemed reluctant to speak English on the job. They all *could*, of course, but that colonel had been infuriatingly correct in his assessment that they often relied on guides and witnesses to translate for expediency.

Guy pointed two fingers at his eyes and then at Matthieu, but he laughed while he was doing so.

'Are we going up to Tour Ronde on Friday?' Guy asked, turning to Yannick. 'Top up your red blood cells and see if we can spot some crevasses? The forecast is for sunshine, so there will be people out next week.'

'Absolutely,' he responded with a nod. 'If I ever get through this report.' He lifted his hands over the keyboard again, his two fingers hovering, ready to go.

'What's that?' Guy squinted over his shoulder at the screen. 'You airlifted a wrist sprain back to base?'

'She was a witness,' he defended himself. 'The helicopter had come to pick us up anyway and she...' He paused to chuckle as he imagined what had happened. 'She tried to reach the victim.'

'Well, don't skimp on the details,' Guy said, giving him another friendly slap.

'No, sir.'

As the others filed out with mumbled farewells, Yannick embraced the silence of the office with a deep sigh. His gaze snagged on the mitten, which looked brand new.

Luna Rowntree was a beginner with bendy skis, who was apparently here looking for a man called Robert Durand. Was he an ex-boyfriend? Had she been hurt or defrauded or worse? Finishing the report quickly, he headed out, tucking the mitten into the lost property box in the corner and shaking off the lingering sense of responsibility for her.

He cut across the helipad and headed for the car park by the river. Unable to resist, he turned and stared up at the glowing half-moon hanging low in the sky above the snowy crags of the Tête

Rousse and the Aiguille de Goûter, as though it was following the normal route of the Mont Blanc summit tour.

He needed a new point of view himself, to marvel at the moon even when everything he'd lost weighed heavily on his shoulders. Up on the mountain, either during an operation or an adventure, he knew what needed to be done and he did it. But in the valley? It wasn't getting any easier to accept that Jim was gone. His second Christmas as a divorced father had been even more difficult than the first. Stressful situations were often easier than what came next.

It was after the adrenaline ebbed that life got difficult.

8

Luna glanced up at the same moon as Yannick as she got off the bus in the town centre. Her wrist was strapped and a little swollen, but the nurses had assured her it would be better in a few days. And her trip to hospital had proven useful for more than medical treatment.

She'd discovered her mum had worked there for a winter as a nurse in the emergency department. No matter how much Luna tried to tell herself it wasn't a disturbing revelation, she felt nevertheless disturbed that she hadn't known.

She'd first tried asking after Robert Durand, but even though the nurses had obligingly fetched 'Dr Durand', who happened to be on shift, the doctor had been no relation. It was a frustratingly common name.

But then she'd thought to ask about June. According to the staff records, her mum had been employed for the winter between 1992 and 1993. Luna had been born in November 1993. *No...* June not mentioning three months spent in Chamonix was one thing, but lying about the identity of Luna's father was entirely another.

An imposing white hotel with Belle Époque balconies and blue shutters was lit up in pink and pumping out music. The sound of voices reached the street from the terrace – hardy revellers fresh from a day on the slopes. Luna clomped past slowly in her boots, juggling her skis in her good hand. Après ski sounded like a good time from her position on the footpath, but she didn't understand how people still had the energy for it.

But perhaps celebrating wasn't such a bad idea. After the ups and downs of the day, Luna was thankful to still be standing, even if it was a little shakily. She'd made herself go *up there*, so the day had been something of a personal success, even though the feeling was probably just the last drops of adrenaline in her veins and she was determined she'd *never* go up again.

Luna reached Silvia's shop just as she was changing the sign to 'fermé'. Luna peered in through the window and waved when she got Silvia's attention. Her friend unlocked the door immediately and gestured her inside.

'What happened to you?'

Luna snorted, brushing a strand of limp, knotted hair out of her face with her strapped hand. 'Do I look that bad?'

Silvia picked up her wrist and exclaimed over the bandage. 'You're injured?'

'Only a little.'

'Come. Let's get a drink,' Silvia suggested. 'You can borrow some of my shoes. I always keep extras here. Have you learned, yet, that life in Chamonix is all about the right shoes?'

'I've certainly discovered what happens with the wrong ones,' she said, thinking of her old brogues with their thin soles – and definitely not about snow boots and crampons and the capable steps of a particular gendarme.

Luna's muscles started to ache as soon as she sat on a bench in Silvia's storeroom and let her friend unclip her ski boots, sighing with relief as she was freed from the thick plastic.

'Nothing has *ever* felt so good,' she groaned. 'You know, I think my legs hurt more than my wrist.'

'Sounds like you had a great day,' Silvia commented.

'How do you figure that? I'm going to be black and blue and I fell over so many times, even on the practice slope!'

'You'll feel better after a beer,' Silvia said matter-of-factly, straightening as Luna leaned down to tie her shoelaces. 'Wait, you have something in your hair.' Her friend's fingers brushed over her head, the tips finding the bare patch at her crown. 'Oh, it's nothing. Sorry I thought you had a twig caught there.'

'No, it's a scar and the hair never grew back in that spot. I fell down the stairs when I was four,' Luna said with a wry smile. 'I've had quite a career of falls. It needed ten stitches and nearly caused the early death of my mother, she used to tell me.' Her smile faded as her own thoughtless choice of words caught her in the chest. 'Perhaps I'm lucky she used to be an emergency nurse, although she switched to working at GP's practices when I was little.' She propped her elbows on her knees and glanced at Silvia. 'One good thing about my visit to the hospital was that I found out Mum worked there briefly,' she added, not game enough to mention the suspicious timing of that short-term contract.

'I'm sorry you hurt yourself, but how interesting that you made your first discovery at the hospital! The rest of the answers are just waiting for you, I'm sure,' Silvia said gently, hauling Luna to her feet. 'Allez, let's go.'

The 'allez' reminded her again of the kind gendarme hauling her up the steep hill and she was glad her cheeks were already red from cold, otherwise Silvia might have asked her why she was blushing. What a day.

* * *

Silvia was absolutely right about the beer. As Luna took a sip of her drink at the bar of a cosy, wood-panelled pub with posters of skiing and paragliding and a 3D topographical map of the area on the wall, all of her muscles softened and melted into aching relief. She felt about five years older after one day up in the wind and the sunshine and the cold.

She slumped against the solid-wood counter and would have groaned again, if she hadn't been certain Silvia would laugh. Rubbing a hand over her face, she discovered that hurt, too, as her sunburn was coming up.

'To your first day of skiing,' Silvia said, holding up her beer.

'To my last day of skiing,' Luna said grimly, clinking her glass with Silvia's.

'You can be proud of yourself, you know,' Silvia said. 'Not all beginners stick with it as long as you did on the first day. I'd say that makes you special.'

Instead of the icy cold, her body seemed to be overheating, now, between the sunburn and Silvia's words.

'I wonder how my mum learned. I suppose I thought it would be easier, because she'd done it.'

'It's much easier when you have a motivated teacher,' Silvia said in a meaningful tone.

'Hmm?' Luna asked, taking a sip of the cold beer and letting the temperature extremes flood through her.

'If you have a boyfriend or a girlfriend who wants you to ski,' Silvia explained with a laugh. 'That's the best way to learn as an adult.'

'I don't think that's any help to me,' Luna said with a laugh.

'Why not?' Silvia asked. 'Cham is a great place to meet people.'

'I'm not here to find love,' Luna said, giving her friend a dubious look. 'And I'm not staying long enough to get to know someone.'

'This is a place where love doesn't always last forever, but it's worth searching for anyway,' Silvia countered. 'You've had so much heartache for someone so young. There's nothing stopping you getting out and having some fun.'

'Fun' wasn't the first thing she thought of when she pictured a romantic relationship. 'Heartache' was more like it, which was why this particular idea of Silvia's was *not* a good one.

Luna froze in thought, wondering if Robert Durand had taught June to ski, if they'd had a temporary affair for the ski season. The possibility that she'd never know upset her more than she wanted.

'I looked up the online cemetery records for you today,' Silvia continued.

Luna turned eagerly to face Silvia, but she could immediately see her friend had had no success. Even that small gesture of respect for her benefactor would not be easy to complete.

'I'm sorry, but there was no listing. If he lived at the address you have, he should have been buried here. I don't understand it.'

'Could he... perhaps he was cremated?' She thought of her mother's ashes on the bedside table at Silvia's. She pictured two urns next to each other, reuniting a pair of lovers, which was sentimental and utterly ridiculous – and exactly the sort of strange thought that occurred to Luna more often than was healthy.

'Hmm, perhaps he was cremated, although usually there would be a place in the cemetery for the ashes, as you aren't allowed to just keep them in the home, in France.'

Luna gulped, imagining Silvia's boyfriend stumbling upon the contraband urn. How was it that she'd accidentally broken the law twice since she'd arrived and kept running into gendarmes? She took another long sip of beer.

Silvia was still speaking, musing quietly. 'But if the ashes were scattered... yes, perhaps. You can ask at the mairie,' she said, referring to the town hall. 'If the ashes were scattered, there will be a record, because you need to request permission to do that.'

'Right,' Luna said with a sigh. 'I'll stop in there when they reopen in the new year, since I won't be able to do the rest of my ski course.' She gestured limply with her injured arm. 'I might be sporting a bandage for the English class on Thursday.'

'You'll be fine,' Silvia said with more confidence than Luna felt. 'I had wondered what took you so long this evening. Another half an hour and I might have called the PGHM!' She chuckled at her own joke, but Luna was gripped by another rush of mortification mixed with the effects of leaching adrenaline.

'You didn't need to call them,' she mumbled. '*I* did.'

Silvia's elbow banged onto the bar as she whirled to face Luna. 'You what?'

'I mean, I called the emergency services – not for *me*!' she clarified quickly. 'A parachute jumper had an accident. I saw it happen, so I called and they came. I just... they were going in the helicopter anyway, so they took me back to base with them.'

A smile spread over Silvia's face. 'I know most of the secouristes, the first responders. Which ones arrived to help? Just one team?'

'It was two rescuers and a doctor, plus the pilot and the man with the rope. They didn't introduce themselves,' Luna said defensively, when Silvia seemed to be waiting for her to say more.

'What did they look like? I might recognise them.'

'Um...' Luna chewed on her lip, pretending she was trying to remember what they looked like, while she was actually thinking of a way to describe her kind gendarme without revealing how much she'd crushed on him. 'One had a beard. A short, light brown beard. He was probably younger than me, so, in his twenties. Aside from that I can only say he had a helmet and goggles!'

'Okay, that was possibly Matthieu. And the other one?'

'Er...' Goosebumps prickled along her hairline. 'A little older, I think, but I can't say for sure. Black hair, dark eyes and a... a smile.' It was a stupid description, but she couldn't exactly say that he reminded her of a teddy bear and had rough fingertips on her skin. Perhaps it would be best if Silvia couldn't work out which one he was.

'Yannick!' Silvia said brightly. 'That can only be Yannick. He's a treasure.'

Despite Luna's iffy description, 'a treasure' certainly suggested Silvia had guessed correctly. So, his name was Yannick...

'You will get to know more of the team. Did I tell you where you are going to teach the class?'

Luna's head spun with the sudden change of topic. 'No, you didn't mention that.'

'The class is a new one for my most important client – the PGHM Chamonix.'

* * *

On Thursday morning, Luna gazed at the building where she would teach her first class, fiddling with the moonstone in the pocket of her wool coat as her heart beat a loopy rhythm. Silvia hadn't known exactly which of the PGHM first responders would be attending her course and Luna vacillated wildly between wanting to see Yannick and feeling mortified at the prospect.

Teaching adults was already out of her comfort zone. That crystal would have its work cut out for it.

She'd expected Silvia to send her to the base, but the address she'd provided was around the corner from the Maison de la Montagne where she'd made her first fruitless inquiries about Robert Durand.

The headquarters of the mountain unit was a squat, sprawling building with piles of snow in the car park, icicles clinging to the eaves and a sign on the façade that read 'Peloton de Gendarmerie de Haute Montagne'. Above the sign was a round, blue emblem with a mountain and something that looked like a pair of crossed swords on it.

'Peloton' meant 'platoon' and it was now obvious to her what the 'HM' stood for: high mountains. Her preparatory research had given her more background on the elite high-altitude unit of the Gendarmerie Nationale, but the more she'd discovered, the more her unease grew.

She was not the right teacher for a mountain rescue squadron. Every time she merely looked at the peaks, she confronted her own mortality and she'd never imagined that people would seriously jump off mountains with a parachute and a set of skis. In the valley, she occasionally managed to stop thinking about hypothermia and exposure, falls and broken bones, but this place was full of thrill-seekers and adrenaline was everywhere.

After making her way gingerly across the icy car park and signing in, she was shown to a classroom that was unlike anywhere she'd taught before. The projector and whiteboard were familiar, but the cabinet at the back of the room wasn't filled with writing materials, but with ropes and harnesses, medical equipment and pulley devices.

A second whiteboard was covered in scribbled text – place names, times, dates, GPS coordinates. Desks lined three walls, with several computers and extra screens, along with telephones and electronic devices whose purposes Luna could only guess at. A door to an adjacent room was ajar and she caught a glimpse of twin beds – presumably for night shifts.

The walls were covered in charts – topographical maps, navigational diagrams and climate data. She approached one chart curiously, marked with pins in different colours, freezing in alarm as she read that the pink pins marked recent avalanches.

She jumped when the door swung open and Guy walked in. He shook her hand warmly and flashed her a charming smile. She'd seen the captain several times at Silvia's over the past week.

'Do you have everything you need?' he asked in French. 'The training we usually have is quite informal.'

'Je crois,' she replied – *I think so*. She had three different lesson plans to choose from after her initial assessment of the level of the class, but it wasn't enough to stop her feeling nervous.

'You tell me if they don't behave,' Guy said, waggling a finger at her.

'Uh... okay.'

He chuckled and clapped her on the shoulder. 'Don't worry. I've threatened them with cleaning duties if they don't actively participate.'

'Oh... great.'

'Eh bien, I'll call them in. Les gars!' From the way he barked the invitation to enter, she wouldn't have been surprised if they'd marched in and stood at attention, but there was no saluting and, after her students filed past and introduced themselves, they took their seats in the chairs she'd hastily set in a circle.

Distracted by the barrage of military ranks in French, in addition to the fact that they introduced themselves surname first and added their first names as an afterthought, Luna struggled to take note of who was who. One with grey at his temples she thought was called Patrice. There was only one woman and Luna missed her name entirely.

She recognised the man with the beard from her rescue and Silvia had luckily already identified him as Matthieu. He paused in surprise when he saw her. 'Content de vous revoir, madame,' he said, shaking her hand.

'It's nice to see you again, too,' she said pointedly in English. From Matthieu's grimace, she suspected Guy's threat about cleaning duties had unfortunately been necessary. There was a strange atmosphere of doom in the classroom, although Luna hoped she was imagining it.

Guy held the door open for a straggler, who arrived at a jog, nodding to his commanding officer. Luna's knees were already wobbly before he turned around. She recognised that thick, straight hair, and the ears that stuck out a little.

No. She would *not* start wondering if there was a reason they'd met and she definitely wouldn't blurt out his name like a schoolgirl with a crush. She was his teacher and she would maintain some dignity.

9

'Yannick?'

He whirled in surprise at the sound of his name before he was quite finished greeting Guy.

Luna. He'd just convinced himself he was an idiot for imagining he might see her again.

She blinked at him in surprise and he belatedly realised he'd said her name aloud – a name he wasn't supposed to know. Another awkward heartbeat passed before he realised *she'd* said *his* name, too. 'Huh,' was all he managed to say.

The back of his neck prickled. He was going to get so much shit for this later. He could feel it in the air behind him, the looks the team were shooting his way. He was a warrant officer in the gendarmerie, a father. He shouldn't stand there staring like a tongue-tied idiot, no matter how pretty she looked with her intent gaze and her dark hair with several strands askew.

'We... ehm.' He rubbed the back of his head. With a cough, he drew himself up – not quite to attention, but enough to remind himself this was a professional situation. 'Adjudant Pasquier, Yannick,' he introduced himself formally.

'It's... nice to meet you – properly.' She cleared her throat. 'Shall we... We should... begin.' She patted her hair nervously, but only made it more of a mess. Turning to the room, she said, 'Please excuse me if I get anything wrong about your job. I've tried to do some research into... mountain rescue, but it's not something I know much about, so... Let's get started anyway.'

She'd arranged the chairs in a circle and to Yannick it suddenly felt like an official debrief. She wasn't to know, but that was only going to make the guys nervous, especially given the situation up on the Grandes Jorasses, which wasn't far from anyone's mind that day. He'd discussed cancelling the course with Guy, but the commandant was right: there was nothing the grounded team members could do in support. Keeping their appointment with the new English teacher made more sense.

But, wow, he felt sorry for her, more and more as the lesson wore on and her attempts to foster conversation stalled at every stage. At any other time, he might have had a sharp word or two for the team, but he understood why they were reacting this way. No one particularly wanted to *talk* right now.

'What do you want us to say?' asked Matthieu, after she'd explained the next activity.

'It's a practice exercise.' She held up the sheet of paper they were all holding or had placed awkwardly in their laps. She'd directed them to scribble a few words down to fill in the blanks on the sheet with some expressions for natural conversation. 'You tell an anecdote using this language that we discussed – something... funny that happened recently.'

He met Matthieu's grim gaze. The hour would only drag on if they couldn't get out of their own heads.

'Why should we tell an anecdote? Why do we need this?' asked Laurent.

'Um,' Luna began, glancing at her shoes. 'Telling stories is...

part of human character,' she said, her voice trailing off. 'I thought that's why people went up mountains,' she added weakly.

'I am not going to tell stories to a victim during a rescue,' Marina said with a snort.

'You wouldn't... use small talk to keep a victim calm?' Luna suggested. 'Perhaps this exercise about the weather would be better.'

'No!' Yannick cut in before anyone had a chance to groan. The weather was the reason four of their colleagues had spent the night in an emergency bivouac at 3,300 m of altitude and still couldn't be retrieved.

'Unless your exercise about the weather can give us words for "le chapeau de Mont Blanc" or "l'effet de foehn",' Matthieu challenged her.

'"The hat of Mont Blanc",' she translated hesitantly. 'The effect of what?'

'The weather in the high mountains is a particular phenomenon,' Yannick explained, 'and a part of our job is to monitor and understand the weather more deeply than "sunny" or "cloudy". The north face of a mountain has different weather to the south face and sudden changes in temperature are common. Clouds like the hat of Mont Blanc can show the weather will change soon. But there's nothing wrong with telling anecdotes,' he assured her. He gave the others what he hoped was a warning glance. 'I can start.' He straightened and took a deep breath, unexpectedly nervous, but there was one topic he could talk about for days. 'My daughter wanted a... poupée for Christmas.'

He glanced at Luna for help, when he couldn't produce the word in English, surprised to see a flicker of dismay cross her features, but she gave herself a shake. 'Oh, a doll,' she supplied.

'A doll,' he repeated. 'Oui. But... hum, funnily enough,' he said laboriously, trying to use the language she'd modelled, 'she says she doesn't like the dolls in the... store and she asks me: "Papa, why don't the dolls have skis?"' He managed a stilted laugh, his hair standing on end at the strange experience of telling the story in front of his peers in his slow English.

That colonel had had a point: unless the whole group was confident using English in a crisis, it could cause miscommunication and errors. He would make the others see that later, as he was the ranking officer in the room.

Patrice cuffed him on the shoulder and chuckled. 'Ta petite,' he murmured fondly. 'Trop mignonne.'

'Thank you, Yannick,' Luna said. 'Your daughter does sound very cute. How old is she?'

'Five,' he answered. Thinking of Maëlys always restored his pride.

The session finally ended with stifled sighs of relief. Luna gathered her things with jerky movements, shoving papers haphazardly into a brown corduroy bag.

Yannick thought she probably wouldn't come back. He'd taken the occasional group of recruits from the gendarmerie school of skiing and mountaineering and it was usually clear which ones wouldn't make it through training. It wasn't easy to watch, but they would face worse conditions – with lives on the line – on the job and some people weren't cut out for it.

But Luna deserved an explanation.

Yannick caught up with her while she was signing out at the front desk. She was left-handed, with a strange pencil grip that reminded him of Maëlys and her painstaking letters that were all backwards. When she looked up at him, her eyes were deep with misgiving. He ushered her outside with a hand at her back.

'I'm sorry,' she began, speaking in French now. 'I'm sure Silvia will find you another teacher before next week. I'm obviously not the right person to teach here. Thank you for trying to help.'

'I wanted to explain,' he began.

'You don't have to,' she said with a shake of her head. 'I'm a French teacher, for kids, not an English teacher for...' Her gaze landed on his boots and made its way slowly up his uniform trousers, to the pale blue shirt, pausing on the patch on his gilet – a yellow, horizontal line with a strike of red through it that designated his rank. 'For gendarmes with helicopters,' she finished faintly.

'It wasn't your fault,' he insisted. 'Four of our group are up on the mountain right now, unable to get down because of winter cloud cover. One of them has a suspected broken leg.'

She gasped, her eyes growing round. 'They're stuck up there?'

'The situation is stable, for now. They've secured the victims, erected shelter. It's just a matter of time before they can be picked up, but... injuries can sometimes take a bad turn very quickly and we would all rather be up there... *doing* something.'

'You'd rather be up there?' She blinked rapidly.

'Perhaps it's true that you don't understand our work and our unit,' he said as gently as he could. 'But you could learn enough to teach us something.'

'I don't know what I—'

'You're exactly right, you know. A lot of people climb mountains so they have stories to tell. The legends are important in this place and I like the idea of telling a story to keep a victim calm,' he explained. 'I knew a man with many stories and I think... it was a good lesson.'

'Well, I've done that material, now,' she said with a wry laugh. 'I'm sorry I didn't realise something had happened. I would have done things differently.' She looked him full in the face for the first time in the conversation, sharing his smile and he was right back at staring when he really shouldn't.

'Will you come back next week?' he asked. 'The others will be down safely by then. Matthieu can tell you the story.'

She hesitated for a moment, but then nodded. 'I'll come back. To be honest, I need the job. I can't let a group of gendarmes scare me away.' She opened her hands in a dismissive shrug, but it didn't stop him wondering why she needed the job and what had brought her to Chamonix in search of a man with a common name.

'We're not so terrifying, when you get to know us.'

She grinned at him again. 'I'll have to trust you on that. But thank you – for everything.'

He gave her a curt nod in response.

'Hey, Yanni!' There was a call from the door of the building and he turned to see Matthieu standing there. 'There was a break in the cloud while we were in class and Choucas is bringing the team down.'

Relief flooded Yannick's body. If Choucas, the helicopter, was in the air again, the team would be down within half an hour.

'They're all going to be okay,' Matthieu continued. 'Maybe the prof should teach us about the weather after all!' He gave Luna a joking salute, his grin stretching across his face. 'You can be our team mascot.'

'She's not a mascot,' Yannick said drily. 'She's a teacher.'

'Either way, it all worked out, today. You going to head over to the DZ to see if they need help?' Matthieu asked as he turned to go back inside and Yannick waved him off with a nod.

'I'll... see you next week, then,' Luna said, 'if not before,' she added with a laugh. 'Not that I'm going anywhere near a ski slope. That was a *disaster*.' She gave an awkward wave and turned to go as though she was bolting, shoving her hands deep into the pockets of her wool coat. She didn't head towards a car, but onto the footpath. He wondered what had happened to her old vehicle with the summer tyres.

And then he remembered. 'Luna?' he called after her.

She whirled round, her flowing skirt following half a second later. 'Hmm?'

'I have your gloves – two different ones. One is here in my car and the other one is at the DZ – the helicopter drop zone. I'm going there now, if you have time to come with me.'

'You rescued my gloves?'

'Hum, I suppose so.'

'Thank you,' she said with a small smile that he couldn't help but share. 'I won't get in the way at the DZ? I'll just pick up my gloves and go. And I'm glad your friends are okay, by the way.'

'You won't be in the way. Perhaps you are a good luck charm.'

'Don't tell me a gendarme like you believes in crystals and herbs and good luck charms?'

'No, of course n—' He realised she was teasing him. 'Do you?'

'The moonstone in my pocket would suggest so,' she said with a sheepish shrug.

A few moments later, she was strapped into his passenger seat, peering out of the window as he drove the ten minutes to the DZ. She clutched the woollen glove in both her hands and appeared to be deep in thought. She always appeared to be deep in thought.

'Have you found the man you're looking for?' he asked casually.

'Not yet,' she replied.

'I knew a man with the surname Durand. I wondered if it was a relative,' he added.

'I'm learning there are a lot of people called "Durand" around here,' she said drily. 'Next stop is the mairie. Silvia tried to help me, but she couldn't find his grave. I'm going to ask to check the register of scattered ashes this afternoon.'

Yannick's stomach flipped and he gripped the steering wheel to steady himself. Blinking, he wrenched his attention back to the road as his skin bloomed with goosebumps. 'This man you're looking for is dead?'

He glanced at her in time to see her wince. 'Yes. It's kind of awkward looking for a dead man.'

'When did he die?'

'In March, according to the extract from his death certificate that I was allowed to see.'

Yannick's breath whooshed out and he shook his head to clear it. 'What relation was he to you?'

If she noticed the unsteadiness in his voice, she didn't react. She gave a pained sort of laugh. 'That's just it. I don't know. I just received a letter informing me that a man I'd never heard of had taken out a life insurance policy with me as the beneficiary. And then he died.' Her voice was brittle.

La lune... Luna. Merde alors. An insurance policy. Half of the picture was suddenly so clear, he'd been an idiot for not putting it together before now, but the other half was only more confusing. The name *Robert* Durand? Damn it, it was possible.

She kept talking while his thoughts churned. 'This probably sounds strange, but I don't want to take the money. I mean, I really need it. But I don't know why he paid the premiums. An inheritance I might have made peace with, but life insurance feels like... he expected to die and I benefited and I hate that idea.'

Yannick's skin crawled as he thought about the way Jim had lived without roots in the valley, as though he'd always thought he'd go up the mountain and never return.

Luna continued speaking, oblivious to his suspicions. 'I can't accept the money until I understand, or at least until I've paid my respects, as pointless as that sounds.' She gave a discouraged sigh. 'That's why I'm here – because I couldn't do anything else.'

That was a feeling Yannick understood deeply. Life could certainly be strange sometimes. He could almost feel Jim toasting them both from beyond.

'Are you all right?' she asked suddenly.

Although he kept his eyes glued to the road, he could feel her intent gaze. He nodded curtly in response.

'Luna,' he murmured. 'I think I can help you find him. Let me get permission from the commandant and I'll tell you all I know.'

10

Luna waited with a strange feeling of reverence as Silvia unfolded a creased and crinkled map after sweeping aside the books and trinkets on the coffee table. It didn't look like any of the Ordnance Survey maps her mum had used to keep on the shelves for their rambles.

Ringed with green valley sections in topographic detail was an enormous area in white, marked with grey ridges in irregular patterns: the Mont Blanc massif. She'd never thought much about the highest mountain peak in western Europe, beyond a trivia question. But here she was, studying the map, wondering if she could get up there.

Not to the peak of Mont Blanc itself. She'd give up today, if that was the place she had to reach. But paying her respects at the place Robert Durand's ashes had been scattered might turn out to be impossible for her anyway. She'd have to think of another way to find some peace about the money. Hopefully Yannick's information, when he'd received permission to pass it on, would answer all her questions. She was feverish with impatience.

'Show me what they wrote down for you at the mairie,' Silvia instructed, holding out her hand.

Luna had been shocked to receive a straight answer when she'd visited the Chamonix town hall that afternoon to look into the register of scattered ashes. Although she still winced every time she remembered that keeping ashes at home was illegal in France, the existence of this register turned out to be a blessing.

The administrator at the town hall had immediately found a request for permission to scatter the ashes of Robert Durand, dated June the year before. And the location: somewhere called Trélaporte.

Silvia pointed out the glacier de Trélaporte, tucked in behind a ridge that was marked with topographic lines so tightly packed that it must represent a sheer rock face. Even the place names sounded beautiful and impossible to Luna. There was the glacial valley of the Mer de Glace, the sea of ice, that carved an enormous path through the massif. Further up, along the border with Italy, was the Glacier du Géant and the Aiguilles du Diable – the devil's needles – and geographical terms in French that she'd have to look up in the dictionary: couloir, arête, séracs and brèche.

'I will never make it up there,' she murmured. 'What good would it do anyway? He's not really there – just his ashes.'

Silvia gave her a pointed look and Luna wished that she didn't understand exactly what she meant. Those words didn't sound like they'd come from the woman who had set off across France because her conscience wouldn't stay quiet. But Luna Rowntree travelling to a glacier sounded ridiculous.

It was frustrating to be so close, and yet have no chance of achieving the one goal that she'd hoped was within her control: visiting his grave.

'I hope Yannick has some more information,' she said morosely. 'I know he doesn't mean to leave me in suspense.' She was proud of herself for saying his name without even the slightest quiver of emotion. Her little crush on the very *married* gendarme had been a typical Luna-like blunder. Of course a man like that would be married.

Silvia peered over her glasses. 'Would you like me to phone Guy?' Luna shook her head. 'I don't mind. There's no way you'll be able to sleep in this state.'

'I just feel like I'm so close,' she murmured. Unfortunately, knowing the location of his ashes hadn't brought her any further in her quest to understand. There would be no plaque, no memorial. It was another dead-end – unless Yannick could fill in the gaps.

He'd had such a strange look on his face as he'd realised something from whatever Luna had babbled – such a troubled brow – and all he'd explained was that he needed permission to disclose details of a mission.

Luna still felt vaguely sick from the possibilities.

When the doorbell rang, she jumped violently. Silvia rose and gave her a firm squeeze on the shoulder. 'Perhaps it's Guy,' she said, as Luna tried to tamp down her anticipation.

She trailed Silvia downstairs to the mudroom, holding her breath. When Silvia turned the lock and swung open the heavy wooden door, it wasn't Guy who stood on the threshold.

Yannick snapped his head up to greet them. He was leaning one hand on the doorframe, his eyes soft and serious as his gaze settled on her. He was still in his uniform and Luna was touched that he'd come straight here to speak to her. Gosh, why weren't there more people like him in the world?

Squeezing past Silvia, Luna rushed to the door. 'You came!' she blurted out. 'Thank you!'

'Guy said I'd find you here,' he said, replying in French. 'I have a lot to tell you.' His flat tone hinted that, whoever Robert Durand had been, he'd meant something to Yannick.

'You'd better come in,' she muttered in English, noticing that Silvia had made herself scarce.

'Sorry, I... can try in English if that would help,' he said stiltedly as he took off his boots and followed her up the stairs to Silvia's colourful living room.

Luna shook her head. 'En français, c'est bon. I might reply in English, but we understand each other.'

With a firm nod, he sat stiffly on the sofa and faced her, lacing his fingers between his knees. It took him a long moment to begin.

'I've spoken to the families of victims many times, but this is different,' he remarked.

'Because I'm not family?' she asked.

'No,' he said, peering at her askance. 'Because he was my friend.' He took a deep breath.

'I'm sorry,' she said, feeling the futility of those words keenly; she'd heard them herself so many times.

Silvia appeared with two cups of her lavender and chamomile tisane and Yannick thanked her with a grateful smile. She gave his shoulder the affectionate squeeze that Luna had wanted to give him a moment ago. She had the unexpected urge to brush her palms over his cheeks and tell him everything would be all right.

'You said he was your friend,' she prompted gently after he'd taken a sip of scalding tea.

'Yes. And it was still a surprise to me when I checked our files and found that his name was actually Robert. Everyone knew him as Jim de Montagne.'

Luna froze, thinking back to the conversation at the Maison de la Montagne after Christmas. *Jim.* Her benefactor had been a mountain guide after all.

'It was the perfect nickname,' Yannick continued, lost in his own thoughts. '"Jim" is so short and modest, especially when you place it before "Montagne". That was just like him: a humble man who knew how to respect the mountain.'

Luna's skin prickled as she soaked in every detail Yannick stiltedly shared.

'He was the man I said told many stories,' Yannick continued. 'He had no family – that we knew of. His brother came from Annecy to collect his personal effects after his death. Jim didn't leave much behind.'

Luna swallowed the lump in her throat. Jim de Montagne hadn't left an inheritance, but he'd paid insurance premiums so she'd still benefit from his death. She wasn't sure how she could ever feel right about it. 'You don't know... who I was to him?'

He peered at her from under his brow again. 'I don't, Luna, and that is another reason why I didn't imagine you meant Jim when you said you were looking for someone. He never mentioned you – except on the day he died.'

The prickle became a flush of goosebumps. It was a strange sensation to grieve for someone you'd never known. 'How did he die?'

The look in Yannick's eyes was enough to make her wary of the answer. 'He was with a group on the Miage glacier, when a snow bridge collapsed and he fell into a crevasse – along with one of his clients.'

'A crevasse is... a crack in the ice?' she clarified.

He glanced at her doubtfully, clearing his throat. 'Yes, in summer the glacier cracks, sometimes very deeply, then winter snow covers it again, so the crevasse is not visible. Often the snow bridge is strong enough to support the weight of a skier, but sometimes... it isn't. We see this kind of accident often.'

Luna tried not to let him see her shudder.

'I was first to march that day, with Patrice – first on duty. The helicopter could let us out near the crevasse, so we were on the scene quickly, but Jim was seriously injured and unfortunately he died before we could get him out.'

There was nothing Luna could say. Yannick clearly felt a sense of responsibility for Jim's death that he shouldn't, but that wouldn't be erased with words and she couldn't imagine how painful it must have been for him to witness his friend's death and be unable to save him.

His grief was obvious on his face, but Luna wouldn't dare take that away from him by offering meaningless platitudes. So, she just nodded and sipped her tea.

He looked at her then, with sudden intensity. 'I thought he was talking about the moon. He wasn't lucid at the end. I thought he said, "la lune". I told you the moon is a mountaineer's companion. When you want to summit Mont Blanc – or any mountain – you often have to leave long before dawn to make it back down afterward. I never questioned why he'd talk about the moon, but when I heard your name, it made me rethink.'

'It's one of the only things I know about my father: he gave me the name Luna Marie,' she murmured. 'Not that Jim was my father – at least, I'm fairly certain he couldn't have been,' she added hastily. She hated the seed of doubt that had crept into those words.

'When I consider it now, Jim wasn't talking about the moon. He was saying your name. He was trying to tell me something, but it was too late. The insurance policy you spoke about was mentioned in his will – well it wasn't really a will, it was some scribbled notes he'd left at the Compagnie des Guides in case of his death. We investigated the accident as per procedure and one of the gendarmes made sure a copy of the death certificate was sent to the insurance company. I didn't... the others took over the paperwork for me, even though I'd been in charge of the mission.'

'I'm sorry to make you go through this again,' she said.

A flash of emotion passed over his features, as though going over the details of that day was something he still did often, but he shook his head. 'I think Jim would be happy you're here.'

'I hope so.' There was so much to read in Yannick's expression: grief, duty, kindness, concern. It was fascinating and slightly overwhelming and she felt too fragile to stare at him for long, but she didn't want to look away.

A noise from the kitchen startled her and she realised she'd leaned forward, drawn in by Jim's story, by the mystery. Pulling back, she admitted to herself that perhaps she'd been drawn in by the kindness in his face, too.

She pressed the backs of her fingers to her warm cheeks. Silvia must have built up the fire in the stove when Luna hadn't been watching.

'Thank you for telling me all this. It means a lot to me.'

His smile broke out – the adorable, toothy one and her heartbeat flipped out again. 'Je suis content de vous l'avoir dit,' he said.

I'm glad, too, Luna thought. 'But I've kept you. I appreciate you coming all the way here in the evening. I admit I was impatient to know, but it was kind of you to rush over. Your daughter must be waiting for you,' she said with a little nod to remind herself that sparks and connections were all in her head, because he went home to his wife every night and she was sure he would be the most devoted husband she could imagine.

But instead of the slightly giddy smile he'd worn as he spoke about his daughter that morning in class, his expression slipped. 'She stays with her mother mostly,' he admitted. 'We share custody, but my shifts...'

'Oh, God, I'm sorry,' Luna said, slapping a hand over her mouth. 'I just assumed—'

'C'est pas grave, Luna,' he reassured her with a touch of amusement in his voice. 'It was no problem to come by.'

Luna rummaged around for some composure while her brain – or was it her heart – latched onto the fact that he wasn't married after all. What did that change? Ultimately, nothing, but it didn't feel like nothing, as her blood fizzed the way it did when she stared up at the mountains.

Nothing, she told herself strictly. She was in a fragile state and gravitated towards this teddy-bear gendarme with his soft voice and capable hands. She was looking for a way forward with her life, not a complex distraction for her heart. She'd learned that with Aiden: sort her life out first. Then she might have a hope of finding someone who loved her for herself – peculiar tendencies and all.

She doubted Yannick could be that person, no matter how sweet he was.

'Everything okay?' Silvia asked, wandering tentatively in from the kitchen. 'Will you take her? To Trélaporte to pay her respects?'

The blood drained from Luna's face and she shook her head frantically at her friend. But it was too late. The suggestion had been made.

11

Who is she, Jim?

Yannick wasn't in the habit of speaking to the dead, but the way his intuition was firing, he wished he could. This woman had meant something to Jim and she'd made Jim mean something to her. It touched him more than he'd been prepared for, the way she reached out for his memory. There weren't many people he knew who would think twice about accepting a financial windfall, but she had explained that she needed to pay her respects, find out the truth if possible. And he would help her in any way he could.

'You want to see the place where we scattered his ashes?' he asked.

She looked faint as she made a strange gesture between a nod and a shake of her head. 'I can't – can I? Remember I fell off the green slope at La Flégère.'

He frowned. 'You didn't fall off. You went down to check on the—'

She cut him off. 'I wasn't a hero. I fell and I happened to see the accident. I can't ski.'

'Du tout?'

She shook her head 'I can't ski – at all,' she repeated. 'That day was the first time I'd ever stood on skis.'

He was torn between praising her for going after the victim and scolding her for the same thing. If she had been Jim's daughter, the old man would have been horrified by how helpless she was in the territory he had made his own.

'Where I scattered the ashes, you probably can't reach.'

'*You* scattered his ashes?' she asked.

He nodded sombrely. 'With another old friend of his, from the summit of the Aiguille du Grépon. One last climb of his favourite route, which is called "Le soleil à rendez-vous avec la lune".' His voice trailed off.

'"The sun meeting the moon"?' she translated into English, her voice soft. 'That's very romantic – for a rock-climbing route. But... you scattered his ashes from the peak?' she repeated, discouraged.

'Yes. You can probably see it from here, although I ascended from the other side.' He didn't imagine peering at the distant peak from Chamonix would be enough to satisfy her sense of obligation.

'You could go to the refuge,' Silvia suggested, 'where the guides gathered to pay their respects. I know it's not guarded in winter, but you would help her reach it wouldn't you Yannick.'

'Oh, I'd never—' Luna cut herself off. 'Would I? Would I make it?'

Yannick had seen a woman with only one arm climb the Aiguille Verte. Luna seemed fairly fit. With him in charge of the ropes, she could probably complete the comparatively easy trek to the refuge. 'That would be up to you,' he said slowly. 'In summer, you would make it no problem.'

She stifled a snort of disbelief.

'In winter... possibly. If you are determined.' He wasn't sure if he meant she would make it if she had the courage, or that he would take her if she truly insisted she had to go. 'You would need to learn and train and practice – and you would need to know the dangers.'

'I can imagine the dangers,' she assured him, 'although I don't really want to.'

'Imagining the dangers is no good. You have to *know* them to avoid them.'

She swallowed. 'Perhaps it's a bad idea. I'll try to find out anything more that I can, now I know to ask for Jim, rather than Robert, and then I should go home.'

She was right, but the disappointment in her voice tugged at him, as well as his sense of responsibility. 'Luna,' he began, leaning forward to make sure he had her full attention. 'Whatever you meant to him, Jim wouldn't have wanted you to feel afraid and alienated in the mountains. He was more at home up there than here in the valley.'

As he spoke, a sense of conviction settled over him. Here was something he could do – for Jim, for Luna.

'Jim was a good friend,' he explained. 'He took me under his wing when I was accepted into the unit and moved here. I'm not a Chamoniard by birth – I'm from Ardèche. If he was still alive, he would have taught you to ski – I have no doubt,' he added. 'Here, I'll show you a photo of Jim.'

She came around the coffee table to sit next to him as he pulled up the photo that had been framed and placed – for an hour – at the foot of the Aiguille du Grépon last year as the Compagnie des Guides had paid their respects.

Jim had been wiry and strong and the only sign of his age were his prodigious wrinkles from hours in the sun. Luna's face lit up when she saw him.

'I wish I could have met him,' she said, her voice distant, 'even if he would have made me ski.'

'He would have stuck you in a harness, given you a piolet – an ice axe – and pushed you up a frozen waterfall, too.'

Her jaw dropped. 'I could never do that.'

'Why don't we start with skiing. Jim's not here to teach you, so I hope you'll let me,' he said tentatively.

'Perfect!' Silvia said, approaching them to take the seat where Luna had been a moment before. 'You can't be afraid if Adjudant Yannick Pasquier is teaching you to ski, hmm?'

Luna gave Silvia a doubtful look. She tucked her hand into the cuff of her oversized knit pullover and patted her cheek, which looked as though she'd been sitting too close to the fire. 'I'm not sure you understand what you're getting yourself in to,' she mumbled, glancing at him.

'I'm not worried,' he said, a smile stretching on his lips. 'I've already decided you're dure-à-cuire – you're tough,' he added in English, when her brow furrowed at the French expression.

'Doesn't that mean hard to cook?' she asked with a laugh. 'I suppose that's better than "easy to freeze".'

'Then, we ski?' he asked in English. 'And maybe we will get to the refuge before you go. Petits pas?'

'"Small steps" sounds good. I only hope I'm as tough as you think I am.'

'If you're connected to Jim, then you must be.'

The look she gave him was heart-breakingly lost. Although he understood she had a mystery to solve, he had to wonder why finding the answers seemed so important to her. Surely she had her own life to live, instead of dropping everything to follow the trail of the past?

* * *

Luna arrived ninety minutes earlier than the time she'd agreed with Yannick for their first ski lesson on Saturday, so she could have her panic attack in peace. Her wrist throbbed, even though it hadn't bothered her for several days. But telling herself something was all in her head didn't help when she prepared for her first descent down the green training slope, her knees knocking.

She could still hear Lydia hyperventilating over the phone when she'd told her cousin her plans for the day. Lyd was even more attached to home and hearth than June had been, which Luna was certain had something to do with apples falling from trees, but her brain was a mess of nerves and she couldn't quite complete the figure of speech.

Silvia, on the other hand, had sent her out the door with a clasp of her shoulders, two kisses on each cheek and the soothing words, 'I know you can do it.'

Not truly believing it would help, she reached into the pocket of her coat and gave the little moonstone crystal a squeeze through her glove. Silvia had insisted she take it with her for strength. Luna suspected she needed more than the power of this humble little rock to stop her making a fool of herself on the slopes today.

Her technique had deteriorated since her lesson the previous Sunday. Or rather, what little technique she'd mastered was no use since she was rigid with nerves. Even the training slope was making hear heart wallop in her chest, as she pictured the sharp drop-off where the accident had occurred.

But she was determined to be 'hard to cook'. Lyd might think she was absent-minded and flighty, Aiden had accused her of being fragile and they had both made very good points, but she could still be tough. She clung to the memory of her mum telling her not to bend to other people's ideas of who she should be, even though it seemed ridiculous to imagine she could ever ski as self-assuredly as the men and women passing her in their colourful jackets and expensive helmets.

Centring herself with a deep breath, she pushed off with her poles and lurched down the familiar slope. Just as she was beginning to freak out about her speed, the gradient evened out and she could push her heels out in the braking position and wobble to a stop at the bottom. Her blood rushed in her ears so loudly that at first she didn't hear when someone called her name while she was waiting for the chairlift. When the voice called a second time, she jerked around, nearly taking someone out with her ski pole, which she promptly dropped into the snow.

Behind her in the queue, she caught sight of Yannick and blinked several times, making her eyes water in the frigid air. Even out of uniform, she recognised him immediately by that wide, gorgeous smile.

Boy, Silvia was right. Having Yannick, her friendly neighbourhood mountain rescue gendarme, teach her to ski would be about the only way she would manage it. Just seeing him cheered her up. She shuffled to the side of the queue to allow others to pass.

He glided effortlessly on his skis, where Luna shuffled like a penguin. He leaned down to snatch up her pole before sliding to a stop next to her. Picking up her arm, he slid the strap of the ski pole around her wrist and then closed her hand around the grip, with the strap between her thumb and forefinger.

Lesson one: how to put the strap on. With a pointed nod, he dropped her hand. Luna wasn't even sure she could replicate what he'd done.

She glanced up to thank him and caught sight of the reason why he was early as well. Clinging onto one of his poles was a small child with curly brown hair emerging from beneath a bright pink helmet with the visor down over her eyes.

'Voici ma fille, Maëlys,' he introduced his daughter in French.

Luna thought back to her first year of teaching where she'd been a supply teacher in a primary school and taught the younger classes once a week. She didn't remember much beyond the constant need for one child or another to pee.

'Bonjour, Maëlys. Je m'appelle Luna.'

The little girl just looked up at her and said nothing – at least Luna thought she was looking at her, behind the visor. She didn't smile.

'Take the chairlift with us,' Yannick said, tugging Maëlys behind him as the queue moved forward. Luna shuffled laboriously after them. Glancing back, he held out his other pole to her and caught her eye with a smile.

With a sigh that shed the last of her pride, she let her own poles hang off her wrists and grasped the end of his, squealing when she shot forward and remembering to bend her knees just in time. His smile was still in place as they waited on the markings for the chairlift.

'Are you laughing at me?' she accused. 'Erm, vous riez de moi?' she translated for his daughter's benefit.

His mouth twitched into an even wider smile and he looked down at his skis. 'Ouais,' he admitted with some colour in his cheeks. 'Don't you think we should use "tu" instead of "vous"?' he suggested, making Luna realise she'd used formal grammar in her question before.

'Are civilians allowed to say "tu" to a gendarme?'

He only had time to raise his eyebrows before the seat scooped them up. Maëlys hopped up like a pro, while Luna plopped awkwardly onto her bottom, juggling her poles as Yannick pulled the bar into place. She gave a startled yelp as the chair was hoisted suddenly upwards on the cable, cursing herself for not getting that little panic out of the way before running into them.

But Maëlys giggled brightly and then all three of them were

grinning as they floated through the crisp air. From the safety of the chair, with her skis dangling, Luna finally remembered to look out. The peaks were shrouded in cloud, the sky patchworked with blue. But the landscape that should have looked barren, frozen under a layer of snow, was alive to her that day. The peaks across the valley called to her in a different way, now she knew she had a connection to the high mountain guide Jim de Montagne.

The rocky crags and the marshmallows of snow, the absolute silence of high altitude seemed to suck her in, making her think about her own body, the chemicals and physical processes sustaining her existence, the resilience of life. What did it feel like to stand up there among the summits?

'Ça va?' Yannick asked, breaking her reverie.

She nodded. 'It's so beautiful. I can't believe I'm up here.'

He squeezed her hand through both of their gloves, but the chairlift was approaching the station and she had to focus. Typical Luna-like absent-mindedness could cause an accident. She shuffled off at the other end, struggling to arrange the straps of her poles correctly.

'À plus tard,' she called out to Yannick and Maëlys, gesturing that they could go on without her and she'd see them later. She hesitated for a moment, wondering if the ski lesson Yannick had offered her would eat into time with his daughter. She didn't want to cost him that, even for Jim's sake.

She watched them set off for the bottom of another chairlift that would take them to the more difficult slopes. Maëlys moved on skis with astounding coordination and alarming speed, but Yannick matched his movements to hers, close enough to swoop down and catch her if she misjudged. Luna wondered what it would have been like to grow up knowing someone would catch her. But thirty was too late to learn to be comfortable with unnecessary risks and she bit her lip in concern at the thought of them careening down the mountain.

She pictured Yannick dangling from a helicopter or climbing in a narrow, icy crevasse and she felt again that he must be another breed of human to be able to go to work, day after day, and face these hazards.

And he'd watched his friend die...

Dismayed by her thoughts, she tried her best to switch them off by practising her skiing. At least the alertness required to remember her technique, to balance and override her instincts, forced all other thoughts away.

The time disappeared quickly. As the appointed meeting time approached, she ascended in the chairlift one last time and caught sight of Yannick on his haunches in front of Maëlys, lifting her visor to peer into her face. Luna tried not to come too close, to give them privacy, but, as she shuffled off the lift, she couldn't help over-hearing.

12

'Maman will be here soon,' Yannick was saying gently as he unclipped her boots from the skis.

'J'irai pas!' Maëlys said, stamping her foot. She caught Yannick's finger under her boot and he stifled a yelp. The little girl didn't want to go to her mother. Luna was far more curious than she had any right to be. 'I *hate* dancing!' Maëlys insisted in her childish French. 'I want to go skiing with you. I hate dancing and I hate that you always *leave*!'

Luna froze, wishing she could disappear before Yannick caught sight of her. It hurt, thinking about his family split in two. She couldn't imagine Yannick being the one to leave. He'd stay, at the cost of his own happiness, she thought with remarkable conviction.

'But I always come back, louloute,' he soothed, tugging her helmet off and pressing a kiss to her hair. 'I'll see you for dinner tomorrow, too.'

'But I want to go *skiing* with you!'

'There will be another time.'

'Not for a *whole year*!'

Luna smiled, but with a shot of dismay at the child-like despair in the girl's voice and her misunderstanding of time – although perhaps a week or two without skiing felt like a year to a five-year-old. As Luna tried not to watch, Yannick hauled his daughter up and held her close, wrapping his arm around her and murmuring something Luna couldn't hear.

Then he glanced up and saw her before she could skulk away. He gestured for her to approach and she shuffled over, but she hit an icy spot, her skis slipped forward and she plopped onto her bottom. Maëlys' tears stopped abruptly and she giggled again, peering down at Luna from her place in Yannick's arms. Luna tried to get up, but her skis clacked together and she couldn't get more than a couple of inches off the ground, groaning with effort. Eventually, she gave up, tugging her goggles up onto her helmet.

Before she could unclip her boots from her skis, Yannick trudged to where she'd fallen and held out his free hand to her.

'Put the skis parallel – no, not like that! Across the slope. Bon, give me your hand.'

He extended his bare hand and she pulled off her glove to help her grip. She didn't understand how his hands stayed so warm. Hers had been inside her gloves the whole time and still felt like ice against his rough skin.

The strength in his fingers was obvious. He had no trouble hauling her to her feet as he held his daughter in his other arm.

'Thank you,' she muttered in English, letting go of him as she steadied herself. 'I'm okay. You have...' She gestured wildly in his direction.

'Her mother will be here soon,' he explained. 'She has a dancing class.'

Luna nodded. 'I heard,' she said apologetically.

'Everyone heard,' he muttered, his lips twitching with a smile as he pressed another kiss to his daughter's hairline.

With a wallop of emotion, Luna marvelled at the pressure he could apply around her heart without even intending to. She should probably take the warning.

'Yannick! Salut!'

They both turned to see a woman approaching in a puffy coat but no ski gear. Luna stood awkwardly by, unable to drift away unnoticed in case she fell over, as Yannick kissed the woman on both cheeks.

Yannick gave Maëlys one more squeeze as he thanked the woman for collecting Maëlys at the top of the cable car. Luna supposed everyone around here had season ski passes.

'Et vas-y,' he said gently as he detached Maëlys' arms from around his neck. He grimaced apologetically at his ex. With the promise of ice cream *before* dinner the following day, he managed to persuade the little girl to go, but she left with clomping feet and a hurt look that Luna imagined caught him straight in the heart.

He turned to Luna with a tired grimace and she attempted to shuffle closer. Keeping a normal, conversational distance was nearly impossible on skis.

'Are you sure I'm not taking up time you would have spent with Maëlys?'

'Absolument pas,' he said with an earnest shake of his head. 'I was glad to find the couple of hours with her. She's too fast on skis and I need to make sure she can control her technique,' he explained in French. 'Wait, I want to try to talk in English.'

'Your English is very good – like all of the gendarmes in class,' Luna pointed out.

'We can all speak, but we avoid it, which says to you there could be improvement.'

Luna tried not to laugh, but she didn't quite manage it. '*Tells* you, not says to you.'

'Hélas! You see? I need practice. I will teach you to ski in English.'

'I didn't realise skiing in French would be different.'

'Everything in French is a little different, non?' He smiled, punctuating his sentence with a shrug that was definitely French. 'On peut commencer? Hum... are you ready to start?'

'As I'll ever be,' she mumbled.

'Okay,' he began. 'First thing, it's very important. You cannot get too warm.'

'I don't think that'll be a problem,' she said drily.

'You do sport, your heart rate goes up – you will get warm,' he pointed out tolerantly. 'It's important not to sweat. If you sweat and then you get cold again, that is when you get hypothermia.'

'Wonderful,' Luna said under her breath.

'If you feel warm, take the zip down a little, but if you have already started to sweat, you need to keep it closed and don't stay too long outside when you are finished.'

'I can promise you that.'

* * *

Half an hour later, he'd watched her technique on the beginner slope several times and she was starting to get the hang of it again. She'd just started believing she might actually improve that day, when he motioned for her to stop in the middle of the slope, rather than at the end, where it was flatter. Luna managed to push her skis out in a wide snow-plough shape, but she couldn't quite come to a halt and he had to throw out an arm for her to grab onto. Her heart was already pounding with alarm, made worse because she was looking straight down the slope, not moving, her skis slipping and sliding as she clung to him.

Pull yourself together, Luna, she berated herself through gritted teeth, glancing apologetically at Yannick, only for her breath to steal away again when she noticed how close he was and how much she liked the rueful smile playing on his lips.

She eventually found a somewhat stable position, her knees twisted uncomfortably and her poles dug into the snow in front of her. Yannick gave her an approving nod from where he stood just below her, totally relaxed.

'Now, we learn how we don't go down.'

'Hmm?'

'Skiing is not going down the mountain.'

'It's not?' She grunted as one ski slipped and tried to turn. She was starting to believe him about the sweating. All of her muscles were tensed with the effort of staying still and not falling. She wondered if adrenaline was warmer than blood somehow, because she had a lot of that swimming in her veins.

'Going down the mountain is called "falling", yes?'

'I bloody hope not.'

'Skiing is controlling the fall. You need to think about the... ligne de pente, euh... the line of slope, maybe?'

'I'll look it up later,' she muttered, her fingers starting to hurt from gripping her poles too tightly. 'Just explain it to me – quickly.'

He held up one arm, his hand pointing to the ground on an angle. 'With skis like this you go down.' He switched direction his hand pointing up on an angle. 'Like this, you go down en arrière,' he said, enunciating the French words clearly.

'Got it. Going down backwards,' she translated with a shudder. 'We don't want that.'

He held his arm straight, clenching his fist. 'With skis like this, you don't fall. You're safe.'

She tried to shift so she was perpendicular to the slope, but she ended up grabbing for his shoulders as her skis tried to leave her behind.

'Ouf,' he said as he caught her heavily.

She was decidedly warm now, especially in her cheeks. 'I'm not good at this,' she muttered. 'I'd better not be Jim's daughter.'

'Nobody is born on skis. We all learn,' he said, his breath tickling her forehead. 'We'll go down a little first. We go down, we slow and turn, we stop and get safe. That is what we will practice, okay? Allons-y.'

He held her while she righted her skis and then he pushed off, giving her no chance to ask herself if she was ready. Partway down the slope, he stopped and turned and barked the instruction for her to do the same. She teetered through a turn and managed to get one ski into position perpendicular to the slope.

'Arms forward, don't lean back! Bon!' he called. 'Have your weight on the valley ski and stabilise with the mountain ski. Oui, c'est bien, juste comme ça – like that. Euh, move the ankle a little and dig the ski into the snow. How do you say "plier"?'

'Bend,' she muttered without thought as she bent her ankle, digging the sharp edge of her ski into the slope. To her surprise, she was at a complete stop and found she was entirely stable – even more stable than when she stood in skis on the flat. Her muscles complained at the way she was standing with one leg higher than the other, but she could endure that for quite some time, she guessed.

She took a long breath in and released it slowly as her anxiety dissipated and the world around her came into focus. The snow-covered rock and wilderness, the icy extremes of nature, it was all so beautiful she could scarcely believe she was privileged enough to see it, to breathe in the air from the habitat of the birds.

What would her mother have said, if she could have seen Luna, now? *I'm safe, Mum,* Luna marvelled. *I'm standing on a mountain and I'm safe.* Why hadn't her mother told her skiing could feel like this?

'Luna? Are you okay?'

She nodded, hoping he couldn't see how emotional the experience had become. Adrenaline had a lot to answer for.

'You want to stop? Are you tired?'

She ignored the ache in her muscles and shook her head. 'Not yet.'

Yannick skied back up to her – Luna nearly did a double-take to see him casually gliding back *up* the slope that had been such a challenge for her to ski *down* that morning. So much for his ligne de pente. He popped his goggles up as he came to a stop in front of her with his skis in some kind of reverse snow plough position that showed just how much she still had to learn.

'We will practice this again, but to practice curves and the safety stop, you need a steeper slope.'

She shook her head vehemently, suddenly annoyed with the smile he gave her as he ducked his head to peer into her face.

'Does it work for an adult if I promise ice cream?' he asked.

She gave a pout to cover the smile that was trying to break out. 'Make it a blueberry tart and you've got a—'

'Bon! Allez!'

She suspected he'd tricked her, but she had no choice but to follow him.

Yannick spoke slowly, in a low tone as they took the chairlift back up to the blue 'easy' piste that looked like a sheer drop in comparison to the green bunny slope. She wasn't even sure he realised he'd switched to French and she didn't want to point it out, because his smooth words spoke directly to her fizzing adrenaline.

'It's very important to relax. Accept the fear in your blood but keep the muscles loose so you can move the way you need to move. Imagine what you *want* to happen. You'll see the edge of the piste and execute a turn and bring yourself back perpendicular to the ligne de pente. Your skis will help you. The edges of your skis are there to keep you safe.'

'I thought that's what *you* were for,' Luna muttered.

He flashed his teeth in a smile and Luna wanted to lean her head on his shoulder. Stupid adrenaline. He nodded slowly. 'You can keep yourself safe,' he said, switching back to English. 'I'm... out of service.'

Luna snorted. 'You're not out of service. That means broken. If you meant hors service, then you're looking for off-duty.'

'I'm off-duty,' he repeated obediently.

As they disembarked the chairlift and made their way past the cable car to the top of the blue slope, he started speaking again. 'Relax the muscles, use the traverse to slow and stop, we will practise coming to a complete stop once. Listen for my command. Nothing can happen because *you* are in control.'

When he set off, cutting slowly across the slope, she followed before her thoughts had a chance to get tangled in her fears.

The speed on the steeper run made the wind rush in her face and her heart strike against her ribs. For a moment, she felt as though she was chasing after herself and every turn was life or death, a scrappy fight against gravity to pull up in time. But partway down, she began to sense a rhythm in the curves, a feeling of balance as she scraped her skis through the snow with an audible crunch.

This mysterious ligne de pente was palpable as she scrambled to catch herself and when Yannick called for her to stop, she didn't want to – she wanted to keep gliding in this dance she'd just learned.

But she pulled to a stop above him, digging in her ski. The sun was throwing long rays over the Mont Blanc massif across the valley and for a moment, her reasons for being here didn't matter. She was in this moment, feeling the cold in her lungs and the warmth on her face and a kernel of trust in her heart.

'Allons-y!' Yannick called, breaking the spell. *Let's go.* Luna grinned and headed off after him, whooshing gently through curve after curve, allowing herself just a little more speed as she controlled her fall. Before she was ready, the slope swerved down one last breath-stealing tilt, ending abruptly at the bottom of a ski lift.

Luna was breathing hard, her blood pumping, as she lurched to a stop near the gates. 'I did it.'

13

Luna had a spot of mayonnaise on her cheek. It had been there for some time, but Yannick hadn't had the opportunity to tell her. Once she'd swiped at a crumb at the side of her mouth and almost reached it, but not quite.

She'd eaten her chips almost without taking a breath, although she'd also been talking non-stop. He wasn't quite sure how it was physically possible. After the challenging day on the mountain, her metabolism had apparently gone into overdrive and her thoughts tumbled out all over each other in a flood that left him pleasantly dazed.

He suspected she was exhausted, but hadn't realised it yet, especially since she'd been reluctant to take breaks once she'd mastered the blue slope, and had skied doggedly until the cable car closed for the day.

'It all suddenly made sense – even though it's entirely counter-intuitive. I mean, you have to lean down the mountain to make sure you don't *go* down. That's crazy, but it's true. It's a huge trust exercise.' Her eyes clouded as she stuffed a forkful of her croûte savoyarde into her mouth. 'That's *it*. It's trust. You can't go up there without a huge amount of trust – in yourself, the technology, other skiers. And, in my case, you.' Her bright smile was a touch apologetic, but it made his chest tight and he glanced away like a giddy teenager with a crush. It was *not* what he should have been feeling with a short-term visitor who needed him in a somewhat professional capacity.

'C'est ça,' he agreed, taking a breath and preparing to mention the dollop of mayonnaise, but she kept talking before he could say anything.

'I always thought it was the danger that gave people that adrenaline kick, that feeling of being *alive*, but it isn't that.'

'Adrenaline *is* a fear response,' he contradicted her lightly.

'Okay, maybe the adrenaline bit is from the danger, but being up there! There's nothing but snow and rock and air and it makes you realise how big the world is.' She paused in thought, but given the searching look on her face, he didn't feel it was the time to mention the mayonnaise. He bit his lip and waited for her to continue. 'You made me think about that,' she said.

'Mmm?' he prompted.

'The moon. Perspective. You have no idea how much those words struck me.'

'I have an idea,' he admitted softly.

'I wish I knew why my mum never told me she used to ski. I mean, I'll never master it, but—'

'Stop,' he interrupted abruptly. He'd enjoyed her chatter washing over his tired thoughts, but he couldn't let that last sentence stand. She immediately sat up straighter, her smile slipping. He tilted his head to study her. 'The problem is not that you can't ski. The problem is that you *think* you can't. I am happy when I can get a skier, or a hiker, down from a dangerous place on the mountain, when I can take them to the hospital to recover. It's not good that they became stuck or fell, but accidents happen in the mountains – and on the roads, on the coast, in *life*. What troubles me is when someone gives up. When I have a victim who thinks they can't move, they can't take my hand, they can't make a jump to save themselves – sometimes I can't rescue them and that *troubles* me. Don't say never.' Perhaps he'd added too much emphasis onto that word, because Luna's heart was in her eyes as she listened to him.

'I'm sorry—'

He shook his head. 'You are right to say that life in the mountains is built on trust. The sensible alpiniste knows he or she should never go alone. That is the single most dangerous thing you can do. In French we call them compagnon de cordée – the rope... companion? Because you are literally connected with a rope for safety – to each other. If I take you to the refuge, I need to trust you, too.'

She seemed to stop breathing entirely and then slowly deflated. 'Wow,' she whispered. 'That... might take some time.'

'You have time, no? You learned to ski a blue slope in two days.' He peered at her with an encouraging expression until her smile returned. There was a particular glint in her eye he was starting to recognise – a little embarrassed, but bright and compelling. He wondered what it meant.

'I don't think learning to trust someone is like learning to ski,' she said.

'Perhaps not,' he agreed.

'I think you have an unfair advantage, though.'

'Hmm?' he prompted with a frown.

'You're the most trustworthy person I've ever met. You're a gendarme and you have that... face.'

'What face?'

With a self-deprecating chuckle, she raised her hand and for a moment he thought she was about to touch him. He froze, holding his breath in anticipation, but she hesitated. 'You could tell me just about anything and I'd believe you because of this face.' After a few false-starts, she darted her hand out and patted his cheek.

He sat up straight in surprise. The brief touch of her cool fingertips flared out through the rest of him. He swallowed, trying to shake off the self-conscious sensation. The only person who'd touched his face recently was Maëlys.

'Would you believe you have a spot of mayonnaise on *your* face?' he finally managed to say.

She glanced up. 'Do I?' Rubbing a thumb over her jaw, she missed it entirely, then paused. 'You're teasing me,' she accused him with a smile, giving him a shove.

'It's true!' he protested.

'I should never have admitted I'd trust anything you said.'

'I'm serious.' Clearing his throat, he picked up his serviette and dipped his head to her level. Tentatively holding her still with two fingers under her chin, he wiped the spot with the serviette, trying to ignore the feel of her wide eyes on his – apparently very trustworthy – face. He smiled wryly at her shocked expression and brushed his thumb briefly over her chin.

'Thank you,' she muttered.

'I have some experience wiping sauce off cheeks.'

'I assume you mean Maëlys and not... other women,' she said with a laugh.

He choked on a cough. 'Of course I meant Maëlys.'

'How long have you and your ex been separated?' she asked, taking a suspiciously casual sip of beer. Her plate was finally empty, although she seemed to be eyeing up his basket of chips. He pushed it in her direction and she nabbed one like a seagull.

'About a year and a half,' he answered, equally casually.

'Were you married?'

He nodded. 'For five years.'

'What happened?' she asked, wide-eyed, apparently giving up concealing her curiosity.

He thought for a moment, crossing his arms and tapping his foot on the footrest of his barstool. 'Perhaps what makes me trustworthy on the mountain makes me... less dependable in the valley,' he said flatly.

She frowned. 'I really can't imagine you as not dependable.'

'You can't? Luna, I'm a military officer. I work shifts. Sometimes I don't come home at the end of my shift. Committing to someone – to a relationship – as well is very difficult. Even the court agreed that Valérie should have the... garde principale for Maëlys – you know what I mean?' He was satisfied to realise he'd switched comfortably to English over the afternoon, although he'd probably mixed in French words.

'Primary custody,' Luna translated with a glum nod. 'But your job wasn't a surprise to her. How long have you been in the gendarmerie?'

'Eighteen years – nearly thirteen at the PGHM. But life changes and she needed stability I couldn't provide. I work for the mountain and the mountain takes what it takes.'

He studied her, wondering if she'd pick up on what he wasn't saying. Some days he didn't make it home from his shift on time – occasionally not until the next day. But there was always the possibility that he wouldn't make it home at all. The plaque on the granite boulder in the car park at Cordial with its roll of honour of sixty-five names was a daily reminder of that.

She answered him with a question that suggested she recognised the foundation of heartache in his explanation. 'Why did you become a mountain rescue officer?' she asked. 'Did you... lose someone?'

He glanced at her sharply, resisting her sympathy for as long as he could. It wasn't long. 'My brother,' he said roughly.

Her hand landed on his forearm, where he'd rolled up the sleeve of his shirt, and he stared at it as she gave him a squeeze, her palm cool on his skin. 'What happened?'

'He was climbing in Switzerland. Julien was the real *alpiniste* in the family. I know exactly what it feels like when someone you love goes missing in the mountains. He was never found. Not long after his death, I was here with my parents and read a story about a German man who died in a crevasse over two hundred years ago. Two local men from a town near Cham trekked up to the glacier and brought his body home and I thought: *That's what I could do.*' He gave a self-deprecating shrug. She was listening to him with her whole body – certainly with those dark eyes that held a hint of forest green.

Before he could explain that his brother's death was twenty years ago and he really should be okay now, the door of the bar opened to admit a group of his colleagues, still in their two-tone blue jackets. It was a different team, but everyone in the unit was tight-knit and he appreciated the opportunity to shake off the conversation that had drifted a long way from casual.

'Hey, Yanni!' his friend Eric called out, approaching immediately to shake his hand and clap him on the shoulder. 'I didn't expect to see you out. Nouvelle copine?' he asked, unrepentantly curious.

The suggestion that Luna was his girlfriend was so far from the truth he laughed with only a touch of heat in his cheeks. 'No, this is Luna, our new English teacher and... mascot.'

'I heard your team got stuck with English classes – don't take that badly, mademoiselle,' he assured Luna.

'I'm just questioning the mascot comment,' she said drily. 'What would I be? An ibex? One of those mountain goats? Oh gosh, I'd be one of those cute little furry things in the souvenir shops, right?'

'Une marmotte?' Eric said with a grin. 'Yes, I see it. The PGHM marmot to go with the helicopter named after a bird.'

'You might be just as cute, but marmots hibernate in the winter and you have to learn to ski,' Yannick quipped, but froze when her gaze jerked to his in surprise. Merde, had he just called her cute? Would she think he was patronising her? That might be better than her suspecting the truth: that he was attracted to her.

Swallowing a grimace, he followed Luna and Eric to a wooden table to join the others, who were winding down from a shift. Luna asked questions and they answered with amused smiles as her eyes grew rounder with each new story.

'Mais... quelle est la profondeur d'une crevasse?' she asked. That she had to ask about the depth of a crevasse reminded him of how little she understood about the high mountain environment. He had some more work to do, but he wasn't a stranger to work.

He felt good about today.

Eric explained the great variance in size and that some crevasses could be fifty metres deep. Yannick had to admit that team three was much friendlier to Luna than team two had been, which only reminded him of his patronising mascot faux pas again.

As the volume of the music cranked up in the bar, his first thought was to go home to be a nearly thirty-nine-year-old ex-husband and father in peace, but Luna was laughing and chatting and he wasn't sure if he had to take her back to Silvia's house in Argentière or if she'd worked out the night bus. He'd stopped drinking at one beer. Not knowing whether he was needed wasn't a position he often found himself in and he wasn't entirely comfortable with the uncertainty.

'I love to dance,' he heard her say to Jean-Marc. She'd switched back into English. 'But I never do. Where I live – or lived or whatever – there isn't really anywhere to dance after you turn twenty-one.'

'Bien, alors, why don't you?' Jean-Marc encouraged her with a smile and a gesture towards the cluster of revellers who'd created an impromptu dance floor between the tables. Luna raised her chin, drank the last of her beer and stood to cheers from his colleagues.

She gave Jean-Marc a pointed look and he stood to follow her with a smile, along with Bast, one of the other younger secouristes. It was the usual mix of dance music and pop songs for the snow-heads, but Luna seemed to like it.

He watched her with a smile on his face that wouldn't go away. Holding her arms above her head, strands of her short hair over her face, she moved to the beat in a style completely her own, twirling and swaying. He imagined her in her own living room, dancing like this.

Jean-Marc and Bast were obviously entertained as well. She was a breath of fresh air, blown into the unit by chance – by Jim. It pricked him, and he wished his old friend could have seen this – and told them all who she was to him.

Whatever he felt when he watched her, it only showed that his grief was still fresh. He glanced back into his mineral water with a touch of sadness that he was more comfortable with.

'Alors,' Eric said with a smile, 'you can forget Valérie after all?' Yannick's dismay must have shown on his face because Eric clapped him on the shoulder. 'She's a nice woman. A bit young for you maybe, but you could do worse.'

'She could do better,' Yannick muttered. He shook his head. 'It's not like that. She's connected to Jim, although she doesn't know how yet.'

'Connected to Jim? As in, family?' Eric leaned close. 'Have you told Jean-Yves? I didn't think Jim had any kids.'

Yannick kicked himself for not thinking to go straight to Jim's sometime rope partner Jean-Yves. The two guides had been close – although not without a streak of healthy competition. 'I haven't told him, but that's a good idea. She doesn't actually know what their connection is. That's why I'm helping her.'

'Not because she's as sweet as a marmot?' Eric said with a chuckle. When Yannick didn't share his laughter, Eric sighed. 'It's... okay to turn the page, you know. It doesn't mean you don't love Maëlys.'

Yannick shook his head. 'I won't even open the book again. I have my family – Maëlys and the PGHM. That's more than enough.'

He didn't like the spark of pity in Eric's eyes. His friend had never been married, didn't have any kids. What did he know about being pulled in different directions?

He glanced at Luna – swaying, enjoying, *living* – and it almost felt like Jim was still there, reassuring him that he'd done the right thing today. He'd found something to honour his friend's memory and, in a small way, make up for the decisions he'd made that day – decisions he hadn't fully explained to Luna. He didn't want to upset her.

He would help her learn to ski and feel safe in an alpine environment and then let her go home. It was the least he could do.

14

Yannick suspected Luna was more exhausted than drunk when he finally drove her through the valley to Silvia's house shortly before midnight. He came around to open the passenger door and her hands were sluggish on the seat belt. Instead of climbing down from the SUV, her forehead fell to his shoulder. A few flakes of snow floated over them.

'Thank you for today,' she murmured in English. Her French seemed to have switched off at about ten o'clock.

His hand came up to swipe her hair out of her face. 'Pas de souci, Luna,' he said gently. After watching her ski with her blood and dance with her soul, he felt unexpectedly soft.

'I'm so tired.'

'You were incredible today.'

'I don't know if you're just being nice,' she murmured with a chuckle. 'I'm only a civilian to you – someone you need to help.' He couldn't argue with that. 'It's not fair.'

'What's not fair?' he asked, peering down at her.

She lifted her head and he was struck by how familiar she felt after such a short time – her narrow chin, wide cheekbones. 'I said you have a trustworthy face, but what I meant was... I like your face. It's a really nice one.'

He blinked at her, trying not to feel anything when he couldn't interpret her meaning with certainty. 'You... like my face?'

Her cheeks flushed pink and she had that spark in her eye again. 'Gosh, today I... breathed so much.'

'I think you need to go to bed, Luna,' he crooned, taking her hand to urge her out of the car.

She shook her head lightly. 'You don't understand. I feel like I breathed today for the first time in months – years, even. I still don't know what I think I'll find here, but... you have such a lovely face.'

He knew that feeling of breathing out, of something loosening that had been wedged tight, releasing the blood flow. And he knew she was mixing up her adrenaline and confusion into something that wasn't supposed to be between them.

'I know,' she murmured reassuringly, brushing her hand over his shoulder and not meeting his eye. 'I'm just on a high from learning to ski today. This is about Jim and my mum and not about... us.' She nodded, as though convincing herself. She stepped out of the car and stretched. 'Wow, look at the moon.'

He followed her gaze to see the gibbous moon shimmering into view high above them, as the clouds parted. Tiny snowflakes caught the light. The air was still and frigid and he looked up at the jutting rock of the Aiguille des Grands Montets above the snow-covered forest. He always found it difficult to look up without being filled with the immediate desire to *go* up.

'It's so beautiful,' Luna said softly. She was looking down on the little cluster of chalets that made up the village of les Chosalets, with their peaked roofs heaving with snow and warm, yellow lights, smoke drifting lazily from the chimneys.

'Yes, it is,' he commented, pointing in the opposite direction, where he'd been looking. She stared up in dismay, teetering as she craned her neck, and he slipped an arm around her. If there was a thump of heady feeling as he drew close, he could be certain it would pass.

He drew back to retrieve her skis and boots from the roof box, dropping them at Silvia's door for her. When she approached, the expression on her face was more like goodbye. Good.

'Thank you,' she said softly again.

'Will you be ready to ski next week? I'm on duty on Saturday, but Friday could work.'

She nodded. 'Whenever you can go up, I'll go up. And I might practice on my own, too.'

'Oh, and Eric pointed out that Jim's old friend Jean-Yves might know something more – or at least he'd probably like to meet you. He's a guide, too. Perhaps you could visit the Compagnie des Guides and they can show you Jim's photos.'

'That's a great idea. I'll do that.'

Dipping his head to say goodbye with kisses on the cheek, he paused, unsure if she was comfortable with that. But she closed the distance, pressing her lips lightly to his cheek.

His head spun a little as he ambled back to the car and got in without looking at her. Had anyone ever told him his face was 'lovely'? A quick kiss on the cheek wasn't supposed to make him feel so warm and wobbly. But he couldn't stop grinning.

* * *

Everything hurt when Luna awoke the following morning. She rolled over and groaned, nerves twinging in her joints and her muscles complaining. Her shins hurt. Her toes hurt. Even her fingers were stiff from grasping the ski poles for dear life.

The one muscle that seemed in fine fettle was her heart, which beat cheerfully along with the earworm of 'I Predict a Riot' that she'd had in her head since the evening before.

She'd done it. She'd skied down a proper slope and *enjoyed* it. She hadn't felt cold or scared or inept. Prying her eyes open, she stared at her mother's urn and asked herself if her mum might have felt the same things, when she came to Chamonix years ago.

'Why didn't you tell me?' she muttered. What had changed to turn the smiling woman at the top of a ski slope into her home-body mother who didn't like to leave Kent?

Despite the aches in her muscles, Luna hauled herself straight out of bed and opened the wardrobe. She'd started to see what she was capable of yesterday, and she wanted to maintain that feeling. She'd even managed to admit her crush on Yannick, so she didn't have to feel so silly around him. Of course he'd looked flummoxed and adorably flustered, as though he had no idea why someone would like his face – although perhaps expressing it in the terms she had might have been a bit weird. Regardless, spending time with him should be much less awkward now.

Except she'd rather liked their kind of awkward.

He'd said she was cute, which was lovely for her ego, even if she knew it didn't mean anything. And she'd kissed his cheek... Phew, adrenaline truly did some strange things to her, because that brief brush of her lips over his bristly skin had been everything she'd wanted in that moment.

The other thing that had got her out of bed surprisingly quickly was her determination to earn his trust. When she'd pictured the visit to the glacier, she'd imagined herself being dragged behind him, slipping and sliding and being an inconvenient dead weight, but when he'd spoken about rope partners, about the trust he'd place in her, that scenario was no longer acceptable.

She *couldn't* be an inept dead weight, so she pulled on a tracksuit to go for a run. It was apparently seven degrees below zero outside, so she wrapped up warm, telling herself it wasn't Siberia and people still went jogging in this crazy town. She'd even seen a few runners out and about herself, amongst the skiers with their clomping boots and the mountaineers, jangling with equipment.

Noticing something hard in the inside pocket of her coat as she pulled it on, she reached in to take a fond look at her little piece of moonstone, but was surprised to discover a different crystal in her hand. It was reddish and rough and she could only imagine that Silvia had hidden it in her coat for strength, or chakras or something Luna didn't understand. But she smiled faintly, because she did understand and appreciate her friend's concern.

Completing her stretches before she ventured to the door, she called out to tell Silvia where she was going and then hurtled outside before she could talk herself out of it. Her feet immediately complained about the cold cutting through her light trainers. Her lungs froze up. But still she pulled her woolie beanie down over her ears and set off with a shudder, clutching her coat.

She usually ran a five-kilometre parkrun once a week and did at least one other jog of a similar length, but she'd barely run a mile and a half that day when her stomach started aching and she felt as though she was about to keel over.

Sitting down on a stone wall, she tried to catch her breath, but she felt so strange, she was worried something was wrong with her and she wouldn't be able to make it back to Silvia's. She heard the wap-wap of a helicopter and shielded her eyes to peer up at it. She recognised the familiar navy blue of the PGHM with a small smile and hoped they would arrive quickly where they were needed.

The short break and the distraction settled her stomach somewhat and she dragged herself to her feet to walk gingerly back to Silvia's, trying to jog for short, painful spurts. She wasn't built for this environment. When she collapsed back into the house, toed off her shoes and struggled up the steps into the living room, Silvia hopped up from the sofa in alarm.

'Luna! You went running like *that*?'

'Like what?' she asked weakly, slumping to the floor because it felt somehow better than reclining on the sofa.

'Weren't you hot?'

'Hot?' she repeated stupidly. 'It's freezing out there.' Luna tugged off her beanie and noticed her hair was plastered to her head with sweat.

Silvia hurried to the kitchen and returned with a glass of water. 'Sip it slowly, tesoro. You are overheated. Running is a big workout,' Silvia explained. 'If you wear too much, your body temperature rises and cannot regulate itself. You are lucky you stopped, or you could have fainted.'

Luna blinked at Silvia in disbelief. She took a sip of the water, suddenly realising she could have guzzled the whole thing. 'I'm really not cut out for this.'

'You didn't know,' Silvia said, patting her arm. 'You got in very late last night.'

Luna nodded and continued to sip the water silently, until she realised that Silvia wouldn't let her get away with saying nothing. 'Another team from the PGHM turned up at the bar,' she explained. 'I had such an amazing day on the slopes that I ended up on the dance floor with Bast and Jean-Marc,' she said with a chuckle. 'My first après-ski experience. It was fun. Skiing is such a high. I kind of get it, now.'

It was Silvia's turn to chuckle. 'I'm glad you got home safe, then.'

'Yannick drove me home,' Luna explained, starting to feel more herself now the nausea was receding.

'Oh, I didn't think après ski was his scene,' Silvia commented.

'He didn't... dance, if that's what you mean.' Luna stifled a laugh, wondering what Yannick would look like if he danced. She was suddenly burning to see that. 'He only stayed because he felt responsible for me.' At least that's what she had to tell herself.

'I thought you might have met someone,' Silvia said casually. 'I have this feeling that your visit here might involve more than just the truth about Jim. Are you sure you didn't like the second crystal I placed in your hand the day we met?'

'Is that the one you sneaked into my coat? Does that have something to do with relationships? Oh, I... No, Silvia. I had a boyfriend when my mum died and... I really don't think I'm in a place where I can get involved with someone. I need to work through my feelings one at a time,' Luna said ruefully, thinking about staying as far away from that stone as possible.

'I suppose that's wise,' Silvia agreed with a sigh, 'but I really thought the carnelian would be something for you. Among its many properties, it attracts the energies of love and passion – to bring something light and fun into your life while you're here.'

Luna stifled a snort. 'Passion? I don't think so. I can't believe you're telling me to have a fling, Silvia.' But she paused, her mind spinning with thoughts of her mum here, learning to ski and perhaps even discovering *passion*, as foreign as that word sounded. 'What about you and Guy?' she asked, changing the subject. 'How long have you been together?'

'Oh, years – off and on. Nearly ten years, perhaps.'

Luna regarded her friend speculatively. No anniversary, no marking the first date. Silvia didn't even know how long they'd been together. Luna wasn't sure what that told her about the relationship as Silvia and Guy always seemed close. 'Neither of you wanted to marry?'

It was Silvia's turn to squirm. 'We are both free spirits, I suppose.'

'When did you meet?'

'For the first time? Years ago, when he first transferred from Modane. He wasn't the commandant back then, of course. I taught a basic Italian class and he was my student. But it wasn't until around five years later that... well, things started between us. I was already over forty and he was forty-seven, so there didn't seem to be any point in commitment.'

Luna digested Silvia's words slowly.

'But we are like the sun and the moon,' she said with a sigh. 'He's always up *there* in winter – looking to be caught in an avalanche, if you ask me. And if I go up with him in summer... We don't work well together when risks are involved.' Her words trailed off, but Luna's heart was already full of dismay. 'I said I love a man in uniform, and all the boys at the PGHM are close to my heart, but it isn't easy caring for someone who sees himself as a guardian of those on the mountain. You have to be a certain kind of daredevil.'

If anything had become clear to Luna during her day on the slopes, it was that she would never be a daredevil.

'I'm glad you had a good day, yesterday,' Silvia said brightly. 'I knew you would learn to ski without too much difficulty.'

Luna nodded slowly, trying to recapture that feeling of confidence, but it was difficult when she'd nearly keeled over just from jogging because she wasn't familiar with the climate. So much for earning Yannick's trust before the trip to the glacier.

'Skiing started to make sense at least. I need to get back up there before I forget that I can do it. I might even go again today, after I stop by the Compagnie des Guides.'

'For the photos of Jim?'

She nodded. 'Yannick also said a guide called Jean-Yves might know something more. I'll try to find him.' She was glad to find her focus again and stop thinking about the PGHM and trust and hearts and daredevils.

15

'This one was taken at the Refuge de Leschaux, when we took a group up Grandes Jorasses a few years ago. Too inexperienced, they were. That was another time we nearly called for rescue, but we got them down.'

Luna soaked up the old man's words in silence, staring at the pictures he set out in front of her. It felt as though she'd been looking at photos all day, but she was still completely absorbed in Jim's life at high altitude.

She'd stopped first at the Compagnie des Guides, where the woman behind the desk had apologised profusely for the confusion the first time she'd stopped by and explained that Jim had been in their database with the surname 'DeMontagne' and no one had even realised his name was Robert Durand.

She'd pulled a small packet of photos out of a filing cabinet and had offered to call Jim's friend Jean-Yves for her. She'd pored over pictures of Jim as a young man, in the days when the glaciers had tumbled further down the mountain, and of Jim with clients and other guides in more recent photos, his face beautifully weathered with experience.

In one old photo, he'd even been rock-climbing with a friend barefoot – two boys who had looked around fifteen. On the back of the photo, written in blocky handwriting, had been written the word 'Robert', making Luna smile wryly.

An hour later, she'd found herself in the small apartment belonging to Jean-Yves, which was filled with bits of wood and rock, old maps and piles of equipment, including several ice axes stacked on top of the shoe rack by the front door.

Jim's friend had given her a gritty cup of coffee that was so strong it could almost hold up the spoon and fetched a box of photos from a shelf.

The photo in front of her showed the two men, Jim blue-eyed, pink and freckled and Jean-Yves tanned, with salt-and-pepper hair. They stood, grinning, on a narrow metal balcony that appeared to hang right over a glacial valley, with the tumbling chunks of ice behind.

'Jim made it a matter of pride that he and his clients rarely got into trouble. Of course, we've all had our share of rescues on the job, but Jim could turn a man into a mountain goat and give him the courage to take those next steps.'

The description reminded her of Yannick on the chairlift.

'I knew about the insurance policy,' Jean-Yves said grimly. 'You're the beneficiary?'

'Yes, I am,' was all Luna could say in response as her mind buzzed with questions.

'The premium was expensive because of Jim's work,' the old guide continued. 'We haven't lost too many people over the years, but the chances are still much higher than for the general population.'

His words made Luna's throat clog with misgiving. She would much rather have known him alive than receive money because he'd died before his time. 'When did he take out the policy?'

'Twenty years ago at least. He must have paid a pretty sum over that time.'

'And what did he say about... me?'

Jean-Yves took a long look at her as his brow knit. With his thick moustache and embroidered felt jacket, he could have stepped out of a photo from the golden age of mountaineering. 'He told me he had no other option, that the insurance policy was the only thing he could do to help someone he had a responsibility towards. I always wondered if he meant you were his child. I thought he might have had an affair with a married woman.'

Luna frowned, only further confused by the man's words. 'Responsibility' didn't sound like paternity. 'My mother wasn't married,' Luna insisted, hearing the defensiveness in her tone and pushing it away as best she could. Jean-Yves didn't deserve anything but her polite respect. 'I don't think he could be my father. My mother told me quite a different story,' she insisted, not sure if she was only trying to convince herself. 'Do you know why he was called Jim?' she asked.

'Oh, that goes further back than I do. I think the story was that his best friend in school was also a Robert, so he decided to be called Jim. One year I had three Roberts in my class, when I was at school.'

'I suppose that sort of makes sense,' Luna said.

'You might... perhaps you look a little like him,' Jean-Yves said softly, a shadow in his eyes. 'Are you sure you're not his daughter?'

The way he phrased the question made her skin prickle. 'I can't say for certain,' she admitted softly. 'I was told my father's surname *was* Robert, but Robert Favre, not Durand. And I thought he was from Corsica, where I was born.' Except her mum had been in Chamonix the winter before, Luna added silently with a wince.

Jean-Yves frowned, his mind working. 'Favre is also a very common name.'

'Unfortunately. But I still don't understand why Jim made me the beneficiary. He even had my most recent address to contact me.'

'Attendez,' Jean-Yves said suddenly. 'The blonde woman – an old friend, he said, but I always interpreted from his tone that he meant an old lover. What was her name? Judy? Something English.'

Luna couldn't speak for a moment. 'June?' she suggested, holding her breath.

'Could be.' He nodded. 'One of Jim's favourite places in the world was the Refuge de l'Envers des Aiguilles, below the Aiguille du Grépon.'

'Yes, Yannick told me. That's where you all gathered for the scattering of his ashes.'

Jean-Yves nodded. 'Jim stayed there often even when we didn't have a group. He stuck a few photos up on the wall there, and one was of her.'

'Does the woman in that photo look anything like this?' Luna asked eagerly, fetching her photo out of her handbag. 'This was my mum.'

Jean-Yves accepted the photo and studied it. 'Could be, but I'm not certain. I haven't taken any notice of those pictures on the wall in years. She had a child in the photo, though.'

Luna sat heavily against the back of her chair, her head spinning. She was on a trail of some kind, but instead of arriving anywhere, she kept finding sharp turns that made her question her destination entirely. The suggestions that Jim might be her father couldn't be ignored and June had obviously glossed over certain things about her twenties, but an outright lie about the identity of Luna's father – and telling her daughter that he'd died years ago – seemed a step too far.

'Perhaps I do need to get to this refuge,' she murmured. If there was a photo of her on the wall, she needed to know.

He nodded. 'The snow will be up to the windows right now – perhaps higher. But it's possible, with the right equipment – if you choose a good window in the weather.'

Climbing to a mountain hut that was under several feet of snow seemed too much of a challenge. She wondered what Yannick would say – something calm and reassuring, definitely.

She would talk to him after class on Thursday and find out more.

* * *

Arriving for her lesson with team two on the second Thursday in January, Luna marvelled at how much had changed in a week – mainly her attitude. She'd skied a blue slope – even on her own, the day before. She'd picked up another two classes that Silvia had offered her and even done a shift in the crystal shop. She'd run a full 5km in some new, breathable winter running gear – courtesy of Jim's money.

If Lyd could see her, now... Actually, her cousin would probably still think she was crazy for hanging around here looking into dead people's secrets with her mother's ashes stored illegally in her room – although at least she'd hidden the urn in her wardrobe now.

Yannick had sent her three photos of Jim through the week, including an eye-wateringly vertiginous view down on the old man from above on a rock face, with ropes dangling. She hadn't immediately realised that Yannick himself must have been climbing above, taking the photo.

But that picture – and the ubiquitous views of the peaks that seemed so wild and formidable to her – had given her an idea for her next class. Instead of worrying that she'd feel like a fraud because she knew nothing about mountain rescue, she'd decided to use that fact to everyone's advantage.

As soon as she entered the training room, she noticed her students' attitudes had changed in a week, too. They shook her hand and apologised and Matthieu even brought her a steaming cup of coffee that looked only slightly less sludgy than the one Jean-Yves had made for her.

Yannick rushed in at the last minute again, clutching a clipboard, and Luna was amused by the little flutter inside her as she was reminded how strapping he looked in his uniform, the collar of his navy-blue gilet brushing his jaw.

She stared at his cheek for a moment, remembering kissing him goodbye on Saturday night, before he smiled and she snapped out of it.

'Hi,' she said, feeling a tickle of lingering embarrassment that she'd hoped she'd banished with her weird admission about his face, but... his *face*. The wide jaw, thick lashes and bright smile showing all his teeth – he looked so sweet she couldn't even form a sentence.

'Hi,' he replied with what might have been a matching touch of colour in his cheeks.

When Matthieu leaned between the two of them with an exaggerated wave, saying, 'Hi,' in a high-pitched, teasing voice, Luna cleared her throat and collected herself to start the lesson. She perched on the edge of her chair in the circle, clutching her mug, and gave them her little prepared speech.

'I know last week didn't go so well. It's fine,' she insisted when the apologies tumbled over each other again. 'I also know you can all speak very good English. I know how precious your time is, so it's important to me to help you in exactly the way you need and not force you to do anything that's not useful.'

'It was useful last week,' Yannick insisted.

'Well, today will be even more so,' she promised. 'You might have realised that I don't know much about the PGHM – or about the alpine environment in general. So, that's what we're going to do. You need to educate me – in English.'

Her gendarme students embraced their assignment even more enthusiastically than she'd hoped. They took her on a comprehensive tour of the operations room where missions were planned and monitored, and even gave her an introduction to basic mountaineering equipment.

By the time the ninety minutes were over, she'd learned that the helicopter could be dispatched within two minutes and took less than five minutes to reach most locations on the Mont Blanc massif and the Aiguilles Rouges on the other side of the valley. She'd learned the emergency medical services were known by the acronym 'SAMU' in French and that a medic travelled in the helicopter on nearly every operation.

She'd had trouble translating the concept they'd explained as 'premier à marcher', the designation of which rescuers were on duty each day to run for the helicopter when calls came in. The direct translation, 'first to walk', didn't capture the call to duty and she had no idea what the English military term for something similar would be.

Luna had held an ice axe in her hand for the first time and flinched continually as the gendarmes had demonstrated the techniques for climbing with the tool. At the end of the lesson, Luna was trussed up in a harness with different kinds of ropes hanging off it, beseeching her students to practise saying, 'slowly,' instead of, 'doucement,' and to remember that they should actually pronounce the 'h' at the beginning of English words.

'Do you feel like a Christmas tree every time you walk onto a job?' she asked, peering down at herself.

124   LEONIE MACK

'I hope you're all prepared to tidy up,' came a voice in French from the door, interrupting the laughter. Guy stepped into the room, studying Luna with his head to one side. She froze in alarm, but he chuckled and leaned down to kiss her cheek. 'Bonjour, Luna,' he greeted her.

It was slightly strange to greet him like a friend in this professional context, but she'd seen him so many times at Silvia's house in civilian dress, that perhaps the greeting was appropriate.

'We're... practising,' she explained.

'Super! Next time you can play the victim.'

The gendarmes reacted with raucous enthusiasm, although the prospect made Luna's hair stand on end.

'That is what I need to talk to you about,' Guy continued, addressing them all. 'Team two is on duty next week.'

'Shall we reschedule?' she asked.

'No, no, but if you can come to the drop zone, we can have an informal class. If it's not a busy day, you'll still have most of your students.'

'Just not the ones who are premier à marcher?' she asked with a smile. Guy returned the smile and she stumbled forward under the weight of all the pats on the back from her students.

'We hhhad good class today,' Matthieu said in English, exaggerating the 'h'. 'She learned a lot. She's our marmot – I mean mascot.' He gave Luna a wink and Yannick a teasing shove that made her realise how easily news travelled within the group.

'I can see she learned a lot,' Guy said drily. 'Now you should get back to work.'

They said goodbye and filed out obediently and it was only as Yannick turned to go that she remembered she was still tied up with equipment. Looking down at the harness cinched around her waist and thighs, she gave an enormous sigh.

'You want some help?' Yannick asked, looking back from the doorway.

'Oh, um, well, I don't know where it all goes in the cupboard.'

'The guys will put it away, don't worry,' he said in French.

She pulled at the strap connected to the avalanche transceiver hanging across her body and managed to scrape it over her head, peering at the device curiously before she set it down. She got a bit caught in the long coil of rope Matthieu had draped over her and Yannick had to help her slip her arm out.

It took forever to unclip each of the carabiners attached to the harness belt, even though she took one side and Yannick the other. She had to squash another dose of self-consciousness when she realised how close he was standing.

'Um, I met Jean-Yves,' she mumbled to fill the silence. 'He knew about the insurance policy and he suspected I was Jim's daughter, as strange as that would be. But he doesn't know for certain, of course.'

'That's a shame.'

'I'm not really sure where to go from here. Mum didn't talk about my father much, although it's hard to believe she would have told me the wrong name.' She sighed, wondering if she'd ever feel that she truly knew who her mum had been. 'Jean-Yves told me about the Refuge de l'Envers des Aiguilles,' she continued.

'Jim loved that refuge. Treated it like his own house in summer. Something about the sunsets, he used to say.'

'Apparently he put some photos on the wall – including maybe a photo of me as a child. He remembered Jim talking about my mother as an old friend.'

Yannick's brow shot up. 'That does sound familiar.'

'Jean-Yves said he thought she was an old girlfriend of Jim's so there might have been something... romantic between them after all. But why keep a photo of an ex-girlfriend on the wall? If he wasn't my father, then why...' She couldn't even finish the sentence.

Yannick continued gently. 'It would be like Jim to keep a photo of her, even after he let her go so she could be with someone else.'

Luna stared at Yannick, as he got back to work again on her carabiners, studying his narrowed eyes and that solid jaw. 'What do you mean? Why would he let her go if she was his girlfriend?'

She had a feeling she knew what his answer would be, now she was beginning to understand the mindset of the people who lived in the shadow of the mountain.

16

'Jim never married. He always said it wasn't his fate.'

'The mountain was his fate,' Luna said quietly. Her stomach dropped when Yannick nodded. 'You think, even if he loved my mother, he wouldn't have married her?'

His gaze flitted to hers briefly, but then stayed rooted to a knot he was untying at her waist. She stumbled as he tugged at the stubborn knot. What had those cheeky gendarmes done to her?

'I don't know for certain,' he muttered eventually. 'But it's possible. I met him when he was in his mid-forties. I can't say what he was like at thirty.'

'What did he think when you got married?'

Yannick's hands paused for a heartbeat, then managed to unfasten the knot and slip the rope out swiftly. 'He didn't expect me to marry the mountain, too,' he commented. He grasped the waist strap of the harness absently. His brow was knit, thoughts chiselled into his face.

Luna waited to see if any of those thoughts would spill out, fairly certain he had no idea his fingers were digging into her waist as he loosened the harness with practised hands. He paused and blinked at the strap, before snatching his hands back.

Turning and running his fingers through his hair, he sighed. 'Jim didn't give advice. He always said we had to make our choices as we saw them. He wouldn't have advised me against marriage, but... he also understood when Valérie and I started talking about separating.'

'He was a good friend to you during that time?' she asked.

Yannick nodded. 'I joined the gendarmerie partly because I... like clear guidelines. Jim showed me it's okay that life sometimes doesn't come with a rulebook. The mountain, too, breaks rules all the time. Assessments of acceptable risk aren't always black and white and the right decision can turn out to be the wrong one, but you have no way of knowing.'

Luna studied him as he spoke softly in French. Yannick, with his rough hands, broad shoulders and dependable jaw, was sad. She didn't fully grasp what he was talking about, breaking the rules and assessing risk, but she could understand how difficult it must be for him to let Jim go. Not only had Yannick lost a good friend that day, but he'd lost a victim in his professional capacity and she was beginning to grasp the complexity of those feelings in him. He'd lost his own brother, as well, without even the closure of a body.

'Climbing a mountain and committing to a relationship: both involve assessments of acceptable risk, huh?' she said, screwing up her face as she thought of the two years she'd wasted dating Aiden, who she'd thought hadn't posed any risk.

'I don't think it's quite the same thing,' he said.

'It isn't? You'd rather climb a mountain than commit to someone again, right? It's an unacceptable risk. For Jim, too.'

His mouth fell open. 'I hadn't thought of it that way.' He picked up a stack of straps with carabiners on each end and headed for the cupboard, glancing back at her. 'What about you? You want to know if there was a love story between Jim and your mother, but what would that mean for you?'

'Perhaps that's what I want to find out.' She slipped her fingers into the waistband of the loosened harness but paused before pushing it down over her hips. 'I'm better at thinking than doing,' she admitted with a laugh. 'Maybe I understand completely why a relationship is an unacceptable risk. I thought Mum was the same. There was a kind of anxiety about her, but now that I know she skied here, that she might have known a mountain guide, I can't help wondering if that anxiety was the result of something that happened to her – if she lost someone. She spoke about my father before she died, when she was on strong medication and I thought she might have still loved him, despite telling me he walked away from us before he died. Why would she have lied about that?'

When her gaze came back into focus, Yannick was there, his head cocked, regarding her with sympathy and warmth and maybe a little bit of fondness that made her want to learn to climb mountains.

'If there's anything to find here, I don't doubt you'll find it.'

She sighed, meeting his gaze with a smile. 'Are you just being kind again?'

'No!' he insisted.

Luna's smile wobbled. 'I still don't know whether I can believe you – even when you use your gendarme voice.'

'I have a gendarme voice?'

'Yep. When you say "stop", too.' She said the word in a mock French accent that made him laugh.

'Passe-moi le baudrier,' he said, holding out his hand.

She didn't understand him for a moment. 'Oh!' she said when he gestured to the harness and stepped out of it, handing it to him.

He held it in front of her. 'Le baudrier,' he said, slowly and clearly. 'Répétez!' he instructed with a poorly hidden smile.

'Le baudrier,' she said, rolling her eyes. 'I thought we were using "tu"?' She hoped her question didn't reveal how disappointed she'd be to return to the formal address with him.

'Baudrier,' he said again, exaggerating the pronunciation of the 'r'. 'And I can't use "tu" in a gendarme voice.'

'Okay, I get it! Was Jim as exacting as you?'

'No,' he said with a smile. 'But it's your bad luck you have me instead.'

As much as she wished she'd met Jim, she didn't think her luck was bad. 'Do you really think I'd make it to Jim's refuge? I'm so curious about the photo. Maybe it's not me at all.'

He considered her question for a long moment and she couldn't decide if that meant it was genuinely dangerous or he was just being careful.

'I could go without you, look at the photo and send you a picture,' he proposed.

His suggestion made a lot of sense, but Luna couldn't convince herself it was the right course of action. 'That would answer one question, but what if there's something else there for me to find? And if there's nothing else, then all I can do is learn about who he was and pay my respects. If I can get there, I should at least try.'

'It's possible, of course.'

'Of course,' Luna agreed wryly. 'Even a cute little marmot could make it with your help.'

'I'm sorry about that,' he said, his pained tone making her regret her joke. 'I didn't mean "cute" like a child. I meant "pretty"... Ehm.' He rubbed the back of his neck, drawing her eyes from his pink cheeks to the firm muscle of his forearm and she was suddenly thankful that gendarmes were apparently impervious to cold and wore short-sleeved polo shirts year-round at head-quarters.

'It's okay,' she said, letting him off the hook and reminding herself he was only being kind to say she was pretty. 'I feel so out of place here, I'd be better off hibernating.'

'Stop!' he said pointedly, in his gendarme voice. 'No negativity, please. Getting to the refuge would involve a short climb and some deep snow. That means an ice axe and crampons, all the ropes and safety equipment.' He watched her carefully as he explained.

'Does that mean... no?'

'My biggest concern is whether you can make it there and back in one day.'

'So that's definitely a no?' she asked. At least if it was out of the realms of possibility, she could try to let it lie and she wouldn't need to think any more about ice axes.

'Not at all,' he said in such a mild tone that she was nearly annoyed with him. 'But I think we'd need to stay at the refuge overnight.'

'I thought it was closed.'

'It's not closed, but there is no guard there, so we'd need to do everything ourselves – bring food, melt snow for water. But there is a wood heater and blankets.'

Luna's mouth hung open, as she imagined people who trekked to this hut in winter for no reason – or no reason she could under-stand. 'Is it safe?'

Yannick answered immediately with a nod of his head. 'Mostly.'

'*Mostly*?'

'Luna, I can't promise you there won't be an accident or an avalanche. I can never promise you there won't be an avalanche. The instant you leave the prepared ski slopes, you face more risk. Sometimes the weather forecast is wrong and you can get caught.'

When he glanced at her, there was a hint of a smile on his features.

'I can promise you, though, that it will be worth it.'

* * *

Yannick had already been on shift at the drop zone for more than two hours when it was time for their English class the following Thursday. Emilien and Patrice had already been out in the hélico, spotting cornices after heavy snowfall overnight. It would be a busy day for off-piste skiers in the Vallée Blanche, given the number of excursions that had been notified to the Chamoniarde and passed on to Cordial.

After he'd finished marking the snow cornices on the map on the wall of the control room, he cross-referenced the new reports of crevasses or damaged snow bridges, marking those as well. It was routine work, familiarising himself with the ever-changing conditions on the mountain, but his eyes strayed continually to the little red house symbol on the map, marking the Refuge de l'Envers des Aiguilles.

As far as he knew, there was no one up there today. Other routes were more popular in winter. He would need a report on the conditions of the snow and ice before he attempted to take Luna.

But he would take her, which would be an interesting experience to say the least. By the end of the afternoon last Friday, she'd managed a few turns on parallel skis and wasn't doing badly, for a beginner, but she had a way to go before they could consider skiing the Vallée Blanche and now she would need to learn basic climbing safety too.

He couldn't be certain she wouldn't give up under pressure. It was extraordinary the lengths she'd already gone to, to find out about Jim, but if there was an easier way, he had to offer it. He'd even called Jim's brother through the week, only to hear that the man had sold or given away most of Jim's things and had found no photos of a mysterious blonde woman with a child. He couldn't recommend that Luna travel to Annecy to meet the man, because it was strange that she had received a tidy sum on Jim's death and his own brother had inherited only his meagre possessions and modest savings.

His old friend had left a puzzle and, if Yannick was honest, he wanted it solved too – enough to take a civilian out to an isolated mountain refuge at more than 2,000 m above sea level in the middle of winter. Perhaps if he worked out why Jim had paid those premiums, he could make up for what had happened that day.

Shaking himself out of his distraction, he focussed on the map. He had twelve hours on shift and then he got to see Maëlys, as Valérie and her boyfriend were going out that night. Even if he only got to put her to bed, he was glad of the extra evening with her.

He noticed Luna arriving on foot through the car park and wondered what had happened to her old right-hand drive car with no winter tyres. He waved to her through the windows and motioned to the entrance. She still clutched her brown corduroy bag full of materials, but she'd given up on her skirts and blouses in favour of a sturdy pair of trousers and winter boots.

Greeting her with quick kisses on the cheek before he thought too much about it, he introduced her to their team leader Philippe, who was coordinating the shift, and showed her into the little rec room, which would be their impromptu classroom for the day. She set down her bag, eyeing his harness.

'Are you premier à marcher?' she asked.

'Second,' he said with a shake of his head. 'Emilien and Patrice are first today, with Marina and Alex – I don't think you've met

Alex. They won't come to class. The chances of a call are high and they need to be watching.'

Matthieu and the others from the team spilled in from where they'd been testing equipment in the hangar.

'La marmotte mascotte is at the drop zone!' Matthieu said with a smile, clapping her on the shoulder. 'The interventions will go good today!'

She grinned at Matthieu. 'If the *missions* go *well* today, then it's because of the expertise of the gendarmes and not because of me – and definitely not because of those hibernating marmots. I don't even believe those ones they call groundhogs in America can really predict the onset of spring.'

Matthieu guffawed. 'I know that film. Maybe you will bring the spring early, too!'

Yannick hoped not, which was a strange thought. He always enjoyed winter, but he felt this one needed to be especially long.

They took her on a tour of the DZ, taking every opportunity to show off the brackets and ropes installed throughout the building for extra strength training. Yannick stood back and let the younger guys show her how they could hang off the doorframes and perform pull-ups that weren't anything special in this unit.

He tried not to be gratified when she asked him, 'Can you do that too?' after Laurent had demonstrated the hang board in the rec room.

'Of course,' he replied, but resisted showing off.

Matthieu introduced her lovingly to 'Dragon' and 'Choucas', the two helicopters, explaining that 'choucas' was a kind of black bird that no one knew how to translate into English. The names were standard across all PGHM units and the individual aircraft were identified by the addition of the département code, in this case Choucas 74, for Haute-Savoie.

Her eyes glazed over as Matthieu tried to explain the specifications of the aircraft. Emilien and Patrice performed more checks while the mechanic steered Choucas out onto the tarmac in preparation for the inevitable first call.

'This is Cecile, the médecin urgentiste for today,' Matthieu said. 'Ceci, this is our English teacher, Luna.'

'I think he means our emergency doctor,' Cecile said with a smile, shaking Luna's hand. She was an experienced paramedic doctor in her forties with as many rescues under her belt as he had.

They were in the materials room when sudden activity alerted them that the real day had begun. Through the window, they saw Emilien, Patrice and Cecile rushing for the helicopter, putting on their helmets as they ran.

Choucas lifted off and, with a quick glance at each other, the English class decamped to the control room to hear what had happened.

'Chute en crevasse,' Philippe muttered.

'Euh, it's a fall... into crevasse,' Matthieu explained. 'Good we checked the equipment this morning.'

The radio crackled to life and news of a second call filled the control room – a skiing injury. Philippe conferred briefly with Cordial and then signed off, turning to look at Yannick. 'Tous les deux,' he said indicating him and Matthieu, 'get ready to support Emilien at the Vallée Blanche. Marina and Alex will go out on this call. Send the doctor back when you go up.'

English was the last thing on Yannick's mind as he switched to duty mode, grabbing his helmet and heading for the hangar with the familiar surge in his blood that was more than a little addictive. He would bring someone down alive today.

17

Despite her decent French, Luna struggled to keep up with the constant, clipped sentences coming over the radio and the team leader's equally curt responses. The helicopter had lifted off and then returned, lifted off again and returned again, leaving the teams up on the mountain to do their job. She should go, but she couldn't bring herself to, fiddling with the moonstone she found in her pocket and thinking stupid thoughts about being the team's mascot.

But, as much as she wished she could, she couldn't influence the outcome of either operation. She'd heard that the victim in the crevasse was conscious and uninjured, but stuck in a crack. The air in the control room felt still and thin. She kept glancing up at the jagged needles of rock, knowing she couldn't see where the rescue crew were, but looking anyway.

'The site is secured; Yanni is preparing to go down,' she heard over the radio and froze. Yannick was going down where? 'Radio communication from now on.'

'Ouais, c'est bon,' she heard Yannick's voice, followed by a grunt of effort and a swooshing sound that probably came from rope moving over ice. 'Descendez-moi, doucement – doucement!' he instructed, telling someone to let him down slowly. He counted the distance to the victim – five metres, then three – and Luna didn't want to know how far he'd gone down. She heard him calling out to the victim, his words punctuated by crunching and swishing that unfortunately allowed Luna to imagine him descending into the icy maw of a deep crevasse.

She didn't realise she was trembling until one of the gendarmes in her class rolled an office chair over for her, pushing her into it.

The rescue effort seemed painstakingly slow as they planned the exact angle at which they needed to extract the victim. But when Emilien reported back that the man had been safely pulled out of the crevasse with no injuries, Luna was startled to discover that the whole operation had taken only twenty minutes.

She was listening keenly for more updates but heard nothing. It was safe to assume that silence meant Yannick was back up, but nobody had explicitly announced it – not in the way they'd celebrated the return of the victim to the surface.

When the helicopter came back with the first pair of gendarmes and a stack of equipment, she nearly hyperventilated when she realised that neither of them was Yannick.

'It's okay, prof,' said Matthieu, using the French term for a teacher, which would have made her smile under other circumstances. 'The victim is okay.'

'And the... team?' she asked, even as her cheeks went pink.

Matthieu threw up his hands. 'It's a little crevasse – only nine metres down. We climb these for fun!'

She tried to tell herself to breathe normally again. 'Right,' she managed to say with a nod, but she glanced at the radio again.

'Euh, Emilien? This is the DZ,' Philippe said into the radio, giving Luna a smile. 'Tout va bien là-haut?' *Everything okay up there?*

'De quoi, DZ?' came Emilien's voice. 'We're packing up and waiting for Choucas.'

'Both of you? Our visitor got worried you'd left Yanni in the crevasse.'

Luna flushed, her hair standing on end and her cheeks hot. They were just teasing her for being worried, she hoped. Emilien's snort of laughter was distorted over the radio. It *was* a little funny how concerned she'd been when she'd seen Yannick in action before, but she still felt lightheaded.

'You okay, Yanni?' she heard Emilien asking with a chuckle.

After a moment's hesitation, 'Je vais bien, DZ,' came the voice she'd needed to hear. *I'm okay,* DZ.

She blew out a careful breath, imagining she could hear her own blood rush with relief. Her anxiety made no sense. It had been a routine operation. He must have been down dozens of crevasses since the day Jim died and been a complete professional about it each time.

She still felt sick.

Trying to pull herself together, she rose to collect her things from the rec room on wobbly legs. She kept dropping her bag as she tried to stuff her unused notebook back inside. She'd officially taught the strangest lesson she could imagine and yet, everything felt like a lesson about life in this crazy place.

Squeezing her eyes shut for a moment, she wondered what her mum had thought of all the risks and why it felt as though Luna was following in her footsteps, even though June had hopefully never witnessed a PGHM rescue.

Luna stepped back into the control room in time to see

Choucas setting down on the tarmac. The door slid open and Yannick and Emilien, in their helmets and goggles, stepped out, hauling heavy bags after them. Yannick draped a coil of rope over his shoulder, hefted a rucksack and a large piece of equipment and hurried out from beneath the blades, ducking his head.

Luna didn't rush over to him. It was so clear he was working, that her feet remained rooted to the spot, despite the compulsion to show her relief. She stopped in the door of the hangar to see him tugging off his helmet, his straight hair sticking up. The ice axe dangling from his harness was caked with snow. He didn't otherwise look as though he'd just climbed into a crevasse, except his shoulders rose and fell with the aftermath of adrenaline and exertion.

She knew that feeling, because she felt it too. She was even sweating – she'd bet Yannick wasn't. Saving a skier from a crevasse was another day at the office for him, whereas *listening* to someone climb down a crevasse was too much for Luna to take.

Patrice clapped Yannick on the shoulder and he was enveloped in the support of his team. He didn't need Luna's worry. She'd probably distracted him on the job, embarrassing him over the radio. Maybe her little crush was more of a problem than she wanted to admit.

* * *

Yannick clocked up three rescues before the end of his shift – a particularly gratifying day. Finishing up the afternoon by belaying Matthieu down to a skier who'd strayed into rocks, he got back to the DZ just in time to put away his harness and ask the others to take care of packing up and paperwork while he rushed to collect Maëlys.

Only when he wrapped his daughter in a hug did he think about that morning – about the wild look in Luna's eye when he'd come back from the first operation of the day. She hadn't approached and he'd been so busy, he hadn't noticed her leaving, hadn't processed why he was disappointed that she hadn't said goodbye.

A bit of distance was probably for the best. He found it far too easy to be drawn into her unique way of thinking, where she blurted out things like: 'You'd rather climb a mountain than commit to someone again.'

Yes, Luna had brought something good into his life – and the promise of doing something for Jim – but it was no good interpreting it as anything more than an opportunity to serve, to perform a duty, his particular specialty.

He drew back to grin at Maëlys, brushing her curls back from her face. 'Ready to come home with Papa, louloute? Maman said you've got a reading book. We can make a fire and look at your book on your favourite cushions.'

'I don't like the book,' she insisted. 'Can I help cut the wood and make the fire?' He felt rather than saw Valérie eyeing him from where she was standing by the open-plan kitchen. It always reminded him of how they'd designed the place together, waiting simultaneously as the builders made slow progress and Valérie's belly grew round.

Maëlys had been born three weeks early, before the house was close to ready, reminding Yannick he could never prepare for all eventualities, no matter how hard he tried.

'She's already eaten dinner because I wasn't sure what you... I know you've been on duty all day.'

'And she needs to get to bed early.' He confirmed the clear message Valérie had given him when she'd asked him to take her on a school evening.

'She hasn't been sleeping at school,' she explained.

'Sleeping is *boring* at school,' Maëlys insisted.

He tugged on her hair affectionately. 'I never slept during the day either.' His daughter's face lit up, while Valérie's froze in alarm and he realised he'd said the wrong thing. 'Sleeping is good for you though,' he added half-heartedly, but he suspected the damage was done. 'Come here, petit cœur.' He hauled her up into his arms and Valérie sighed again.

'I've been trying to explain to her that I can't pick her up any more,' his ex-muttered.

'*I* can,' he said as gently as he could. 'She won't expect it from you.' He turned to his daughter. 'Are you growing? I think you're getting heavy.'

'No, it's...' Valérie turned towards the window. 'You know we're trying for a baby,' she said under her breath.

That knocked the wind out of him. If Valérie had hinted at the possibility before, he'd missed it or blocked it out. Yannick stood completely still, waiting until his knees were stable again and forcing himself to breathe. He wanted to be happy for Maëlys' sake. They'd been so stretched with one child, a second had only ever been a distant dream, but his daughter would gain a little sister or brother and the thought filled him with wonder.

But it also pushed him further away. He'd been the problem after all – putting the job above his family. They'd deliberated for years before deciding to have a child, but the decision had obviously been easier with Fabien, her new partner.

'I hope everything... goes well,' he said softly, kissing her cheek. She peered up at him warily, as though she had more to say – as though she might still think about everything they'd lost. But she turned away again.

'Thanks, Yannick.'

After he settled Maëlys into her bed at his house later that evening, he couldn't tear himself away. Sitting on the floor and leaning against the bedframe, he stared at her face, with her little cheeks and Valérie's chin, marvelling at the gift he'd been given: the duty to love this person with everything in him.

He committed his time to the mountain and his heart to his daughter. It was more than enough.

18

'I can't...' Luna panted out a few breaths before she could even finish her sentence. '...hold it.'

'Avec les jambes. Use your legs. To the left, find the foothold.'

Luna flailed out with her left leg, listening for Yannick's calm prompts until her foot snagged the little grip and she could shift her weight. An hour into her first climbing lesson the week after her visit to the DZ, she was dripping with sweat; her fingers ached and her arms were throbbing. At least if she focussed on her shortness of breath, she wasn't thinking of the drop.

It was completely safe. She was attached to a long rope that looped through an anchor point high above her. On the other end of the rope was Yannick, who would have to be dead before he would let her fall. But her animal brain still protested strongly at her attempt to haul herself several metres vertically off the ground, clinging only to a set of tiny grips.

It was nearly February and, although she was doing tolerably well at the ski resort, practising doggedly several times a week, if she had to climb to get up to Jim's favourite refuge, she wouldn't make it. She'd keel over with exhaustion or she'd get hypothermia; she was sweating so much with effort.

She managed a few more grips, before her foot slipped and she slammed into the wall, knocking her cheek. The rope was immediately taut and she barely fell an inch.

'Take hold of the other rope like I showed you,' he instructed from below, 'and sit back in the harness, feet on the wall.'

Blinking sweat out of her eyes and wrangling her instincts back under control, she remembered the tutorial he'd given her at the beginning and grasped for the rope attached to a deceptively simple-looking belay device.

'Have you got it?' he prompted.

She blew out a deep breath, knowing he was waiting for her to confirm she could let herself down. She forced herself to nod.

'Talk to me, Luna!'

That was part of the problem: she was trying not to talk to him so much. After realising she'd been a bit of an idiot to get so starry-eyed over Yannick, she'd been trying to work on her boundaries. She was trying not to notice his muscular arms in his sleeveless gym shirt, determined to ignore the flow of ideas for her imaginary calendar: twelve months of competence. But it was difficult not to swoon a little as his capable hands looped ropes together and tied knots and he stood close to check her straps and carabiners, close enough that she could appreciate the faint woody scent of him and the way she could feel the air distorting between them.

She found him attractive, that was the problem. But she would get over it without spilling her emotions all over him. They could build enough trust for this madcap journey she felt the need to undertake without her going gaga over someone who didn't need her hero worship.

She gripped the rappel rope tightly in the locked position. 'I've got it!' she called down to him.

'Let it out now,' he replied and her stomach dropped as she jerked down the first couple of feet. 'Hand over hand – slowly!'

'I know,' she called back through gritted teeth. 'Everything is "doucement", right?'

'Tout à fait.' *Absolutely*.

She muttered something about how infuriatingly calm he was as she made her way painstakingly down, but she had to admit she felt safe. The strength required to descend by the ropes was surprisingly little compared to hauling herself up. When her rubber-soled climbing shoes touched down on the mat, she collapsed onto her bottom. Yannick's knees entered her peripheral vision, then his arms and hands as he dropped to her level.

She lifted her gaze ruefully to his, but he was smiling at her with his head tilted. 'Good climb,' he said, brushing his thumb over her cheek, which was probably covered with dirt and chalk from the wall. 'Allez, up you get.' She groaned when he grasped her hands and hauled her to her feet. 'One more time.'

Staring up at the wall, she swayed as she muttered, 'There had better be a damn photo up in that refuge,' and grasped the first grips again.

'Hop, hop!' he called out.

'I'm not an army recruit!' she called back, almost snarling.

'No, but I have to collect Maëlys from school soon.'

That got her moving. She was certain she could feel every tiny muscle in her limbs – and the big ones, too – as she dragged herself up. Surely there was no way that June Rowntree had done this. Her mum had got nervous on a ladder. It was only because of the gendarme at her feet that Luna wasn't a trembling puddle of nerves herself.

But if her mum had had Jim... It was still difficult to imagine.

Luna made it far enough that, when she glanced down, she freaked out and slipped, dangling spreadeagle once more from

Yannick's rope. She grasped for the rope and called down when she had a secure hold.

'That was good,' he said when she landed. 'Really,' he added, cocking his head. 'You can believe me. Look at my face.' His expression was comically earnest with a touch of self-deprecating humour and her knees were wobbly again. 'We'll do some more practice with the ropes, learn some knots, and then you can go to the Mer de Glace to practice.'

'The glacier?' she repeated in alarm.

He nodded, casually drawing down and looping the belay rope attached to his own harness. 'Climbing at the glacier with crampons isn't so difficult.'

'Easy for you to say,' she murmured. Peering at the strap and carabiner that were still attached at the top of the wall, she asked, 'How do you get the rope back up there?'

'The same way we get a rope up there on a rock face.' He gestured out the window to the needles of rock just visible.

Luna blinked. 'And how's that?'

'You use anchor points as you climb. Some are permanently installed and others you put there yourself – different devices for different places on the rock – and your partner takes them away again. In the gym, the tethers stay there, but you understand the idea.' She didn't really and her silence seemed to tip him off to that fact. 'I could show you.'

'Shall I time you?' she joked.

He nodded eagerly and she found herself returning his puppy-dog smile with a puzzled one of her own. She retrieved her phone from her pile of things and looked up to find him tensed and ready to start, holding the rope loosely in one hand.

'Belay me?' he said, gesturing her forward.

'Um,' was all she could say to that. Before she could protest, he'd set up the belay device attached to her harness and retied a knot on his own. She put her phone down so quickly she nearly dropped it, fumbling for the rope.

'Don't get a cramp,' he said, briefly squeezing his hand over hers. 'Keep the rope fairly loose unless I fall.'

'Wha— erm.' But he'd already turned for the wall, rolling his shoulders. 'Wait! I need— I can't—'

When he froze and turned to her with a nonplussed expression, she realised she'd said the wrong thing. 'You can't?'

Her breath stalled. She wished she didn't realise what he was asking. He'd been about to trust her and she was letting him down.

Gripping the rope with a huff, she shook herself and met his gaze. 'Okay. I remember everything you told me at the beginning.'

His face bloomed into a smile and perhaps it wasn't wise for Luna to belay him right then, because her legs weren't entirely stable.

'Ready?' he asked.

Luna crouched to tap her phone screen, starting the timer. 'Um, go?' she said, holding her breath.

Her jaw went slack watching him. He pulled himself up the first few grips just with his arms, the muscles straining and his powerful hands clinging to the wall. Pausing occasionally to look up, his concentration palpable, he reached a strap and slipped his rope into the carabiner before continuing the ascent. He gave the occasional grunt of effort, but otherwise looked as though he'd been built to climb and not to walk, hauling himself up steadily. He grabbed the strap from the bolt at the top in what felt like the blink of an eye, but he'd never hurried, just calmly flexed those muscles and pushed and pulled himself up.

Luna needed a twenty-four-month calendar.

She swayed on her feet just watching him.

'Give me lots of slack!' he called down after he'd reached the top and grasped the rope tightly at his hip to rappel back down –

much more quickly than Luna was comfortable with. But she didn't take any of his weight at any moment – which was probably why he'd allowed her to belay him after only a brief explanation. He jumped onto the mat with a satisfied sigh and looked up eagerly for his time.

'Under five minutes!' Luna said with a gasp as she looked at her phone.

Yannick leaned close to peer at her phone screen with a frown. 'Five minutes? I've done this wall in less than three,' he said with a wince. 'I need more practice.'

'I'm glad you were careful. I don't understand how I could catch you if you fell,' she admitted.

'With the help of the equipment,' he answered. 'Can I show you? Two climbers usually belay each other. When we go to the refuge, I'll belay myself with a rope brake, but you should know how to do it if we need to.'

'I'm sure I'll need more practice.'

'Exactement,' he said with a small smile. 'It's just practice. The rope helps take the impact and the belay device as well. Use them correctly and you can take my weight.'

The idea was so preposterous that she laughed, but she wasn't laughing a moment later when he headed for the wall again, slipping his rope into an anchor point about halfway up. Luna gulped, accepting that he was actually going to do this – he would let her hold his safety rope while he intentionally fell. The ball of panic in her throat was about as big as her pounding heart as she pulled slack through the belay device, promising herself that she would catch him.

'C'est bon?' he asked. 'I can let go?' He turned and met her gaze as he clung to the grips.

Checking the belay device once more, she said, 'I've got you,' her voice wavering. She stared up at him, her mind processing the image in slow-motion as he let himself fall. Her harness dug into her back and thighs as the rope pulled taut with a creak. She waited to see if she'd go shooting up to the ceiling, or perhaps the rope would break or her hold would slip. But it wasn't her hands holding him up. All she'd done was set the belay device correctly and kept her feet planted and... she was quite comfortably supporting his weight.

After hanging for long enough to prove that she could do it, he rappelled back down and gave her that bright, warm smile that had caught her in the ribs the first time she'd seen him. She was alive with sensations: the rush of adrenaline, the pinch of attraction and an overwhelming feeling of accomplishment that wasn't just hers – it was *theirs*.

She gulped, staring up at him as his smile slipped, and wondered what he'd do if she took his face between both of her hands and planted an enormous kiss on those lips. She wasn't supposed to be indulging the attraction, but her blood was singing and she was so *present*. There were no questions, or considerations or distractions – just the moment.

Perhaps at that unique point in time, enveloped in their incipient trust, she would be allowed to kiss him? Just once?

19

'I... euhm,' Yannick began, stepping back so suddenly that he tripped on the rope. His face was hot and his breath was tight, even though he'd barely done any exercise.

'Oh, gosh, you need to go, right?' she said, looking around as though she could just grab her bag and take off. She took a step away, but he was holding the rope and she bounced back with a grimace.

Murmuring an apology, he hurriedly untied the knots at his harness and fed the rope out of the belay device. He'd tied her in and it was clear she wasn't sure how to undo the figure-eight climbing knot, so he set his jaw and came close again.

It had been easier to stand so near before he'd suddenly thought about kissing her. He struggled with professional distance when she soaked him up with her eyes the way she had a moment ago, as though she saw more in him than anyone else did.

It was difficult to resist brushing his fingertips over her cheeks. He refused to look at her mouth, even though he'd watched her face so often now that he could picture her lips anyway.

He fumbled with the ropes, trying to pull himself together. He needed to get back out on the mountain. It was always the best place to clear his head.

By the time they'd packed up and changed, he didn't have time to drive Luna back to Argentière before collecting his daughter, but they were too far out of town for him to leave her to take the bus or the train.

'If you wait a moment while I collect her from school, I can drive you back,' he said as they climbed into his SUV.

'Of course that's fine. Why do you have to pick her up so early?'

'It's Wednesday,' he answered absently, pulling out of the park.

'And...?'

'School doesn't finish early on Wednesdays in England?'

'No!' she said, gaping. 'That sounds amazing. I wonder if we could introduce that – for French teachers, at least.'

'Maëlys would have finished even earlier today except she's in the lunch club.'

'Do you have to work half-days on Wednesdays then?' she asked.

'Valérie does, but she has an appointment today and I'm not on duty, so it worked well.' He tried to keep his voice even. 'She's having fertility treatment,' he added without quite intending to.

'Oh,' was all Luna said at first. 'Wow.'

He nodded and kept his eyes on the road, changing gears as they approached a roundabout.

'How... do you feel about that?' she asked warily.

The school was just up ahead and he wasn't sure if he was relieved or not. He cleared his throat and flashed her a quick smile. 'I don't know yet,' he admitted. Pulling into the car park, he unclipped his seatbelt and reached for the door, but Luna's hand on his arm stopped him.

'Hmm?' he prompted.

'Just...' She squeezed his forearm and then patted it awkwardly. 'Just thank you and...' Her hand settled on his shoulder for a moment and with a click, his emotions fell into place and he was thinking about kissing her again. All he'd have to do was lean over and cup her cheek with one hand and...

She leaned closer and his mind blanked. *Merde*, he didn't want any broken hearts, and, with the way his was pounding, that was the direction this was heading. But he stayed where he was, trying to remember to breathe as she approached... and kissed his cheek.

He managed to get out of the car somehow and wander towards the school in a daze. With Maëlys safe in his arms, he carefully un-clicked the moment with Luna and focussed his attention on his daughter.

'Do you want to go to the swimming pool? Or the park?' he asked her. After a few mild days in the valley, the playground was no longer covered in snow.

'Aren't we going skiing?' she asked as she hopped up into her child seat in the back of his SUV.

He couldn't help smiling, even though Valérie probably wouldn't be happy. She thought they should foster a range of interests, rather than indulging her fixation on the slopes. His ex was undoubtedly worried he'd raise another PGHM first responder and she'd never escape the stress that had ended their marriage. 'How about we do something else?' *For once.*

'But *she's* here, the moon woman. Aren't you teaching her to ski?'

Luna snorted a laugh at being called, 'La femme lune,' by his daughter. 'Today, I learned—'

'We can go skiing,' Yannick interrupted Luna before she could say another of Maëlys' magic words: escalade. He muttered to Luna as he clipped his seatbelt in, 'You don't say that word unless you want to spend another few hours at the wall belaying a five-year-old.' She shared his grin and more unpremeditated words spilled out of him. 'Tu viens?' he asked. *Will you come?* He meant come to the resort, not that they'd all ski together – at least, that's what he hoped he'd meant. 'I-I'll have to watch her. We could just go up together. I can't—' He couldn't quite find the end of that sentence. But the headline was appropriate: *I can't*.

'I'll go up to practice too,' she said with a nod.

* * *

When Yannick accepted a tisane from Silvia later that afternoon, he was wondering how he'd managed to spend all day with Luna, when he'd been trying to keep his distance – emotionally at least. She now sat watching Maëlys intently as his daughter made little piles with some loose stones Silvia had produced for her to play with.

He smoothed his hands through Maëlys' hair as she hummed absently, moving the stones with abstract focus.

'When did she learn to ski?' Luna asked, her brow furrowed. Her expression reminded him of the moment Maëlys had headed off down the black run after they'd planned to ski the blue together.

'I started taking her up when she was two – that's when she could stand in her boots. But she stayed inside my skis mostly until the next season, when she was three.'

Luna hesitated, her expression pinched. 'I suppose you... get used to the feeling of watching them take off at speed?' she said softly. 'My mum used to freak out when I rode a bike. I'm pretty sure I've inherited that from her.' She shook her head as if to clear it.

Leaning forward, she parted her messy hair and ran her fingers over a patch of scar tissue on her head, a few centimetres wide. His throat tightened imagining what that had looked like when she'd first sustained the injury. He'd responded to his share of rockslide accidents.

'I fell down the stairs when I was younger than Maëlys and I needed stitches. I don't think Mum ever recovered.'

'I can imagine. I think it's difficult for mothers,' he said, hoping she didn't notice how the words pinched a nerve. 'At least, that's the impression I get from Valérie.'

'She doesn't like Maëlys skiing?'

'No, no,' he assured her. 'You do get used to that when you live in Cham. But... I think she's worried Maëlys will turn out like me.' He said it with a smile to cover the way those words made him feel cold. 'I don't think any parent wishes their child to have a dangerous job.'

'You manage the risks... don't you?' she asked with a grimace.

'Of course we do. You wouldn't realise exactly how much.' His answer reminded him of the mission where he'd lost Jim. If he told her exactly how that mission had played out, she might understand a little better about the complexity of managing risk on the mountain.

Perhaps he should tell her, although he could only imagine how soft-hearted Luna would react. At least she might not look at him as though she thought he never made mistakes.

'But we take risks as well,' he reminded her pointedly. 'Once you've been up the mountain...'

'It owns you!' Guy said, interrupting them and placing sliced baguette with melted cheese on the coffee table. Maëlys snatched one and stuffed the first bite into her mouth without looking up from her stones.

'The mountain owns you?' Luna repeated doubtfully, watching

Guy as the commandant took a seat on the sofa next to Yannick. 'That doesn't sound good.'

'Oh, but it is,' the commandant insisted. 'You become part of it – the mountain becomes part of *you*. Even when people get into trouble on the mountain – trouble they could have avoided with better preparation – we don't get angry, because we understand why people want to be up there.'

'*I* don't understand,' Luna admitted. 'I still can't believe I have a connection to someone who was known as Jim de Montagne.' She turned to Yannick. 'But you said you didn't grow up here. How did the mountain come to own you?'

'My parents loved the mountains,' he explained. 'We came here on holiday several times a year. I was seventeen the first time I stood on the summit of Mont Blanc. You can't go back from that – you have to go forwards and push yourself.'

She stared at him in dismay as Guy commented loudly in approval. That was the look he should remind himself about when he thought about Luna, as he found himself doing increasingly often. He would only disappoint her.

Luna stood to help Silvia in the kitchen and Guy turned to him and asked, 'You have exercises scheduled for next week, don't you?' Yannick nodded around a bite of grilled cheese. 'Take Luna with you.'

He nearly choked on the baguette. Hurriedly chewing, he swallowed and said, 'What for? We're due to head to high altitude Friday night.'

'I'm not suggesting you take her up high,' Guy reassured him. 'But don't you have crevasse training with the military school at Grands Montets? Training in English would do you all some good – practice under pressure. That's the point of the class, isn't it?'

'What's the point of the class?' Luna asked, as she returned with a roll of goat's cheese on a plate.

Yannick hesitated, waiting for Guy to explain, but the boss said nothing. His mind raced. Did he want Luna with them on exercises, when she'd looked so horrified after they'd returned from the routine rescue the week before? He'd been hoping to introduce her to the ice a little more gently.

'Next week during class, we have scheduled practical training exercises. Guy suggested we take you with us and practice our English under pressure – on the Argentière glacier.'

Her mouth dropped open. 'Um...'

Guy piped up, 'I think Yanni understands you well enough to take you on the exercises next week and it's a challenge that will do the team good – and perhaps you, too, Luna.'

'You would be roped in at all times,' he assured her. 'We're used to securing civilians on the glacier. And there are some safety issues I need to show you before we go to the refuge – some practice with crampons.'

'In that case,' she responded slowly, 'let's do it.'

Did he discern a flicker of anticipation in her eyes? 'We'll make an alpinist out of you after all,' he mumbled. It was supposed to be a joke, but when he imagined her embracing the mountain, it felt suspiciously like accepting *him* and he'd just convinced himself there was no way that would happen.

'That's a bit step up from the team marmot,' she quipped with a wry grin. 'When do you think we'll be able to go to the refuge?'

'Not for a few weeks at least. The avalanche warning is too high and I'd like some better updates on the conditions before we try. In the meantime, you can train and practice and we should be able to ski down the Vallée Blanche, rather than walking up the Mer de Glace in snowshoes.'

She gulped but didn't express any doubt.

'Have you thought about what you'll do if it's your mum in the photo – and you?'

She grimaced. 'I've thought about it so much I'm going around in circles. I'm happy to have the refuge as a goal, because I don't know where to go from here. Mum was only here for a few months before she moved to Corsica, where I was born.'

'I didn't realise you were born on Corsica!' Guy exclaimed. 'It's a beautiful place. Most of us have spent a few weeks there on assignment with the PGHM,' Yannick explained.

'There are mountains there?'

'Bien sûr. A large part of the island is a mountain massif. I was deployed there six years ago for a season,' Yannick confirmed.

'Oh,' she said, as though that had surprised her. 'I always assumed Mum was drawn there by the beaches.'

'The beaches are nice, too,' he insisted.

'But where you were born is inland,' Silvia mentioned as she arrived from the kitchen with more plates: bread and goat's cheese, olives and chopped apples.

'You were born in Corte?' Yannick asked. 'I was at that hospital a lot during my detachment there.'

'That's what it says on my passport. I assumed my mum worked at the hospital.'

'That's a coincidence,' Silvia said emphatically.

'You love coincidences,' Luna teased with a smile.

'Only because they so rarely are coincidences,' Silvia replied, giving Luna a meaningful look.

'Perhaps you are not only the mascot of team two, but of the entire PGHM of France, all 250 secouristes!' Guy said with a grin.

'I'm not sure that's a responsibility I want,' she responded wryly. 'You guys can jump out of helicopters with your own luck.'

Guy shook with laughter and slapped his knee, but Yannick tried to interpret her words as a warning.

The warning didn't help half an hour later when she walked him to the door, giving Maëlys a smile and leaning up to press a kiss on his cheek. He wondered what it would be like if she let him pull her close and his heady thoughts scrambled – a mess of confusion and questions he couldn't deal with.

Clutching Maëlys' hand, he gave Luna only a tight nod in farewell.

20

'You're doing *what*?' Lydia bellowed over the phone. 'Who are you and what have you done with Luna?'

'It's for a class,' Luna explained with a grimace, thinking she'd been right to keep quiet about her winter adventures in Chamonix so far. It did sound unbelievable that she was heading to a glacier that morning with a bunch of mountaineering soldiers. 'I have to practise, too,' she continued. 'The only clue I've found about the insurance money is a photo in a mountain refuge, so I'm going up there soon. Robert Durand might have been connected to Mum.'

Lyd's gasping choke suggested Luna's attempt to explain had only made her cousin more concerned. 'What's come over you? I hate to play this card, but what would your mum have said? She'd hate to think of you doing something so risky.'

Luna winced, glancing at the wardrobe where she'd stuffed her mum's illegally-kept ashes. 'Mum would have understood,' she insisted. 'And I won't be in danger. I'll be going with a... guide.' She just managed to stop herself saying she'd be going to the refuge with a gendarme who was lovely and gallant and sweet with his solemn little daughter and she found it difficult to stop herself from touching his gorgeous face all the time.

'If you think this guy Jim might have been your father, there are easier ways to find out, Lu. Have you even checked your birth certificate?'

Of course scatter-brained Luna hadn't thought of checking her birth certificate. 'That would be too simple a solution,' she said with a self-deprecating laugh. 'I haven't seen my birth certificate in years. Mum always kept both of my passports up to date when I was younger, so I never needed it.'

'If it will save you a trip in the ice and snow, I'll search through your things to find it for you!' Lyd insisted. 'Just promise me, when I find it, you won't go up there. How am I supposed to take it, knowing you could fall or freeze or get lost? I just want you home with us.'

'I... thanks, Lyd,' she managed, glad she'd been saved the necessity of lying. If it turned out Jim was her father – a possibility that was still difficult to believe, even though she couldn't stop thinking about it – then she still needed to go to the refuge. The journey was symbolic and impractical and possibly dangerous, but it was a gesture she needed to make. She still felt out of place among the confident mountaineering crowd that filled the bars in the evening with their rustling high-tech coats, but the people connected to the mountain – Silvia, Guy, even Yannick – understood her starry-eyed reasoning. 'I'm looking forward to seeing you all, too,' she assured Lyd. 'I'll be home at Easter, at the latest. Two more months.'

She was surprised to realise she hoped this would be a long winter and it wasn't only because she wanted answers.

* * *

'If I wouldn't have been wearing a helmet,' Matthieu said with a dramatic pause, 'I would have had broken my skull – no doubt.' Since that first lesson, he'd shown great aptitude for telling stories in class, but today Luna was struggling to concentrate.

Teaching wasn't supposed to be an adrenaline-fuelled profession. Sure, there had been moments in Luna's early career where her heart had pounded in her ears as she'd tried to think of the best thing to say to keep an unruly class under control. But surely no teacher in the history of the profession had had to explain grammar at 2,300 metres of altitude in a glacial bowl full of snow – while strapped to her students with a rope.

'If I *hadn't* been wearing a helmet,' she corrected Matthieu over the rush of the wind as she trudged behind him. 'In the "if" clause, you don't use "would".'

They'd trekked up from the top of a chairlift in the ski resort set above Silvia's chalet, off-piste skiers swerving to avoid the rope team. As they'd passed the colossal icefall at the tail of the Argentière glacier, Luna's jaw had dropped as she'd marvelled at the mass of ice, riven with crevasses and slowly collapsing into the enormous gully below.

Now in the icefield, the rocky peaks extended out in all directions, emerging from the ocean of snow. The towns tucked in the valley were a distant memory in this world of giants. Each step felt both tiny and heroic.

Matthieu nodded and continued his story of a rockfall the year before that had left him in hospital after losing consciousness. 'Luckily enough, I had my helmet on,' he finished, giving her a wink as he repeated the language she'd taught them weeks ago.

'Stop here!' came a call from up ahead. They'd been moving slowly using crampons that helped with grip but didn't stop her struggling through the deep snow and punishing gradient. She kept hearing Yannick's words about hypothermia and sweating.

One of the gendarmes sank a stake into the snow and hammered it in. In the space of less than a minute, they'd rigged up a safety system on the steep slope of the glacier.

'Matthieu, can you tie Luna in?' Yannick called from where he was juggling a large metal pipe.

With a nod, the younger gendarme approached, slipped the rope from her shoulder and tied a knot in her harness with quick hands. She recognised the climbing knot Yannick had tied at the gym, but when Matthieu tied it, there were no blushes or any awkwardness.

Lyd would have a good laugh if she saw how Luna was losing it over a guy just because he was kind to her – not to mention how ridiculous she looked in a helmet and mountaineering gear.

Her rope attached securely to the system of stakes, Luna was able to take her eyes off her own feet and gaze up the slope at the majestic valley between tall, jagged summits, that had been carved over centuries by the movement of ice.

The glacier was an enormous frozen river, as though time sped up with the altitude. Mere humans didn't notice the violence of the ice flows as they cut through stone, leaving bare rock faces and snow-covered rubble in its path.

Her life was little more than a blip of colour and sound in the landscape, that could be ended at any moment by any number of dangers – buried crevasses, avalanches, rockfalls – but would come to its natural end quickly enough in comparison to the millennia these rocks had seen. Even the ice was older than she was.

'You have sunglasses?' Yannick's voice was surprisingly close when she snapped her attention back to the present.

'*Do* you have sunglasses,' she corrected absently, noting that he wore his own pair of wraparound glasses with reflective blue lenses, with his goggles up on his helmet.

His mouth twitched in a smile. 'Do you have sunglasses?' he

repeated. The 'h' was completely lost, as usual. She shook her head. His hands came up and lowered her goggles into place and she kicked herself for swooning when the backs of his fingers brushed her face. 'The sun is bright at this altitude and you will damage your eyes. Next time bring sunglasses, too.'

'Yes, sir,' she said with a faint smile.

'While the others set up the equipment for the crevasse exercise, I need to show you "self-arrest".'

She nearly mentioned keeping her mother's ashes in her room, amused by the idea of Yannick reluctantly arresting her for possession of human remains. But of course he wasn't talking about that kind of arrest – that was her own loopy sense of humour.

'When walking in a rope team, if one person falls, it's important the others don't fall too.'

'Oh my God,' she muttered. 'I hadn't thought of that.'

'If you feel sudden tension, go straight down into the snow and dig in your crampons and your... coudes. What are these in English again?'

'Elbows,' she supplied. 'Okay, dig in crampons and elbows.'

'You probably won't be in front, so you need to go down onto your... behind. You want as much surface as you can make – you know what I mean?'

She couldn't resist. 'You mean there's a lot of surface on my behind?'

'No, no!' he said in alarm, lifting his hand as though he could snatch back the words.

'I'm messing with you, Yannick,' she said drily. 'It's okay.'

'Euh, I— Ah,' he said with a choked sigh, scratching the back of his neck.

She was reminded of the time he'd called her cute and was tempted to reassure him, but she took pity on him and let the subject drop. 'Surface, okay – or surface area, more specifically. And go down bum-first. That makes sense.'

'Okay, go!'

She should have expected it when he tugged suddenly on her rope, as she'd experienced his inner drill sergeant before, but she was caught by surprise and went down on her stomach, flopping into the snow. When she rolled over with a groan, his face appeared above her, upside down.

He held out his gloved hands and helped her haul herself up, the snow falling from her coat in chunks. Muted applause made her glance up to see the rest of the team laughing at her.

'You won't be laughing when we spend the entire next lesson learning how to pronounce a "th"!' she called out, to more guffaws from the team.

'Try again,' Yannick said with a smile in his voice. 'I'll give you a warning.'

She was ready this time when he pulled on the rope and she threw herself into the snow, landing with a poof. She felt as though she was trying to swim backstroke in a pile of candy floss.

The tension on the rope didn't let up and she slipped a few inches with a squeal. 'Dig in!' Yannick called. Kicking out, she stamped her heels into the snow and dug in her elbows.

She still felt the tug of the rope, but she didn't budge, and when Yannick said, 'Très bien,' she flushed with pride that was probably overblown, but made her smile.

He helped her up, pulling off his glove to brush snow from her out of her neck warmer. She shivered, colder than she'd realised, now a trickle of snow was making its way down her neck. It was definitely the cold and nothing to do with his tenderness. Yannick must have realised how loath she was to take off her gloves, so he was carefully removing the snow with his own warm fingertips and she was trying her hardest not to purr at the gentleness of the touch.

When a suggestive whistle rose from the rest of the group, Yannick jerked his hand back in a hurry. 'Good,' he repeated curtly this time.

He motioned for her to follow him up to the others, showing her how to use her rope slings to remain clipped in at all times.

'How do you know it's safe here?' she asked, tramping after him.

'I don't – not for certain. But you can be watchful. Look.' He gestured at the incline above them as a skier appeared from behind a rocky outcrop, zooming down the unprepared slope. Yannick tensed, watching, but relaxed again a moment later when the skier made a sharp turn before passing them and continuing on their way. 'Where the skier turned, there is a section with interesting shadows. I would not go anywhere near there. The way the snow lies can give indications but learning to detect crevasses takes much longer than learning to stay up on skis. For now, you stay behind me and walk where I walk. If I fall in a crevasse, you know there is a crevasse there.'

She gulped, shivers racing over her skin at his casual statement.

'Come and see, prof!' Matthieu called as they approached and Yannick double checked that she was clipped into the lifeline. '*This* is a crevasse.'

He pointed to what looked like a small hole in the snow, less than three feet long and only half as wide. Luna frowned and shuffled closer to look, but Yannick snatched the back of her coat to stop her. 'Go down on your hands.'

She dropped onto all fours, staring at the innocuous gap in the snow. As she peered over the side, she gasped and a fresh shot of vertigo washed through her. Under several feet of snow, sheer, glowing blue ice walls dropped in a haphazard manner, cracked and jagged and decorated with enormous icicles.

It was beautiful and terrifying as she stared into the chasm as though looking directly at mortality. When she glanced away, she searched out Yannick's gaze, remembering his casual commentary over the radio two weeks ago as he'd descended into one of these cavities to pull someone out.

He held out a hand to pull her up and she had the fleeting thought that she wanted to bury her face in his coat and wrap her arms around him. It was so beautiful, so deadly, so *brave* of him to think he could change the fate of someone who found themselves down there, looking up at the stalactites.

Instead of hugging him with all her might, she blurted out, 'Jim died in one of those?'

21

She wanted to take the words back as soon as Yannick's smile faded. She'd caught an odd look on his face occasionally when they'd talked about Jim's death. It must have upset him greatly, and yet she would have thought he'd lost victims down crevasses on numerous occasions. After nearly a year, it was worrying that it still haunted him.

It was also strange that he was taking so much time with her, not that she was willing to dwell on that. If she was taking advantage of his overdeveloped feelings of guilt, she'd be faced with yet another dilemma and she had too many of those already. He'd said the client survived, but Jim didn't. The more Luna thought about that, the more questions she had.

He nodded slowly. 'Yes, Jim died in a crevasse, but not here. He died on the Miage glacier, on the other side of the massif.' As though he realised she had questions, he watched her warily, but she wouldn't press him today, not in the middle of the training exercise.

The group leader, Philippe, called out instructions to secure the edge of the crevasse. Luna tried to resist, but, as the moments wore on, she found she couldn't. She reached back for Yannick's gloved hand, wanting to give it a reassuring squeeze; whatever had happened that day, she was certain he must have done the right thing, even though the outcome had broken his heart.

But before her hand could brush his, he moved away to show some of the trainee recruits the equipment. It was probably for the best.

* * *

The expression 'chilled to the bone' had never had as much meaning to Luna as it did that afternoon, waiting for Choucas to collect the equipment and the couple of gendarmes who hadn't made the trek back to the chairlift. She was so cold, she almost felt like part of the frozen landscape – fresh and ageless and a little glittery.

It had been a good day. The sunshine had made the sub-zero temperature mostly bearable. The team had embraced the challenge of completing the training exercises in English and Luna had a whole list of new topics to cover in class that might be helpful to ensure clear communication on the mountain when the victim didn't speak French.

One advantage of the freezing outdoor classroom had been the ability to practise the pronunciation of the 'h': if the gendarmes couldn't see their own breath, they hadn't pronounced it correctly. It was a small point, but she could imagine a victim who was less than lucid taking several critical moments to understand what the rescuer meant by, 'You 'ave 'eadache?'

Ready to head back into the valley, her blood was fizzing again and she could almost understand why people chased the feeling. As ridiculous as it was, she almost felt like part of the group and that was an even headier emotion.

Matthieu stood next to her – Yannick had probably told him to babysit her while he communicated with the helicopter. 'You will come out for a beer later?' Matthieu asked.

'A beer sounds perfect,' she said with a sigh. 'I need to warm up first though. I understand the sweating-hypothermia thing, now.'

'What? You need to tell us if we go too fast. That's the rule in the mountain: complete honesty and no being a hero. If we were out overnight, you could really get hypothermia. Don't make me tell Yanni,' he added with a grin.

'I've learned my lesson,' she assured him, glancing to where Yannick stood, peering at the snowy cornices, his expression inscrutable in his sunglasses. He was too far away to talk to, but she was just as aware of him as if he were still attached to her with a rope.

The throb of the helicopter sounded in the stillness a minute before the aircraft appeared and the few remaining gendarmes burst into action. Matthieu pushed her head down and waited with her while the others packed Choucas full of equipment.

'Is that the winch, then?' Luna asked, pointing to a heavy-duty hook attached to an orange beacon near the door.

'You want to try?' Matthieu suggested with a grin. 'Just a little winching?'

Luna's eyes bugged out. 'What? No!'

But Matthieu was already calling out to the others. 'Hey! Can we take Luna up on the winch? That'll really show her what we do all day.'

Yannick's gaze snapped to hers in question and she shook her head firmly.

'Vas-y!' Matthieu encouraged. 'Go up with Yanni. He needs the practice anyway.'

'Surely it's not safe for a civilian?' she continued weakly.

Matthieu shrugged. 'We test this equipment several times a

day, prof, and we trust it with our lives. I hate to admit it, but gendarmes are just as fragile as everyone else.'

That made Luna smile. 'Surely not.'

The winchman waved as she approached with Matthieu. 'You want to try? We could just do a few metres.'

She turned to Yannick again, needing to interpret from him whether it was too much for her. He met her gaze with a tilt of his head and a facial expression that was part shrug.

'Uh, okay then.' Panic rose in her as soon as the words were out and she glanced urgently to Yannick again.

He nodded calmly. 'You go on, Matthieu. I'll go up with her.'

The helicopter lifted off as Yannick settled his microphone in front of his lips and tucked the earpiece in place, keeping up a smooth flow of communication with the pilot and the winchman. He checked her harness thoroughly, making Luna gulp.

She stared up in dread as the hook was lowered from the hovering helicopter. The past few minutes had gone by in a blur, even though all her senses were heightened. Yannick didn't hesitate but clipped them both in twice with thick straps and then raised his arm to signal to the winchman.

A moment later, the cord yanked them into the air, leaving her stomach behind on the ice and drawing a choked squeal from her mouth as she swung right into Yannick so she was almost sitting in his lap.

The light breeze felt like a gust off the ground. She lost all orientation as they started to spin and she felt as though she were being pulled in different directions. The pressure on her lungs was unbearable.

'Open your eyes,' Yannick said gently and she felt as though she had to prise her lids apart.

But when she looked her breath rushed out and then whooshed in again as she took in the glistening landscape, the violent icefalls in strange, irregular shapes, unspoilt fields of snow and the enormous sky above the dignified peaks.

Whimpering with disbelief, she swallowed and blinked the tears out of her eyes. She wasn't sure if she was allowed to touch the straps, so she closed a hand in Yannick's coat and focussed on breathing.

They sat in their harnesses, legs entwined, as though it was a bizarre, intimate picnic high up in the air, suspended over another world.

'Are you okay?' he asked in her ear.

She nodded manically. 'This is incredible,' she muttered. She glanced up to see a broad smile on his face and her own stretched unexpectedly. 'We're flying!' she said, her voice high.

It was over almost too soon as the helicopter reeled them in and Yannick stepped calmly onto the runner, grasping Luna around the waist to steady her until the winchman could usher her inside. She spilled onto the floor in an undignified manner, wondering if she'd ever recover, until a pair of strong hands heaved her upright and deposited her into a seat.

'What did you think, prof?' Matthieu asked as he clipped her into the safety cable. He slipped a pair of headphones around the back of her neck and over her ears, tucked under her climbing helmet.

Luna forced her eyes open again, kicking herself for being disappointed it wasn't Yannick helping her. She'd just been plastered to him while they sailed through the sky. She should have had enough by now, but the longer she was attached to him with various mountaineering paraphernalia, the more she felt his absence when she wasn't.

'That was... wow,' was all she managed to say, making the winchman chuckle.

Luna was just coming back to her senses, thoroughly ready to return to the safety of the valley, when the radio blared to life with a call from Cordial, the control centre. The helicopter banked again, diverting to somewhere Luna hadn't quite caught, to pick up an off-piste skier who'd hit trouble and needed an urgent rescue before he fell.

'Yanni, I'll drop you and Matthieu down and then take the others back to the DZ. The approach might be difficult, depending on where the victim is. We don't want to catch him in the rotor wash,' she heard the pilot say through her headphones. Her stomach dropped again when the air in the helicopter changed as the team switched to rescue mode.

Every ravine, every needle-like peak in the massif seemed to have a name – and the pilot knew them all: Pointe de la Fenêtre, Col du Tacul and Petit Rognon. As the aircraft slowed, the rescuers and the winchman all scanned the area thoroughly, searching for the tiny figure of the victim among the snow and rock below.

'Le voilà!' Matthieu said, spotting the skier. Luna craned her neck to look, feeling a jolt of alarm when she saw the victim perched precariously on a rock above a sheer drop. The gendarmes calmly discussed their approach and, what seemed like only a moment later, the helicopter touched one runner down on a snowy patch above the stranded skier, churning up ice. Peering up, Luna gaped to see the rotors nearly touching the rock and she clutched her seat in alarm.

Yannick leaped down from the helicopter and sank a metal stake into the snow to set up a lifeline for the rescuers, but it slipped and he grunted in frustration over the radio as he tried in vain to secure it in the snow.

'J'abandonne,' he said, tugging the stake up again and climbing back into the helicopter with a wash of icy snow.

After more discussion, Luna realised they'd decided to winch to a different spot. A moment later, the winchman opened the door and Yannick swung out. Luna felt as if her breath stopped. He spun downwards through the air at an alarming rate.

Her own experience had been nothing compared to what the gendarmes performed every day. She wondered if their hearts still pounded or if they'd all been rewired after years of perilous stunts like this.

She kept Yannick in view as he landed deftly and sank the stake successfully into the snow this time. Waving his arm in a circle, he let go of the hook and the winchman reeled it back in.

'Don't worry. We do this all the time,' Matthieu said as he headed for the door. Luna was exceedingly glad he would soon join Yannick and at least they wouldn't be alone on the desolate rock face down there.

When Matthieu had been safely delivered, the helicopter turned back for the valley, leaving them behind. Luna watched for as long as she could, but they quickly became two tiny specks on the snow – and voices in the radio, keeping everyone apprised of their progress.

When Choucas arrived at the DZ, Yannick was beginning the descent to the stranded skier, with Matthieu belaying him from above. The two recruits who'd travelled with them climbed out of the helicopter, but Luna was glued to her canvas seat, listening intently to the radio as Yannick's voice, tight with the effort of climbing, gave intermittent updates.

The pilot turned to her with a sympathetic smile. 'Go inside and listen in the control room,' he said in French. 'I'll be there to pick them up as soon as Yanni's secured the victim. He's one of our best climbers you know. He'll bring the skier down safely.'

On wobbly legs, she made her way into the control room. A few minutes later, Yannick confirmed he'd clipped the stranded skier onto the lifeline and was waiting for extraction.

When he returned in the helicopter fifteen minutes later, Luna felt as though she'd lived about two weeks that day – of someone else's life.

A large part of her wanted to throw her arms around him as he jogged into the hangar, ruffle his hair and press kisses to his face, but she was also jittery and weak from nerves even though the mission had ended in success. The intensity of her feelings scared her, even though she assured herself it was only the effects of adrenaline, heightening every sensation.

This had always been her weakness, living by her feelings, even when they led her astray, as they were doing in that moment. She barely knew Yannick. But she'd never wanted a cosy cottage as much as she wanted to fold him in her arms right then.

22

'I heard you're planning to take her up to the refuge to see Jim's things.'

Yannick glanced at his companion and gave himself an inward shake. He'd been watching the dance floor when he was supposed to be talking to Jean-Yves, who he'd run into when the team had piled into the bar.

There was something about Luna's dancing that was simultaneously wonderful and terrible, especially since she'd changed into the flowing skirt she'd worn the night he'd met her. But she was having so much fun laughing with Emilien and Marina and one of the recruits that it was difficult to look anywhere else.

He forced his gaze into his half-finished beer and nodded. 'It will be a challenge for her, but I think that's what she wants.' He understood that feeling at least. 'Jim's dead, but she wants to find a way to make it okay that she received the payout. If climbing up to the refuge can do that, then it's worth the trip, even if it turns out she's not the girl in the photo – or if we don't find out anything else. At least then she can go home with a clear conscience.'

'Do you think it'll make you feel better, too? God knows there's nothing else the rest of us can do for you.'

He nodded darkly. 'You're right. I'm taking her up there because it's the only thing I can still do for Jim.'

'Like you said, Jim's dead, Yanni,' Jean-Yves said baldly. 'He's gone up the mountain for the last time. He was a guide, not a gendarme. You don't need to preserve his memory carved in stone and pull it out every year, like you do with your own fallen heroes. You don't need to hold the rope when he's already dead. You can just let him go. He would have wanted you to let him go – and maybe to go and dance with *her*.'

'What?' The statements about what Jim would have wanted resonated too much inside him, but he was pulled out of his reverie by the sudden mention of Luna.

'If she is his daughter, don't you think it would make Jim happy if you two... you know. If something happened there?'

Yannick snorted his sip of beer. 'Why would you say that?'

'You obviously like her,' Jean-Yves said with a grin. 'Maybe Jim is setting you two up from beyond the grave.'

'He is not,' Yannick said in a rush. 'He stayed single his whole life and I understand why.'

'Because Valérie hurt you.'

'We hurt each other. I can't bring Luna into all of this – the divorce, the job. Her mum died recently and she's working out her life. She only needs me to tell her about Jim and take her up to the refuge.'

Jean-Yves clapped him on the shoulder. 'All right, I wasn't suggesting you marry her.'

Yannick grimaced as he swallowed a sip of beer. That was part of the problem. He'd never been good at judging how serious a relationship was.

'Have you had any reports from the area?' he asked, changing the subject. 'I need to find a time when conditions are good and I have a couple of days off together so I can take her up.'

'Would it be easier if I take her?' Jean-Yves offered. 'I knew Jim at least as well as you did.'

The lump in Yannick's throat was persistent. His gaze drifted back to where Luna was bopping to an electronic beat, Emilien copying her with a smile. It didn't make sense that he would feel jealous of Jean-Yves taking her instead.

'I want to take her,' he replied.

'Because of Jim?' Jean-Yves prompted.

Yannick nodded. 'You're probably right that he wouldn't want me to hold the rope, but I haven't worked out how to let it go yet.' Jean-Yves didn't know all the details of what had happened that day. The article in the newspaper, Jim's eulogy, none of that had captured the choices Yannick had made. 'But I also want to see her get up there,' he admitted quietly. 'I want to be there when she does it.'

Jean-Yves regarded him thoughtfully over his glass before draining it. 'This old man is done for tonight. I'll pass on any reports I hear about the climb to the refuge. Let me know when you're going and if I can help.'

'Thanks,' Yannick muttered. 'I should go home as well.' He glanced back at where Luna was now swaying to the music on her own, the gendarmes collecting more drinks.

'Because you're an old man too these days?' Jean-Yves teased him. 'You're not even forty yet, Yanni. You've got a long way to go before you should be sitting here with me.'

'Getting closer every year,' he mumbled, thinking of his approaching birthday as Jean-Yves went to collect his coat.

The door of the bar opened with a gust of cold air and Silvia appeared, her hair blasted from the wind, which didn't bode well for rescue conditions tomorrow. Her gaze swept the bar, pausing on Luna with a faint smile and continuing until she found him. She headed in his direction, greeting him with a kiss on the cheek.

'I was just going.'

'I'll get Luna home,' Silvia said.

'Of course. I'm sure she could get herself home,' he mumbled.

'There's no one in your team secretly waiting to walk her home and steal a kiss?' Silvia asked with a smile.

Yannick carefully schooled his features, hoping Silvia wouldn't be able to see that *he'd* thought about kissing her – as foolish as that seemed to him right then. 'She's been adopted into the team – that's all. No one's going to break her heart.'

'Good,' Silvia said with a dismissive laugh.

He stood abruptly, slapping the bar – perhaps to stop Silvia studying his face, which he was fairly certain had turned pink. 'I'll see you later.'

Surely, one month from his thirty-ninth birthday, with a failed marriage behind him, he should be past these flustered feelings. It didn't matter if he liked her anyway, there was no time for anything to happen between them.

But a lingering worry wore a trail over his thoughts as he drove home. Sometimes an instant was all it took to change someone's life.

* * *

Silvia linked her arm with Luna's as they strolled through the illuminated streets of Chamonix under a light shower of falling snow. It was so quiet, the sound dampened by the heavy moisture in the air and the pillows of white covering the town.

'Next week the school holidays begin,' Silvia told her. 'Cham will be busy for a month as all of France takes its turn to come and ski. I might need your help in the shop.'

'Of course,' Luna responded immediately. 'I love working there, even if I still don't know what half of the crystals mean.'

Silvia smiled broadly, a twinkle in her eye. 'Did you check in your pocket tonight?'

Luna frowned, tugging off her glove – one she'd lost and Yannick had found – and rummaged in the deep pocket of her borrowed jacket. She'd felt like dressing as herself that night, in her old skirt and tights. She looked a little strange with a technical winter jacket over the top, but it was so much warmer than her wool coat.

Her fingers brushed a cool stone with rough edges and, before she even drew it out, she knew which stone it was. She chuckled, shaking her head. 'You and your carnelian, Silvia. I might be walking in my mum's footsteps, but I don't need to repeat her mistakes regarding "love and passion",' she said firmly, glancing warily at her friend in case Silvia suspected that Luna was blowing smoke with those words.

'I know, Luna, but sometimes things just happen, especially here in Cham,' Silvia said pointedly. 'It might do you good to remember that life isn't serious all the time. You had fun with the young secouristes. I enjoyed watching you getting out and living your life.'

Luna frowned. Was that what she was doing? She'd thought she was here to put the past to rest, not to forge a path ahead. But Silvia was right: in this town of adventurers, life hurtled along regardless of whether you were ready. But she was a long way from learning not to be serious – especially about relationships. It was clear that Silvia did *not* mean Yannick, but he was the only one in Luna's mind.

'Check your other pocket,' Silvia said.

Luna rummaged again, her fingers finding a crinkling packet

with a distinctive square shape. 'Silvia!' she admonished, pulling her hand back quickly. 'You didn't!'

The older woman shrugged and kept walking. 'You never know, chérie. The carnelian is for life, courage and sensual experiences. You might not be ready for a long-term relationship, but life is too short to miss out on... something because you don't have a condom,' she said with a wink.

Luna gave a choking laugh. 'Is that a well-known saying among mountaineers?'

'No, but perhaps it should be,' Silvia said with a toss of her hair. 'But Luna, do you truly think it was a mistake that your mother met your father? You were born as a result. I'm certain she couldn't have regretted a thing. I had a feeling when we first met, that there was more for you here than just the truth about Jim. I think après ski agrees with you and a little... mistake wouldn't hurt, especially now you have a condom.'

'Do you have any idea how weird it is to think of my mum accidentally conceiving me because she didn't have one?' Luna said, burying her face in her hands and giving her head a shake.

'You did say you didn't want to repeat those mistakes,' Silvia pointed out.

'Gargh! I don't know that I was conceived here anyway,' Luna responded, her words trailing off. 'Besides, I think she really loved my father.'

'Did you say your cousin was looking for your birth certificate?'

Luna eyed her. 'Lydia looked through all of my boxes, and my mum's things, but she didn't find it. If Jim was my father... I don't want to imagine the kind of hurt that led to Mum never mentioning his name ever again.'

'What does your intuition tell you?' Silvia prompted.

Luna bit her lip against the surge of conflicted feelings that rose within her. 'That I can't rule out the possibility,' she admitted.

'The more I learn, the more I see of the mountain, the more I feel connected to it – to him. And the fact that his last words were about me...' Her skin tingled every time she thought about that.

'Do you think you could accept the money now?'

'Isn't that the biggest question,' Luna muttered, although it didn't always feel like the biggest question any more. She had so many questions and they only bred more questions and no answers. Her dreams of her own cottage were further away than ever, but she was strangely accepting of that. 'I'd still like to know if it was guilt that led him to pay the insurance premiums. If so, then... I suppose accepting the money would be like absolving him and I'd be more than happy to do that.'

'Even if he hurt your mother?'

She nodded. 'My mum wasn't the type to hold a grudge.'

'I can imagine that,' Silvia said gently. 'If she was anything like you.'

Luna gulped, imagining she was just like her mother. With hindsight, she suspected June had suffered in silence for years, missing 'Robert', the love of her life. That was a mistake Luna definitely didn't want to repeat.

23

The stars aligned at the end of February – well, if not the stars, then the meteorological and alpine conditions and Yannick's shift pattern. Luna had to cancel her Friday class at the leisure centre, but Silvia had assured her that wouldn't be a problem. The date for their departure for the Refuge de l'Envers des Aiguilles was set for 29 February, which Luna found somehow appropriate: a date that didn't come around often for an event that was likely to occur only once.

Silvia's chalet became a revolving door of visitors the night before they left. Jean-Yves and another mountain guide appeared bearing gifts: an ice axe of Jim's that she accepted with an enormous lump in her throat and a brown fleece with the logo of the Compagnie des Guides on it.

'Jim was always out at sunrise and sunset,' Jean-Yves told her. 'He liked to sleep in the top bunk near the window in the winter dorm.'

'Thank you,' she said earnestly.

'Greet him for us,' Jean-Yves said, his voice rough and she could only give him a solemn nod in reply.

The owner of the sports shop across from Silvia's boutique arrived with a pair of climbing gloves that looked a lot like the pair she was used to seeing hanging from Yannick's harness. The shop owner too had known Jim. Even the publican from the wood-panelled bar arrived briefly to pay his respects. The following week, it would be the anniversary of Jim's death and Luna was touched that something positive seemed to have come from her wild scheme to ease her own conscience.

'You'll contact us from the refuge,' Guy said firmly as he was sat with Luna in Silvia's lounge drinking tisane. 'I've told Yanni to stay in touch with Cordial, but there's mobile phone reception up there, so you can send Silvia a message too. Have you packed the extra power pack for your phone? There's no electricity at the refuge. Yanni has a radio to contact us if anything goes wrong.'

'Nothing is going to go wrong,' Silvia said reassuringly. 'Here, take this.' She handed Luna a polished crystal the colour of a stormy sky, riven with cracks under the surface. 'Smoky quartz, from the Talèfre glacier, right near the refuge. It's a grounding stone, for calmness and strength and emotional healing.'

Luna held the small stone in her palm. 'A miracle worker, then?' she murmured.

'The crystals only focus what is already inside you. It's not a miracle, it's a... wish, Luna. You understand what I mean.' Luna shared her smile and gave a nod. She was good at wishing, at dreaming – and she was in need of some grounding. Tomorrow, she would find out if she truly was the child in an old photo that hung in a remote mountain refuge.

Silvia turned to Guy, patting his thigh. 'Do you think we can sneak one into Yannick's pocket?'

'He doesn't need any more calmness and strength,' Luna pointed out.

Guy tilted his head in thought. 'He's been stuck since Jim died

– actually, since Valérie left him. I've wanted to give him a shove in the backside all year, but he has to do it himself.'

The doorbell rang once more before Luna could process Guy's words and Silvia led Yannick himself up the stairs to the living room, still in his uniform, an eager smile on his face. Luna sprang to her feet, unable to temper her excitement, even though she was holding the little grounding stone. It was excitement about tomorrow – she told herself, despite the sigh she had to swallow when he greeted her with a kiss on the cheek.

'I wanted to double check your equipment,' he said.

She glanced back at him numerous times as she led him to her room. 'You're looking forward to tomorrow,' she marvelled.

'Of course. You might discover why skiing the Vallée Blanche is so popular.'

'Even though you have to take *me*,' she continued.

His eyes crinkled endearingly. 'Yes, Luna. I'm looking forward to skiing with you and climbing up to the refuge with you.'

And staying overnight...

Luna hadn't allowed herself to follow that train of thought to any conclusion beyond the fact that it would probably be fifteen degrees below zero and the refuge was not a luxurious mountain cabin with a jacuzzi – to say nothing of the fact that she was fairly certain she was the only one who thought about kissing whenever he came close.

She opened the door to her wardrobe to fetch her trekking backpack and quickly closed it again when the first thing she saw was the little decorative urn. She hesitated for a moment too long, stifling a laugh.

'Quelque chose ne va pas?' he asked. 'Something... wrong?'

'You might arrest me,' she muttered.

'Quoi?'

'I am supposed to be completely honest with you, right?' She opened the wardrobe door again. 'I didn't exactly plan this, but I'm illegally keeping my mother's ashes in my wardrobe,' she said with a grimace.

Her statement was greeted by silence behind her. When the silence stretched until she couldn't bear it any more, she turned to look at him in dismay, but he had a soft smile on his face. 'I'm not going to arrest you.'

He lifted a hesitant hand to her face, reminding her of the second time they'd met, when he'd brushed his fingers under her chin and chided her gently for attempting to reach the victim, while smiling that teddy-bear smile that made her glad that he existed. This time, he tucked her hair behind her ear, his thumb lingering on her cheek, affecting her balance so much she had to lean against the wardrobe door.

'Is it... comforting to have her with you?' he asked, studying her.

'Yes,' she admitted, 'when I'm not feeling guilty for breaking French laws. I don't have anyone else to talk to sometimes,' she admitted. None of her secrets were safe when his dark eyes were on her. She would never dare to tell Lydia, but Yannick was also holding onto grief when others told him to let it go. She could *feel* that he understood.

She needed another one of those casual touches Yannick did so well. In all honesty, she needed a hug. Silvia was good with hugs, but she really needed a big, safe, enveloping hug from a mountain rescue gendarme with an overdeveloped sense of responsibility.

'Did you talk to her about tomorrow?' he asked. 'Tell her you're nervous? Afraid?'

Mum, we're finally heading up to the glacier tomorrow, to see Jim's resting place. I've been thinking about that photo for so long, I almost don't believe that we'll see it. And I'll probably screw the consequences and kiss Yannick. I can't stop thinking about it. Gargh.

She swallowed a rueful smile. 'Yep. But I'm pretty sure she knows that being afraid won't stop me.'

* * *

Mont Blanc was wearing its wispy hat of clouds as Luna stood in the square in front of the Téléphérique de l'Aiguille du Midi the following morning, her knees weak and her teeth chattering with more than cold. She'd seen the needle at the top of the cable car, perched on a lonely rock 2,800 m higher than the elevation of the valley, from Silvia's window for the past two months. She could scarcely believe she'd be up there, today, where the air was thin and the black birds of prey spread their wings over the icy landscape.

From Silvia's, the summit of the Aiguille du Midi looked frozen and desolate, like the end of the world, even though thousands of visitors took the cable car up every day, many of them even skiing down the treacherous terrain of the Vallée Blanche. Today, unbelievably, Luna would be one of them.

Her nose stung as she considered what she was about to do. Sure, her mum had apparently skied, but she'd bet June had stayed on the slopes, even if Jim had tried to take her off-piste. If they had had a relationship, there had obviously been limits – like Guy and Silvia, Luna thought sadly. Or even like Yannick and Valérie.

She shook herself, trying to clear her morose thoughts. She couldn't afford them, when she would be undertaking the adventure of her life and might possibly find out how she was connected to Jim.

Catching sight of Yannick striding across the square, the fizz started up in her veins again. She should be used to looking at him by now, given how many times a week she saw him between English class, climbing training, skiing and even the occasional run, where she was panting and exhausted, while he looked as though he'd taken a Sunday stroll.

She'd seen him often in his uniform, either the blue polo shirt and gilet for office duty or the navy-blue utility vest and heavy-duty trousers when he was first or second to march. Today, he wore civvies – black ski trousers and a red jacket – but the rest of his gear looked familiar: harness, carabiners on straps, gloves hanging off one side and several ropes draped over his chest. Like Luna, his skis were strapped to his backpack.

He greeted her with a kiss on the cheek and hunkered down to look her in the eye. 'Comment tu te sens?' he asked in a low voice. *How are you feeling?*

'Okay,' she said with a nod. He prompted her with a lift of his brow and she remembered the numerous lectures from various members of the PGHM about honest communication. 'Nervous,' she admitted. 'But not quite afraid.'

'How is your gear?' They shared a grin since she'd taught him the word 'gear' instead of saying 'equipment' all the time. She'd never been able to stop blushing whenever his hands moved over her harness, which was a continual source of irritation. 'Turn around,' he instructed curtly and she followed the order without question.

'Did I pack the shovel right?' she asked. The grip stuck out of the backpack, even though the handle of the rather basic avalanche rescue tool collapsed to almost nothing. She was trying not to think too much about needing that shovel. If she had to dig Yannick out of an avalanche, she'd rather be in there herself.

'Yes, it's good,' he confirmed.

Tugging on the straps of her backpack, he checked the position of the sharp ice axe and crampons. It still amused her that she, Luna Rowntree, was carrying her very own mountaineering equipment.

'Something is funny?' he asked, rather scarily in tune with her wobbly feelings.

'I feel like Edmund Hillary,' she admitted with snort of laughter. 'You can be Tenzing Norgay, my Sherpa guide. I saw a photo of the two of them, once. Tenzing had a smile like yours.'

'He did?' Yannick said casually as he turned her back around and checked her avalanche transceiver, strapped to her chest inside her coat. But his mouth was turned up in a smile. It wasn't quite the bright, toothy one she loved, but it was enough to warm her up from the inside. 'You want to take a photo before we go up?' he asked.

She nodded and handed him her phone, beckoning him to stand next to her and make it a selfie of the two of them. The little image on the phone gave her a jolt. They looked like real rope partners: casually trusting, easy with each other and... attached.

'If people had known about selfies back before you were born, you might not have so many mysteries,' he joked, tugging her out of her emotional reverie. His smile faded. 'Luna,' he hummed softly, 'ça ira. You can do this.'

Ça ira... It's fine. She was fine. She could do this. *I can do this, Mum. Truly, I can.* She nodded jerkily, her eyes stinging.

She took a deep breath. 'Let's go,' she said, her jaw tight.

With an approving nod, he took her hand and squeezed it and they headed for the entrance to the cable car. Luna didn't let go. She probably should have, but she didn't want to and she'd embarrassed herself enough times in front of him already that once more wouldn't matter.

Instead of loosening his hold, he wrapped his hand around hers and they walked to the turnstiles like that.

Boarding the cable car with the crowd of skiers and mountaineers, Luna felt entirely out of place. There were enough British accents that that wasn't the reason, but the other passengers didn't seem to be shaking with fear at the thought of facing the mountain. They were telling stories and laughing raucously – and swearing liberally, she noticed with amusement.

The cable car whisked them up above Chamonix in the blink of an eye, the cosy cluster of snow-covered roofs nestled at the junction of two enormous mountain massifs. A few minutes later, Luna's familiar ski slopes at La Flégère and Le Brévent seemed suddenly a long way below them as they ascended and ascended.

The sky was a piercing blue, reminiscent of a summer's day. Without the protection of thick cloud cover, the temperature had plummeted over the last couple of nights, resulting in good visibility and a rigid snowpack; conditions were perfect for skiing down a glacier.

After the mid-station, the cable car seemed to go almost vertically straight up. Luna pressed her nose to the glass as they drew level with granite rock faces, too steep to support snow, and she gazed down on the rubble of glaciers and up to endless stone summits, tickled by cloud. Chamonix was an insignificant bundle of vulnerable humanity far below this unforgiving world of ice and snow.

The beauty of the mountains was almost painful, knocking the air from her lungs and the strength from her legs before she'd even attempted to negotiate the remorseless landscape. No longer worrying about embarrassment, she groped for Yannick's hand and he threaded his fingers through hers, saying nothing, but tilting his head close to share the view.

As they disembarked at the top, Luna's head felt heavy from the quick altitude change and she swallowed to relieve the pressure in her ears. The station was built into a rocky outcrop that seemed to teeter above the steep valley. She caught glimpses through the panoramic windows of the needles of the neighbouring rocky peaks and the white dome of Mont Blanc in the distance.

'You'll have to come back up if you want to go up to the very top,' Yannick said casually as he led her through the station building. 'There's a lift, but we don't have time today. We need to make it down the Vallée Blanche before the sun weakens the snowpack making crevasse falls and avalanches more likely – and then up to the refuge before you get too tired.'

'So much down and up,' she muttered.

He gave her a smile that seemed to settle her stomach. 'That's what you do in the mountains.'

They crossed a windblown steel bridge, white with the growth of ice crystals on the metal handrails and she couldn't help looking down at the dizzying drop between the needles of rock, swallowing a whimper as the world seemed to sway.

Clomping through a freezing corridor carved out of the stone, they followed the signs for the exit to the Vallée Blanche, through a tunnel made of snow and ice. A turnstile led out of the station and then... Luna struggled to breathe. A narrow, snow-covered ridge stretched before them, strung with stakes and a rope to help the trickle of thrill-seekers on their way down to the valley. On either side of the ridge – nothing but white and a sheer drop.

I can't do this...

24

The past two months flashed through Luna's mind in arresting, vivid colour, from her first view of the enormous moon over the mountains, to Silvia's shop, her class of gendarmes, the ski slopes, the climbing wall and that glittering blue crevasse. But mostly, she remembered Yannick telling her he couldn't rescue someone who said they couldn't.

'The arête, this ridge, is quite safe, now the stakes and ropes have been set up, but I'll rope you in to my harness, just in case,' she heard Yannick saying smoothly in French, right beside her.

His words snapped her out of her terror and she could breathe out again. With one of his expert knots in the carabiner at her hip, she could at least accept that going down was the only way forward.

'This part is the most intimidating. After we've walked down the arête, it's a lot of fun, I promise.'

'You're lucky you have that face, or I'd never believe you,' she muttered under her breath, settling her goggles over her eyes.

The wind smacked into her as she followed him out into the blinding terrain. Vertigo assailed her, jumbling her sense of what was above and what was below. She felt tiny and helpless and desperately afraid.

'One step down,' she heard Yannick's voice over the wind. 'Hold the rope. Hold my hand. You can do it.'

She gripped his gloved hand tightly as he eased her down the narrow ridge and she focussed on their boots, the solid snow under her feet and each simple step. Then she was halfway down without quite understanding how it had happened.

'Look up,' Yannick encouraged her. She gazed at him, first, the hint of a smile under his goggles, then he gestured outwards and her breath hitched again.

Before her, spread the 'roof of Europe', the unforgiving landscape of ancient rock and ice and snow. She was up here, not pitting herself against the mountain, but honouring it somehow.

She grinned at Yannick, glad he couldn't see her blinking back tears beneath her goggles. He settled his helmet against hers – only a brief moment, but the gesture wrapped itself around Luna's heart.

When the ridge flattened out, they stopped to put on their skis. This was Jim's territory, his reason for living and each breath she took of the thin air gave her more perspective on the man who had left her a mystery and a legacy – and a challenge.

She was humbled, both by the enormity of the landscape, but also by the memory of the man who had lived quietly to the rhythm of the mountain. A sudden desire to see the spring here – the summer and the autumn too – struck her deeply.

Yannick untied the rope and coiled it up again while Luna tried not to dwell on the fact that she was standing alone and untethered in this enormous landscape. He detached her skis from her backpack and dropped them into the snow with a slap, swinging his pack down afterwards for his own skis. His bag was bulky, full of their food for two days, and Luna's climbing boots were strapped to the top. He was apparently able to climb in ski touring boots – he could probably climb in clown shoes with a ball and chain hanging off one ankle, he was so ridiculously competent.

'C'est bon?' he asked brightly.

She gave the only answer that would do. 'C'est bon,' she murmured, taking the ski poles he held out to her and trying not to get a cramp from grasping them too tightly.

Heading across the top of the Vallée Blanche for the 'Voie Normale', the easiest route down, she trekked after him, pushing along in her skis, past enormous boulders of glimmering blue ice, under a blanket of snow, and past an open crevasse. Strange organic ice formations rose suddenly in a choppy sea of blue and white and grey rock that looked perfectly still, glistening in the morning sun, but also proved the violence of the slow-moving glacier.

She had never imagined places like this existed in the world, or that so many people could stand here and look around them in awe.

'A crevasse is a crack in glacial ice,' Yannick called out over the whistle of the wind. 'And that is a serac,' he explained, pointing at one of the protrusions of ice. 'Both features we track and monitor for safety. A serac fall in this area is rare but can be very dangerous.'

Luna nodded with a gulp, but she was learning the word 'dangerous' had a slightly different meaning for Yannick and the people who came to this mountain for their livelihood. 'Danger' had always been a sign for Luna to keep well away, but she'd learned that sometimes it could also mean, 'Proceed with caution; it might be worth it.'

After they'd trudged slowly around a column of rock, the next descent came into view, not as steep, but still pockmarked with shadows and ice waves that even Luna could guess would be dangerous. But others were swooshing down ahead of them, swerving to avoid the obstacles.

'We'll stop for a rest just there.' Yannick pointed to a spot that looked the same as all the rest of the enormous snowfield to Luna, but she nodded. 'But if you need more rests, shout to me. It's better to take it slow than rush down and leave you no energy for the climb to the refuge.'

The sun was already high in the sky and she realised their traverse had taken over an hour, even though it had felt like the blink of an eye. Excitement bubbled in Luna's belly, tangling with the dregs of fear.

'I'd make a joke about racing you down,' she began, enjoying his swift look of alarm, 'but I'm not that mean. I'll follow you down carefully, not straying at all.'

He rapped on her helmet. 'Allons-y!'

Then she was flying after him, the landscape rushing up towards her as she held it back with her skis. The crunch of the snow slowed her descent and the figure of Yannick ahead of her, swooping gracefully on his skis, kept her focussed on the task and not overwhelmed by the enormity of the world around her.

It was hypnotic to watch him swinging through the curves, touching down elegantly with one pole as he turned. It felt like dancing as she matched him, curve for curve, floating on gravity and the icy air. She had to pull up sharply twice, when speed nearly got the better of her, but Yannick was in her thoughts again, reminding her of the ligne de pente – the fall line, as she'd later learned it was called in English – giving her the power to control her own destiny.

When they reached the place where they would stop and rest, she was breathing hard, but not at all tired. The descent wasn't for Jim or her mother or her increasingly indistinct future. It was for her present, for the fleeting moment that was hers – and Yannick's. She never wanted it to end.

* * *

The sound of a helicopter overhead made Yannick slow to a stop on the left bank of the Glacier du Tacul in the early afternoon. The red-and-yellow helicopter of the sécurité civile, Dragon, appeared over the grey peaks, thundering past on its way to a rescue. Luna juddered to a stop behind him, her movements a little ragged.

The descent, aided by gravity, could be accomplished quickly with speed but the Vallée Blanche required concentration and was surprisingly physical. He couldn't push Luna when they still had to negotiate the snowy track to the refuge.

She hadn't needed any pushing so far. It hadn't been a chore at all to lead her down the valley, stopping regularly to catch her elated smiles and share her sense of wonder. He felt as though he'd achieved something too, even though he'd made this descent on an exercise with the team just last week.

But it was different, today, because he'd watched her start to believe she could do it.

Her dilemma, her grief, the way she'd spent the past eighteen months since her mother died treading water – he understood those feelings too well. He'd lived them too, letting life buffet him like the wind on the snowpack. He'd languished in his crevasse, giving up, the way Jim had.

But Luna had searched everywhere for answers, for a way forward, to the point that she was so far out of her comfort zone she'd had to turn everything she thought about herself on its head.

She lived from her heart and he could watch her ski all day, the way she wobbled and caught herself, frowned and smiled and whooped. How many people would be up here with him today, after this chain of events? He suspected the answer to that was: only Luna.

Yannick was unbearably touched and they hadn't even reached the tiring part of the day.

Scanning the terrain, he beckoned for her to follow him right to the edge of the glacier flow, where miniature icefalls formed a skirt along the edge of the protruding needles of rock.

'First stop,' he called to Luna, lifting his goggles. Watching her reaction carefully, he told her solemnly, 'This is the Glacier du Tacul. And that,' he said, pointing to a broad needle of rock stretching far up into the sky above them, 'is the Aiguille du Grépon, where I scattered Jim's ashes last year. There's a statue of Maria, the virgin, at the top. Jean-Yves and I had to leave just after dawn because it's a climb of several hours to the top, and the guides gathered up there to watch us and listen to his eulogy.'

She looked thoughtful for a moment, her gaze fixed on the needle of rock. 'The sun meeting the moon? Was that the name of the route?' she asked. 'I suppose it's a sad sort of name, because the sun and the moon are independent and only meet rarely.'

'A couple of times a year at an eclipse,' he added. 'You can't see the refuge, but it's up on that ledge.'

'Up there?' she repeated, shading her eyes in an attempt to see. 'I didn't think it would be so close.'

He chuckled. 'It's not close. It's five hundred metres higher than our current position. We have to descend further and climb back up because it's not safe from here.'

She nodded, turning again to take in the grand intersection of slopes and crags, all powdered in snow. 'So this is Jim's territory,' she said softly.

'Does it feel how you expected?'

'Does anything ever feel how you expect?' she murmured in response. 'It should have been harder.'

He knew that feeling too, but for her, he could wish it away. Perhaps if he wrapped his arms around her as he'd been dying to do since she'd admitted to keeping her mother's ashes in her wardrobe the night before, he could make her see that she'd done more than enough.

Instead of giving her a hug, he handed her an energy bar. It was a good sign that she wolfed it down.

'We need to keep going. You feel okay?' he asked as casually as he could. She looked a little more worse for wear than he'd expected. It was probably the altitude. She'd never been up as high as they'd travelled that morning.

She glanced at him. 'I don't 'ave 'eadache, if that's what you're asking,' she said with a laugh. 'Let's go.'

The wind picked up as they descended the next part of the valley, where the Glacier du Tacul met the rapidly retreating Glacier de Leschaux and they merged into the main flow of the Mer de Glace. He was glad they weren't still up in the Vallée Blanche, especially when he noticed the multiple trips of the helicopter overhead, but they still had the climb ahead of them.

Coming to a stop near the beginning of the trail to the refuge, he detached his skis and swapped them for a pair of crampons. Putting Luna's skis to one side, he crouched down to help her change into the insulated mountaineering boots he'd insisted she have for this trip.

She stared up at the rock rising beside the rubble of the glacial valley. 'We're going up there?'

'There's a ladder and some permanent cables, but we'll have to see if it's safe and if not, we'll use the snow.' He didn't miss the shudder that went through her. 'These are good climbing conditions because we are later in the season and the névé has formed.'

'The what?'

'The snow is changing to ice, but not finished, yet. It's good for grip.'

'I didn't realise there was a word for that.'

'It's easier than the climbing wall at the gym,' he assured her. 'I took Maëlys up here last summer.'

'But she's a better climber than me,' Luna pointed out with a smile.

A sudden gust blasted through the valley, picking up loose snow, and she flinched. A few clouds had blown in and, without the sun, the temperature was biting.

'Are you warm enough?' he asked her. She nodded, but it was too quick to have been a considered answer. He had to remember that she wasn't familiar with this environment.

He set up the ropes, checking and double checking the knots and testing both belay devices. His own had a brake in case she wasn't in a position to catch him, but it was an easy climb with few vertical sections.

With one last, long look to make sure she was set up, he approached the rock.

By the time he'd ascended the first icy ladder and anchored himself, he realised the conditions weren't ideal after all. The wind was stronger than the forecast had indicated and it was bitterly cold on the exposed rock.

He called out for Luna to follow him up. Her goggles were around her neck now the sun had gone down and her eyes were dark and full of misgiving as she approached. It was a short climb, but, in the wind, pressed against ice and rock and without the advantage of years of experience, he could see she was struggling, panting and gritting her teeth. He wished he'd taken her skis from her, but she'd insisted she could manage.

'Take a rest,' he said, pulling the slack through the belay device again to give her some support.

'I... can't. There's nowhere—' She dug her toes into the ice with a grunt. 'I can't get a hold.'

He guided her to a position where he'd seen some pockmarked concave sections in the ice that were probably an indication of other climbing activity in recent days, but even there, she didn't feel secure enough to rest.

'Then rest in the harness,' he called down. 'I've got you.'

Clinging to the ice-covered ladder, she nodded and he felt her weight on the rope as she closed her eyes, panting. Giving herself a shake a minute later, she started climbing again.

At the top of the ladders, he took out one of her ice axes and handed it to her. She brandished it with a wry smile. 'I still can't believe I need this. "Ice axe" sounds like a murder weapon.'

'You could just call it a piolet like we do.'

'"Piolet" doesn't sound quite murderous enough.' She breathed out on a long huff. 'I think I'm ready to keep going.'

Grappling for the cables, swinging the ice axe and occasionally resting on the support of the rope, Luna made her painstaking ascent to the snow-covered traverse that would take them to the refuge. Yannick located a good spot to rest, knotted into the anchor and looked back for her.

'This is the most difficult part,' he called down over the wind. 'You're nearly there.'

'You've said this is the most difficult part more than once today,' she shot back, her voice quavering. 'Argh.' Her foot slipped and the rope went taut, but she swung the ice axe and found enough purchase to scramble up to him, struggling to dig her crampons into the snow. It was messy and desperate and completely lacking in the techniques he'd taught her, but she made it, collapsing at his feet.

Dropping to his haunches, he grasped her arms and hauled her up, snapping the carabiner of her resting sling into the anchor.

Pulling off his gloves, he lifted her face. Tears streamed down her cheeks and she was pale and shivering but she had half a smile on her face.

For a moment, he felt a shifting sensation like falling, although his feet were firmly planted and he was anchored to the rock. Nothing had prepared him for this kind of fall.

'We don't want these to freeze.'

Luna's eyes drifted closed as Yannick's familiar voice cut through her swimming emotions and his thumbs mopped up the tears on her cheeks. His palms were warm, his fingertips gentle on her skin and she could have stayed hunched on that ledge forever, soaking up the tenderness.

It was worth the cold and the wind and the screaming muscles in her arms and legs to be up here, sharing gusting breaths with Yannick.

Her own breath had never felt so precious and she was certain that Jim would have been happy for her. He and her mother were gone, but she was *alive*. She felt as though she had the whole world at her feet.

She grasped Yannick's forearms, partly for balance and partly because she needed to keep hold of the feeling. She wanted to express everything inside her, trusting he'd understand, but she suspected anything she said would upset the moment rather than sharpen it.

So she simply murmured, 'I need some water.'

After a few sips out of the frigid bottle from her pack, she hauled herself to her feet, almost enjoying the spinning vertigo as she stood on a strange angle, anchored to the mountain. Checking the ropes again, Yannick unclipped and went ahead along a snowy traverse with barely enough space for a single shoe, but at least it climbed gently, rather than requiring a scramble to the top.

Once he'd located the next anchor point, she unclipped and followed him, assailed by dizziness every time she looked down. They continued like that for what felt like a lifetime, pausing to press into the rock when the wind squalled.

The path opened out to cross a little snowfield and Yannick gave a shout and pointed up ahead. Luna squinted, struggling along behind him, and caught sight of a slanted roof emerging from a deep snowdrift. She was filled with both disbelief that the refuge was not just a trick of her overtaxed eyes and awe that someone had built the little stone building on this desolate ledge. 'Refuge' was an appropriate name for the partly buried structure. Only a row of windows in a stone wall was visible, with a chimney poking out of the snow on top.

'Is that it?' she asked, her voice croaky and high.

Yannick's grin was bright in the swirling snow and dappled sunlight. 'That's it!' he confirmed. 'We have to climb down and around, but you've nearly made it!'

She hurried after him, slipping with a squeal. The rope went taut in an instant and she dug her crampons in before she slipped more than a few feet.

'Not now, Luna!' Yannick called out with a wry smile. 'Stay focussed!'

She scrambled back up to the traverse, where their footsteps had made deep tracks in the snow, and matched his sedate pace this time. One more burst of focus was required to navigate a narrow gully and then she was standing in front of the grey stone refuge that looked as though it had stood there for centuries, part of the landscape.

A terrace ran along the front of the building, providing a dizzying view of the entire valley. It was mostly filled with snow, but someone had dug a path and it had only been partially covered by a fresh fall.

Yannick stood at the edge of the terrace and gestured for her to step up to the building first. With hot tears stinging her eyes and pressure in her chest, she stumbled through the snow to the refuge, bracing herself against the stone wall and crumbling inside.

She'd made it.

She tore off her gloves and helmet and settled her palm against the wall. The wind whipped her hair and the icy air bit immediately into her fingers, but she'd climbed up here with little more than her guts and she felt *good* – tired and capable and *strong*.

The crunch of Yannick's boots behind her made her whirl round and she stared at him, unable to tamp down any of her emotions. She probably looked wild, but perhaps it wasn't such a bad thing to live by her feelings, if her feelings could lead her to moments like this – moments where she could look into this person's face and see the whole world.

In two steps he was next to her, gathering her up, holding her together, in the hug she'd been longing for. His arms were tight, as though he knew she needed that pressure to keep her on the ground. She threw her arms around his neck and squeezed him back, breathing unsteadily into his ear when he lifted her a few inches off the ground.

'I did it,' she croaked.

His hand brushed her face, smoothing her hair after he put her back down. 'You did it,' he repeated softly.

Any minute, he would loosen his hold and she'd have to let go, but she clung on for as long as she could, tightening her grip on him, and marvelling at how immeasurably precious he felt.

But he didn't let go. One of his hands curled around the back of her head and she noticed the flutter of his pulse at his neck. With a fresh surge of adrenaline, she lifted her face. His eyelids seemed heavy as he peered at her, his expression taut. He came closer and stopped again, his chest rising sharply. Light-headedness assailed Luna and it definitely wasn't the from the altitude this time. After one last gulp of frigid air, she tipped her chin up and pressed her lips haltingly to his.

She'd intended to draw away again to gauge his response, but from the moment her mouth finally met his, something inside her – inside both of them – unlocked and she didn't want to stop. His hand tightened in her hair, holding her where she was. She groped for his face as her blood rushed and everything tilted a fresh wave of vertigo. It wasn't a gentle or tender kiss, but fraught and hungry and utterly perfect. He pulled away briefly, heaving in a breath and blinking back uncertainty, but he dipped his head again, stealing another eager kiss as though he couldn't help it.

Her palms scraped his stubbled cheeks and she clutched the collar of his coat as she stretched up to him. He muttered something between hard kisses and panting breaths that she was too lightheaded to understand. The way he kissed her was fierce and aching and turned everything she'd thought about their relationship on its head.

Straining closer, she opened her mouth and her stomach dipped, falling as though she was still on the steep slope. She could feel him against her skin, even though they both wore layers of clothing, not to mention all the mountaineering equipment.

He broke off to suck in a breath, turning his head away for several heartbeats, before swallowing and settling his forehead heavily against hers. When his eyes opened, they were wary again under his eyelashes.

Okay. Right. It was the adrenaline again, blurring the boundaries that should have been clear.

He drew back to peer at her and she realised she'd said those last words out loud – because that was the kind of weird thing Luna Rowntree said after the kiss of her life.

She didn't seem to be able to stop there either. 'Sorry,' she murmured, brushing her palm down his cheek – how did the man have such gorgeous cheeks? 'Wow, that was just way better than I imagined. But I know it's... We should stop.'

He blinked those thick lashes a few times and a baffled smile flirted with his lips. 'You imagined kissing? Me?'

If he hadn't noticed, she shouldn't have said anything. 'Yes, you,' she said, giving him an awkward pat on his shoulder and extricating herself, which was harder than she'd expected since he seemed to have forgotten he was holding her in a bear hug. 'But don't worry. I know you can't... and I'm misinterpreting... stuff. You just feel a duty to me and you're big on duty. I know. I appreciate it. I really appreciate everything. Having someone here for me – *with* me – it's a real high and we got carried away. I won't read too much into it. I promise.'

She chuckled and ducked her head, still slightly embarrassed by her feelings, when everyone probably developed crushes on these gendarmes when they were 2,500 m above sea level in a snowy wonderland.

He was silent for so long that she took another peek at him, despite her embarrassment. His brow was thick with something like dismay.

'Seriously, it's okay,' she said. 'Adrenaline, right? We just had a crazy day. I know you do stuff like this all the time, but you probably don't have to drag a civilian beginner with you.'

He breathed out and glanced down at his hands. 'C'est...' was all he managed, starting in French. 'It's an honour, Luna,' he said, his voice firm, 'to watch you do this for Jim.'

His words rippled through her, mixing with the torrent of thoughts and emotions that already assailed her and, before she could even absorb the experience of this gorgeous person telling her it was an honour to be with her, she registered an unexpected feeling of disappointment – followed by guilt.

She wasn't standing on this terrace to kiss Yannick and bask in the sweetest moment of her life. She'd come here for Jim. *Yannick* was here for Jim, because of his own guilt that she didn't fully understand.

'I suppose I should go inside and find the picture,' she muttered, hoping he couldn't tell she'd forgotten about the photo for a moment, while they'd kissed. It would be far too easy to love him. Yannick gladly gave his assistance, but she sensed he was not so generous with his heart.

* * *

Yannick had to shovel snow away from the door before they could get it open. Inside, they found themselves in a utility room which looked cosy, although the air temperature was frigid. Luna shuddered, her mind expecting warmth where there was none.

'I'll light the stove,' Yannick muttered. 'There's a common room through there, with the wall of pictures and a guest book.' She nodded silently, suddenly wary, now she was finally here. What would it change, if she was in the picture? What would it change, if it turned out her father was Jim de Montagne and not another dead man she'd never known? 'Luna?' Yannick prompted, with that tone she loved, where her name sounded precious and wonderful. 'Shall I come with you?'

She shook her head but then whirled back to him. 'Actually, yes.'

He didn't question her but nodded and dropped the wood he'd grabbed from the pile. Going through the door ahead of her, he held it open for her, then strode to the wall, where a whiteboard had been wiped clean at the end of the summer season.

A shelf with a guestbook was set beneath the whiteboard, a little pile of stones balanced on top of each other on one end. Pinned into the wood panelling were postcards and photos and notes from years of visitors: smiling faces of men and women, young and old, and a few children.

Luna skimmed her gaze over them, searching for a face she would recognise every moment of her life, no matter how much time passed after her death. Her eyes settled on a different photo first: a picture of a smiling toddler with a pair of sunglasses on upside down. She had dark brown curls around her face and a toothy grin.

Yannick lifted the tack and pulled the photo off the wall with a wistful smile.

'It's Maëlys,' Luna guessed.

He nodded. 'Jim hung it here. He taught her to call him Grand-papi. He loved kids.' He gave her a sympathetic look before pinning the picture carefully back in place.

High up in the corner was an older-looking photo, with a softer focus and printed with rounded corners. Luna hopped up on her tiptoes to reach it and Yannick lifted the tack for her. When she held the photo in her hands, her vision swam and her stomach dropped and all her questions mattered again, because she was looking at the face of her mother – a younger version, with a jaunty blonde ponytail and a bright smile.

June was standing on a beach with dramatic rock formations behind her and on her hip was a toddler with a crop of wispy dark hair to her ears, a pink dummy in her mouth. Feeling Yannick's arm snake around her waist, she dropped her head to his shoulder as she stared at the photo.

'I hadn't taken much note of that photo before,' he said softly. 'I would guess it's Corsica. I assume that's her – and you.'

Luna nodded wordlessly. Flipping the photo over, she found a note in careful block letters in the bottom right corner: Luna Marie, 1995.

26

He had to stop thinking about the kiss.

Luna was quiet, her gaze alternating between the photo in her hand and the view out of the small window onto the wide valley, making him glad he'd wrestled the shutters open over a mound of snow. She was grappling with questions about her past and future and he respected that, giving her distance.

If only he could stop thinking about the kiss, though – and about her admission that she'd thought about kissing him before. His ears still heated thinking about it. The tightness in his chest hadn't let up since the passion flaring between them had caught him by surprise.

She'd apologised, but the truth was, he'd kissed her just as much as she'd kissed him – and he wanted to do it again. He'd thought about kissing her before today too. He shouldn't have let her apologise, but he couldn't think of anything to say when she was right after all. They were misinterpreting the closeness that came from hours spent together on a mission.

He just hadn't expected it to feel so good, holding her close, her fingertips on his face and her mouth eager and sincere. He hadn't expected to be so moved, and it hadn't had anything to do with Jim.

But Jim was the mission and he knew about staying focussed on the mission. He'd thought she'd be pleased the photo was of her and confirmed that she had some kind of relationship to Jim, but she seemed strangely deflated and there was nothing he could do except keep busy and leave her to her turmoil. He hurried to light the stove and soon there was a comforting warmth inside the room, allowing them to shed some layers. He set containers of snow by the stove to melt for water.

She was tired – he could feel it. He helped her out of her jacket, hung up her avalanche transceiver and set out some of their food on the table nearest the stove. She ate slices of dried saucisson with walnuts as though in a trance.

'I'll call Guy and Silvia,' he murmured, switching on his phone. She picked at her food while he connected the call, reassuring Guy that they'd made it safely.

'And?' the commandant asked. 'Have you found anything about Jim?'

'It is Luna in the photo,' he confirmed. 'Maybe we'll find something else,' he said gently, knowing she was listening. She scooted closer along the bench all of a sudden, and Yannick didn't stop to question it before wrapping his arm around her. She nestled her head on his shoulder and his breath caught. He wouldn't have moved for the world.

'And Luna? Is she okay?'

He tightened his arm. 'She's fine – tired, but she did well today.'

'The wind picked up this afternoon,' Guy commented. Yannick briefly thought to ask about the day's interventions, but he didn't need to know just then.

'Yeah,' was all he could think of to say. He leaned his head back against the wall as softness stole through him. 'We'll be back tomorrow,' he murmured.

'All right, then,' Guy said. Yannick disconnected the call and sat as still as he could. He began to wonder if she'd fallen asleep, but she sat suddenly upright.

'Jean-Yves said Jim always watched the sunset. Have we missed it?'

'No. It's not even six.'

'I can't believe I'm going to say this, but let's put our boots on and go back outside.'

She threw on her jacket and gloves and rushed out again, staggering when the wind and the cold greeted them. Her hair blew into her face and he tucked it back before tugging a beanie down over her ears.

'You need to stay warm,' he said sharply. She nodded sombrely and he was pricked afresh with guilt for kissing her when there was already so much uncertainty in her life.

'Look,' she said softly, gazing across the valley to the tooth-like needles of les Drus, two granite peaks, one a rock face over a kilometre high. The last rays of the sun cast the jagged wall of rock with an orange glow. Snow clung to the lower slopes, glistening and fragile and ephemeral in comparison to the vast frozen valley. 'It's so beautiful, I almost can't believe it exists,' Luna murmured.

'That peak,' he said, pointing to the right of les Drus, 'is called the Aiguille Verte. It's a legendary climb. Jim and I did it together once, years ago. It was another of his favourites and he loved taking clients up.'

'It was a good thing you did for him, scattering his ashes somewhere he loved,' she commented.

He stifled a sigh, trying not to think about that day when he'd said a final goodbye to his friend, trying not to think about his own part in Jim's death. 'Jim had an apartment in Chamonix, but his home was in this spot: between the valley and the peaks.'

She fell silent and he gave her time, hoping she'd tell him what she was thinking and feeling.

'I came all the way out here,' she began, 'but it still feels like a gift Jim gave me, not the other way around.'

'You don't owe him anything. He wouldn't have wanted that.' Several people had told Yannick the same thing, but his situation was different.

Her exhale was slow. She leaned her head on his shoulder once more. 'Thank you. I needed to hear that.'

'Are you disappointed that it's you in the picture?'

'In a strange way, yes. If it had been someone else, then I'd have hit a dead end and I could try to make peace on my own, now I've paid my respects, but it seems like I meant something to him and I... I don't know what to do about that. If he's my father, I don't know what that changes, although it feels like it should change everything.'

'Would you mind if it turns out he's your father?'

She squeezed her eyes shut and he almost regretted asking. 'I don't know. I'd hate to think Mum died keeping such a big secret from me.'

He didn't think she realised she was crying – or how deeply she was still grieving. Her grief – for her mother, for Jim, who she'd never even known – touched him so deeply, he promised himself that he'd protect her to the best of his abilities, even from him – especially from him.

As the sun disappeared behind the mountains to the west, a chill descended with the shadows. A few languid flakes of snow ranged through the air around them, but Luna didn't move from where she was huddled against him, looking out with her head on his shoulder.

'We need to stay warm,' he murmured.

She nodded reluctantly. 'Where is the moon?' she asked suddenly, scanning the sky.

'Perhaps it hasn't risen, yet.'

She took one last, longing look at the sky, before trudging back through the snow to the door of the refuge. 'I would like to have seen the moon from up here, even if it's only an illusion that makes it look bigger.'

* * *

'How much stuff did you carry in there?' Luna felt a fresh shot of guilt every time Yannick produced something else from the backpack. He'd carried water and food for the day – brown bread, that divine salami with walnuts, a packet of rice and a tin of vegetables, dried fruit and nuts and energy bars – as well as a bulky first-aid kit and the two sleeping bags he'd just dug out from the bottom. He unpacked one of the sleeping bags and handed it up to where she was hunched on the top bunk – Jim's bunk.

'You always carry a bivouac bag when you make an expedition in the mountains, even if you don't plan to stay overnight. It means survival if you get stuck.'

'Wouldn't the PGHM come and rescue me?' The stern look he gave her made her smile.

'Sometimes the hélico can't fly due to wind or fog. Bad weather can come unexpectedly. That's why these refuges – and the permanent bivouacs – exist in the Alps.'

'I don't think you need to worry about me,' she said. She peered around the small dorm room in the refuge. Yannick had lit the stove in the room, but she suspected it would still be a cold night. 'I suppose this will be the only time I ever come up here.' It was strange how sad that thought made her – even stranger how tempted she was to see more refuges and bivouacs and dangerous traverses with sheer drops.

She could come back if she wanted to. She could visit, but she sensed that this moment would be gone – this moment sharing a mission with Yannick.

Luna set out the sleeping bag on the lumpy mattress that felt like five-star luxury after the day she'd had. Perhaps her cottage could look something like this refuge, with its rough stonework, gabled roof and wooden shutters. She liked that idea – something to make the dream of the cottage her own and not just something that made her mum's absence more bearable.

She picked up the photo again. She would put it back tomorrow morning before they left – she'd already taken photos of both sides – but she'd tucked it into the bunk bed frame for tonight. The light from Yannick's small lantern was too dim to make out the details of her mother's face.

'I'm a little worried that I'm not actually looking for Jim here, but for my mum. What a stupid quest,' she mused aloud, hearing a quiet rustling as Yannick moved around below.

'You found a photo of her,' he pointed out.

She glanced down at him with a smile, only to freeze, when she saw he was peeling off his fleece and was down to a skin-tight thermal base layer. She tried to force her eyes away, but they refused, instead studying the definition of muscles on his torso and the breadth of his shoulders.

He glanced up and caught her looking. She only hoped she'd schooled her features in time. 'Get in the sleeping bag and stay warm. I'll put more wood on the stove through the night, but it'll still be chilly.'

Phew, he mustn't have noticed her soaking him up with her eyes.

Tossing her up two rough woollen blankets, he continued, 'Put these over you and tuck the sides underneath.'

She did as he instructed, resting on the blow-up pillow Yannick had carried for her, and was soon comfortably warm for the first time since they'd left the cable car station that morning. She felt as though she'd lived a lifetime that day, as though one Luna had gone up the mountain and another would come down tomorrow.

She'd spent that lifetime with Yannick. It wasn't a committed relationship; neither of them was in the position to *commit* to anything. But it was *something* and it made her restless to think that something would dissolve again when they retreated to the valley tomorrow.

The bunk shook slightly as he climbed in below her. Although she tried to ignore it, to get lost in her own thoughts, she was aware of every movement he made as he rolled over in his sleeping bag.

'Did you ever sleep there while Jim slept here?' she asked, not ready to let him fall asleep yet.

'Yes,' he said with a chuckle. 'He snored. I always knew I wouldn't get much sleep if I went up with him.'

'Isn't it dangerous to be sleep-deprived while climbing?'

There was more movement on the bunk below. 'Being sleep-deprived is part of climbing. Sleeping is cold and uncomfortable and you leave and arrive at odd hours. You get used to it – like shift work.'

'Do you get many call-outs at night?'

'Not in winter. In summer, it depends. Many interventions are needed early in the morning for mountaineering groups who set out in the dark – or late-night searches for climbers who don't return to the refuge when expected.'

She shuddered involuntarily. 'Did you... rescue Jim on other occasions? Or just that last time?'

He went worryingly still and Luna wondered if he'd ever tell her why Jim's death still bothered him. 'I pulled him and a client off a cliff face a few years ago,' he said. 'The client blacked out unexpectedly. It was probably the altitude. But Jim was usually a good judge of his clients and helped them to pick activities within their abilities,' he said with a tired sigh.

'So he probably wouldn't have brought me here,' she said wryly.

'You made it. Jim would have been proud of you.'

The words warmed her and she settled under the blanket with a faint smile. Perhaps this was the first step to moving on with her life – a way to accept the money and live with the mystery of not knowing. The insurance policy hadn't been a mistake. Jim had known who she was and chosen to name her as the beneficiary; he would have been proud of her for paying her respects.

Then Yannick turned her thoughts on their heads again. '*I'm* proud of you, Luna.'

27

Her blood rushed and her skin prickled and those words did so much more than warm her. Even though she'd spent the day in the footsteps of people who'd died, she felt so *alive*. She wasn't sure she wanted the feeling.

'Bonne nuit,' Yannick murmured as he shifted again.

'Good night,' she echoed, her heart still pounding. She rolled over and tried to lie still, but her thoughts were tangled and she was worried she was losing sight of her quest. She was also aware of every movement Yannick made below her – and assailed by the feeling of being alone as the wind whistled outside and she wrestled with her priorities. She sighed loudly. 'Yannick?'

'Mmm?' he responded.

'Is it cold down there?'

'It's fine,' he mumbled. 'Are you cold?'

That was not the answer she'd been looking for. 'I'm... Isn't it efficient to share body heat or something?' She was embarrassed before the words had even left her mouth.

He hesitated and she heard a little cough that might have been an amused chuckle. 'If you conserve your own body heat, you'll be okay. Tuck the blanket more tightly.'

That was a clear answer if she'd ever heard one. No more cuddling. He'd let her rest her head on his shoulder enough times today. She tried to give it up, roll over and sleep, but she felt so strange up there in Jim's bed with Yannick below her, too far away.

'Well that's... disappointing,' she mumbled.

'What do you mean?' The was a catch in his voice.

'I suppose... we've been attached by a rope for most of the day and it feels strange now that we're not.' She'd taken this requirement for honesty a little too far – typical Luna-style. 'And I thought mountain cabins and sharing body heat were a natural combination,' she added, although the joke didn't do much for her mortification.

But when he responded, he said something entirely different from the gentle logic she'd expected – the logic that still would have felt like rejection. 'I... it does feel strange,' he said, as though his words surprised him.

'I... You... Well, not that it's... Um, you could...'

'You want me to rope you in?'

'With... your arms?' Her face was hot now and she regretted ever starting the idiotic conversation. 'Sorry, that was stupid. Forget about it.' She tucked her face into the sleeping bag to try to pretend she didn't exist.

She heard rustling below and the bunk shook. When she braved a glance out over the hem of the sleeping bag, she saw another sleeping bag appear on the bunk next to her, then a woollen blanket, and finally Yannick's head.

His hair stood up in messy spikes and he gave her a soft smile when he caught her eye and she wasn't sure she'd ever liked someone as much as she liked him. He spread his sleeping bag next to hers and scooted his legs in before settling two woollen blankets over them.

'We can share body heat,' he said quietly. 'That's a very sensible idea.'

Luna was so relieved she could have cried – again.

Pulling a blanket around both of them, he slung his arm over her and she sank deeply, contentment stealing over her. His breath tickled her ear, spreading over her skin. Perhaps they could stay up here melting the snow they needed for water and pretending the rest of the world didn't exist.

'Thanks,' she whispered, sleep already calling to her, now he was close again.

Luna wished she could open her arms and pull him to her, convince him he could trust her with more than just a belay rope, but she was tucked inside her sleeping bag, with his arm holding her still and sleep making her eyelids heavy.

He squeezed her tighter for a moment. 'I needed a hug, too,' he murmured so quietly she wasn't sure he'd intended for her to hear.

* * *

It had been a long time since Yannick had shared body heat with someone – or at least used that as an excuse.

He understood what she'd meant about the rope. He'd chosen the bed directly beneath her because it had been the nearest he could choose without being brave enough to admit she felt too far away. Luna had been the brave one and then she'd fallen asleep in his arms so quickly, he'd asked her if the cuddle was okay, expecting an answer, but had only received a contented snuffle in response.

He stayed awake longer, trying to berate himself for the sudden switch from 'protect her from him' to 'hold her while she sleeps', but he had no energy for the guilt. His last wakeful minutes were spent marvelling at the privilege of feeling her chest rise and fall with her breath.

It was an honour to lie beside her and give her shelter with his own body. It was also a joy he'd never expected and probably didn't deserve.

That joy was the feeling that greeted him early the following morning when his instincts woke him before dawn. Falling asleep at altitude was a dangerous exercise – in sleep, you don't notice the onset of hypothermia – and usually he woke several times, but he could tell it was nearly sunrise by the frigid air. He'd spent a peaceful night.

He needed to get up and light another fire, since he'd failed to add more wood during the night. He needed to check the weather, plan the descent. Most importantly, he needed to find his perspective. He was out here for Jim's sake – and for Luna's. Cuddling and listening to her breathe simply because it brought him joy was not part of his mission.

But he struggled to move, held back by a mix of thoughts and emotions he thought he'd buried. Luna was pressed tightly to his side, curled towards him. He could feel her breath on his cheek and the pressure of her body against his. A surge of happiness washed over him to realise that she'd sought him out in sleep.

Luna... It was an unusual name, but somehow perfect for her – an unusual person. Thinking of her name, written in Jim's handwriting on the back of that photograph, reminded him of his friend's last words and it was almost a relief when some of the joy receded.

He needed to get her home safely. He'd done what he could and now he could only support her as she decided her next steps – the steps that would lead her away from here. She would be happy, living near the cousin she spoke about with a lot of fondness. That's what Jim would have wanted for her.

He slipped out of his sleeping bag as smoothly as he could. Quickly dressing, he made a fire in the stove and headed out to check the weather from the terrace. The sky was still black, pierced with stars. Only a few smudges of cloud blurred the points of light. The air was motionless and vast, the snow turned to crystal in the overnight freeze. His gaze ranged over the valley and up to the needles behind the refuge and there was the crescent moon, suspended above the formidable Aiguille du Grépon.

He had to wake Luna. She wouldn't want to miss the moon. He found her sitting up in the bunk, looking dazed. Seeing her mussed and sleepy made him pause to suck in a much-needed breath.

'What's up?' she asked, her voice gravelly.

'Come outside and see the moon.'

She blinked at him and frowned. 'Did you sleep at all?'

'More than I usually do,' he admitted. 'Vas-y! It will set soon.'

She stumbled and groaned as she pulled on her snow trousers and boots, her neck warmer and the thicker fleece scarf and her two pairs of gloves. 'It will set before I've got all my clothes on again. Why did Jim love this place instead of some nice thatched cabin in the Seychelles?'

He chuckled, pretending he didn't take her comment personally. The mountain was harsh; he couldn't pretend otherwise. She didn't have to love it the way he did.

'You could go to Corsica next: the Mediterranean, clear water, sunshine. You can see the moon from there too.'

A surprisingly grim look passed across her face. 'Since my cousin can't find my birth certificate, I might have to. Maybe the PGHM there needs English classes?' she mumbled. 'Right, I'm finally ready,' she said with a huff. When he opened the door, she staggered back with a gasp. 'Oh shit, I'd forgotten how cold it is.'

'The problem with warming up too much at night – the change in temperature is a shock.'

She wrapped her arms around herself and stepped out into the dawn after him. Her wide-eyed gaze roamed the dim valley, the shades of snow and rock and sky, and then settled on the moon, when he pointed it out.

'Do you really think it would be better to spend the night cold and not sleep well?'

'Yes,' he replied without hesitation.

'I'm sorry for screwing up your self-discipline,' she muttered. 'But I'm glad I was warm and comfortable, even if it meant I got a shock when I came outside. It was worth it.'

He stared at her, but she didn't return the look. She studied the sky as the first hints of dark blue glowed over the snow-dappled peaks of the Grandes Jorasses to the east.

'People can't be tough all the time, you know,' she said. 'Even PGHM secouristes – even *you*, Yannick.'

'I have to be,' he replied immediately.

'Yeah? But you needed a hug too – you admitted it.'

His skin prickled with the awareness of something running ahead of him that he couldn't control. 'I shouldn't have,' he insisted.

'You shouldn't have needed it? Or you shouldn't have admitted it?' She whirled in his direction. 'What happened to this complete honesty you expected from me? Doesn't it go both ways? And if you need something, it's no good pretending you don't. You're not superhuman.'

'I *have* to be, for the sake of the team. You don't understand.' Valérie hadn't understood either. He shouldn't have kissed Luna;

he shouldn't have held her while she slept. He was supposed to be coming to terms with the loneliness of his choices.

He started to draw away, go back inside, but her next words stopped him. 'Tell me, then,' she said with a firmness he'd rarely heard in her voice. 'If I don't understand, tell me why you put all this pressure on yourself, why you can't be human.'

Why you can't be human... Her words made a little tear inside him. He'd felt intensely human last night, sharing a bed – and warmth and breath – with another person. But he knew exactly what to say to make her understand. Perhaps he should have told her the full story from the beginning.

'Luna,' he began, her name almost painful on his lips this time. 'Jim is dead because of me, because I chose not to save him.'

28

Luna grappled for balance as her emotions took off in different directions. The stark words, '*I chose not to save him*,' echoed coldly in her mind, but what hurt the most was the knowledge of just how much Yannick had tortured himself for what she could only believe had been a necessary decision. She was also frustrated to realise she couldn't just wave her hand and take away all his hurt – his very *human* hurt.

'Tell me exactly what happened,' she prompted gently. Her fingertips were going numb inside her gloves, but she wouldn't move if going indoors meant he closed up again. 'Tell me in French. I'll understand.'

His expression smoothed and she suspected she was seeing Adjudant Yannick Pasquier, the gendarme with eighteen years of military service, reporting for duty. 'I wasn't first to march that day,' he began, following her suggestion and speaking in French. 'Patrice and I were second. Matthieu and Marina went to the glacier first, while we prepared the equipment and planned the intervention.'

'Did you already know it was Jim?'

He nodded. 'He called it in himself, the tough old man.' He squinted for a moment, but the hint of emotion was gone again in an instant. 'I'll never forget hearing his scratchy voice, reporting that he and a client had fallen into a crevasse. We knew even before Marina reported back that it would be a complex rescue and we... made our initial assessment.'

'Assessment?'

'We suspected that Jim was badly hurt, that the chances of saving the client were better.'

Luna gulped. 'The chances...'

He looked up sharply. 'This is normal procedure. In dangerous situations, where every minute matters, we leave the weakest. Two years ago, I left a man to die four hundred metres from the summit of Mont Blanc. It was the only way to save his partner. I went back up a few days later when the weather improved and dug out his body.'

And he did that wholeheartedly, Luna thought to herself, because he knew what it was like to lose someone and never even see their body.

She fumbled for the wall of the refuge to support herself. He'd been right. She didn't understand how much he had to deal with – he'd protected her from it. A few English classes with the unit, watching a practice exercise and she'd thought she grasped something of the burden he carried, but the reality was much more upsetting.

She was so confused. How could she admire him for his dedication and ability on one hand, but be horrified by the cost he willingly paid – the cost of his own wellbeing? She understood Silvia's and Valérie's positions more deeply than before – and Jim's wariness of relationships. Yannick was right – he couldn't afford to be human.

'At least Jim understood the situation – perhaps too well,'

Yannick continued. 'He suspected he was going to die as soon as I reached him. He knew I would save the client first.'

He stared out at the valley, his face still impassive. 'We had to hurry. There were too many variables – the condition of the victims, the stability of the crevasse and the seracs. It was a nightmare operation. I went down first and the doctor prepared to follow. You know the chain of command is different on the mountain. We make decisions as a team, so we discussed the next steps constantly.'

'You all decided to prioritise the client?' she prompted gently when he paused.

'I was hoping we could get the doctor down to stabilise Jim while I freed the client – or maybe Matthieu would join me and we could take one victim each, but as soon as I made it down five metres, I knew we wouldn't have time for any of that. The seracs were unstable. I wouldn't have brought another gendarme into that situation, let alone the doc. So I ignored Jim. I actually remember he said something about insurance and I thought he was talking about his client's. But I wasn't listening.'

'You were saving the client,' Luna filled in when Yannick didn't say it himself. 'What did you have to do to get him out?'

'He was trapped under a fallen serac – both of them were, but the client was only pinned by his leg. I could see Jim's head and one arm and he'd obviously been badly crushed. Do you want me to continue?' he asked suddenly. 'I'm only telling you this because you asked. You look... disturbed.'

'Keep going,' she said immediately, swallowing to settle her roiling stomach. Perhaps she wouldn't have wanted to know if he'd warned her his explanation would be so graphic, but she was here now – with him. She couldn't back out.

He looked at his boots with a distant expression. 'The client was screaming in pain. I made the judgement that the victim needed urgent retrieval rather than medical care in situ. I didn't call down Matthieu or the doctor,' he said, pausing to swallow, 'I had to ask them to send down the chainsaw instead, and I started cutting him out as fast as I could.'

There was a long silence and Luna watched a muscle move in his jaw, the twitch of his brow as he tried not to feel anything and didn't quite succeed.

'Freeing his leg was only the beginning, unfortunately.' He stared at his gloved hands. 'I've seen these accidents before. As soon as the pressure was off, the blood started spurting. He needed a haemostatic compress and a tourniquet to stop it enough to get him lifted.'

Luna's stomach turned again, not wanting to imagine him in that situation, alone in a dangerous crevasse, covered in the victim's blood.

'The problem is, our equipment can only support the weight of two people – two ropes. If I'd brought Matthieu down, one of us would have to have gone back up before bringing the victim up, and I judged that he didn't have that kind of time. So I kept the second rope free to bring him up quickly and... left Jim dying.'

'But what else could you have done?'

'That's the question I ask myself every single morning when I wake up.' He closed his eyes for a moment. 'What if I'd picked Jim? The haemorrhaging could easily have killed the client anyway and Jim was still lucid. What if I'd taken the time to get Matthieu down to reach him? We might have had a few minutes. The client had pressure on his wound. He might have survived another ten minutes down there while we worked on Jim. I made an assessment and... then I had to live with it.'

'And it was so much harder because it was Jim,' she whispered. 'That's not your fault.'

'But it was my decision,' he said in a clipped tone. 'What if I ignored Jim because I was worried about not being impartial?'

She wasn't sure if he wanted an answer but she sensed a shift in the conversation. He was no longer giving her a stark explanation to scare her off. He wanted her to understand, to say something – perhaps even to comfort him.

'The team wouldn't have sent you down if they'd been worried about your decisions,' she said firmly.

When he glanced at her, his brow knit, she knew she'd said the right thing. 'I had to be down there.'

'You don't think your colleagues would have been able to do the same job?'

'It's not that,' he muttered. 'At least with me down there, Jim wasn't alone at the end.'

'Can you tell me more? About those last moments?'

'I had to bring the other victim up in a stretcher because he was barely conscious, but I handed him over to the doctor and went back down for Jim.' His pause was more pained than usual. 'After I begged the doc for a vial of morphine and a needle.'

Luna grimaced but his story was no longer for her, so she reined herself in.

'By the time I got back down, he had no colour in his face. He'd been groaning in pain for a while. Jim used to say he didn't feel pain.'

'Everyone feels pain,' Luna murmured, looking out over the valley. 'Some are just too proud to admit it.' She felt Yannick's gaze on her and found him studying her with an intensity she hadn't expected.

'You're right, of course. He was in a lot of pain. I tried... I got a rope around a piece of ice and we managed to move it a little, but he was pinned into the crevasse. He was dizzy and drifting in and out of consciousness. He was losing blood but I had no hope of stopping it because I didn't know where it was coming from. When he let me give him the morphine, I knew it was all I could do, but I wanted to keep digging. I wanted to pull him out alive more than anything.'

Her tears fell, hot and silent, down her cold cheeks. Perhaps she should have been crying for Jim, her mysterious benefactor, a man who'd meant something to her even though she'd never met him. But she was crying for Yannick, although he'd never let her if he knew.

'He grabbed my hand and he said, "Je reste ici, Yanni." Just that: I'm staying here. He probably didn't even want his body to be pulled out.'

'I'm glad he had you there. I'm sure he was glad to spend his final moments with you.'

'Luna,' he said in a pained tone, as though he wished she hadn't spoken.

'Is that... Do you need a hug?' she asked, peering at him.

He tilted his head in half a nod and it was all the confirmation she needed to bury her face in his chest and press tight. His arms came up, clutching the back of her head with his gloved hand and she hoped he felt how wonderful it could be to be human.

'The moon is setting,' he murmured, turning so she could see it without moving from her position against him.

'It really does look huge,' she marvelled. 'Are you sure Jim *wasn't* talking about the moon?'

His arms tightened around her, which made her unexpectedly content. 'The moon wasn't in the sky that afternoon. I thought he was talking about the afterlife or something – the alpinist's afterlife. But I'm sure, looking back, that he said "Luna" and not "la lune". And now you're here, where we laid him to rest.'

Luna closed her eyes. Would Yannick truly be able to lay Jim to rest? He'd brought her here out of his own feelings of guilt. Both of them were searching for a way to put the past to rest. She couldn't meet Jim. She might never find out who he was to her, but holding onto Yannick while he pretended he didn't feel pain was a step forward. She needed that – and so did he.

It might hurt, when their lives tore apart the little rope team they'd built for this treacherous time in their lives, but for now she wanted to stay warm in his arms and deal with the pain of separation later.

29

A storm blew in late that afternoon, shadowing the Mer de Glace with the promise of more snow, but Yannick had already brought Luna safely down the glacier to the cog-wheel railway that would deliver them back to Chamonix, and civilisation.

The poor, magnificent glacier had retreated so much in recent years that they had to climb five hundred steps just to reach the cable car to the Montenvers railway station. Luna pressed her face to the glass at the window of the little train, as though soaking in her last glimpses of the icefields.

The Mer de Glace wasn't visible from Chamonix. Perhaps today would be her last view of it.

He grasped their skis and stepped off the train with studied casualness when they arrived at the valley station. He'd parked there yesterday before walking to meet her. All he had to do was hand over her skis, kiss her on the cheek and say goodbye to the two strange days where he'd felt like someone else – someone who liked warm blankets and hugs and deep conversation and a pair of dark eyes that looked at him in a way no one else did.

He'd managed to leave Jim behind at the refuge this time. He'd

232   LEONIE MACK

told her he woke up every morning reliving his choices, but that morning he hadn't. That morning, he'd woken up thinking only of the opposite of loneliness – whatever that was.

Leaving Luna and everything they'd shared would be more difficult, but he'd do it. She had her dreams and her future. She didn't need him, even though she might have forgotten that when they were roped together, sharing footprints and misty breaths and surges of adrenaline.

She followed him out to the forecourt, where the historic locomotive sat dormant under a thick layer of snow, and paused, clutching the straps of her backpack.

'Do you want a lift to Silvia's? I parked on the other side of the station.'

She nodded, but still seemed hesitant about something. Was she embarrassed by how close they'd been while under the influence of altitude and adrenaline? She was such a soft soul, she'd obviously been moved by his story about the day Jim had died and that had probably made this feeling of intimacy even worse. Perhaps he shouldn't have told her after all.

Trailing him to the car park, she waited while he stowed their skis in the roof box and then she settled into the passenger seat. He started the engine and switched on the heated seats.

'Oh, wow, I'd forgotten this kind of warmth existed,' she said with a groan a few minutes later. Her head lolled and he couldn't stifle a smile. 'Did you say something about a sauna?' she asked.

He nodded. 'I have a barrel sauna in my garden.'

'That would be amazing right now.'

He opened his mouth but paused. What happened to the cheek kisses and goodbye? 'You want to use the sauna?' he offered.

'Would that be okay? I feel like I'm going to be cold for a week.'

'Yes, it's okay,' he answered immediately, turning the car in the direction of his own house and fighting off eagerness. 'Do you want to get some things from Silvia's first?'

'No, no,' she said too quickly. 'I mean, if I can borrow a towel? Argentière is out of your way isn't it?'

'Of course you can borrow a towel.'

Snow was falling when he pulled up on the gravel outside his house. It was built from dark wood with some rendered stone on the ground floor. He'd become so used to seeing things through her eyes, that the view of his own home felt different. What would she think of the little chalet that was too small to be a family home, but had a swing set full of snow in the garden and wobbly pictures of Disney characters in window paints decorating every pane?

His favourite spot was the balcony off his bedroom on the upper floor, with a view of the Bossons glacier. But if he showed her, that would mean standing in his bedroom and the thought of that made the back of his neck hot. He was trying to clear his head, not cloud it with fruitless questions about what was going on between them.

He was also conscious of the renovation projects he hadn't had time for: the red paint peeling on the shutters; the rickety mudroom tacked on to the front door. Inside, he'd barely decorated. There hadn't seemed much point, when no one would see it except himself and Maëlys.

She gave him a cheerful smile as she tugged off her boots and his skin tingled with something giddy like happiness. He quickly turned up the heating and set a fire as she wandered the sparse living room. He might have been faintly embarrassed that there were more ropes in the room than decorations, but she took everything in with a smile, studying the few photos on the wood-panelled walls: a portrait of Maëlys from last year; ski tracks on the pristine snow of the Glacier du Géant; a view of the Mont Blanc massif from across the valley in summer, with the icefall tumbling down the mountain in ultra slow-motion.

'Did you take these?' she asked and he nodded silently in reply. 'You're a photographer?'

'When you have these subjects, anyone can be a photographer,' he said with a shrug. 'You can take a shower and I'll turn the sauna on to warm up. It'll take about half an hour.'

When he'd sent her off into the main bathroom with a towel and a selection of clothes that wouldn't fit, he raced for the tiny kitchen, assembling a plate of cheese, saucisson and olives and wishing he'd stopped for fresh bread, before peeling his own layers off and stumbling into the tiny downstairs shower.

His heart was pounding strangely, as though something important was going on, and he felt as if he was trekking through a winter fog up on the mountain. Had she really come for the sauna? Or did she feel the pull too?

He emerged from the shower, his hair still dripping, to find her perched by the plate of food, evidently trying not to guzzle.

'Eat it all if you want,' he said.

She glanced at him guiltily and then froze, her gaze dropping and then jerking back up, and he realised he only had a towel draped around him. They might have been attached by an invisible rope, but that didn't stop him feeling faintly embarrassed to have her wide eyes skimming over him.

He bolted for the stairs, clutching the towel. 'I'll be back in a minute.'

* * *

Luna blinked into the fire in the stove and sat on her hands. The food that had engaged all of her senses a moment ago had lost some of its appeal.

She'd known, when she'd made him bring her here under slightly murky pretences, that she wanted more closeness – another kiss, more intimacy. She'd almost lost courage several times, knowing he would never make a move unless she asked him to.

Then he'd emerged from the shower and she'd realised the enormity of what she wanted – but she wanted it badly.

She'd never seen him without layers of winter clothes, except for the hint of a forearm when he was on office duty at Cordial and that one time in the climbing gym. But she'd known he would be perfect in his skin: built for endurance, with fine, dark hair on his chest. Taking a deep breath, she bit her lip and gathered her courage to talk to him when he came back down.

In a T-shirt and tracksuit bottoms, he was somehow just as attractive as he'd been a moment ago wearing almost nothing. But his words immediately threw cold water over Luna's plans to open the subject of going to bed together – which had already sounded unbearably awkward when she expressed it like that in her own mind.

'The sauna will be hot in another ten minutes or so, but you could go in already. It's good to get used to the heat gradually.'

Ah, the damn sauna. Her conscience wouldn't let her waste all the electricity it had already consumed. 'Um, okay.'

'You can get changed in the little bathroom down here. I'll get you a fresh towel t-to sit on.' He raced off again and she peered after him, suddenly noticing his nerves. He returned with a clean towel and a pair of Crocs that were far too big for her – to match the jogging bottoms that fell down every time she took a step.

'Um,' she blurted rather stupidly. He glanced up, meeting her gaze, and her head spun. 'Wouldn't it save electricity if we go in together? I-I mean, keeping the towels on, or... I would be happy to do that anyway.'

'You... want to save electricity.'

She nodded earnestly, kicking herself for another half-truth. She was so *bad* at this; she should probably just give up, except she also couldn't face the thought of leaving.

'Ah, c'est bon – okay. You get changed first.'

When they were sitting on opposite benches in the cute little sauna shaped like an enormous barrel, Luna felt like laughing. Perhaps there was an element of relief in the heavy heat, as though her skin was breathing out. But mainly it was the spectacular view of Yannick in front of her in a towel, giving her the occasional, slightly embarrassed smile – her teddy-bear gendarme with shoulders for days and packed muscle all down his arms and chest.

'Ça va?' he asked.

She breathed in deeply and sat back against the curved wood. 'Ça va,' she repeated with a smile. 'Bien,' she added – she was well.

He mirrored her pose, his head back, and she was both gratified to see him slowly relax and attracted to the cordons in his neck. In fact, she was attracted to just about every part of him – especially his soft, loyal heart.

After they'd sweltered quietly for fifteen minutes, she sat up and leaned her elbows on her knees. 'Yannick?' she prompted quietly.

He cracked an eye open. 'Mmm?'

'Did you know Silvia has a sauna? I haven't used it before.'

'But maybe you will, n—' He realised what she was hinting at before he finished his sentence. 'Sh-she has a sauna?'

Luna nodded as confidently as she could. 'Sorry I made it sound like that's the reason I wanted to come here.'

'Je te pardonne,' he said immediately with a puzzled half-smile. Of course he would forgive her without hesitation. 'But what... is the reason, then?'

'You,' was the first thing that tumbled out. 'It's the rope. I can't untie it yet. I want to...' She squeezed her eyes closed so she could get the words out. 'I want to just be – with you. And kiss you again and... I'll understand if you don't want—'

He sat up suddenly, grasping her face, and cut her off with a kiss.

Luna barely had time to register her relief before it was replaced with the thrill of understanding from the weight of his hands cupping her cheeks, the pressure of his mouth on hers. He wanted this, too. She leaned into him, inviting more.

The kiss deepened and they both pulled back with a surprised gasp. He had time for a twitch of a smile before she kissed him again.

The chaotic dash back to the house was cold and wet across the snow-covered lawn, but they shared stirred-up smiles, clutched their towels with one hand and tangled their fingers with the other. He shepherded her into the shower and she experienced none of the awkwardness she'd expected when she dropped her towel and pulled him into the cubicle with her.

He smiled too much for her to feel embarrassed – and kissed her too often – and his hands on her skin weren't strange or new. She felt just as secure as she had the night before, falling asleep next to him. He washed her with gentle efficiency, which she still found arousing, but it was her touches on him that pushed them into intimacy. He stifled a groan when her lips wandered up his neck. His breath stalled as her palms ranged over his chest.

He switched off the shower and swiftly dried off. Wrapping her up in her own huge towel, he hefted her into the air with a clipped, 'Hop,' that made her laugh. Then he ran for the stairs, kicking open his bedroom door and dumping her onto the bed.

She grabbed for him and he let her drag him close. Cradled in his arms, it didn't feel like the first time she'd felt his skin against hers. He dipped his head, dragging his mouth over her breast with a groan and she felt as though she was flying.

But he groaned again, this time in frustration, dropping his head to her sternum. 'I don't... I haven't slept with anyone since Valérie,' he admitted. 'I don't have a préservatif.'

Luna pressed a hand to her mouth to stifle a smile. He looked so sweet and earnest, looking up from where his chin rested on her naked chest, telling her he didn't have a condom. 'Would you believe Silvia gave me one?' she said, losing the battle with a smile. 'She sneaked it into the pocket of my jacket and I never took it out.'

He leaped up comically quickly, dashing downstairs naked to raid her pocket. His grin when he returned made her heart stutter. Climbing back onto the bed, he brushed his nose along her neck and whispered, 'I don't know how Silvia knew, but I'm grateful,' and Luna's hair stood on end hearing the hunger in his voice.

From giddy smiles and laughing touches, they both fell into the building intensity of the moment. He encouraged her above him and she clung to his neck and shoulders, grappling for him as she tumbled through her feelings.

Tugging his hands down to her hips, she gave him the wordless instruction to let go and was rewarded when he tightened his hold with a ragged exhale, his face at her neck. With her fingers in his hair, clutching him close, she guided them both through the descent into what felt to Luna like uncharted territory.

30

Luna was only slightly awake twenty minutes later when Yannick's phone rang somewhere downstairs. He stirred behind her, satisfyingly lethargic, before hauling himself up, pausing only to brush his palm down her back.

She rolled over and peered through half-closed lids at his retreating – and very naked – back. Grinning to herself, she sighed and stretched and wallowed in the memories she felt in her skin and her muscles that had nothing to do with careening down a mountain this time.

'Hé, patron,' she heard Yannick say. She knew the gendarmes called their commandant 'patron', meaning 'boss'. He was talking to Guy.

The realisation made Luna sit up suddenly and run a hand over her dishevelled hair. She hadn't told Silvia they'd arrived back safely. She'd been so caught up in this bubble, escaping real life, that she'd forgotten there were people worrying about her.

She peered out of the sliding glass doors to the balcony as she swiped her towel off the floor. The sky above the snowy peaks already showed hints of dusk, and snowflakes caught the yellow light of the streetlamps.

Wrapping the towel around her a little sheepishly, she headed for the stairs. She'd grasped the banister and was about to take the first step when she paused, hearing Yannick's next sentence.

'No problems. We arrived back safely. We just... stopped for... un petit débriefing. And a drink, en fait.'

Her stomach sank even as Yannick's words amused her. A debriefing? That was one way to describe it. Of course, he was right – they couldn't tell Guy they'd just been cuddling naked in bed. Silvia and that blasted carnelian would have a field day if she found out. Neither she nor Yannick was usually the type for adrenaline-fuelled sex and there was no answer to the questions that would ensue if they admitted what had happened, but she was still disappointed.

'I'll get Luna to call Silvia. Sorry we forgot to turn her phone back on.' He was such a terrible liar.

She tiptoed down the stairs as he disconnected the call and caught sight of him, a silhouette against the light from the sliding doors of the living room. He was still naked except for a pair of boxer shorts.

'Debriefing? Is that what that was?' she asked and he whirled to face her.

His grimace almost made her regret her teasing, but when his fingers slipped into her hair and he lowered his face earnestly to hers, she didn't regret anything. 'I'm sorry. I thought you wouldn't want him to know. I don't— I've never—'

She cut him off with a touch of her fingertips to his lips. 'I know. I haven't either.' She pressed a quick kiss to his mouth, enjoying the way his chest rose in response. 'You don't have much of a sense of humour you know,' she said drily.

His mouth dropped open. 'I think they train the sense of

humour out of the new recruits at military school,' he said with a straight face. 'Luna,' he continued, dipping his head to whisper, 'you're not wearing any clothes.'

She peered up at him. 'Neither are you, officer.'

Then he leaned the rest of the way down and kissed her thoroughly. Whatever she'd been expecting, it hadn't been that. With his mouth achingly soft on hers, she almost believed she was everything he wanted – which was ridiculous, because he didn't allow himself to want anything.

After a few minutes of giddy kisses and heavy touches proving that whatever this was, it wasn't finished, he drew away again with a halting breath. She saw it in his brow: he felt guilty for allowing their relationship to progress when it had no future.

'Don't feel bad,' she said firmly, pressing a kiss to his cheek and stealing one last breath of him. She strode to where she'd left her pack, stuffed with her clothes from the trek, and wrinkled her nose at the thought of pulling on her rather whiffy shirt. 'No matter what comes next, I would rather that we... debriefed than not.'

She pulled her shirt on over her head so she didn't have to see his reaction to her words.

'I'll take you back to Silvia's?' was all he said in response.

Luna waited for as long as she could, pulling on her trousers and willing him to ask her to stay, even if they didn't have a future, but he said nothing. 'Thanks,' she murmured. 'I suppose we should go then.'

When he cut the engine of his SUV in front of Silvia's chalet, he turned to her restlessly, his expression earnest, but adorably confused. His hair was a spiky mess from their haphazard shower after the sauna – memories of which were still keeping her warm.

But before he could say anything, Silvia burst out of the door and he snapped back in his seat. Luna reluctantly opened the car door and allowed her friend to wrap her arms around her.

'Well?' Silvia asked eagerly. 'Guy told me it was you in the photo. Did you find anything else?'

Only a bit of fleeting happiness, she thought to herself. 'The mystery is not solved, but it meant a lot to go and see Jim's territory.'

She had to content herself with an intense look and a jerky wave from Yannick instead of a kiss goodbye. Silvia helped her stow her skis and she dumped her backpack in the laundry before accepting one of her friend's restorative tisanes.

Silvia asked carefully, 'Don't you think it's more likely Jim is your father, now? He had a photo of you and paid all those insurance premiums.'

'I suppose it is one of the likeliest explanations,' Luna admitted. 'Perhaps I can order a copy of my birth certificate. Will that be difficult?'

'I think you can do it online, but they will have to post it from Corsica and I have no idea how long that will take,' Silvia explained.

'I'll look into it tomorrow. Perhaps there will be a simple answer after all,' she said, her thoughts muddled. 'But was he really the kind of man who wouldn't have *any* contact with his only daughter for nearly thirty years? Yannick said he loved kids – he made Maëlys call him Grand-papi.'

Her friend sighed deeply. 'There's a difference between playing grandfather and *being* a father. Perhaps your mother asked him to stay away.'

'She wouldn't have done that,' Luna insisted.

'Not even if he'd broken her heart?'

Luna swallowed a lump in her throat, thinking of those reminiscences when her mother hadn't quite been herself in her last days. She had loved Luna's father and June had been a lot like Luna herself – warm-hearted, living on dreams and easily hurt.

Rowntrees were not superhuman.

Silvia's smile held a touch of contrition, as though she realised what she'd said about broken hearts had disturbed Luna. But all she said was, 'I suspect you'll need a good half hour in the shower.'

'Uh, yes,' Luna agreed, trying not to blush – or think of the two showers she'd already had, the second of which had been one of the loveliest of her life.

'I'll cook something, hmm?'

'Thank you,' Luna said, smiling faintly at her friend. 'Guy's not here?' He was usually the better cook.

'No,' Silvia said, her tone flat.

Luna paused, peering at Silvia. 'Is everything okay with you and Guy?'

'Yes,' she said, her voice still tight. 'He's going up with a group to the Goûter refuge next week for altitude training and... well, he has to sleep at his house when he's going to do things like that. I don't like goodbyes and I don't like thinking of the risks. It's easier when you're the one taking them. He can come back when he's down again.'

'Oh,' was all Luna could say. Silvia's words made her unbearably sad.

* * *

Yannick had a strange week with too much time on his hands. He should have expected a degree of post-adrenaline fatigue but although he was accustomed to a short bout of depression or anxiety after a stressful mission, he hadn't realised he could experience something similar after a different kind of mission – one that had lasted weeks, not hours. And a post-adrenaline crash had never made him miss a person before.

It was especially strange since the mission had ended well.

He'd brought Jim's beneficiary to pay her respects. He'd performed one last act of service for a man who hadn't deserved to die and he'd shed a little of his guilt by sharing the whole story with her. He didn't know who she was to Jim, but he'd played his part in her mission, felt the rope slipping through his fingers and left his old friend where he'd wanted to stay.

But he hated that he had no excuse to see Luna.

When Emilien commented that Yannick was grumpy that week, he asked himself if it had been a bad idea to sleep with her. He hadn't felt so close to another human being – so equal – in a long time. It was screwing with his head. He wasn't good at casual relationships, which annoyed him, because he wasn't good at serious relationships either.

He hoped Luna was still happy that it had happened and wasn't eating herself up about it as much as he was.

When Thursday finally came around, he was nervous enough that even Matthieu noticed. 'Has your English gone rusty since you haven't had any extra practice with Luna?' he teased. Yannick only managed to mumble something in response.

He found excuses to wait near reception until she arrived, greeting her stiltedly, even to his own ears. Then she smiled and a goofy grin grew on his face.

'It was really strange not to see you this week,' she said with a soft laugh and the tension drained out of him in a second. He pressed a kiss to each of her cheeks, trying not to linger, but it was difficult when he remembered skimming his mouth down her neck. He was very bad at this.

'I know what you mean,' he muttered back.

He did his best to concentrate on the lesson, but her hands were pretty, as she gestured and gesticulated and she looked just as good in one of her flowing blouses and a skirt as she had in technical gear holding a pair of ice axes. He got distracted remembering how she'd looked wielding those ice axes: a little comical, but very determined.

He decided it wouldn't be so strange to walk her out to the car park, but when he found himself carrying her corduroy bag and hooking it over her shoulder for her, he realised he'd possibly gone too far.

'I've got it, thanks,' she said with the same little smile she'd given him when she'd arrived.

'I seem to be in the habit of looking after you.'

'I won't complain,' she said gently.

'You don't need looking after though. You've learned about life in Cham.'

'True,' she agreed, heading for the footpath.

'What happened to your car, by the way? I forgot to ask.'

'I never arranged winter tyres, so it's just sitting at Silvia's. Perhaps I haven't quite mastered life here,' she said with a grimace.

'Hmm,' was all he could manage, but it slowed her leaving. 'It's the anniversary of Jim's death tomorrow.'

Her eyes clouded, which wasn't the response he'd wanted, but it was his own fault for bursting out with it. 'Will you be okay?' she asked.

'Ouais – yes, of course.'

'There's no "of course", Yannick. Pain and pride, remember?'

'I remember,' he murmured. 'But the anniversary of his death... We're going to celebrate, not suffer. We'll meet for a drink at the bar. Maybe you'll find some people to dance with.'

'Okay, thanks for the invitation.'

He wondered if she had as many things she wasn't saying as he did. Mainly: *I missed you and I don't know what to do about it, since you're probably planning to leave soon.*

'I ordered a copy of my birth certificate,' she told him. 'It was surprisingly easy. It should arrive in a few days, although Guy says it will be slower than that, coming from Corsica.'

'That's... soon,' he said. 'You might have your answer after all.' He wanted to ask if she would still stay until Easter, which was at the end of the month, but he wasn't ready to know the answer. He didn't feel at all superhuman right then, especially not when she reached a halting hand out and squeezed his arm.

'I missed you this week,' she said with spots of colour in her cheeks.

Ouf, his resolve broke up like ice in summer. With a quick glance around, he grasped her hands and tugged her closer. She made him smile, with her big feelings.

'Do you find that funny?' she grumbled.

His smile grew. 'I missed you too,' he murmured.

'Oh, yeah, I'm sure you missed me lots when you were out saving people. You must have really missed going on the blue runs at La Flégère and holding a rope for me.'

'You don't need me for the blue runs and... sometimes watching you from the other end of the rope was an extreme sport.'

'I got your adrenaline pumping, did I?' she asked with a small smile.

All he could do was nod and drag his gaze back up from her lips when he caught himself sneaking a glance.

'Well, I'll see you tomorrow night at the bar,' she said stiltedly. She turned to go and he realised he was still clutching both of her hands. He didn't let go immediately.

He couldn't keep the question in. 'Are you still planning to leave at Easter?'

She froze, her eyes flying to his in alarm. He could read her well enough to guess the answer: she could leave any time her old life came calling.

'Why are you asking?'

He found himself wishing that her birth certificate got lost in the post. 'I—' He took a deep breath and forced the honesty he owed her. 'I want you to come to the bar tomorrow night for Jim – but mainly for me, because I want to see you. I'm just... thinking about whether we have some time to...'

He hadn't expected her to smile brightly at that. 'Debrief?' she said, lifting her face up. It was so hard not to kiss her, even as her joke made him frown.

'I'd be happy with a drink – or dinner sometime. I just want to see you.' That sounded disturbingly eager. 'Before you leave,' he added with an embarrassed cough.

Her smile widened. 'Officer,' she said softly, making him grumble under his breath at her playfulness when part of him wanted this conversation to be serious. 'Take me home with you tomorrow night.'

He sucked in a deep breath. 'D'accord, if you say so, madame,' he agreed with a hopeless smile. He rubbed the back of his head, feeling adrift, except for his other hand that still clutched hers.

31

Yannick had been right: the gathering for the anniversary of Jim's death was not a sombre affair. The pale green Génépi liqueur flowed liberally and the conversation was raucous. The word had spread that Luna was the girl in the photo at the Refuge de l'Envers des Aiguilles and she heard so many stories about Jim, shared so many toasts of the tangy, herbal liqueur with mountain guides, that she felt she'd almost met him.

If it turned out Jim was her father then that would make her happy – proud to carry something of him into the future.

She was happy full stop, especially when she caught Yannick's eye where he was perched at the bar nursing a single beer and chatting with Jean-Yves and then a string of PGHM colleagues.

He seemed relaxed, which was another source of satisfaction. Going out to the refuge might have been a hare-brained plan, but he'd gained something from it too. Sitting at the bar with a smile on his face was a far cry from the anguish in his brow when he'd told her about Jim's final minutes. She hoped he was beginning to remember how his friend had lived and not just how he'd died.

As the evening wore on, she grew distracted by her exit plan. She sensed Yannick didn't want anyone to know they'd been more than just rope partners and that was fair enough. It was his home; she was just a temporary guest in it. But it did present a challenge regarding their departure together from the bar.

As usual, the volume of the music ratcheted up at around ten and the dance floor called to her – literally, as a few familiar faces from the PGHM and some mountain guides she'd just met beckoned for her to join them.

'Uh, I'm a bit tired tonight. And I have a class tomorrow.' It was true. Silvia had offered her more and more hours of short courses for various clients until she was teaching nearly as many hours as she had in her part-time job in the UK.

Are you still planning to leave at Easter?

She supposed she was, even though the dream of her own house, of financial independence and finding joy in her job again, was as indistinct as ever. Yannick was a much clearer feature in her life right now, but he'd been careful not to make her any promises and she respected that.

Poor, superhuman Yannick. She'd make him human for a few weeks and then she'd go before anyone got hurt – before *she* got hurt, because it was always Luna who got hurt.

'Would you like a lift home?'

It took all of Luna's effort to keep a straight face as she heard Yannick's voice behind her. 'Thanks, that would be great.'

A PGHM officer who'd been introduced as Eric shook Yannick's hand goodbye. 'Same time in twelve days, non? Here? Or would you like to try one of the cool new places the young kids go?' he said with a wink. 'Twentieth of March, right?'

Yannick grimaced. 'Yes, but there's nothing much to... I'll save it for next year, hmm?'

'Next year will be forty and I don't want to celebrate that when I'm only three years behind you.'

'De quoi?' Luna asked what they were talking about.

Eric clapped him on the shoulder. 'Yannick's birthday. He spent a miserable one last year with the investigation into Jim's death and I always said he should make up for it this year, even if he is only thirty-nine.'

'Sounds like you need to celebrate,' she said, smiling when he sent her an urgent shake of his head. 'Don't worry,' Luna added. 'I'll make sure he's here.'

'C'est bien, c'est bien,' Eric said, laughing. 'You keep him in line, prof.'

'Why don't you want to celebrate your birthday?' she asked as they dawdled to his car through a light sprinkle of snow. Winter had decided to stay until the bitter end, making Luna think of silly jokes about marmots seeing their shadows in a French version of *Groundhog Day*. Piles of snow still lined the footpaths and every peaked roof was a potential avalanche on unsuspecting pedestrians when the temperature rose in the afternoon.

He shoved his hands in his pockets in typical Yannick reticence. 'What would I be celebrating? I gave up on birthdays a few years ago when everything was going wrong with Valérie.'

'How about being alive, Yannick?' she said drily, meeting his startled gaze. 'I'd celebrate you being alive.'

His lips twitched. 'C'est bon,' he said, draping an arm over her shoulders. 'You can celebrate. And I'll try.'

Her heart stuttered, stupidly affected by his words, his smile, his touch. 'Trying is all you can do,' she said softly.

* * *

If Silvia's worried looks were anything to go by, her friend knew why Luna disappeared some nights and didn't come home. After all her friend's encouragement to get out and have a fling, Luna was unexpectedly reluctant to give her any details – possibly because Luna was trying to forget everything Silvia had said about love not always lasting forever in Cham.

It was odd knowing Yannick's boss probably also knew they were sleeping together – now that Guy had returned from his expedition in one piece and was allowed back in Silvia's house.

But Luna would put up with a lot of embarrassment for the sake of the time she spent with Yannick, which was never quite enough. Another duty week had arrived and he spent long days on shift at the DZ, and when he'd had Maëlys for two nights at the beginning of the week, Luna had suspected she wasn't welcome, which hurt a little.

She felt guilty for feeling hurt, when it made complete sense for him to keep his emotional distance. If only she could do the same, but every time she saw his soft smile, a little more of her heart broke off.

It didn't help that whenever she tried to do something nice for him, it backfired. She'd burned the cheese on toast, wasting a tragic amount of goat's cheese and Beaufort, and her attempt to light a fire in his stove had ended in a singed lock of hair when she didn't realise how well the little rolled-up firelighters worked.

Yannick was tolerant and gently amused, but she almost wished he'd yell at her – feel *something*, like he had when they were up on the mountain.

Although her birth certificate still hadn't turned up, Easter loomed, making every message in urgent capitals from Lydia about cottages and schools sting sharply. She was looking forward to celebrating Yannick's birthday – but two weeks later was Easter

Monday and after that was the start of school term in Sheffield. The start of her new life.

In the early hours of Thursday morning, she was startled awake by his phone ringing. He hauled himself up immediately and after the barest of conversations, he was out of bed, pulling a blue uniform shirt over his head. A few minutes later, without explanation, the front door opened and closed and he was gone.

Luna slept poorly after that, waking in a fog when her alarm went off. She was teaching her class at the DZ that day, but Yannick's early departure had given her prickles of misgiving.

She headed back to Silvia's to change and collect her things and her friend surprised her by wrapping her arms around her in a tight hug. Luna clutched her back.

'What's the matter? I have to get over to the DZ.'

'I don't think there'll be a class today,' Silvia said, her voice sombre. 'I thought you would know what's going on.' Luna shook her head numbly. 'There's been an avalanche; all of team two is up on the mountain searching for survivors.'

Her stomach twisted, remembering Yannick's tone as he told her about Jim, and about leaving a man to die up there. Worrying about his feelings for her suddenly seemed petty and insignificant.

'I'm... going to go to the DZ anyway,' she mumbled. 'Just in case.' That was her excuse.

'Luna,' Silvia said in a warning tone. 'Are you sure you want to get involved in this? They might bring bodies down and depending on hospital capacity, they might even end up at the DZ.'

Her stomach lurched. Of course she didn't want to get involved. She was a soft-hearted, squeamish language teacher, not a super-human secouriste. But she *was* involved.

'I'll just go and see what's happening. I won't stay long,' she lied.

The river next to the drop zone was rushing that day, the crystals of old snow turning to puddles underfoot. As soon as she turned into the driveway, the activity was obvious. Choucas was being prepared for take-off and two gendarmes, one with a dog on a leash, raced for the doors.

Guy was there, barking orders to more gendarmes, and an emergency doctor appeared to be treating a victim with minor injuries right outside the hangar. Luna made her way gingerly to the doors, determined to stay out of the way.

The control room was a hive of activity, with maps laid out and marked and satellite photos on every computer screen. She saw Eric and Bast from team three and waved apologetically when they noticed her.

'Are they all right up there?' she asked.

Eric smiled encouragingly. 'Ouais. The avalanche area seems stable for now.' That didn't exactly allay her fears.

'There were three parties of mountaineers heading for Mont Blanc,' Bast explained. 'Twelve climbers. It's a large number for so early in the year.'

'Are there reports of any... deaths?'

The gendarmes hesitated, before Eric took a deep breath and nodded. 'One confirmed death. There will be more as we find them.'

'The avalanche happened at 4.06 this morning, just after they set out. It's too long for anyone to survive up there under the snow,' Bast explained impassively.

'Is there anything I can do?' she asked, feeling more helpless than usual.

'We have everything under control,' Eric said kindly. 'Although.' A thoughtful expression crossed his face. 'Perhaps you can talk to the victims? We have five here with minor injuries – two Norwegians, two Americans and one German. We need to get as much information as possible about where the groups were standing when the avalanche occurred so we can target the search. We'll have to call it off before the team gets too fatigued.'

Forcing back thoughts about the tragedy on the mountain, Luna found herself in the rec room with the five avalanche survivors draped in emergency blankets, with cuts on their faces. Jean-Marc was there too, with a map.

'Our guide was at the front of our team,' said a wiry, grey-haired woman from Germany who was clutching a steaming mug of tisane.

Luna listened intently as they recounted their departure from the refuge early that morning and the moment the ominous crack and rumble had sounded in the darkness. She focussed on the story, helping Jean-Marc understand the group's progress before the tidal wave of snow had rushed at them.

The lack of emotion struck Luna. The instinct for survival must have overridden anything the victims felt. The German woman's partner was still on the mountain, missing, but the enormity of what had happened was obviously too much for any of them to take in after the shock.

She heard Choucas land and take off again and the dim voices from the control room, exchanging updates with Philippe, the team leader, who was up on the mountain today. Her thoughts returned over and over to the place on the map where the avalanche had occurred – where Yannick and the team were currently searching in the devastating rubble of snow and ice.

'Are you sure Jean-Yves said you were heading for the Dôme du Goûter?' Jean-Marc clarified.

Luna froze, her brain a few seconds behind her panicking heart. 'The guide was Jean-Yves?' she asked in a small voice.

'Yes, he notified the Chamoniarde of his departure,' Jean-Marc said casually, while Luna tried not to hyperventilate. She grabbed

Jean-Marc's sleeve and the gendarme turned to her in confusion. 'What's wrong?'

'Is he... Jean-Yves. He's...'

The victims had had their own ordeal to numb their feelings, but Luna had no such protection. Nausea washed through her stomach and her mind raced ahead, imagining if it had been Yannick, how that would wrench her heart out.

'Luna, Jean-Yves is in the hospital with minor injuries. He was the one who called us in this morning,' Jean-Marc said gently.

Luna's bones seemed to turn to liquid as relief surged through her, along with a wash of misgiving. Perhaps Silvia was right to protect herself, as much as it pained Luna to think she was holding back, keeping her distance in the relationship

When she stood to stretch her legs, she peered out the window to see the first body bag being unloaded from the helicopter and it punched her in the gut once again. *That could be Yannick next time.*

After the doctor took charge of the survivors, Luna felt she was only in the way. Part of her wanted to stay and listen to the radio, but she couldn't change anything and the gendarmes were now busy receiving a local politician and a TV crew. What use was a mascot in a real crisis?

She ran into Guy as she was heading for the gate. 'It's been a difficult morning,' he said after kissing her cheek in greeting. 'You're not waiting for Yannick?'

'Well, I... No. I can't. Is he coming down soon?'

'We're winding down the search, but it'll be a while longer. Yanni adapts to altitude well, so he'll be one of the last ones down.'

'Thanks for letting me know,' she murmured.

'Don't expect too much from him today,' the commandant warned.

She thought of the German victim, of her impassive voice as she spoke about her partner, who was probably in one of those body bags. No wonder Yannick stuffed his emotions into a corner, believed he needed to be superhuman and was afraid to open up to people.

She understood, now. But it didn't stop her from realising how much she loved him, anyway, how difficult it would be to stuff her own feelings away.

'I won't,' she assured Guy. 'I won't expect too much from him.'

32

Two hours earlier, Yannick had been squinting through his sunglasses as the brilliant snow reflected bright light directly up at him. He pulled his probe back out and moved along the line with the other rescuers, plunging the thin pole back down through three metres of snow.

A shout went up from the dog handler and Philippe called for Yannick to break rank and help. He'd been up here for hours, searching methodically and as tirelessly as the 4,000 m of altitude allowed, desperately hoping to find someone – and also fearing it, because whoever he found now, hours after the event, was unlikely to be alive.

When his probe met resistance right where the dog was barking, at a depth of about a metre, his stomach sank. Setting his jaw, he lifted his shovel and started digging, Matthieu and Marina joining him. What he uncovered was exactly what he'd expected. The cuff of a blue jacket became an arm, then a shoulder.

They uncovered four more bodies before Philippe called off the search for the last missing mountaineer. It took two hours to get everyone down, Choucas ferrying people and equipment. He and Philippe were the last to return to the valley, both of them still staring at the steep field of tumbled snow as though they could miraculously find the last victim alive under there.

Philippe clapped him on the shoulder. 'Good job, Yanni.'

He just grunted in response. Every rescuer dealt with days like this differently and he felt as though he'd forgotten how he did it. He was supposed to shut it all down until he was able to file it away, but he was thinking of Luna's eyes when he'd told her about Jim's death. He was thinking about the enormity of everything he felt when he hugged Maëlys goodbye at Valérie's house.

Maybe Guy was right to consider moving him to a desk job if he couldn't handle digging bodies out of the ice any more. But those bodies had been someone's father, someone's partner – maybe someone's *brother*. If he didn't bring them down, someone else would have to and it was all he'd ever wanted to do, bring people home.

Jumping down from the hélico, his muscles complained, even as his lungs rejoiced to be back in normal air pressure. Tugging his helmet off, he hauled the gear towards the hangar, but stopped short when he heard Eric behind him.

'Team two is back on solid ground! Your mascot is still working, I see.'

He lifted his hand to shake Eric's. 'What do you mean? Luna's here?'

Eric shook his head. 'But she was earlier. She helped us get those last coordinates. It looked like she was worried about you.'

Yannick was too tired to examine his feelings – or stop them from welling up. He accepted Eric's offer to clean the equipment and pack away and fumbled for his phone.

'I hope you weren't too worried,' he babbled as soon as she accepted the call. 'Thank you for helping today.'

She hesitated and he held his breath, needing to hear her voice. 'I was glad to help. I'm even more glad you're down safe.'

'Luna,' he said on a sigh, not even sure what he needed to say.

'I understand if you want to be alone, but if you need to...' she began hesitantly, trailing off.

'I need to,' he said with relief that she'd opened the door for him. He needed a hug. He needed to kiss her until this intense awareness of his own mortality faded. He probably shouldn't take out his hard day on her. But he was going to do it anyway and hope she was tough enough to withstand everything he felt right now.

'I'll meet you at your house,' she promised and Yannick couldn't get there fast enough.

When he didn't even wait until they'd taken their shoes off, she thankfully didn't seem offended, hooking an arm around his neck and hanging on as he pressed her into the door from the mudroom into the house so he could kiss her harder.

'Are you okay?' she asked with a gasp as his lips settled on her neck, breathing in.

'No,' he said, surprising himself as well. 'Argh, yes, I am okay, but also... no.' He kissed her again, for longer this time, drawing it out. He hoisted her into his arms, holding her up while he tugged off her boots, toeing off his own and carrying her into the house.

She surprised him too by taking up where he'd left off, pressing kisses to his neck, his ear, his cheek, with a hint of desperation. His skin tingled and his blood rushed and he didn't understand how such an awful day could end like this, with her lips exploring his dirty skin.

'I haven't showered,' he pointed out with a grimace.

'I don't care,' she replied, kissing his jaw. 'Don't you dare let go of me now.'

He stumbled, her words knocking the breath out of him when he'd only just got used to breathing at a comfortable altitude. He took her at her word, carried her upstairs and dropped her onto the bed, shedding his clothes.

There were too many layers and he was too impatient to even peel her out of her thermal shirt, simply shoving his hands up, sliding his palms over her skin. She felt like the sunshine on his face in summer. When he nipped at her neck, she tasted like life.

She stayed with him, responding to his rough touch, granting him the freedom of her body and he couldn't help asking himself how he'd ever deserved this – or how he ever could. As he kissed her shoulder, panting, after they'd finished, one thought settled heavily in his mind: he would go through a lot to have experienced that moment with her.

* * *

Luna arrived back at Silvia's the following morning with the same sense she'd had when she'd come down from the mountain, of experiencing a lifetime in a day, when only an afternoon and an evening had passed in the real world.

Yannick had left early for his shift that morning, after a thorough goodbye that still gave her tingles just thinking about it. She was one of the only people in the world who'd seen the fierce soul Yannick kept under his calm exterior. He'd handed her his vulnerability and she promised herself she'd protect it with everything she had.

Guy looked up from the croissant he was dipping in his coffee.

'Bonjour,' she said hesitantly.

'Bonjour.' Guy nodded. 'Thank you for your help yesterday.'

Silvia bustled in, giving her an enormous hug and sitting her at the table. 'Sit down and relax, tesoro, and no need to talk about what happened if you don't want to.'

Luna nodded but she caught Guy's gaze as Silvia headed back into the kitchen with the empty cafetière.

'Comment va-t-il?' Guy asked quietly.

'He's okay,' she responded, giving Guy's arm a reassuring squeeze.

'Now, prepare yourself, chérie,' Silvia said, sitting down next to Luna, joyfully mixing her endearments as usual. 'Your letter arrived.'

Luna sat bolt upright as Silvia produced the A4 envelope, post-marked Corsica, shaking it gently when Luna didn't immediately grasp for it. She took the letter gingerly, an unexpected bolt of dread shooting through her.

'Coincidence that you were born in Corte,' Guy said absently. 'I know the commandant of the PGHM unit there. He's coming for a conference just before Easter.'

'Your mother was a nurse, no?' Silvia asked. 'Perhaps the commandant from Corsica knew her.'

'It's possible,' Guy agreed, sipping his coffee, but Luna couldn't see past the unknown contents of the letter in her hand.

'You can take it down to your room if you like,' Silvia said gravely. 'You don't have to open it in front of us.'

'I have a class this morning anyway,' she choked out. 'I think it'll have to wait.' She set down her half-eaten croissant, feeling guilty, but her stomach churned so much, she wouldn't be able to keep down another bite.

Stowing the letter in her bag, she was glad of the distraction of the class with staff from a holiday rental village. She texted Yannick on her way there, trying not to notice how little snow now lay on the footpaths as spring crept over the valley.

On peut se voir ce soir?

It was somehow easier to ask if she could see him tonight in French, as though she could pretend her inhibitions didn't exist, as she pretended to be French. His reply didn't drop in until after her class.

I have Maëlys again tonight.

She tried not to sigh in disappointment. Perhaps she shouldn't be leaning on him the way everyone else did. But he followed up that message with another an hour later.

But I'd like to see you if you don't mind dinner with a five-year-old.

He greeted her that evening with his bright, bashful smile and a furtive kiss and she still couldn't believe she was fortunate enough to have him in her life. He dropped her hand before they stepped into the living room, where Maëlys appeared to be tearing paper to shreds.

'Eh, louloute,' he said gently, ducking to get her attention as he beckoned Luna over. 'Remember my friend?'

Maëlys glanced at Luna without acknowledging her. 'Oui, la femme lune,' she said, returning to her task. Luna knew she had no right, but she was strangely gratified to be known as the 'moon woman' by this little girl. With her serious eyes and sparse words, Maëlys was so obviously a part of Yannick that it was difficult for Luna to stop thinking of her more fondly than a mere 'friend' of her father's should.

It took some effort to coax the little girl into bed after dinner and when Yannick padded downstairs again, still in his blue uniform shirt and heavy-duty trousers, Luna wondered whether it was fair to make use of his emotional stability for the task she had to accomplish. He paused, tilting his head and studying her.

'Je suis content que tu sois là,' he said simply and that was all it took for her worries to flee. *I'm happy you're here.* 'Do you believe me?'

'Yes,' she said with a wobbly smile. 'I believe everything you say with that face, remember?'

He gave her an earnest look that faltered just enough that she knew he was about to joke. 'I say everything with this face.' His grin broke out and Luna wished the letter away again.

She patted the sofa next to her and curled into him when he sank down. She hesitated just long enough for his eyes to drift closed and for more words to emerge from his lips that seemed designed to make her heart break.

'Elle me fait peur,' he murmured. *She scares me.*

Luna suspected he didn't mean because it was so difficult to get Maëlys to go to sleep.

'She's so important to me, but I can't make her any guarantees.'

'Nobody can make guarantees,' she said softly. 'My mum didn't do anything more dangerous than driving a car, but she was still gone before she was sixty.'

His expression was distant. 'Looking at her while she sleeps is like looking down from halfway up a climb – or maybe it's like looking at the sky from a vertical rock face above. The world tilts and I can't tell which way is up.'

'I think that's... feelings, right?' she said, biting her lip. It was *love.*

'Perhaps you're right,' he said, turning to rest his chin against the top of her head. 'Je suis content,' he repeated softly. 'What about you? Do you need something?'

She wished she could reassure him that the only reason she'd asked to come was because she wanted to spend as much time with him as she could before she had to go. It would have been the truth, but she wouldn't have been brave enough to send that text without another reason as well.

'I got the letter from Corsica,' she murmured.

His head came back up. 'What? What did it say?'

'I haven't opened it, yet.'

'That's why you wanted to come tonight,' he commented.

She hesitated for a moment. 'Part of the reason,' she admitted.

'Alors, do you want to open it?'

'Not really,' she mumbled, fetching her bag from where she'd left it beside the sofa.

'Mmm?'

All he had to do was lower his thick brow and all her confusion came tumbling out. 'I know I have to open it if I'm going to try to do this thing people call "moving on".' She sighed deeply. 'If Jim is my father, then it's all solved. I can be certain that accepting the money is the right thing to do and I'll have some second-hand memories to treasure. But I'll also have proof that my mum kept secrets from me.'

Not to mention no reason to stay in Chamonix any longer – except for the reason that was sitting beside her, and she wasn't supposed to count him.

'But if Jim isn't my father, I'll be in exactly the same position I was in when I arrived: no idea why he made me the beneficiary and not convinced I should take the money.'

'Do you really think you're in the same position as when you arrived?' he asked.

'Of course not,' she admitted, struggling to meet his grave gaze. 'But if he wasn't my father, then what do the past three months mean?'

His sigh was as deep as hers had been. 'I think you should open it.' Trust Yannick to stay focussed on the practical.

She coaxed open the envelope and drew out the single piece of paper. This was one time in her life she needed to focus on what was in front of her and not the fog of distraction.

It was a surprisingly simple document, with 'Mairie de Corte' on the letterhead and a few lines of text. As soon as she saw the information about the 'enfant' at the top, she froze. Blinking back surprise, she scanned the rest of the document with information about her father and then her mother, including addresses – matching addresses – in Corte.

'What is it?' Yannick asked, squeezing her arm.

'My parents were married,' she muttered, wondering if she'd simply assumed her whole life that her birth had been something of an accident. She cradled her forehead in her hand, staring at the document in her lap. 'I wasn't born Luna Rowntree at all. Look at this: Luna Marie Favre. Jim was not my father.'

33

Her mum hadn't lied; her father's name had been Robert Favre, a man who was even more of a mystery to her than Robert Durand – and a man who possibly had no connection to Chamonix, except the suspicious timing of Luna's conception.

'You still needed to get to know Jim,' Yannick pointed out evenly. 'You might not have all the answers, but he was an old friend of your mother. You can accept the money and move on.'

How difficult she found that prospect: moving on. She'd hoped to find something of her mum here, but she'd only found more mysteries. Even worse, she might never know why Jim had done what he'd done, why he'd hung a photo of her on the wall of a remote mountain refuge – and she might never be able to use his money with a clear conscience.

She thought, with a shot of dismay, that the birth certificate might not even be correct. Wasn't there a chance she'd been conceived here, but then her mother married Robert Favre in Corsica? Luna was so sick of contemplating her mum's heartache.

Her choices were to shove her conscience and learn to accept her windfall, or stick to her quixotic guns and perhaps donate the money to a local cause. Even Yannick, who'd seemed to at least tolerate her idealism, was telling her to take the money.

But who was Robert Favre?

'Shhh, Luna. Tout va bien.' His voice was low in her ear as he assured her everything would be all right and she realised she'd tucked herself into him and tears stained her cheeks. How ridiculous that he'd brought dead bodies home yesterday and here she was leaking all over him because she didn't know anything about her father – a fact that was not news.

'I don't know what to do,' she muttered. Poor Yannick. If he hadn't been so solid, so incredibly steadfast, he might not have had to put up with her outburst.

'What do you want to do?' he asked gently.

The answer, unfortunately, came to her in an instant. 'I want my mum to be alive.' She braced herself for the lecture on grief that she was accustomed to hearing – from Lydia, from Aiden, from concerned strangers who realised she was a thirty-year-old woman who couldn't cope with losing her mother.

But all he did was wrap his arms around her and she remembered how she'd felt at the refuge: insignificant and fragile, but so alive in every miraculous cell of her body. She'd hoped she'd carried something of her mum with her to that refuge, but perhaps the place had meant nothing to June.

It meant something to me.

The next surprise came in the form of Yannick's whispered words to her. 'I wish I could bring her back for you.'

A fresh tumble of tears wet her cheeks. 'You can't,' she pointed out baldly. 'Even you, gendarme secouriste, can't bring her back.'

'I know,' he murmured. 'But I still wish I could.'

He drew back to study her. 'Because I know how you feel, Luna. I've spent twenty years wasting energy wishing someone was alive and if I knew how to stop it, I'd tell you.'

'Yannick,' was all she could say. She wasn't even sure if she was chiding him or feeling for him.

'I was thinking about that yesterday, during the avalanche search,' he murmured. 'Perhaps I'm more human than I thought.'

She tucked her head against his shoulder and patted his gilet, just over the patch with the yellow stripe denoting his rank. 'It's kind of attractive when you're superhuman, but I like it better when you're mortal with me.'

His hesitant smile took a few tries before it stretched. She loved that smile. If she could package it up and take it home with her, she would. 'You make me want to be mortal.'

Her heart stuttered and she wanted to say something stupid like: *That's the most romantic thing anyone has ever said to me.*

'I'd hate to think I made you mortal at just the wrong moment,' she said softly, tracing his rank insignia.

'It's not your responsibility,' he countered.

No, but what if you were my responsibility? She shook off the tempting thought.

'But what will you do, now? You've paid your respects to Jim. What more *can* you do? Will you go to Corsica? You have a few weeks before you're supposed to start your job.'

That thought hurt. She didn't have anything more she could do here, but she'd stay until the last moment, if Yannick would keep holding her like this.

He frowned suddenly, lifting his arm from around her and snagging the paper that sat limply in her lap. 'Attends, did you see this?' He stilled, his gaze roving the piece of paper, but he was much further away in his thoughts. 'I know why the name is familiar,' he marvelled under his breath.

'What?'

'Robert Favre,' he said slowly. 'I thought I'd heard the name before and now I've seen this on your birth certificate, I know where: on the memorial stone in the car park at Cordial.'

'What?' She leaned over the paper as he pointed to the section where the details of the father were set out. Under the heading, 'Profession' was listed: Maréchal-des-Logis-chef, Gendarmerie Nationale. Her skin prickled. 'Robert Favre was in the PGHM,' she realised with a gasp.

* * *

After finding Robert Favre in plain sight, she could piece his life together at the click of a button, when Guy released his personnel file as she was his next of kin.

Silvia appeared at Cordial to sit with her while she read the file on the computer on Monday and Guy hovered in the background.

'If I'd heard your father's name before this, I might have put everything together sooner,' Guy commented. 'We hold a memorial ceremony every year for our officers who died in the course of their duties.'

'Are there many?' Luna looked up to ask, trying not to feel the flash of Yannick's face as she did so.

Guy shook his head. 'In the sixty-five years of operation of the PGHM Chamonix, sixty-five gendarmes lost their lives, but in recent years, there has only been one terrible accident here on the massif, during a training exercise.'

Luna gulped. One was enough now she'd got to know the men and women of this unit. She turned back to the computer to read, wondering if she was going to wish she'd left everything a mystery.

Born in Aix-en-Provence in 1960, Robert Favre had joined the Gendarmerie at twenty, and had been assigned to the PGHM when he was twenty-six. He'd been an avid climber and spent three months convalescing from a bad fall during a private climb when he was thirty.

She had to imagine when he'd met her mum, as there was no specific information. Guy suggested he might have met her delivering victims to the hospital. Robert's marriage was noted in his file: 29 March 1993. June would already have been pregnant with Luna by then. He was transferred at his own request to Corsica in June 1993 but returned to Chamonix at the end of 1995 – without June and Luna, she suspected, although his change of marital status wasn't noted in the file.

The circumstances of his death in early 1997 were recorded in extensive detail, not all of which Luna understood. He had rescued a group of climbers whose route had been cut off by an avalanche and who were clinging to a rock face, only for a secondary avalanche to sweep him away.

He'd been airlifted alive to the hospital in Annecy, where he'd subsequently died, and his body had been released to his family in Aix-en-Provence.

'But look, chérie,' Silvia said, pointing at the screen. 'It says, "The group was led by mountain guide Jim de Montagne."'

Luna's heart sank and her vision blurred, even as the answer to her quest had now fallen into her lap. She wasn't happy that answer was *guilt*. There was too much guilt, too much pride, too much risk in this crazy town already for that to be her answer.

The report attributed no fault to Jim but Luna understood something of the people who lived in the shadow of the mountain and she knew Jim would have felt guilty even if he hadn't disconnected her father's rope himself.

A flash of intuition brought the memory of Jim's photos to mind, particularly that startling picture of two boys climbing barefoot, with 'Robert' written on the back. Flicking through her photos on her phone, she compared the handwriting on the back of each, which was all the confirmation she needed of something she already understood in her heart. Jim had written 'Robert' on the back of the photo, because it was a photo of him and Robert Favre – the other Robert, the reason Jim had adopted his nickname.

Luna hated the thought of an old, precious friendship torn apart in the blink of an eye, but if Jim had been good friends with her father, it would explain why he'd hung a photo of June and Luna at the refuge, why he'd felt a sense of responsibility to his friend's child after Robert's death.

He'd paid the insurance premiums for years on the macabre chance that he would die, too, and he could make up for an accident that had happened when Luna was only three years old.

'The commandant of the unit in Corsica will be here next week for the general's visit. I believe he's been stationed in Corte for years. Perhaps he remembers your father? Otherwise, I will think about who among the retired secouristes was assigned here during that time. I'll ask around to see if we can find out anything more.'

Luna wasn't sure she wanted to know what had gone wrong between her parents. Even hearing that they'd been madly in love at one time would hurt – if it was true. But if she didn't find out the truth, she'd be in danger of projecting her own feelings onto the memory of her mother and that wouldn't help anyone, especially not her.

Silvia squeezed her shoulder. 'But it's good to know, right? You are the daughter of a gendarme secouriste. That is special.'

'No wonder team two adopted you as their mascot. You're one of us,' Guy said with a smile.

The memories of everything she'd achieved since Christmas washed over her. Teaching the gendarmes of the PGHM and learning from them would be one of the highlights of her life – something she would tell her grandchildren about over and over again until it became a joke: '*Aw, Grandma's going on about the peh-jeh-ash-ehm again. You didn't really jump out of a helicopter, Gran.*'

But her mother hadn't told her a single story about her work at the hospital – or falling in love with a gendarme called Robert Favre. Had the end of their relationship been so hurtful she never wanted to revisit it? What did that mean for the imminent end of Luna's own Chamonix romance?

'Let me take you home and make you a tisane,' Silvia said, tugging her to her feet. 'You've been on quite a journey.'

'It does feel like it's been a journey,' she muttered. Unfortunately, her destination had only become less distinct over time. Did she even want a cottage, or was it just because a house signified stability and she and her mum had always talked about gardens and living in the countryside?

As she fetched her coat, Yannick ducked into the room, rushing over to greet her with a quick kiss. 'I thought I saw you. Everything okay?' he asked. Everything was better for having seen him. She clutched his gilet.

But Luna only had time to nod before Silvia appeared, glancing between the two of them with a knot between her brows. Any other time, Luna would have admired the faint blush on Yannick's cheeks, but she was so mixed up, uncertain what she was supposed to be feeling.

'Hum, I'll... talk to you later,' he mumbled.

'We'll see you on Wednesday,' Silvia said brightly – too brightly.

'Wednesday?'

'Your birthday,' she reminded him with amusement. 'Guy mentioned it.'

'Ah, ouais, c'est ça. I'll see you' – he glanced briefly at Luna – 'there.'

Luna stretched up to press a soft kiss to his lips. 'I'll see you soon,' she whispered.

The trip back to Argentière in Silvia's jeep was quiet and Luna stared out the window as the forest flew by, speckled with green and brown, white and grey as the melting snow dropped from the trees, revealing the skeletons of larch interspersed with lush, dark pines. Sunshine speckled the rocks above the treeline and a dramatic swoosh of cloud had descended over the peaks.

Silvia couldn't refrain from commenting for long. 'I had a feeling about you, Luna,' she began.

'I know,' Luna responded with a smile.

'I was certain that you would find a lot more than just answers to your questions.'

'Which is why you gave me the carnelian and the condom – I did realise this, Silvia,' she said fondly.

'But I did *not* expect it would be him,' Silvia said flatly. 'I didn't mean for you to break your heart.'

Luna glanced up at the sky, at the top of the enormous formations of rock that made up the lower peaks of the Aiguilles Rouges massif, on the opposite side of the valley from Mont Blanc. Wafts of cloud meandered across the sky and, for a moment, she felt as though she was looking down.

He might well break her heart, but she murmured, 'How could it be anyone else?'

34

If Yannick had realised that celebrating his birthday could bring so much joy to others, he might have done it more often. Half the unit had turned out, as well as the guides, hospital staff and ski patrollers he knew best, but rarely had time to socialise with. The bar was full of animated chatter, every stool and bench taken, as people discussed the imminent end of winter at the resorts and the beginning of the spring ski touring season.

Yannick perched against the bar with a beer, talking to Guy and Eric, with Maëlys on a stool next to him slurping raspberry cordial. Valérie and her boyfriend Fabien were talking to one of the pilots. It was surprisingly straightforward socialising in a large group with his ex-wife and her new partner – even less awkward than meeting in private. He would look for other occasions where it might be possible, not least because he was proud to have Maëlys with him, as though he were a normal father.

He had Eric to thank for making his birthday party happen, but Luna as well. She sat with a group of secouristes who seemed to be enjoying making her gape at their latest exploits. Jean-Marc had dragged her to their table when she'd arrived, explaining that his year at military school had honoured her father in a ceremony as part of their graduation.

She'd been a little dazed at that explanation. The complex rituals of honouring the fallen in the gendarmerie would seem strange to an outsider. Yannick had sensed she'd been off-balance, even sad, ever since Friday night, when she'd discovered Robert Favre had been a gendarme in the PGHM – and especially on Monday after learning that Jim had been present when her father had died.

Or perhaps he was projecting his own uncertain feelings about her imminent departure onto her. Easter was in ten days. She'd found her father, learned about Jim, answered her questions. She would have to conclude that she'd fulfilled her mission.

And he would compartmentalise his feelings – somehow.

'We should go soon,' he heard Valérie say behind him.

He turned and squeezed her arm. 'Thanks for coming.'

She must have felt the genuineness of his comment because she gave him a wistful smile. 'It's nice to see everyone again. But I didn't get to meet the moon woman,' she said, casting a pointed look at Luna.

He opened his mouth to make excuses for Luna's presence in his house last week, but he couldn't work out what to say. Obviously Maëlys had mentioned something. Valérie probably suspected the truth: that Luna had stayed that night, the first woman he'd been with since the separation. 'Luna's too popular at the moment,' he decided to say instead, 'since everyone discovered her father was a secouriste.'

Valérie let the topic go. 'I'll meet her next time,' she said.

He swallowed, wondering whether to tell her there wouldn't be a next time.

'Oh, Yannick,' she muttered. 'Still making excuses to keep your distance?' She turned to Maëlys before he could answer. 'Time to go, poussin,' she said, pressing a kiss to the top of their daughter's head. 'You've got school tomorrow.'

'Thanks for coming, louloute,' he said, scooping her up in a hug before she could express the discontent he could see in her wobbly lower lip. 'We'll go skiing soon.'

'Can I have another sirop de framboise when we go skiing?' she asked.

'That was a treat for my birthday. Thanks for helping me celebrate.' Giving Valérie a kiss goodbye, he set his daughter down and waved them off.

Eric ordered him another beer, but he quickly overruled his friend. 'I have to drive home.'

Hands on his hips, Eric faced him. 'Not tonight, you don't. Luna told me she would drive – and she told me to order you another beer. It's *your* birthday old man. Say thank you and act happy.'

'I am happy!' he insisted.

Eric gave him an amused look. 'I almost believe you for once,' he said with a wink, pushing off the bar after he'd paid for Yannick's beer.

Jean-Yves, recovered from his avalanche ordeal, took Eric's place a moment later, ordering schnaps. Yannick raised his beer and Jean-Yves mirrored the action with his cognac glass. They fell into conversation about the state of the routes and the snowpack, the usual topics.

After a pregnant silence, Jean-Yves said, 'So she's not Jim's daughter after all. I thought I saw something, but it must have been wishful thinking. She's dark, while Jim was blond. I didn't know Robert Favre, but he and Jim were friends, I believe.'

'If Jim put a photo of Luna in the refuge, they must have been.'

'What happened out there at the refuge?' he asked, casually sipping his liqueur.

About to protest that nothing had happened, Yannick paused

to consider. 'I left him there, as he would have wanted,' he muttered. 'I took Luna up and she paid her respects and then... You were right. I had to let go of the rope.' He didn't mention the other part of the journey to the refuge that had given him closure: his dawn confession that should have shocked Luna and had instead led to him holding her close that night – and many nights since. 'Jim was there when Luna's father died. Those insurance premiums were a kind of rope for him too.'

'Holding another rope these days?' Jean-Yves asked with a toothy smile.

'Mmm?'

'You can't take your eyes off her.'

He blinked at Jean-Yves. 'She's leaving soon,' he muttered. He could see the truth in her eyes whenever they spoke about Easter .

The guide downed the last of his schnaps and clapped him on the shoulder. 'But she's here now – or are we both imagining her getting up to dance?'

Yannick's gaze landed on her without effort – since Jean-Yves was right and he'd been searching her out all evening. She was saying something to Bast and Matthieu as the three of them stood to join the crowd forming on the cramped dance floor. A faint smile crossed his lips.

He nodded in farewell as Jean-Yves stood to leave and leaned back on the bar, still marvelling at the fact that so many people had turned out for his wretched thirty-ninth birthday. At least it would make him smile next year when he wasn't game enough to celebrate his fortieth – except maybe at the top of the Grandes Jorasses.

Silvia approached the bar, closely followed by Guy. 'Here, Yanni,' Guy said, passing him another beer. 'Happy birthday.'

'Merci, patron,' he said. One didn't turn down a beer from the commandant.

Guy shook him by the shoulder. 'You've done well for yourself. Cute kid. You've made Warrant Officer.'

Yannick could almost hear him add, 'Got married, got divorced,' but Guy hadn't said it and it was probably only Yannick himself thinking it.

'Are we still heading up to Tour Noir next week? Stay over at the Swiss cabin to check in with their side of the border?'

Why was Yannick's first thought that he'd miss a night with Luna? She wouldn't stay every single night until she left anyway, and he was supposed to be compartmentalising.

'You're going up *again*?' Silvia exclaimed, but apparently immediately thought better of her outburst and studied her cocktail with too much interest. 'Just let me know when, as usual, so I don't send out a search party,' she continued coolly.

Yannick thought of everything Luna had told him about her friend and his commandant. She'd been preoccupied with whether or not they were in love – a question Yannick had said didn't have the black-or-white answer she assumed it would, especially not with these two hard-nosed lovers.

But what if it was black and white to Luna? She would love the same way she danced – with her whole being. What if she loved *him*? He didn't often indulge in wishful thinking, but the thought unravelled before he could stop it.

She would smile at him on the days filled with paperwork and wrap her arms around him after a demanding shift. She would adore Maëlys just as she was, with no expectations of making her talk or act like other kids. She would *protect* him, although that was a strange thought. What did he need protecting from?

The place where his thoughts snagged, was on the realisation that she would give up anything – change everything – if she loved him. And what could he give her in return? Bad days when he couldn't save a victim; long, unpredictable hours away and the emotional distance to do his job – if his job didn't get him killed and leave her with a pension to go with the insurance payout she hadn't wanted.

What if *she* left *him*? What if he started to hope he might get that wedding band tattoo after all and then she *left*? Like Valérie – like his *brother*?

He found himself wishing she might love him and also hoping she didn't. She couldn't, surely. They'd only known each other three months. Even if they'd accidentally tied the first loops of a love knot, she could still untie it.

He stared at her from across the room. She was so beautiful when she danced – utterly unique. Her hair had grown a little longer since December and nearly brushed her shoulders – not quite neat, as usual.

'Are you going to join her?' Silvia asked and Yannick realised he hadn't been following the conversation. 'I think everyone has realised there's something going on between you two.'

He shook his head with an awkward laugh. 'I can't dance.' His thirty-ninth birthday didn't seem like the time to start. 'She's having fun,' he added when both Silvia and Guy gave him sceptical looks.

'She could be having fun with *you*,' Silvia pointed out wryly. 'You could be having fun.'

'Why does everyone think I'm not having fun?' he muttered.

Guy squeezed his shoulder. 'Because we've been with you these past couple of years. And you know what it's like to hear the word "can't", Yanni.'

He met the commandant's gaze for a brief moment of understanding. Was that what he'd done to himself? Had he given up?

'She's leaving soon,' he insisted.

'We're all leaving soon, right – one way or another?' said Guy thoughtfully.

Luna caught sight of him from where she was swaying, her arms high. Tilting her head, she gave him an inviting smile. With a questioning gesture, she beckoned for him to join her.

What would it be like to dance with her between the tables? He pushed off the bar before he could change his mind. He suspected it would feel like *living*.

* * *

Luna couldn't stifle a delighted laugh when Yannick came striding towards her from the bar. She hadn't expected him to join her. She hadn't been certain what he wanted from her at his party and had managed to avoid clinging to him all night, even though his friends and colleagues all felt like cheap substitutes for what she truly wanted.

Bast and Jean-Marc turned to see what had made her smile and good-natured whistles and cat-calls followed. Yannick didn't hesitate, although he did crook his head in that self-deprecating shrug she knew well and colour grew on his cheeks.

She reached out and drew him into their midst when he came near enough. He was surprised and hesitant at first, his hands settling tentatively at her waist, but letting go again quickly.

With a self-conscious laugh, he listened to the music and let his body follow. He was an adorably bad dancer, shuffling and bobbing and occasionally missing the beat, but she guessed he was just tipsy enough to let it happen and to her, he'd never looked finer.

Pounding dance music all sounded the same to Luna, but was certainly good for moving. His gaze settled on her again and again, occasionally accompanied by that smile that suggested he couldn't believe his luck.

It wasn't adrenaline surging through her veins, but it was *some-*

thing, as she danced her carefree steps with the sweetest, most gorgeous person she'd ever met. She wasn't sure which of them made the first move, but Yannick was suddenly closer as the song changed to something less frenetic. She looped her arms around his neck and his hands slipped around her back. The cat-calls spread around the bar and his blush deepened. But instead of hiding, he dipped his head and brushed his mouth over hers in a brief kiss.

The cat-calls became whistles and she wrapped her arms more tightly around his neck to hide her face. She caught his grin and lifted her chin again for another kiss. This one was longer – aching and tender with everything she felt for him.

Pressing two quick kisses to his lips as they tried to break apart again, she framed his face with her hands and whispered, 'Happy birthday.' Another kiss. 'I'm so glad you're alive.'

35

'It's Good Friday in five days, Luna. School starts in three weeks and Mrs Goode has already retired.'

'Hello to you too, Lyd. I don't have much time.' Luna didn't have any answers to the questions her cousin was sure to ask either.

'Why not? It's Sunday. You don't teach classes on Sundays, do you?' Lydia had been outraged that Luna had taken the odd Saturday morning language workshop.

'Of course not. Erm...' It took her a moment to decide how to explain where she was going. 'I'm off to a military parade.' It wasn't a parade exactly, but she still wasn't quite certain what kind of ceremony it would turn out to be.

'A what?'

Luna sighed, realising how much she had to tell Lyd – about her mum, about Jim, and she wasn't sure what she could tell Lyd about Yannick that would make sense. 'It's a long story.'

'You can tell me when you get here. When are you leaving?'

'I don't know exactly. It's such a long drive.' And every time she thought about starting her car again, she imagined Yannick appearing and arresting her for driving without winter tyres. At least, that's what she wished would happen when she turned her car in the direction of the motorway. She felt oddly guilty for thinking about leaving him, but he had never asked her to stay.

The number of times she'd considered throwing a few crystals into the wind and deciding to stay... But it wasn't just her risk to take. She'd learned to love Cham, but it would only be home to her if Yannick was part of that and she couldn't be certain he'd let her stay for him. She wished she hadn't built her safety net with the job in Sheffield starting after Easter. If she'd just taken off for the wilds of the Alps with no plans to go back, she could have pretended she was staying for any other reason and not expected anything from a man who'd lost so much that he might not trust again.

'Would you believe it, that cottage has come back on the market, Lu,' Lyd continued enthusiastically. 'The original sale fell through. It was meant to be. I bet there's a grumpy but handsome neighbour who'll be captivated when he sees you gardening and start smiling again.'

Luna choked, hoping it sounded more like a scoff. 'Anyone who falls in love with me because they saw me as a sweaty mess from gardening would definitely have a screw loose.'

Was the charming, comfortable little cottage her future, or was there something much bigger, more frightening in store for her?

'I've got to go. I'll let you know how I'm getting on,' she said evasively.

'Enjoy your military parade,' Lyd replied sceptically.

Luna drove into town with Silvia, trying to ignore the mildness of the air when they got out in the car park. The forests boasted a faint tinge of lime green over the brown winter larches. The spruces showed their deep colour, now the snow had been banished from the lower slopes. She could even make out the greyish white tongue of the Bossons glacier across the valley, the tail of the icefall dipping below the spring snowline.

The square in front of the Maison de la Montagne was decked out in the two-tone blue of the PGHM, as well as banners and ribbons from the civilian rescue services, the guides and other local clubs. Luna and Silvia arrived a few minutes late and the ceremony had already begun.

'You'll know which one is the general because of all his decorations,' Silvia had said on the way down. Luna had thought she'd meant military decorations for many acts of service, but when she saw the man standing at the lectern giving a speech, she supposed Silvia might have meant the buttons and pins and ribbons and stars all over his uniform, not to mention his cylindrical hat with its gold embroidery and bright red stripe.

On one side of the square stood the gendarmes secouristes – all forty-eight from the Chamonix unit, minus the four who were on duty at the DZ. Luna picked out Yannick immediately, standing to attention in the second row, looking rather quaint in a beret and a mountaineer's uniform of navy-blue three-quarter-length trousers and woolly socks above a pair of hiking boots. He wore a white decorative rope braid as a sash over his bright blue jacket.

The square was dotted with other personnel in dress uniform in various shades of blue and black, with gold buttons and funny hats. Members of the public – local families and gawking tourists – gathered on the street.

The general passed over to the commandant from Corsica, Captain Breuil, who gave his own rousing – and mercifully short – speech, finishing with a quote that made Silvia roll her eyes. 'As the explorer Paul-Émile Victor said, "La seule chose qu'on est sûr de ne pas réussir est..."'

Luna's mind raced to translate the convoluted sentence: *The only thing you're certain not to succeed at, is...*

'They always mention Paul-Émile Victor at these ceremonies,' Silvia muttered and Luna missed the second half of the sentence. 'That and honouring the fallen, like it's some kind of consolation prize for dying – at least you know your name will be spoken by generations of gendarmes who come after you.'

Luna swallowed, thinking of Robert Favre and the list of names on the memorial stone around the corner at Cordial. It seemed right to honour them, but Silvia had a point that it was a poor consolation prize – especially for their families.

'Sometimes I think...' she whispered to Silvia, uncertain whether she should have said anything. 'I wonder whether you really like men in uniform at all,' she finished with a wince.

Silvia smiled in response, but it was a dim smile, her eyes clouded. 'You are beginning to understand,' she said, as though the thought made her sad. She glanced away quickly.

'Silvia,' Luna began, grasping her friend's arm. 'Have *you* lost someone?'

Her friend's only response was to look down. 'Haven't we all?' She swallowed and a moment later, her chin was up again, the frailty banished and Luna's question unanswered.

After Captain Breuil was finished, the general called two gendarmes and a winch mechanic in dress uniform to the front and pinned ribbons above their breast pockets while Guy announced the reasons for the medals for bravery.

'That was Yannick last year in the autumn,' Silvia murmured. 'He received a medal for the intervention where Jim died.'

All the breath escaped Luna's lungs as she glanced at Yannick, who stood impassively with no hint of the discomfort she knew he must feel. She could just see the ribbon above his left breast pocket in the colours of the French flag with a medal hanging beneath.

After the ceremony there was a reception at Cordial, which Luna imagined was a much tastier affair than it would have been in England. Although she would truly have enjoyed a custard cream right then, the pistachio macaron and a tiny pain au chocolat that melted in her mouth made up for missing a biscuit and a cup of tea.

She was dipping her pain au chocolate into her coffee like a real French person when Yannick approached, giving her a kiss on the cheek in greeting. 'Nice uniform,' she said with a smile, tweaking his thick felt beret. 'I would never have guessed you had this in the back of your closet.'

'Are you embarrassed to be seen with me?'

She shook her head vehemently. 'It's cute,' she insisted. '*You're* cute,' she corrected with a wink that earned her another kiss on the cheek.

'Come and meet Captain Breuil,' he said, taking her elbow.

The Corsican captain was around Guy's age and greeted Yannick by name and with a warm handshake. After Yannick briskly explained Luna's identity, the captain turned to her sharply. It took him several moments to collect himself enough to speak.

'Your father was Robert Favre?' he asked, his voice high. 'But that means you're the baby... who fell at Calacuccia.'

Luna couldn't react at first. He was supposed to be talking about her father, not *her*. What did he mean by *fell*?

Yannick's hand closed around her arm and she suspected she'd been swaying. 'Perhaps we can discuss this in an office, Captain?'

'Certainly, I...' The captain studied her again. 'I never thought I'd find out what happened to you. This is marvellous.'

What was marvellous to him was disturbing to her. Even after she'd sat down and taken a gulp of coffee to clear her head, she felt stunned.

'I don't know what you're talking about,' she admitted.

The captain drew back in surprise. 'Your mother never told you what happened?'

Luna shook her head in dismay. There was so much June had never told her.

'I served with Robert in Corte. He was a passionate climber – he opened several new routes for us in the Restonica valley. Luna – that's your name, isn't it? A good name for a mountaineer's child. Robert brought you to Cordial quite often. I think he tried to help your mother. She was alone with a young child and we were a small team in Corte. Robert was called out a lot.'

'But you mentioned a fall?'

His eyes grew grave. 'He took you with him one day, to a climbing area. He went with some friends, so you were well supervised. He even had a full-body harness for you so you could scramble on the rocks.'

Luna felt faintly sick. It took all her effort not to brush the scar on her head that had suddenly taken on a horrible new meaning. 'But there was an accident,' she managed flatly.

Captain Breuil nodded. 'The friends testified that you were either in the carrier or clipped in to a rope at all times, but perhaps you were more dexterous than they'd realised and you unclipped yourself.'

Luna's nose stung, even though she was only just beginning to understand what had happened – and guess at what the repercussions had been. She thought with dismay that it could have been the first time in her life someone had called her 'dexterous'.

'You fell fifty metres,' Captain Breuil said solemnly.

Yannick shuddered next to her, turning away with a gulp. He braced his elbows on his knees and clutched his head in his hands.

'What happened then?' Luna asked.

'I arrived in the helicopter with a doctor,' the captain continued. 'It was one of the most heart-breaking missions of my life. You, a tiny child with injuries that looked so serious and Robert... He was in shock.'

'I hate to think how my mother reacted.'

'Not well, I'm afraid,' he confirmed. 'I'd never seen a family member so distraught – but you were also the youngest victim I'd ever attended. You were in hospital for a month and needed surgery. It was nothing short of a miracle that you walked out, but the doctors wouldn't rule out permanent brain injury, given your age at the time.'

Luna stared, her skin crawling. It was bizarre to think she'd been so badly injured and known nothing about it, that she could have died. Her mum's anxiety, her wariness of new places and new activities, it had all been because of Luna and the combination of mistakes and good fortune that had changed their lives in a matter of seconds.

She'd grown up in the shadow of the mountains and she'd never known it.

'I'm truly pleased to see you a healthy adult,' Captain Breuil remarked. 'Robert would have... it would have helped him to know you were well.'

'What happened after I was released from hospital? I know my parents must have divorced.'

'The accident was investigated and it was a difficult case. It's not unusual for hikers to take children in carriers and harnesses, especially experienced climbers like your father. He'd done it before apparently.'

'But that wasn't enough for my mum to accept what had happened.'

'It wasn't enough for your *father* to accept what had happened.' Captain Breuil sighed deeply. 'He started drinking too much and came close to failing his psychological assessment when he applied for the transfer back to Chamonix. To be honest, I was saddened, but not surprised, to hear he died a year later.'

Luna's throat closed and she couldn't stop them this time when the first tears tumbled down her cheeks. The captain hadn't been surprised that Robert had destroyed his own life because of *her*. She was dogged by other people's guilt – how was she supposed to release them all when it was too late?

Her mum had died feeling guilty for keeping so much from Luna. Robert had died guilty for allowing his daughter to get hurt. Jim had died after spending years in the turmoil of guilt at his friend's death.

Yannick would feel guilty for allowing her to fall in love with him, when he couldn't offer a happy ending.

She hated to think of team two calling her their *mascot*. It seemed she'd caused problems for everyone who'd ever loved her.

Sucking in a ragged breath, she stood to go. She had to get out of this place before something else happened to make people suffer. She should buy a damn cottage and never think of tragic accidents, bloody victims or frozen corpses for the rest of her life!

36

She felt like impulsive, incompetent odd duck Luna Marie again two hours later, sitting in the old Astra with her forehead pressed to the steering wheel in frustration. She'd thrown her clothes hurriedly into her suitcase, grabbed her mum out of the back of the closet and raced for the old vehicle – her escape route – only to find that the damn thing wouldn't start.

Her first thought was that Yannick would probably be able to fix it with a paperclip, but she couldn't ask him. She was running away from him and every terrifying thing she felt for him. She didn't know what to do. It seemed a little dramatic to walk to the train station in Argentière dragging her enormous suitcase and she didn't know when the trains ran, or where to. It had grown dark alarmingly quickly, even though the days had lengthened since the chilly December night she'd arrived.

Before she could work out where else she could run, a familiar SUV turned into Silvia's driveway with a flash of headlights and her heart stopped. She wasn't ready for this confrontation. She didn't know how to explain her feelings, her disappointment at the truth of the past and why it made so much difference to her future.

She wasn't sure she could stop herself blurting out how much she loved him, even though the admission would solve nothing.

Yannick climbed out of the SUV, his expression creased with dismay, and looked up at Silvia's front door. He hadn't seen her yet. She could still make a dash for freedom – but just seeing him standing there in his ridiculous uniform, the beret now missing, grounded her panicking brain. She shoved open the door and hauled herself out with a sigh.

'Luna!' He strode quickly to where she stood, his boots crunching on the gravel, and dipped his head to look into her face. His palms landed on her cheeks and the tears pricked her eyes again. 'You want to leave? Now?' His brow was slanted and she'd bet if she asked him to drive her to Paris this very evening, he'd do it. 'Parle-moi. Tell me what you feel.'

She had no hope of holding herself together. Her forehead dropped to his chest and she shuddered, overcome by hurt and second-hand grief, with only more of the same to come. He spoke to her the way he had on the ski slopes – in his calm, mountain-rescue voice. It soothed her as intended, but also made her bitter. Wasn't he the least bit disappointed that she had to go?

Sighing deeply, she searched for perspective. She wanted him to compartmentalise. He was right that he needed to be able to keep control of his emotions to do his job and, when a split-second misjudgement could lead to death or serious injury, she wouldn't wish him anything less than total control.

She peered up along the valley at the brilliant white peaks of Mont Blanc and the Dome du Goûter. It was a clear evening with the pinpricks of stars in full twinkle. She turned slowly, searching for the moon, but she couldn't see it. She would like to have seen that enormous mountain moon one last time – the one she'd been named after.

'It's all my fault,' she declared. 'No, I know that's nonsense, but you asked me what I feel and... I feel some stupid things sometimes.' She felt his lips on the top of her head and sank into him.

'I've watched you feel some beautiful things too,' he said softly.

Most of them with you. 'I'm just... tired,' she began. 'So many people have died. I'm tired of hurting. I need lessons from the PGHM about how to deal with shock.'

'I don't think that's a class that anyone ever passes with full marks.' He sighed. 'You need to go home,' he commented flatly. It wasn't a question.

'I think I do,' she murmured. 'I followed my conscience here, but I have to find a way to let it all go. I wish I'd never found out about my accident.'

'That *definitely* wasn't your fault.'

'It *was*,' she contradicted him gently. 'But I'll have to forgive myself for it, since I wasn't even two years old.' She grimaced. 'I wish my history wasn't so sad. It was bad enough grieving for Mum for way too long—'

He gave her a sceptical look that reminded her of his confession that he'd been grieving for his brother for twenty years.

'I suppose I can't live in the past,' she reworded carefully. 'I'll have to make my own way ahead, without always looking back.' That would be even harder, when looking back was what she'd have to do to see this face.

'Do you know what you want?' he asked, his voice hesitant.

'I have no idea,' she admitted, her hand coming up to clutch his uniform. *Maybe you.* What would he say to that? Would he put on his gentle gendarme voice and kindly point out that she'd taken a wrong turn? Even hearing him admit, with some feeling, that they'd shared a lot and he'd always remember her was more than she could take right now.

'You'll work it out,' he murmured, wrapping an arm around

her. 'Don't forget you skied the Vallée Blanche and climbed to the refuge in winter.'

She swallowed. 'It feels like it was a different me who did all those things. I wanted answers to make myself feel better, but all I got were answers that made everything worse. It's typical. I always screw things up.'

'No, you don't.' There was his gendarme voice – not the gentle one but the bossy one. 'Without you, I wouldn't have left Jim in peace where he wanted to rest. You reminded me to celebrate my life and maybe convinced me I deserve good things sometimes too.'

'You deserve the best things,' she murmured. Not a mixed-up, sentimental person who'd only just learned to ski.

'Whatever you decide, remember... you touched all our hearts. Especially mine.'

'I love you!' she said on a hiccough.

Shit, damn. She'd known she'd do something stupid like say that. His mouth dropped open but she pushed away from him before she could read any more of the damage done in his expression.

'I mean, I know... we shared some intense moments and I'm probably not thinking clearly. You don't have to say anything and don't you dare feel guilty about this.'

'Luna—' The crack in his voice was more than she could take. 'I'm not—'

'I know,' she cut him off. 'I truly didn't say that to make you change anything or admit anything. You are who you are and I love you for that, but I also know why it wouldn't work, so... I have to go.' She turned away, giving the Astra a frustrated tap. 'Except the stupid car doesn't work.'

'Winter tyres are required until—'

'I know, I know! I imagined you arresting me and...'

'Sunday,' he finished. 'After next Sunday, I wouldn't have anything to arrest you for.'

'Except my mum's ashes on the back seat,' she said with a grimace.

'I'm not going to arrest you for that,' he said with a hint of a wry smile. 'It's a civil offence.'

More's the pity. She opened the back door and hauled her suitcase out again. 'I didn't pack properly anyway.'

'But don't leave – in a hurry,' he said stiltedly.

She bit her lip and turned back to him. Nodding, her emotions wobbling again, she closed the door and met his gaze. 'I'll get the car fixed and wait until I can drive it legally.'

'And stay at mine until you go? I don't... We could stay warm a little longer.'

Her breath whooshed from her lungs and she abandoned her suitcase to rush at him. He dipped his head, meeting her for the kiss she'd wanted since the moment he arrived. His arms were tight around her and the kiss deep and hard and fraught. She realised he was upset, too and wrapped her arms around his neck.

'I'm so glad you're alive, Luna.' He repeated her words from the night of his birthday, pressing light kisses to her lips. His fingers found the scar on her head and brushed over the spot with a slight tremor. 'So glad.'

* * *

Luna awoke in the dim early light of her last morning in Chamonix to see Yannick's dark eyes across the pillow already open and watching her. He didn't say anything and neither did she. His gaze flickered over her face, so she studied him in return – that broad, square jaw, shadowed with stubble, his straight hair sticking up in places.

She hoped he wouldn't regret giving them both this last week together, even though it would make the shock of her departure more jarring. She wouldn't have exchanged that week for any number of cottages – just as she could never imagine exchanging his face for another.

'Do you think we leave little bits of our soul around the place?' she asked with a self-deprecating laugh.

'It feels that way,' he replied. 'Where have you left bits of your soul? In the Vallée Blanche, no?'

She nodded. 'On the terrace of the refuge, looking out over the glacier.'

'Me, too.'

She snuggled closer, enjoying the idea of the little pieces of their souls spending eternity together in that frozen place where time passed differently. 'At La Flégère as well,' she added. 'With Mum.'

'And at Cordial and the Maison de la Montagne,' he pointed out. 'You know we aren't going anywhere – except up. You could come back if you want. You're welcome here, all the time.'

He meant 'anytime' surely, but his comment made Luna's throat thick and she sat up, her hair falling around her face in its usual early-morning chaos. 'I would like to see the glaciers in summer,' she said with a smile. Hopefully he wouldn't notice it didn't reach her eyes.

'And the forests in autumn.'

'I'll miss Cham,' she said, turning to him, 'but not as much as I'll miss you.' She would have liked to enjoy his blush, but she hauled herself out of bed so she didn't start blubbering. 'I have to get back to Silvia's to pack. Will I... are you coming to say goodbye?'

He hesitated for a moment too long. 'Yes,' he eventually said. 'I'm not looking forward to it, but I'll be there. Can I drive you to Silvia's now?'

She shook her head. 'I'd like to take the bus and walk up one last time. You lounge in bed,' she teased, knowing the instant she was gone he'd be off on a run or perhaps head to the climbing gym.

Collecting her toothbrush and the other small things she'd left at his house over the past few weeks, she felt the sting behind her eyes and tried not to look too closely at the photos, the fireplace – *anything*, because everything in Yannick's house held memories for her. Giving him a quick kiss at the door and one wild look, she tried to escape before the tears fell.

As the gravel crunched under her boots, she struggled to walk away. Although she'd see him in a couple of hours, her intuition insisted she might never see him again. Stupid intuition. It had been misfiring from the moment she'd landed in this place.

Resisting one last look at his house, she stuffed her hands in her pockets and kept her head down. Just before she left his front garden, seemingly of its own accord, her hand grasped the woollen glove that had lived in her pocket since the colder days of winter and tugged it out. Dropping it onto the footpath, she took a deep breath and forced herself to keep going.

Her composure didn't survive arriving back at Silvia's to be wrapped in a hug. She buried her face in the other woman's wild, curly hair as Silvia thumped her on the back.

'If it's so bad, why don't you stay? I can always find you more work if that's the problem.'

She shook her head. 'I just... I need stability. I don't belong here. I'm not built for taking risks.' *With my heart*. 'You understand that.'

Silvia studied her in dismay.

'Did the crystals say I'd stay?' Luna asked, grimacing when she heard the bitter scepticism in her own tone. If she'd been looking for signs over the past few months, she unfortunately had too many now: the cottage was available; it was the new moon so she couldn't see it again before she left; her heart just about broke every time she thought of Yannick.

'The crystals would only say you'd stay if that's what you wanted. You know they only bring out and enhance what's already inside you.'

Luna thought back to her earliest days in Chamonix, where the simplest things had been a challenge and she'd fiddled endlessly with her moonstone, hoping it worked. She barely recognised that Luna, even though learning about her accident had felt like setting herself back a year in her attempt to live life like a normal person who didn't feel everything so deeply.

'Part of me does want to stay,' she admitted. 'But look what happened to my mum – to my dad! I don't know if I'm strong enough to try. Like you said, everyone's lost someone, here. I can't hold it all in like you can.'

Silvia's expression progressed to alarm. 'Don't compare yourself to me. I underestimated you when you arrived, but I was delighted to be proven wrong. We won't be the same without you – Guy and me, the team at the PGHM, *Yannick*. What intuition I felt about your love life was guesswork, because Chamonix is the kind of place where relationships often come and go and that's what some people want – perhaps that's what *I* have experienced. But you surprised me by choosing Yannick because you travel your own path. You are bold and kind and you know what life is beyond the thrill of the moment.'

Luna blinked at her, wondering who this person was that Silvia saw. Luna was just the absent-minded daughter of June Rowntree, who'd created problems from the day she was conceived.

'I don't want to hurt anyone or get hurt. I have to be sensible,' she murmured, to herself as well. 'I've got a few last things to pack.'

Luna trudged downstairs, saddened to be saying goodbye to

her little room. She wanted to escape instead of enduring all the goodbyes – the way Yannick and Valérie had decided she shouldn't say a final goodbye to Maëlys as it might upset her routine. What about Luna's routine? She was upset.

With shaking hands, she picked up Jim's ice axe from the little pile of equipment she'd accumulated over the past few months. She'd sold her skis and boots, but the ice axe was a fresh dilemma. She wanted the token to remember Jim by, but it only reminded her of the journey she'd undertaken – and what she'd achieved. She studied the blade, brushing her fingertip over the jagged teeth. She'd really scrambled up a rock face covered in packed snow and ice. It almost didn't seem real any more.

Folding the axe in a travel towel, she tucked it among her clothes in the suitcase. She'd just have to make sure she kept it safely away from Lydia's kids. She didn't want to imagine the questions Lyd would ask if she saw it. Her time in Chamonix was another life – another her. She knew exactly how her mum had felt all those years ago.

Luna had sealed the urn with strong tape, but she still grimaced when she packed her mum's ashes into the bottom of the bag. She had to find somewhere for June to rest. It was one of the many practical tasks she'd neglected over the past year. She thought she'd feel guilty about saying a final goodbye, but she was fresh out of guilt. It needed to be done.

Meeting Silvia by the door, she heaved her suitcase to the car, trying not to allow her thoughts to flash back to Christmas night, her wrong turn and her first glimpse of a face that had become precious to her.

She took one last look around the valley. Not only had the moon hidden itself the past two nights, the mountain peaks were missing that day, covered in a thick layer of fog that began just above the treeline.

Luna wasn't surprised when Silvia pressed a stone into her hand. 'Citrine,' her friend murmured, 'for optimism. You deserve the brightest future Luna, and I'll miss you.'

Luna held on as her friend gripped her tight, ignoring the tears that began to fall.

'Is Yannick coming?' Silvia asked.

She nodded, mumbling, 'Any minute.' He had to give back her glove.

'Well, I'll... leave him to say the final goodbye, hmm?' she said, giving Luna one more squeeze before she disappeared back inside.

Except, Yannick wasn't there a minute later. He didn't arrive at all.

37

Uncertain of what to do, Luna waited twenty minutes, checking her phone, her finger hovering over the call button. She didn't want to go without seeing him again, but hadn't she just been railing against the necessity of a messy goodbye? Perhaps he was just being merciful – or thought he was being merciful, the great, compartmentalising oaf.

Had he thought the glove was a souvenir, instead of a weak attempt to force him to come, when she'd sensed his reluctance? He didn't want to get hurt either.

She needed to leave if she was to make it to Troyes before it got dark. She glanced frantically around her as she opened the car door, reason telling her that if he hadn't arrived in the past twenty minutes, he wasn't going to arrive in the next ten seconds – and what would a final goodbye bring her anyway?

With a deep, fraught huff, she plonked down into the driver's seat and tugged the door closed with a finality that scared her. Seeds of doubt sprouted in her mind – in her heart. She knew what she was running away from, but what was she running *towards*? The cottage was her mum's dream and Sheffield was her cousin's home.

What did *she* want?

Part of her hoped the car wouldn't start, even though it had been serviced through the week. Hoping for a sign, she turned the key in the ignition – and the stupid engine roared to life immediately. Driving carefully down the winding road that was thankfully no longer icy, she headed for the motorway, her thoughts swirling.

What had her mum felt when she'd left Chamonix with Robert – pregnant and newly married? Luna waited for the familiar comfort of imagining she was following in June's footsteps, but it didn't come. She didn't want to follow in her mum's footsteps. She didn't want to spend the rest of her life safe, but alone, with only memories of loving someone.

She was being dramatic and sentimental – as usual. She was only thirty. She had every chance of meeting someone, even if it wasn't the handsome neighbour Lyd had joked about. Maybe she'd even have her own kids – and she would bore those grandkids with all her stories of Chamonix, of the time when the glaciers still extended to the lower altitudes.

But whoever she met in the future would have to live with the knowledge that she'd loved Yannick first.

Her brain foggy with her mess of emotions, she was surprised by the sudden splutter of the engine. Panicking, she took the next exit off the motorway and pulled over at the first safe spot. She'd forgotten to tell the mechanic about the broken fuel light and she hadn't filled the tank since... the last time she'd been in Troyes.

With a bleak laugh, she realised she'd just used up the last of Yannick's petrol.

She pulled out her phone to check where she was and noticed that she had a voice message. Seeing it was from Yannick, she fumbled in her rush to open the app. Her hands shaking, she pressed play and listened with her heart in her throat.

'Luna, désolé,' he apologised in clipped French, rustling noises and the throb of a helicopter in the background. 'I was called in for a rescue caravan on Mont Maudit. We're going up now. I don't know if I could have changed anything... I wanted to give your glove back, but I also didn't want to give it back,' he admitted, as though he wasn't entirely sure what he wanted to say. 'I can't ask you to wait because I don't know when I'll get down – *if* I'll get down. I can't ask you,' he repeated. 'But I wanted to,' he said in a rush. 'I have to go.'

* * *

Yannick hurriedly stowed his phone in his jacket pocket, zipped up over his avalanche transceiver and ran for the helicopter, popping his radio receiver back into his ear. He couldn't be sure he'd done the right thing, sending that entirely inadequate message, but it was done and he'd pick up the pieces later. For now, he had a job to do.

He was the last to climb aboard and greeted Marina with a grim nod, clipping into the safety cable and attaching his heavy pack as well. Choucas lifted off the ground as the winchman drew the door closed and they ascended swiftly over the forest.

'*Choucas, this is Cordial,*' he heard over the radio. '*Weather conditions remain unstable. Dropping Yanni and Marina at the refuge might prove difficult. Winching to an alternative drop could be necessary at your discretion. Matthieu and Patrice are in place to provide anchor and rope support.*'

Yannick had followed the progress of his teammates via radio after they'd been dropped up to the Cosmiques refuge. Matthieu had muttered about the crap visibility and Patrice had been cursing the wind. A helicopter runner drop had been ruled out at the last minute and they'd had to winch down.

His blood was pumping already, and it wasn't only because of the imminent drop into high mountain conditions. Between the briefings and the urgent packing, the route planning and strategy meetings, he'd missed Luna's departure.

It shouldn't have made any difference. She was leaving and he would never have stopped her. But missing her had taken away his final chance to... he didn't know what.

When he'd found her glove in his garden, the sting of memory had given him a glimpse of everything he was about to lose. He'd stared at the accessory, flooded with bittersweet feelings and the sudden desire to share all his fears and suffer her reaction, whatever that would be. But he'd already been called in and only had time to stuff the glove into his pocket.

Team two had pulled together admirably. There had been ample volunteers, but it had been clear who would lead. In low visibility, at high altitude, for a laborious rope caravan rescue effort, Yannick was the logical choice. Philippe hadn't even questioned it – hadn't even asked Yannick. He didn't need to.

Two ski tourers had got lost at altitude, with heavy fog and storms forecast, one already showing signs of altitude sickness. Yannick would accept missing Luna for the chance of saving someone's life, but he hadn't been able to go up without first sending her a message, even though it probably wouldn't change anything.

She'd already left. She'd interpret his message as a missed-chance, one of those poignant moments in literature, and she'd have the comfort of knowing she'd meant a lot to him too.

But she didn't understand how much. If Luna had been sitting across from him in the helicopter right now, the way she had on New Year's Eve when they'd met for the second time and admired the moon together, he might have told her he loved her.

Conditions were as bad as they'd feared up there and he shared a brief look with Marina as they accepted that they'd have to winch down. The wind roared in his ears as he swung out of the helicopter, glad of his goggles and his mask, that quickly iced up from his breath. He gritted his teeth through the dizzying spins of the winch drop and landed with a shot of adrenaline onto crunchy, crystalline snow.

In thirty seconds he'd sunk an anchor and tethered, and he signalled for the winchman to draw up the cable. He could barely see the ridge in front of him, let alone the refuge he knew should be on the hill above. All around him was swirling sky, as though nothing existed – maybe not even himself.

Marina dropped down a few metres away and he roped her in swiftly, signalling when she could unclip the winch hook. Without words, they trudged along the ridge in the rhythm of sinking stakes, clipping in and unclipping. Visibility was so poor that it took a few extra minutes to find Matthieu and Patrice.

'*Yanni, give me a report. Is it safe to proceed or do we need to pick you up again?*' came the team leader's voice over the radio.

'Do we have an update from the victims?' Yannick asked.

'*Yes, no change. We have approximate localisation from their phones. The second victim is still conscious, but immobile. The first victim is lucid and mobile.*'

They'd already decided in the valley, as a unit, that saving the second victim was unlikely to succeed with the helicopter unable to fly in the area and visibility too poor to ski among the avalanche fields, crevasses and seracs. Yannick needed to focus on the safety of his team and the chance of bringing the first victim home.

'Stand by Philippe' Yannick said as he took his time with the assessment. Checking his GPS and Matthieu's backup device, he peered at the snow and along the route they'd follow to reach the two stranded skiers.

'Okay to proceed?' he called out to the other three, receiving a round of thumbs up. 'Philippe, this is Yanni,' he said into the radio. 'We're going to proceed. Keep me updated on the storms.'

Checking the ropes one more time and switching on the powerful headlamps on their helmets, they set off into the white-out, in silence for the first few hundred metres. It was slow going, requiring concentration and an ice axe in hand.

Despite the last-minute decision to contact Luna, Yannick's focus was sharp. His goal was clear, each step made with care to bring everyone down again in one piece.

All his concentration was required as they moved further along the ridge. Visibility deteriorated and he began to doubt their ability to get back via the same route, calculating the distance to the nearest refuge, just in case a storm hit without warning.

'Cordial?' he radioed in. 'How's the weather looking? It's fucking foggy up here.'

'*Hé Yanni,*' he heard in reply. '*Nothing new on the storm. You've got a few hours at least.*'

'What about the hélico? Current conditions?'

'*Laurent is worried about the wind. Chances are bad for a hélico pick-up. You guys all right up there? Not going to get lost?*'

'I could put a pin on the map where we're currently standing. I just don't like the idea of camping out tonight with a pair of strangers who snore,' he joked, but it wouldn't be the first time he'd bivouacked with a group of victims through a storm. It would be better if he knew with certainty the condition of the second man, though. 'C'est bon, Cordial,' he confirmed. They were okay – for now.

38

Screw being sensible. Luna jumped out of the car so quickly, she nearly ended up sprawled on the concrete. Abandoning her suitcase – and her mum's ashes, she raced for the little wooden shelter that looked like a bus stop, only to find it was a tourist information board.

She should never have left! She should have realised that, if he hadn't showed up, his work could easily have been the reason. She'd been self-centred and sad and stupidly sensible, when she should have followed her gut, abandoned her departure and gone to find him.

Frantically scanning the map, she discovered she wasn't far from the Saint Gervais train station, but her phone informed her she'd just missed a train. She kicked herself for not realising sooner that she wasn't supposed to leave. She called Silvia.

'Did you know Yannick had been sent up to Mont Maudit?' she asked before even greeting her friend.

'I'm so glad to hear from you, *chérie*. I knew you wouldn't go through with leaving. Where are you? Quick, meet me at Cordial and we will see what the news is.'

'Um,' Luna said with a gulp. 'I did leave,' she murmured. 'But I... ran out of petrol. Could you come and get me? I'll text you where I am.'

'I'll be right there.'

Luna paced furiously under the shelter as a few drops of rain fell, wondering how she could have been so stupid. Running away couldn't keep her or Yannick safe. He'd still be somewhere up on that cursed mountain right now, even if she hadn't known. She'd thought running away would help her not to care, but it was far too late for that.

She couldn't keep him safe, but she could be there when he came back down. If he'd been overly conscientious in showing her the pressures he faced, then it was partly because he was afraid of being hurt, too, but she wouldn't have fallen in love with him if she couldn't face the realities of his job.

Bad luck, Yannick, she thought with a shake of her head. *I'm not keeping my distance.* She meant something to him, he was just too scared to admit it, scared that he'd lose her, or that she'd *leave*.

Argh, she was so annoyed with herself for being so dense.

She raced for Silvia's jeep the moment it pulled up, stowing her suitcase and jumping in. 'Quick!'

Silvia turned to her with a grave expression. 'Luna, he's not going to be back for hours yet.'

'What? Why not?' Her skin prickled with misgiving.

'It's a land caravan. The helicopter couldn't fly above the cloud. They're bringing the victims down on foot.'

The look Silvia gave her suggested Luna's expression was a little wild. 'I'm just saying you will have to wait to see him.'

'But at least if I'm waiting at Cordial—' She cut herself off as the helplessness threatened to wipe away all the perspective she'd gained in the last half hour. 'I left before I'd thought things through. I don't want... anything to happen to him before...'

Silvia's lips twitched. 'Before you tell him you love him?'

'I already did that,' Luna mumbled. 'But then I ruined it again by talking about leaving right after. I don't want anything to happen to him before I've *shown* him what the "I love you" means. Maybe then he'll believe me.'

'Or maybe he's learned to believe you in the meantime,' Silvia said lightly as she put the car into gear and headed for Chamonix. Luna heard his message again in her mind.

'I didn't try to really get through to him,' she reflected. 'I said "can't".'

Silvia chuckled. '"La seule chose qu'on est sûr de ne pas réussir est celle qu'on ne tente pas,"' she quoted wryly. 'Paul-Émile Victor,' she added. 'I never thought that damned quote would come in handy one day.'

'The one from the military ceremony,' Luna remembered. '"The only thing we are certain not to succeed at is the thing we don't attempt,"' she translated carefully. 'You talked too much and I missed the second half! Maybe I would have got the message in time and not sent Yannick out into the mountains thinking I don't love him enough!'

'Enough? For what?'

Luna didn't hesitate over her answer. 'To wave him off every time he goes on a mission. And to be there when he comes back.'

Silvia squeezed her hand briefly. 'I suppose it can be that simple.'

* * *

'Qu'est-ce qui ne va pas?' Luna asked urgently in the first quiet moment after she walked into in the operations room at Cordial. As soon as she and Silvia had arrived at the quaint old building, it had been clear that something was wrong. There were people everywhere: rescuers, support staff, volunteers from the civilian groups. She'd picked up a hint from Yannick's tone in his message and from Silvia's warning that this wasn't quite a usual mission.

'No, no, everything's fine,' the officer sitting at the radio assured her with a quick smile. She caught sight of Emilien in the corridor and pulled him aside.

'They're all right,' Emilien confirmed. 'The weather isn't playing along, but we're used to that. They haven't reached the victims yet.'

'*Cordial, we have a visual on the victims*,' she heard crackling over the radio, and her heart leaped. '*West face of Maudit. We're making our way there, but it's tough. A lot of wind.*'

'Bien reçu, Yanni.' The radio operator spoke into the radio as two others hastily added a pin to a map and compared the topographical representation with a live graphic of wind and storm conditions on the computer.

Silvia left to reopen the shop but Luna was so distracted she barely reacted to her friend's kiss on the cheek. She felt Emilien's hand on her shoulder and realised he'd fetched her a chair. 'Don't worry, he'll be back soon. A little bit of wind never hurt anyone,' he said with a wink that didn't reassure Luna in the least.

The radio traffic went back and forth, time passing in slow-motion, as Yannick described the situation in detail. She gathered the outlook for one of the victims, who was only barely conscious, was grim. An agonising ten minutes passed while Yannick conferred with a doctor on the ground and they administered medicine, as well as oxygen.

The team leader, Philippe was also on the radio from the DZ, piping up with suggestions. Luna peered up at the sky that seemed to darken even in that moment.

'*Hélico is grounded,*' Philippe confirmed. '*Descend to Cosmiques and we'll try to get a doctor up to you from the cable car, if you think he can make it.'*

Yannick made a grunt of effort over the radio and said in English, *'Hey, mate. Chris. You think you can make Cosmiques? I help you.'*

A shiver went through Luna as she heard his wonderful, ungrammatical sentences in English with the 'h' left off.

'Cordial,' he continued quietly, *'I don't think he'll make it. He needs to descend more than he needs a doctor. We'll have a better chance of getting him down to Grands Mulets and it's another 500 metres lower.'*

'Yanni, is that wise?' Philippe asked from the DZ. Luna listened in alarm as they weighed options and the weak voice of the victim insisting he would try could be heard in the background. She realised he must be suffering from acute altitude sickness and felt faintly sick herself.

After a few more minutes of deliberation, Yannick's caravan prepared to set off again, with both mountaineers, for the quicker, more dangerous descent.

The afternoon wore on, but Luna was glued to her chair, jumping when the radio crackled to life with Yannick's regular updates. She didn't know how he could find his way in the thick cloud that had descended further into the valley now. The threat of a storm lingered.

A timer on the wall ticked over to five hours and the conversation from the support staff analysing the weather turned grim, with words like 'windchill factor' and 'hypothermia' bandied about more frequently. Guy strode into a room asking for an update, sparking a tight smile for Luna in greeting.

'Yanni,' he barked into the radio after the support staff had updated him. *'Keep the radio on now.'*

'Pigé, patron,' he said, confirming he'd understood.

Luna wasn't sure if it was better that she could hear everything, now radio contact was being maintained. Every heavy breath was audible, every time someone swiped a hand over their face it made a screech. Emilien poked his head back into the room, coming to stand by Luna.

'Putain!' sounded suddenly at one point in a strained mutter. 'He's heavy.'

Matthieu offered to take a turn with the sick man and Yannick agreed to hand him over in ten minutes.

'I didn't know Yannick swore,' Luna whispered to Emilien.

'Everyone swears at 4,000 metres, prof,' Emilien replied with a smile. 'Even Yanni.'

The calm in the room started to feel artificial as the light dimmed outside with the imminent sunset. The sound of the wind, picked up by the helmet microphones, became more violent. Yannick's updates became clipped but more frequent, remarking on seracs or rocky outcroppings that made Luna wonder how many times he'd completed this trek.

If she'd been exposed to all this on day one, she might have run in the opposite direction, but she was in too deep now, and she would have to find her own way through her feelings for a man who led rope caravans and hauled sick men through windstorms at 4,000 metres of altitude.

With a flurry of radio conversations, Luna understood that Chris's condition had deteriorated to the point that he'd fainted and was barely able to move. Yannick and Matthieu were supporting him with ropes and their bodies and a pair of guides who were staying at the refuge were heading out to meet them in support.

There was a worrying growl of, *'Where's the fucking track?'* from Yannick, followed by loud scuffles and beeping from what she assumed was the GPS. Luna held her breath, refusing to imagine them wandering around aimlessly as the light faded.

'You getting lost up there?' the radio operator asked with artificial brightness.

'*No, no. Found it. Visibility is shit. On the final ascent, unless we find those crevasses Jean-Marc mentioned last week. Please tell me we've got twenty minutes of weather.*'

'Uh, take the short cut!' called out the gendarme in the corner with his eyes glued to the weather projections.

Yannick groaned over the radio and Luna peered out the window in alarm, jumping when a lightning flash illuminated the steeple of the church by the Maison de la Montagne and the forested hill behind. A few raindrops splattered on the windows. It was worryingly dark outside and Luna was shocked to discover it was nearly seven o'clock.

How long had they been up there now? The timer showed over seven hours. She could only hope they were as impervious to the perils of altitude and the cold as everyone seemed to think they were. She hadn't even thought about how they would get down if the helicopter remained grounded.

Her endurance would be put to the test already and it seemed she would have to wait to wrap her arms around him and tell him she'd been wrong to leave. She glanced at Guy and then at the twin bedroom with ugly checked duvets she glimpsed through a connecting door. That was where she would be sleeping tonight.

Just let them try to kick her out.

39

'We have visual contact on the refuge – finally. It's only twenty fucking metres away,' Yannick said between panting breaths. His powerful headlamp created a strange, luminous halo in the dense fog ahead, but he could make out the outline of the Refuge des Grands Mulets, perched on a protruding rock amidst the icefields. His hand ached from the grip he had on the victim's jacket. 'Chris is still with us – just,' he added, patting the man on the back, where he swayed on his feet.

'*Okay, you can stop chatting now, and get inside,*' Guy's voice came over the radio.

Yannick and Marina worked together to haul the barely conscious victim up the short, final climb to the door of the refuge and they spilled inside on a gust of snowflakes and piercing wind. The refuge hadn't officially opened for the season, but the guardian was already there preparing and another team had climbed up to meet them. They'd already melted water, prepared blankets and the emergency hyperbaric chamber for Chris. Even though the winter annex wasn't heated, simply coming in from the wind was a shock of relief that made him realise how much his skin stung, after giving Chris his mask about two hours ago.

'That was the slowest descent in history,' Marina mumbled, untying Pavel, the other stranded skier, from the ropes. Their colleagues took charge of Chris, helping him into the inflated canvas tube where they could pump oxygen and add air pressure to relieve his altitude sickness enough to get him through the night.

Food, water and minor first aid took up the next hour, the wind whistling fiercely outside and blowing snow against the window panes. Feeling gradually returned to Yannick's skin at the same rate as the adrenaline retreated and his first thought was a flash of memory: Luna's hands on his cheeks.

I like your face... I love you.

His breath escaped in a rush as he paced slowly back and forth, keeping his blood flowing to help warm his body. He'd been an idiot to not recognise what they'd meant to each other, even with no expectation of a future.

Stuffing his hand in his pocket, he clutched her glove. It was a heady feeling, imagining coming back down to her after a difficult mission, but what if he didn't come back, like Julien? What if *she* didn't come back?

She'd admitted she'd imagined kissing him and he'd responded that it was an *honour* to spend time with her. Quel imbécile! Why couldn't he have told her that he yearned and *wanted* things whenever she was close? With a gulp, he realised why he hadn't said any of that. It sounded horrible. He didn't know how to express these things – he barely knew how to *feel* them.

It was all too late anyway. She'd be in Troyes by now, arriving at her new home tomorrow, to buy her cottage and never think about snow boots and goggles and ice axes – or avalanches, rockfalls and rescues – ever again.

Patrice clapped him on the shoulder and passed him a cup of hot, sweet tea. 'It's a devil of a storm out there. Glad I was behind you. I bet they'll even get some snow in the valley tonight.'

Yannick's only reply was an inarticulate grunt. It was better than saying what he was thinking: Luna wasn't in the damn valley anyway.

'Spring skiers will be out tomorrow. More work,' Patrice continued, rubbing his hands together and blowing on them. Yannick tried to say something about crevasses or cornices – or *anything* – but he drew a blank.

'She left today, didn't she?' Patrice said, his tone changing. 'You going to be okay?'

No, he wasn't – not until he'd spoken to her. Frowning, Yannick reached into his coat for his phone and switched it on. It took a while to find the weak signal at the refuge, but, when it did... nothing. He had no messages. His voice message was marked as opened, but there was no reply.

'*Ah, Yanni?*' he heard suddenly over the radio. There was a hesitant tone in Guy's voice. Was there bad news on the weather?

'I'm here, patron,' he answered, glad of the distraction.

'*Très bien. I just needed confirmation that you're okay.*'

'The other team just got Chris out of the chamber and he's eating – a bit more aware. He'll survive the night. The other victim, Pavel, is a bit shocked, early hypothermia, but no signs of frostbite.'

'*Well done. That's good. I'm getting regular updates on the victims, I was just checking in with you.*'

His brow knit. 'Me?'

Guy chuckled. '*Yes, team two's lucky mascot has been pulling her hair out all afternoon and I'm trying to convince her to go home.*'

Yannick stilled, wavering on his feet as though he'd been hit with an updraft on a rockface. The thrill that shivered through his body was difficult to bear. He'd never wanted to be down in the valley more, but it was also enough knowing she was there.

'She's... refusing to leave?' he clarified hesitantly. The annex had gone quiet and he noticed Patrice, Matthieu and Marina all watching him.

'*Eyeing up the beds at Cordial, yes. Do you want to say something?*'

'Oui! Non, en fait. Hmm—' His throat closed. 'Luna?' he began, trying to forget the presence of his entire team either in the room up here or down there with the commandant. He loved the shape of her name on his lips, the connection with the moon. 'Don't go – anywhere,' he said in English. 'I'm coming down – for you.'

Guy chuckled over the radio. His colleagues stifled grins and amused looks and Yannick stared at the ceiling as his cheeks heated.

'*Is that a promise or a threat?*' Guy asked. '*But you were supposed to tell her to go home! I'll have to charge her half-board and endure her complaints about the quality of the coffee.*'

'I'm not going to tell her to go home!'

'*Home to Silvia's, you idiot! Or maybe to your house. Either way, I think it's a lost cause. She's grown roots in the chair at Cordial. Hmm? You want to tell him something? She heard you swearing for the first time, Yanni. Now she knows you're not perfect.*'

He snorted. Luna was well aware that he wasn't perfect, and that's what made it so unbelievable that she was there, listening to him curse the weather and breathe too loudly.

Her voice came over the radio, a little distant, as though she wasn't close enough to the microphone. '*Don't worry. I'll be here.*'

'Luna?' he began again. If there was one thing he should have learned years ago, it was that sometimes life didn't wait for you to say what you needed to say. The words bubbled out of him: 'Je t'aime très fort.' *I love you so much.*

Laughing cheers and applause rang out both in the annex and

over the radio, giving her no chance to respond – not that he needed a response. He felt better just for saying it.

Finally, the din quietened enough for him to hear her take a deep breath and say, '*You know I love you too. But get down safe and let me hear you say it in person.*'

'Oui, madame,' he said and stood automatically to attention, a smile breaking out on his face.

'Boss, if he keeps smiling like an imbecile, he's going to hurt himself,' Patrice said into his radio, giving him a shove. 'It was fucking cold out there and he's got windburn.'

'*All right, someone wrap him in a blanket and make sure he doesn't get hypothermia. Silvia would never forgive me. Check in every three hours unless something changes and we'll see if we can get that hélico off the ground tomorrow. Cordial terminé, les gars.*'

Silence fell in the annex as the transmission ended and Yannick felt every eye on him – even Pavel and Chris were watching.

'What?' Yannick asked the team, his lips still twitching with a smile trying to escape.

'That was... touching,' Marina said with a snort.

'I expect an invitation to the wedding,' Matthieu said earnestly and then burst out laughing. 'Your face, Yanni!'

'All right, all right,' he said, holding up his hands to quiet them. 'But you heard her. I'm feeling pretty damn good right now.'

* * *

Luna forced herself awake during the night every time the team up at the refuge checked in, but there was nothing to report and she went groggily back to sleep. Silvia woke her early the next morning with coffee and a plate of pastries, reminding her of Guy's joke about half-board the evening before – which brought back with a flush of emotion the memory of Yannick telling her he loved her.

The moment had felt surreal – the crackly, disembodied voice, filled with more emotion than she'd ever hoped to hear, especially when he was still on duty.

She just needed him to come down again, and everything would fall into place.

A fresh coating of snow covered Chamonix when she peered out the window. It was a strange place, a frontier town at the edge of the great glacial wilderness, unconquerable by the insignificant hands and feet of humans. It was a place that forced you to look up – a perspective Luna would never lose, no matter what happened in the future.

The spire of the little church was also dusted with snow, the trees on the hills powdered white one last time before the onset of spring. Over the rooftops, she saw the ski lift heading up to La Flégère and thought of the urn in the bottom of her suitcase. A fresh sense of peace settled over her when she considered the prospect of her mother's ashes staying here with her. Not in the urn, but scattered here in Cham, the place where June had fallen in love, staying with Luna as she started living her own life now.

Her phone rang and she grimaced when she realised it was Lydia. In the tumult of the day before, she'd forgotten to message her cousin again.

'What time do you get in this afternoon? Are the roads okay?'

'Er, Lyd?' she began hesitantly. 'I'm not coming.'

'Whaaat?'

'You know me,' Luna said, not quite stifling her laugh. 'I'm staying here. I'm sorry about the job. I should have decided earlier, but... I've decided now.'

'What happened? You were about to set off yesterday!'

'Oh, the usual. I fell in love. He told me he loves me too,

although he was at altitude at the time and was in danger of hypothermia, but... I'm staying, anyway.'

In the silence, she imagined her cousin gaping as she tried to find words. 'But your mum! Your parents! After everything that happened...'

Lyd didn't even know the worst of it. 'After learning about everything they lost, I realised I don't want to lose the person *I* love, even if it's difficult.'

'It doesn't have to be difficult!'

Luna sighed, glancing out the window to see a sudden patch of blue between the clouds, and a hint of a jagged peak that disappeared again in an instant. 'Some of the best things in life are difficult, Lyd – including love. I'll come and visit soon – I promise.'

She grumbled something that sounded like, 'You'd better,' and Luna ended the call. She had a mountain rescuer to kiss and a new life to begin.

After the torture of the day before, the morning flew by with preparations for the descent. The wind had died down, but cloud was still a problem, requiring careful planning for a pick-up. Yannick and the team deliberated at length before deciding to descend 500 metres further to a safe spot for the helicopter.

Visibility still wasn't ideal, and it seemed to take some effort to dig themselves out of the refuge, but they reached the pick-up point successfully by mid-morning. Then began the logistical operation of bringing everyone down.

As soon as Luna heard the thump of the helicopter rotor in the sky, she raced for the door. Guy called out to stop her and she turned reluctantly, but he only wanted to toss her his car keys and give her an encouraging smile.

'You can't take the bus today,' he said. 'Not with such an important mission.'

She arrived at the drop zone in time to discover that the two victims had been successfully loaded and were on their way to hospital with Matthieu. Sunshine battled through the cloud, glinting off the layer of fresh powder and the river rushing by the DZ, newly replenished by rivulets of melting snow from high ravines. Crocuses pushed their heads through the blanket of white on the riverbank.

Winter was over and spring had arrived in the valley. Luna felt the same change in her own heart, although she'd also discovered that winter could be a challenge to embrace and not a season to hide away from.

Choucas ferried people and equipment laboriously down from the mountain. Luna heard Yannick's clipped voice often, directing the operation, her soft-hearted gendarme in 'chef de caravane' mode. Matthieu and Patrice arrived, followed by the other two who'd climbed to the refuge in support the afternoon before.

Luna's leg began to bounce as Choucas took off again, finally ready to bring Yannick back to her. She'd missed lunch but she didn't care. Silvia and Guy arrived together, sharing a look when they saw her, a wrecked ball of nerves.

'This isn't going to happen every time he goes up, is it?' Guy asked.

'No,' she said with a wild smile. 'Just this time. Don't worry about me. This is exactly where I need to be.'

She was staring too intently out at the helipad and missed the meaningful look and brief, tentative kiss that Silvia gave Guy.

When Choucas came back into view, thundering over the valley, she leaped to her feet and raced outside, lingering in safety by the hangar and shielding her eyes from the sunshine. Her blood rushing and her head spinning, she watched as the aircraft touched down and the door slid open.

40

And then, Yannick was climbing out, all six-odd precious feet of him, hauling a crazy amount of equipment, yet more tools and gear hanging from his harness – like the first time she'd seen him, except it wasn't a moonlit winter night this time, but a mild spring day.

Nothing could have stopped her. Feeling every inch her impulsive, sentimental self, she launched herself across the tarmac at a run. He noticed her and dropped his bags in an instant, ready to catch her when she sprang into his arms.

Wrapping herself around him, like a climber on a rock face, she registered his, 'Ouf,' of surprise, but he held her tight, so tight, and laughed, his chest quaking.

Somewhere between his helmet and the goggles that hung around his neck, she found his mouth and pressed kiss after happy kiss to his lips. He tried to kiss her back, but she was too quick, moving across his cheeks and even pressing a kiss to his nose.

'Luna,' he said, but she cut him off.

'Shhh, just let me kiss you for a minute and then it's your turn.' After lingering a little over one last kiss, she drew back and fumbled under his chin for the clasp of his helmet, sweeping it off to reveal his mussed hair.

Dropping her to the ground, he took his helmet from her and swept off his goggles as well. He looked exhausted, his neck warmer coated in ice and his face weathered.

'I'm sorry I left,' she began, knowing she had to get through this part. He shook his head, but she didn't let him contradict her. 'I knew you were trying to protect me from all of this. But I don't want to be protected because I love you. I know this life comes with risk, but it's worth it. *You're* worth the risk, to me. Of course I was scared to know you were up there in the storm, but it was worth it for this moment – even for the chance of this moment, for the *memory* of this moment. It was all worth it.'

At first, all he did was press his forehead to hers and breathe, and it was still everything she could have wanted.

'I love you,' was all he said at first, 'so much, the thought of losing you scares me.'

She drew him tight against her again. 'I know it does. But I want to stay. For as long as we have, I want to stay with you.'

'That's good,' he said, glancing away as his bright smile touched his lips, 'because I never worked out how to untie that rope.' He slowly met her gaze. 'I loved you from the moment you cried during the climb at the l'Envers des Aiguilles. I've never seen anything so beautiful in my life.'

It was Luna's turn to drag in a wobbly breath. 'I think I loved you from the moment you smiled at me on New Year's Eve at La Flégère,' she murmured.

'You barely knew me,' he pointed out.

'Yes, but you know me,' she said softly, smoothing her hand over his poor cheek. 'When something's right, I feel it and I follow it.'

'Une chance pour moi,' he whispered and gave her another

kiss, still soft and slow, but aching with tenderness. *Lucky for me*, he'd said, and Luna couldn't help feeling fortunate as well. 'You lost your glove – again,' he added after he'd pulled back.

'Actually, I dropped it on purpose,' she said sheepishly. 'I didn't want to break that thread, either, but I didn't expect it would go out on a mission with you.'

'Would you like it back? Although,' he began, glancing down to hide his self-conscious smile, 'it was nice to have it with me, when I couldn't come down.'

'You keep it then,' she said, leaning up to press another quick kiss to his lips. 'I like knowing something of mine was up at 4,000 m.' She grinned at a sudden thought.

'Quoi?' he prompted.

'Something of mine regularly goes up above 4,000 m.' She wrapped her arms around him. 'My gendarme secouriste, my love, my human.'

EPILOGUE

'Quick, get it done before I pass out!'

Lyd leaned heavily on Guy, swaying every time she looked to her right and saw the dizzying drop over the treetops into the valley – or the imposing rocky massif on the other side, crawling with climbers and glinting white in the summer sunshine.

'I can't rush this!' Luna snapped back, carefully cradling the ceramic urn that had stood on a shelf at Yannick's for nearly five months, an illegal elephant in the room that he'd been too considerate to bring up until she was ready.

'Would you like me to say a few words?' Silvia offered. Touched, Luna nodded with a relieved smile. Silvia cleared her throat. 'We are here to honour the life and legacy of June Rowntree by scattering her ashes in a place she once visited, a place where she found love and hardship and moments of beauty that we will never know all about. Although I didn't know June, it's clear to me that the most precious thing in her life was her beautiful daughter, and that's why her final resting place will be here, watching over Luna's new home, with her devoted husband and step-daughter.'

Luna's cheeks heated at that part, but her eyes were swimming with tears and she'd forgive Silvia for her bias. Yannick's hand squeezed hers – his left hand, which bore his thick wedding band and the tattoo beneath, for the days when climbing meant he had to take it off. He hadn't been satisfied until they were legally united as well as emotionally. She hadn't expected anything less from her duty-conscious gendarme, who didn't do commitment by halves.

She squeezed his hand in return and then untangled her fingers from his to step forward. Tugging off the lid of the urn, she paused for a moment, as though the tears dripping from her chin were preparing the ground, and then she tipped the urn gently into the breeze. 'Bye, Mum,' she whispered. 'I love you.'

'C'est quoi?' came Maëlys' curious voice from behind Luna.

Yannick dropped down to his haunches. 'Remember what I told you at home? When a person has died, sometimes they're buried and sometimes their body is burned,' he explained softly in French.

'Ah, Luna's maman died and that's her cloud,' Maëlys responded solemnly. Luna glanced back to see him smile and place a kiss on the top of his daughter's head.

Her mother's cloud dissipated quickly, most of it onto the scrubby ground, but some was picked up by the wind and carried high over the lake at the top of the chairlift at La Flégère where they'd gathered to put her to rest. Luna hoped June would have liked it, but more importantly, Luna could visit at any time of year and still feel connected to her.

'I'm glad you're all here,' she said softly, her gaze settling on her cousin, who'd made the journey despite loudly complaining about it, then on the faces of her dear friends in turn, especially Silvia and Guy. 'Now, I think Mum would have wanted us to eat tarte aux myrtilles in her honour.'

'I knew I had a lot in common with your mum, Lu. Those blueberry tarts are divine!' Lyd said, giving her a quick squeeze. After everyone had bestowed their hugs and kisses, they began the descent back to the valley in single file, a rope team in spirit, even though the route didn't require actual ropes.

Luna descended last behind Yannick, enjoying the view. Gazing over the roofs of Chamonix and across the valley, she could pick out the needle of the Aiguille du Grépon and gave a nod to Jim. To the right, bright white, with a swirling cap of clouds, was the dome of Mont Blanc. And on the other side of the great mountain summit glowed the crescent moon, pale and unassuming in the summer sunshine.

It was a good day to be alive.

ACKNOWLEDGMENTS

The rescue I wrote in the final sequence of this book is (very) loosely based on a mission that really happened in July 2020. A group of PGHM secouristes rescued a pair of mountaineers from Mont Blanc in bad weather, with a storm approaching, and managed to bring both home against the odds after supporting the sick and exhausted mountaineer for a long trek to a refuge.

The incredible work of the pilots and winch mechanics, the secouristes and all of the support staff formed an amazing backdrop for this story and I was inspired from the first moment I began researching the PGHM.

I am not a mountaineer (I am a mere hiker and a bad skier), so this book wouldn't have been possible without the many stories, pictures and documentaries behind it, as well as the resources of the Chamoniarde and the Deutscher Alpenverein here in Germany (shout out to the Sektion Würzburg).

Of course any errors in the technical mountain rescue aspects are entirely my own!

This book would definitely not have happened if it weren't for my family, for (usually) sharing my enthusiasm for the mountains and letting me drag them up to see the glaciers in Chamonix (and for them dragging me to the ski slopes a few years ago to learn as an adult).

My editor Sarah and the whole team at Boldwood have done another fabulous job helping me refine the story, as well as Lucy

Keeling with her insightful critique – I value your feedback so much, my friend.

A very special mention also this time to my good friend Tatiana for putting up with all my French questions, for sharing in the book excitement as the story came together and helping me to keep believing!

ABOUT THE AUTHOR

Leonie Mack is a bestselling romantic novelist. Having lived in London for many years her home is now in Germany with her husband and three children. Leonie loves train travel, medieval towns, hiking and happy endings!

Sign up to Leonie Mack's mailing list here for news, competitions and updates on future books.

Visit Leonie's website: https://leoniemack.com/

Follow Leonie on social media:

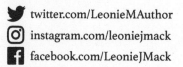

twitter.com/LeonieMAuthor
instagram.com/leoniejmack
facebook.com/LeonieJMack

ALSO BY LEONIE MACK

My Christmas Number One

Italy Ever After

A Match Made in Venice

We'll Always Have Venice

Twenty-One Nights in Paris

A Taste of Italian Sunshine

Snow Days With You

Boldwood

Boldwood Books is an award-winning fiction publishing company seeking out the best stories from around the world.

Find out more at www.boldwoodbooks.com

Join our reader community for brilliant books, competitions and offers!

Follow us
@BoldwoodBooks
@TheBoldBookClub

Sign up to our weekly deals newsletter

https://bit.ly/BoldwoodBNewsletter